LINDSTROM

UNBOUND

Volume Three of the Lindstrom Trilogy

For Marianne

Enjoy!

all the best

A STONEWOOD IMPRINT

JOHN MOSS

IGUANA

Published by Iguana Books
720 Bathurst Street, Suite 303
Toronto, Ontario, Canada
M5S 2R4

Front cover design: Meghan Behse

A Stonewood Imprint

Library and Archives Canada Cataloguing in Publication

Moss, John, 1940-, author

   Lindstrom unbound/ John Moss.

Issued in print and electronic formats.
ISBN 978-1-77180-334-2 (softcover).--ISBN 978-1-77180-335-9 (EPUB).--ISBN 978-1-77180-336-6 (Kindle)

      I. Title.
PS8576.O7863 L56 2019   C813'.6

This is an original print edition of *Lindstrom Unbound*.

for Beverley because I love her

1 BORA BORA

THE HORIZON BURST INTO FLAMES AS THE TROPICAL SUN
edged into the sea. Harry Lindstrom shifted his weight, reshaped the sand
to his contours, and closed his eyes. A welcome drowsiness crept through
his mind but was disturbed by a woman who stopped between him and
the smouldering light. He didn't open his eyes, he didn't want
complications. He turned his head slowly away, and when he turned back
she had vanished. The scent of her perfume lingered and merged with
the overripe odour of luxuriant vegetation. He pushed against the ribs of
a towering palm and slowly boosted himself upright. Finally, he looked
in the direction she'd gone.

Down the beach that ran the length of Matira Point torches had already
been lit near an open pavilion across from the Muana Kea International.
Briefly isolated in the flickering glare, a woman in a floral pareu was
staring directly at Harry. A pair of sandals dangled from one hand. She
wore a strand of Tahitian pearls that glinted when her dark hair lifted away
from her neck as she turned and disappeared into the glittering lights of
the hotel.

A cluster of Polynesian kids played in the gentle surf and pretended to
ignore the guests who gathered on the pavilion behind them. When the
band started playing the kids danced on the wet sand, keeping to the
shadows at the edge of the light. They showed a beauty and vitality the
hotel guests who were resplendent in new pareus and pearls, dress shorts
and pressed shirts, would have died for, had they noticed. Harry watched
for awhile, until the sun was extinguished and the children disappeared.

Wondering why the woman had stopped in front of him, and why she
had moved on without speaking, he retreated to his tiny thatched cottage.
Chez NoNo was not a luxury resort but it was comfortable enough and the
price was right. Continental breakfast at any of the high-end hotels on the
island cost more than what he was paying per day. He lay back on the bed.
It creaked and groaned with familiar sounds. Ten years previously, he and
Karen had spent part of a belated honeymoon on Bora Bora and stayed at
Chez NoNo. They had made noisy love through the nights. Each morning

they encountered neighbouring guests who would avert their eyes, others who would smile broadly, and one elderly gentleman from Paris who would hold up a number of fingers, his estimation of how often they had shaken the springs.

Harry stared into the darkness and tried to ignore the sadness, resolved to catch up on the sleep he had missed during the interminable flight from Toronto. He woke with a start when the music stopped.

He listened to the sounds of the night and thought of the woman with the pearls and the long dark hair. He envisioned her in random images that gradually coalesced into brief scenarios, like film clips with no sound. She had walked into his life while he was waiting for a connecting flight in Los Angeles. He was travelling tourist class, but since he had a four hour wait he upgraded to the private lounge. While thumbing through a copy of *Vanity Fair* he saw her come in, wearing spike heels and a blue linen suit. She was pushing a wheelchair. The occupant was well-dressed and frail with cords of translucent skin running the length of his neck, transfixing his head so that the movement of his eyes as they flicked about seemed uncomprehending, furtive, feral.

Harry couldn't quite make out the connection. Surely she wasn't a nurse or a paid caregiver. She walked on towering heels without wobbling, much like a ballerina *en pointe*. She projected an aura of casual wealth. She didn't show the affectionate condescension of a distant relative or the grieved solicitude of a close one. Mistress was hardly a possibility, given her ward's cadaverous condition.

What about wife, Harry? She's wearing a million dollar bracelet and a platinum wedding band.

When his mind was still, Harry could feel Karen's presence and when he was agitated or distressed or contemplative she spoke to him. Not always in words but in ways he could usually comprehend. She wasn't there and yet she was, that was the uneasy paradox that defined Harry's life.

She's married to somebody, maybe somebody else. She could be his friend.

It had not occurred to him a woman so aggressively glamorous would have friends. He had already accepted she was the old man's wife.

Later, when the incongruous couple was whisked through for advanced boarding on the same plane, Harry noticed how close the woman stayed to her charge, even though a steward was pushing the wheelchair. Harry followed immediately behind as he was seated near the back. At the entry hatch the steward had trouble manoeuvring the heavy spoked wheels over a curb and Harry reached forward to help but was waved away. He stood back and watched as the invalid was placed in a first class seat and his attractive companion settled into the adjoining space.

When Harry walked by, trundling his carry-on behind him, the woman glanced up at him and smiled with unexpected shyness, then quickly looked away.

At the Faa'a terminal in Papeete, he had watched as the couple moved into the open-air shade and waited for the same Air Tahiti Nui flight to Bora Bora he was taking. The man wore grey flannels, a navy blazer, and a school tie of some sort. His expressionless face had a waxy pallor and his lips appeared to have been lightly rouged. He was strapped into the chair so he wouldn't slide out. The woman had changed into a flouncy cotton dress that boldly concealed while it discreetly revealed. She had exchanged her city shoes for strappy high-heeled sandals. She still moved like a dancer. She had a lithesome figure. She looked up and caught Harry's eye across the open terminal. Embarrassed for staring, he looked away.

She was very beautiful. A few years younger than Harry. Mid-thirties. He was in his early forties.

You're very beautiful, too, Harry, in your own peculiar way.

He wasn't sure of an appropriate response.

You should get to know her, you have a lot in common. You're both married to ghosts.

When they landed on the atoll beside Bora Bora, on the airstrip the Americans had built during World War II, Harry helped lift the wheelchair onto the ferry bound for the village of Viatape. Bending over then standing upright his vision momentarily intersected with the invalid's in the chair. Harry felt an unexpected chill when he caught a momentary flicker that might have been anger, or anguish, or confusion in the old man's reptilian eyes. Or perhaps, he thought, it was a trick of the sun.

On the village quay there were a couple of hefty Polynesians to load the wheelchair into a private hotel van along with two Louis Vuitton bags inscribed discreetly in gold with an indiscernible flourish of initials and a large soft sided sports bag with no insignia.

Harry stepped up through the back door of the battered blue bus that would drop him at Chez NoNo and taking a seat he watched as the old man was positioned in the van. Their eyes again met, this time through two layers of glass. Harry tried to hold the man's gaze but then realized the invalid was looking right through him. His eyes nearly opaque signified nothing.

Eyes that say nothing, Harry? Like eyes in a mirror.

He looked again but the wheel chair had been turned and the tight ridges of flesh running from the man's cheeks to his temples seemed to have swallowed his eyes in their tenebrous folds.

The dark haired woman settled next to her husband. She seemed perfectly self-contained. She had the aura of a woman who assumed her innermost desires would be accommodated without having to make them known, a privilege of the inordinately wealthy and the immoderately attractive. She seemed isolated, mysterious, a little dangerous, defiant, sad, almost pathetic. Harry smiled, this time only to himself. They lived in different worlds and Harry had no desire to know hers.

And then she came along and blocked out the sun.

Had she recognized him from the trip, his pale northern body stripped nearly naked? Was she curious about why he was travelling alone? Was she afraid of disturbing him? What could she possibly want?

Harry fell back into a thick sleep and woke at dawn with the shriek of a rooster crowing on the other side of his woven reed walls.

After cursory ablutions, he walked up the beach past the pavilion across from the Muana Kia to a little restaurant poised between the road and the water where he and Karen had breakfasted on warm croissants with guava jam and steaming bowls of *café au lait*, which is exactly what he ordered and it was as satisfying as he remembered. Then he returned to his hut and sorted through his scuba gear, with ten minutes to spare before the van arrived from Topdive to pick him up.

Diving was not something he and Karen had ever done. An old friend Miranda Quin, the Superintendent of Homicide for the Toronto Police Service, was a scuba diver. Her former partner, David Morgan, followed suit and had become zealous. His enthusiasm was infectious. Harry and Morgan had spent quite a bit of time together after Harry resolved a recent case in Vienna, which involved a girlfriend of Morgan's in a morally ambiguous conflict that she side-stepped by entering a nunnery. Under Morgan's aegis, Harry took up diving.

Once over the initial shock at breathing in an alien and deadly environment, Harry became a devotee. In a matter of months he earned his

Open Water and Advanced certification. He chose to train with congenial professionals outside Toronto, driving regularly to Adventure Divers in Peterborough an hour and a half away, eventually joining them on an excursion to the Honduran island of Roatan. Bora Bora was his first dive adventure on his own, without either Morgan or his instructor, Randy Timms, at his side.

The Topdive van picked up other divers at their luxury hotels on the return route to the dive shop in Viatape. There was a lot of congenial chatter but Harry had no desire to make friends. He focussed on the ordinary lives of the islanders, revealed in brief glimpses as the van jounced along the shore road. He slouched in his seat and stared up at the volcanic spires draped with vegetation that spilled in lush green waves down into tangled thickets reaching the edge of the road. On the seaward side a fringe of palms shaded narrow white beaches marked here and there by outrigger canoes in various stages of disrepair that betrayed an entirely different economy than the casual wealth he perceived inside the van. He gazed over the azure lagoon at the coral atoll rising here and there into low motus populated with exclusive resorts as it circumscribed the entire island, isolating it from the open sea.

Viatape was much the same as when he had been there with Karen. Several of the black pearl shops were more richly appointed behind discreetly ramshackle facades but few new buildings had been allowed to desecrate the rustic ambience. Apart from polished limousines delivering tourists from smaller resorts that didn't have pearl shops of their own, it seemed a sleepy haphazard town with a thriving central market, given over to pedestrians, the occasional street-merchant, and a blend of Polynesians and vagabond tourists. Dominating everything were the volcanic green spires as a backdrop on one side and the dazzling lagoon on the other.

Loneliness and his apprehension at diving in a new place disappeared when the van pulled up in front of the Topdive shop at the far end of the village. He had been diving long enough to shift his attention wholly to the task at hand. The safety of diving is in the details, and without safety there was no pleasure.

While he busied himself preparing his gear, Harry was astonished to see the mystery woman walk through from the street. His concentration wavered. She was already fitted up in a shorty 3 ml wetsuit, obviously cut to measure. An aid from the hotel carried her equipment in a big soft-sided black bag. She nodded to Harry. He nodded back.

My God, such intimacy, Harry.

She's not my type.

She's female, Harry. The most female female I've ever seen.

He grimaced.

On the dive boat he was buddied with a tubby Australian who spoke an unintelligible dialect of what Harry assumed was English, and the mystery woman was assigned to a Japanese woman who didn't speak English at all.

While they donned their gear, Harry noticed the most female of females withdraw a band of stretchy black material from her dive bag and slide it over a bracelet that glittered with so many diamonds their uniformity seemed almost conservative. One large diamond was flashy; a bunch of them equally large but set in neat rows was restrained opulence.

He wondered if the black band was to protect the woman from attracting undersea predators or to keep her jewellery safe.

It amounts to the same thing, Harry.

The first dive was uneventful.

During the decompression break, despite protestations of a dive boat assistant, the mystery woman heaved her own tanks around, preparing for the next dive. The ripple of her triceps indicated unexpected strength, while the action itself suggested a streak of determined self-sufficiency.

Harry had been content to accept help.

The woman came forward into the deckhouse shade where Harry had retreated from the sun. She picked up a chunk of fresh pineapple from a common tray and slurped it down, lasciviously, he thought, and wiped her hands on a stray towel. She looked towards Harry, who slid over on the bench, and settled into place beside him.

"Teresa Saintsbury," she said. "Most people call me Tess. That's my professional name."

"What's your profession?" he asked.

"I'm an actress."

"Should I know you?"

"I doubt it. Third rate stuff with aliens and monsters. I'm not very good."

"Then why the career choice."

"It was thrust upon me, so to speak. I have a perfect body."

"For what?"

"For being a third rate actress."

Harry swivelled on the bench to look at her face to face. This was the closest they'd been and he was amazed. Her ebony hair was plastered against her skull, her cheeks were smeared with salt residue, her forehead was creased from a tight mask, her lips were pale, and her eyes were utterly without makeup. She appeared even more stunning than when she had been in jet-set mode.

Her eyes thrilled him. They had the blue-black lustre of Polynesian pearls, with pupils absorbed into the darkness of irradiant irises so that their elusive colour seemed huge against the surrounding white.

"I'm Harry Lindstrom."

"I know, I saw your name on the dive-list. My husband doesn't dive. Would you be my buddy?" she asked, leaning closer.

Husband, then. And no, Harry didn't image he dived.

The woman had stripped her shorty wetsuit down to the waist and he was aware of her perfect breasts poised within the minimal constraint of her bikini top. "For the next dive? Please. My Japanese friend ignores me and goes wherever she wants."

"Of course," said Harry.

"Good," she said. "I've already arranged it with the dive master. I told him we're friends. Your chubby Australian has been reassigned to my Japanese. We're going to Anua reef to see manta rays."

"Big ones?" said Harry, stupidly.

"They always are. Like pigeons in a park, you never see babies. They appear fully grown."

"Let's go then, they're calling us."

"Stay close," she said, turning her back to him so he could zip her up.

"Of course."

Of course!

At a depth of sixty feet they swam into unusually murky water laden with phytoplankton. The dive master motioned for the divers to settle on the sandy bottom between clusters of coral. Before long, a squadron of rays with twelve to twenty-foot wingspans swooped overhead, blotting out the sun. As the rays drew water into their giant maws and filtered the nutrients, Tess Saintsbury reached for Harry's hand and they both squeezed, sharing their exhilaration. The rays slowly disappeared into the silent opaque sea like a great apparition. The sun again beamed through the waves above, and the divers moved back into crystal clear water.

As they swam over spectacular staghorn coral, Harry heard the summons of the dive master's clicker. He swung to the side and saw a huge solitary tiger shark moving towards them. He reached for his buddy's hand and drew her down as he settled onto the bottom, trying desperately not to do any damage but as desperately concerned with not attracting the attention of the prowling leviathan.

Heart in his mouth he waited. The shark swam close. It was vast. It's mouth was gaping in a ferocious grin, showing rows of razor-sharp teeth. Harry looked at Tess, trying to make out her face through the distortion of her mask. Her eyes were creased at the corners. Slowly she swept her free hand in the direction of the shark. Harry watched as the depthless disc of the eye nearest them swivelled in their direction. Harry looked back at Tess. She was grinning, air burbled out the sides of her mouthpiece.

She removed her regulator from her mouth and extended it towards the curious shark, then she pressed the exhaust diaphragm and a great burst of bubbles exploded. The shark's dorsal fin rippled as it changed direction and swam leisurely away. The rest of the divers resumed their explorations among the massive accumulations of staghorn and boulder corals. Harry and Tess moved on.

"So what do you do when you're not diving?" she asked after they had showered back at Topdive, changed, and were waiting on the wooden steps out front for their rides.

Harry hesitated. He had been working as a private investigator for over three years. He specialized in murder. He didn't much like to talk about himself.

"I'm a philosophy professor," he said.

"Really," she said. "Where?"

That was the way people outside academe asked for your credentials. Not what's your area of specialization, not how many papers have you published, how many books, where were they reviewed? No, it was 'who employs you?' Are you real?

"A small college at a large Canadian university," he said. "Huron, the University of Western Ontario. It's not as provincial as it sounds."

"I'm sure."

Remember, she's comfortable teasing a tiger shark.

Her car from the Muana Kea pulled up in front of the dive shop. A silver Mercedes. While the driver loaded her gear into the trunk, she held her hand out to Harry with awkward formality. Her eyes flashed black.

She seemed reluctant to release her grip, as if there was something she needed to tell him but couldn't remember what it was. She turned to climb in the car, then speaking over her shoulder she said, "Sorry I can't offer you a lift, Harry Lindstrom. Perhaps we'll run into each other again."

Harry nodded. There was no one else in her car.

He gazed up at the volcanic spires piercing the sky and tried to think of nothing at all.

2 BLOODY MARY'S

AFTER A COUPLE OF BANANAS AND A COLD HINANO BEER for lunch, Harry slept through much of the afternoon in the shade of coconut trees on the sand in front of Chez NoNo. Neither his body nor his mind were reconciled to the time differential with Toronto. He wasn't up for an afternoon dive and the evening walk he had promised himself seemed pleasantly remote A zephyr of cooling air drifted onshore and countered the intense heat.

About five, the breeze died, just as the lowering sun was slipping under the trees and creeping up the length of his body. The day manager of Chez NoNo roused him with a note that had been hand delivered from the Muana Kea.

Harry
Please join me for dinner. A car will pick you up at eight. Dress
informally. Tiger shark will not be on the menu.
Tess

Apparently an RSVP was not required. She was sure of herself. But my God, did this mean dinner with her husband as well? Was Harry being brought along to assist? Or to amuse?

Or maybe she wants you to expound on the universe, Humphrey.

He preferred when Karen thought of him as Slate, not Bogart. The character, not the actor.

I didn't lie, Sailor. I was once a philosopher of modest renown.

But you're not a philosopher anymore, Harry. Not even modestly.

During long winter nights in their stone farmhouse on the Sanctuary Line near Granton, they used to listen to old radio programs on the internet. Their favourite was a show from the early fifties called "Bold Venture" with Humphrey Bogart as Slate Shannon and Lauren Bacall as Sailor Duvall. They had searched out all 56 episodes still available of the original 78 and fell effortlessly into the characters because they were pure sound and because romance, intrigue, mystery, and adventure in sultry settings were so different from their own lives, back when Harry was a philosopher and Karen was a literary critic and cultural theorist, both at Huron College.

Harry was relieved when Tess turned up without her husband and he felt guilty for it.

They were both comfortable with silence and didn't talk on the drive to the restaurant.

Bloody Mary's burst from the darkness of the coastal road in a splendid explosion of ambiance. From the sanitized sandy floor to the palm branches artfully draped and the bamboo neatly arranged, all beneath the compulsory thatched and woven roof, it promised revellers who had ventured beyond the confines of their expensive resorts an evening of indulgence with a tantalizing hint of adventure.

They were escorted to a reserved table near an open wall on the seaward side. The spectacular view was drowned out by the flare of torches in the garden.

Tess Saintsbury's hair flickered with highlights of fire, her ebony eyes picked up the sheen of the pearl studs in her ears, complemented by the iridescent smoky black pearls of her necklace, and her diamond wristband glistened with countless dancing points of illumination as she gestured while she talked.

They sipped mango daiquiris as an aperitif. Harry was content to admire her lips as they shaped words like bubbles being blown between them. She wore nothing more than a light cotton dress, mid-thigh length with tiny straps that slipped off her shoulders at the slightest provocation.

"You're very quiet," she said. "I expected a philosopher to be loquacious."

"Sorry to disappoint."

"Not at all. What do you really do?"

"I'm a private investigator. Canadian. Murder, mostly."

She didn't seem surprised. She asked, "Are you here on business or pleasure?"

"At Bloody Mary's? Pleasure."

"On Bora Bora."

"Because it's Bora Bora."

"It is very special isn't it. My husband has been here a number of times."

"I was here with my wife ten years ago."

"But you left her at home?"

"No." He didn't want Karen to become dinner conversation. "She's gone," he said. The woman was genuinely trying to engage. "Her name was Karen Malone. She died in an accident."

"Car?"

"She drowned." He paused, then awkwardly added, "I survived."

"Do you have children?"

Harry shifted in his chair and gazed through the flickering torchlight, trying to see the water along the shoreline that he could hear lapping on dead coral outcroppings over the din of the restaurant. Tess leaned forward and whispered condolences.

"It's okay," said Harry.

It's not, it's not. He could hear the words echo.

"Your husband?" he asked. He wasn't sure how to phrase the question. He didn't want to seem like he was retaliating. "Was it recent?"

"A stroke." She seemed relieved that he asked. "One day he was sharp as a razor, his ability to communicate was his primary asset, and then overnight he turned into what he is now, more dead than alive."

He was surprised she had been married for a measurable length of time. Perhaps her story was more ordinary than he'd imagined.

She smiled. "You must think I'm very cruel."

"No," said Harry. "Life is."

He wondered if he spoke with enough irony or sufficient conviction to make his statement less trite than it seemed.

She said nothing for a moment, then continued. "It would have been easier to grieve over his death than to watch every day as he struggles to comprehend that he's alive."

"Does he do that?"

"I don't know. The doctors say there's cerebral activity but no one can say what he's thinking."

She leaned forward into the candlelight. Her eyes had filled with tears. He wanted to reach over and brush them dry but his wife and her husband were too much present to permit such an intimacy.

"Sometimes it's difficult," she said.

"I'm sure it is."

"To tell the difference between life and death."

"Yes," Harry agreed, "Sometimes it is."

After a lull, while she seemed to be waiting, he continued. "But death is unequivocal; life, not so much."

"I've heard of a woman who lives in seclusion near the base of Mount Everest, a Buddhist nun who recites the same prayer over and over, that's all she does, and she's done this for over forty years. Is she alive, Harry?"

"We're talking about her, perhaps that's all she wants."

"But is she alive?"

"Maybe in her own mind she has transcended."

"Transcended what? Not if she eats, sleeps, poops, and applauds her own holiness, which of course she must or she'd move on to another prayer. There is no transcendence but death."

"Death is an absence, not an achievement."

"That depends on your point of view, doesn't it." She toyed with the platinum band on her ring finger. It might have been burnished silver. Harry wasn't good with precious metals.

"Perhaps we should order," he said, hoping to channel the flow of their conversation into less murky waters.

They checked out the seafood display but resisted the familiar parrotfish, red snapper, and jacks, fish they'd been swimming among that morning. Instead, Harry ordered grilled mahi mahi fillets in vanilla sauce and Tess ordered broadbill swordfish, grilled, as she requested, to perfection.

They drank an unusual bottle of white Chateauneuf du Pape and had fresh local fruit for dessert.

"Tell me about your acting career," he asked over coffee.

"It didn't amount to much." Past tense. "Aren't you curious to know who he was?" Again, past tense. "Someone tried to kill him a year ago."

Harry didn't want to consider what she was saying. He had enjoyed his dinner. He was on one of the most idyllic islands on the planet. Murder was an unwelcome intruder, no matter how comely its disguise.

"I'm sorry," he said. It crossed his mind that they had not reached this point by accidental increments.

"I'm told it was a tincture of aconite root. Easy to come by and hard to detect. Wolf's bane or devil's helmet. It's in the buttercup family. Monk's hood is another name for it. The effect was devastating but he didn't die. This was before I came along."

"So you didn't know him when he was, as you said, *razor sharp.*"

"William was not so sick when I met him, Harry. I was using a figure of speech. Since then he has had what they call a cerebral vascular accident, several in fact. He has slipped a great deal."

Whether the old man reached a vegetative condition in stages or at what point Tess appeared during his decline was more than he wanted to know.

"Do they have any idea who did it?" he asked.

"No charges were laid."

William Saintsbury. Harry dredged through a mental inventory of tycoons he might have encountered on the financial pages of *The Globe*. Until entering his current profession, he never read about commerce and now, only when there was an untoward death. His business, after all, was murder. The name tolled no bells, and barely reverberated as he turned it over in his mind.

"We met in California. At the Mansion."

Harry imagined she meant Hefner's.

"Silicon central," she confirmed. "I was the only woman there with real boobs."

She glanced down and Harry's gaze followed hers. She wasn't wearing a bra.

"William rescued me," she continued. "From a tacky crowd, from a tacky career, from a commonplace life. He was no more incapacitated than our host. We had a short time together as husband and wife. And then, this."

The way she said *this*, William Saintsbury was conjured to mind in his present condition. For some reason he couldn't fathom, Harry wanted to know how old the man was. He didn't ask.

"Were you really a philosopher?" she said.

"Were you really an actress?"

"In another life."

"Ah, you believe in reincarnation," he said, hoping to lighten the mood.

"Of a sort. I believe in altered trajectories, burned bridges, fresh starts."

"The transmogrification of psyches, but not of souls."

"You talk like a professor."

"I suppose I do," he responded. "Except I no longer profess. And nobody pays me to think if there's not a dead body involved."

He could see his own eyes reflected in hers, shining like shards of cracked amber. His hair was close cropped and prematurely grey. Strong features, good teeth. Lips narrow, not thin, and a good chin, as his Aunt Beth used to say, a good Lindstrom chin.

"I do have a Canadian connection," she offered. "I went to summer camp near Haliburton, Ontario."

She didn't strike him as a camping alumna.

"Canoe tripping, mostly," she continued. "For eight summers. In camp, we had to pretend we were Indians. Not real Indians, Hollywood Indians. It was embarrassing, even then. Out in the bush, we cut the bullshit disguise, we did campcraft and survival stuff, worked hard, ate well, tanned in the buff."

He did not want to talk about camping and canoes, which would inevitably lead either to an oppressive silence or to revelation and confession about a nightmare he wanted to avoid.

"You must have started when you were very young. Where were you from?"

"Here and there," she said. "We were military, we moved around. Camp kept me grounded, that's what my parents thought. Of course, I was grounded in an alien country and an appropriated culture."

"I have trouble thinking of Canada as alien."

"You would, wouldn't you."

She glanced at her watch. He was still wearing his dive computer but she had changed hers for an exquisite Swiss chronograph that was surprisingly austere, given the glittering diamonds on her other wrist above a faded scar in the shape of a cross on the back of her hand.

"Let's have another drink," she suggested.

"I'm diving tomorrow, I think I'll pass."

She leaned forward and dipped her shoulders seductively. "Just one more. We'll drink it slowly."

Is she trying to get you drunk or is she just stalling for time?

Harry wondered. He could think of no reason for either.

Karen whispered a sultry response but he couldn't make out what she said.

"Or we could drink it fast," she said. "It depends on the desired effect."

You're on your own, Harry. Good luck.

The woman signalled to a waiter and they ordered two more drinks. Harry asked for Dewar's Signature on the rocks and she insisted on something called a monkey la-la.

She slouched back in her rattan chair, projecting an aura of languorous intimacy that was rendered more provocative by her self-mocking smile.

Harry retreated into the depths of his own chair. There was something predatory about this woman that made him uneasy, something feline, that made her attractive.

They chatted amiably over several more drinks. Karen seemed to be absent. As the evening wore on and the dinner crowd thinned, his companion made an observation that in retrospective seemed a judgement of their entire time together.

"You're unusual, Harry. You're not afraid of women," she said.

It hadn't occurred to Harry he was either unusual or afraid.

"Really," he responded.

"Most men are."

"It's a cultural inheritance I try to suppress."

She shifted, drawing the thin material of her dress tight against her breasts.

"Do I frighten you, Harry?"

He didn't smile. Did she frighten him? Possibly. A little.

"You didn't answer me, Harry."

"If you did frighten me, I'd deny it."

"Denial is the sure sign of fear."

So what is that all about?

Harry had no idea. Just talk, jockeying for position.

When they got back to the Muana Kea International, Tess invited him to join her for a nightcap. First, she wanted to check on her husband and asked Harry to go with her.

"It's time you met William," she said.

She led him through the extravagantly appointed hotel pavilion, past the prying eyes of guests poised by the bar to observe the comings and goings of fellow guests whose lives were more interesting than their own. A man in livery, looking like he'd stepped from the pages of a Victorian novel despite his Polynesian features, approached from the side.

"Will you need more ice, Mrs. Saintsbury?"

"*Merci*, Jean-Claude, I have enough."

What an odd exchange.

"William has a good soak in freezing water at least once a day," she explained. "It seems to make him feel better."

About what?

"You manage to lift him into a tub?" His question seemed uncomfortably familiar but he didn't know what else to say.

"Yes. And onto his chair, into bed, onto the toilet, whatever is necessary. I am quite strong. I have to be."

Harry imagined her devotion required strength and patience and the ability to override instinctive revulsion. He had never attended slow death, to know how readily affection overcomes aversion, even disgust. Death for those close to him had been swift and violent. He admired her gentle forbearance.

"Will he be asleep now?"

"He never sleeps. He rests, but he is always there."

A hint of resentment, perhaps?

Candour.

She wants you to like her.

I do.

Side by side they walked along the illuminated wooden causeway that snaked its way over the water, providing access to a village of rustic cottages on pylons. Each unit was clad in woven mats and thatch, so they looked much like larger versions of his own at Chez NoNo.

When they reached the cottage farthest from the hotel, Tess stopped, leaned close to Harry and smiled up at him. He could feel her warmth. It was all he could do not to take her in his arms, but her invalid husband was a few steps away. He felt strangely conflicted. Attracted, revolted, enticed but touched with dread. He stayed still. She backed away, turned, and walked through the door and into the light.

"Harry," she called back to him, her voice tremulous.

He went in, astonished at the luxury, amazed there was no sign of William Saintsbury.

"I left him here in his chair."

"Perhaps someone came to get him."

"That's not likely." Her voice quavered, she was shaking.

"What else? Where could he have got to," said Harry in his professionally reassuring voice.

"I left orders he wasn't to be disturbed."

Harry looked at the darkened glass panel in the floor.

"You can watch the fish," she explained, following his gaze.

"At night?"

"There's a floodlight."

Harry looked around and spotted the switch. Feeling queasy, he reached over and turned it on. The glass panel flared into a rippling glow.

Tess stepped back. Harry leaned forward, forcing himself to look down into the shaft of illuminated water.

From ten feet under the surface, William Saintsbury gazed up at him, eyes agape. He was secured in his heavy wheelchair with straps and a pair of neckties. Fish nibbled at his face and hands. So far, none had ripped into his sodden white flesh.

"Phone the police," Harry said.

3 MELVILLE

"CALL ME QUEEQUEG," SAID THE MAN IN THE SHADOWS.

"Call me Ishmael," said Harry, standing close to Tess Saintsbury as they leaned on the railing outside her cottage. The policeman didn't smile. Harry couldn't decipher the unsettling display of shadows across the man's face until he turned into the light cast from a lamp on a post near the door. Harry froze. From brow to chin and down the length of his neck the man's skin bore intricate swirls of blue-black tattooing that left little of his golden complexion exposed. When he turned his face, the other side was pristine. The division was absolute, the one side a mask of horrific complexity and the other untouched.

"I am Inspector Queequeg," the man repeated.

"Of course," said Harry, embarrassed by his inappropriate flippancy.

"I am here about a murder."

Given the man was followed by an entourage of uniformed gendarmes, emergency personnel, and hotel staff, Harry hardly considered the explanation necessary. He was surprised that it was in English.

"Je m'escuse," said Harry. *"Je ne parle pas très bien français."*

"No problem, *monsieur,* I speak English quite perfectly."

"The body is inside," Harry said. "In the water."

"I see," said Inspector Queequeg. The contradictory directive did not seem to surprise him. "And is this the man's wife?"

"I am," said Tess, pulling away from Harry. She had obviously been crying although Harry hadn't noticed any tears. Her eyes were red and strained at the corners. Her mouth was smeared. She seemed unaware of the policeman's disfigured face. Karen would have been fascinated. For Harry, the intentional anomaly was vaguely confusing.

Tess held out her hand to Queequeg. Her voice was strong. "I am Mary Saintsbury."

Harry looked at her sharply. She wasn't dissembling. If her name had been Tess, apparently now it was Mary.

"Where were you when Mr. Saintsbury died?"

"Do you think we could get him out of there," she said. Her tone was quietly imperious.

"Of course," Queequeg responded but made no move.

"Well," she said, adopting a conciliatory warmth, "I was at dinner with my friend. We spent the entire evening at Bloody Mary's. This is Harry Lindstrom. We discovered him together."

"I assume you made no attempt to move him."

"Of course not," said Harry.

"But you were sure he was dead."

I don't like the implication, Harry.

"Inspector Queequeg, Mrs. Saintsbury and I just met. We had dinner, we came here, her husband was in the water, obviously thoroughly dead. We called you."

"I see."

They entered the cottage, followed by the entourage, and stood at the edge of the illuminated column of water. The surface of the water glistened. The old man's eyes gazed up through the glimmering light.

"Well, let's get him out then," said Queequeg in a commanding voice. "*Dépêche-toi, dépêche-toi.*"

Two burly paramedics immediately stripped to undershorts, folded the glass panel back, and plunged feet-first into the water. They had no difficulty bringing the chair and its occupant to the surface, but when they tried to hoist it up the gap of a foot or so and manoeuvre it onto the cottage floor, the old man slumped against his bindings and his head lolled grotesquely. Harry felt sickened. Tess leaned into him and shuddered violently. He led her outside.

"I am so sorry, Harry," she murmured, "I did not mean to get you into such an ugly situation."

Before he could respond, Inspector Queequeg emerged from the cottage. Stepping past, he announced they should follow him back to the lobby, where he sat them down on a matched pair of sofas and offered to have someone bring them a drink. They both declined.

Tess Saintsbury seemed poised for a grieving widow but Harry knew from experience that sorrow wore infinite guises. Queequeg asked conversationally if she had her passport with her.

"Of course," she said and reached into a leather handbag, which she had exchanged at some point for the small purse she carried at dinner. She handed Queequeg her passport. He examined it and handed it back, and requested Harry's, which Harry had left in his room.

"I will check on you later, Mr. Lindstrom," he said.

Harry and Tess exchanged glances.

"He has nothing to do with this," said Tess with a stridency bordering on anger. "We just met."

Queequeg shrugged. "I see from your passport that you were legally married."

"Were you in doubt?"

"Your name is Mary, but I understand you are known as Tess."

"For Teresa, yes."

"You are thirty-four years old. An American citizen and a housewife. What does that mean?"

"Housewife, housekeeper. I have many skills and am paid for none."

"Are you a mother?"

"A step-mother. My husband was previously married."

"You were his primary caregiver. Are you a nurse?"

"No."

"You were not married for a long time?"

"Not long, no."

"And what about him? He was successful, yes. Successful men have enemies? Did he have enemies?"

"At least one, I'd say."

"Have you any idea who could have done this?"

"Inspector, it would hardly have been worth anyone's effort. Are you aware of my husband's condition?"

"The night manager told me he did not communicate."

"Did not, could not."

"Then why did you come here?"

"It is Bora Bora," she said.

"Yes, and?"

"I needed a holiday, Inspector."

"And yet you travelled with the cause of your fatigue."

"We both needed to get away."

"Get away?"

"From the people hanging on, hovering, watching, suffocating. He loved Polynesia, he had been here many times in the past. He was a friend of Mr. Brando and his wife. He used to stay on Tetiaroa, or at one of the resorts on the Bora Bora atoll. He was happy here."

"So there is no reason you would have wanted him dead?"

Harry sat forward on the sofa.

"Harry, it is all right," she said, laying a restraining hand on his forearm. "The Inspector needs to ask his questions. The answer, Inspector Queequeg, is yes, sometimes I would have preferred him to go. His life was extremely limited."

"For you, too."

"Sometimes. That does not make me a killer."

"No, of course not. He was very miserable, no?"

"He was not capable of the sustained effort to be miserable. Nor to be happy, for that matter. He simply was, in the moment. He was a man haunted by the absence of ghosts."

"I see."

"Do you? And do you see that I'm haunted by the absence of dreams."

"I'm not sure what you mean?"

"Neither am I."

"Of course."

"I occasionally wished he would die. As for killing him, euthanasia may have an abstract appeal. In real life, it is abhorrent."

Chilling, how articulate she is for a B-movie actress.

They're not mutually exclusive, limited talent and a functioning brain.

"Mr. Lindstrom? Do you agree?"

"No." Harry had to draw himself back to the interview: "I actually believe in euthanasia. Sometimes."

"Believe?"

"That it can be the most humane alternative."

"To what?"

"To a life that is merely endured."

"Would you have regarded Mr. Saintsbury as a likely candidate?"

"For dying? I couldn't say. I never met him alive."

"And in any case, you have an alibi."

"I do."

"And Mrs. Saintsbury has an alibi. I am sure the time of death will prove to have been while she was with you. Very fortunate, yes?"

"Not for the dead man."

"Perhaps not."

Unless he wanted to die.

Harry recalled the brief instant in Viatape—it might have been a trick of the midday sun glaring up from the pavement—when his eyes caught in the old man's empty gaze the glimmering hint of a distinct human being. Harry looked across at Queequeg. The man's face seemed devoid of emotion. The muted light of the deserted lobby had erased the hard line between the tattooed and the unadorned sides of his face.

"Inspector Queequeg." Tess Saintsbury spoke with her hand still on Harry's arm. "Dr. Lindstrom is a detective."

"A policeman?"

"No," said Harry. "A private investigator."

"From Canada, yes? Do you have a license?"

Harry reached into his pocket and withdrew a crumpled, soiled, tattered, worn business card. "Only this," he said. "It never occurred to me I'd need professional credentials. I'm here on a holiday."

"From Toronto? You have a partner, Karen Malone. Your email address is *lindstromalone.com*. Very subtle, she has left you. And you are a doctor, what is your specialty?"

"Murder," said Harry.

"Ah, very good. You joke about death."

"I was a philosophy professor."

"And now you explore murder. That is what you might call a fall from grace."

"I prefer to think of it as an elevation."

"I too studied philosophy. Very briefly. But if you are a detective, perhaps I am a philosopher."

Hostility, Harry?

He saw me staring at his face. He is a proud man.

Overweight.

Relevance?

None. His English is good.

Quite perfect.

Nothing is perfect. Who knows that better than you. He's talking, pay attention.

"Tomorrow, *monsieur le professeur*, we will check your papers. For tonight, perhaps you could stay with your close good friend."

"I'm fine," said Tess in a voice that declared the suggestion absurd. "If you would allow me to return to my cottage for a few things, I will have them transfer me to another suite."

"Of course," said Queequeg. "Mr. Lindstrom will accompany you, yes?"

"Dr. Lindstrom is not staying at this hotel."

"Ah then, of course, he will go. Where are you staying, Mr. Lindstrom?"

"Chez NoNo, just down the road."

Queequeg seemed for a moment nonplussed at such an unlikely residence for a friend of the Saintsburys. That pleased Harry.

Queequeg got up slowly; he was a heavy man.

"I will leave someone on watch," he said.

"There's no need," said Tess.

"Yes, there is," he shot back, before nodding to them both with exaggerated cordiality. Harry realized he had not seen the man smile. In the full light of the hotel lobby, with his head turned to the side as he walked away, Mephistopheles had been supplanted by a knight of the mournful countenance. What Harry found disquieting was that he had shown extremes of emotion and no feelings at all.

Just after daybreak the next morning, Tess Saintsbury appeared at Chez NoNo and invited Harry to join her for breakfast back at the Muana Kea. While he would have preferred to sleep longer, having been tormented by recurring images of death through much of the night, he felt obliged to be congenial, even compassionate. They walked up the Matira Point laneway silently, like old friends whose intimacy made words superfluous. They were going through much the same thing, albeit from different perspectives. She had lost her husband, Harry had found the body.

Hardly comparable, Harry.

Logically, no. But that's how it seemed. We were together when the old man died.

Not quite but near enough to make strangers seem intimate.

The police guard in the lobby seemed surprised to see them come in through the main entrance. He had apparently not noticed her leave. A sleepy-eyed *maitre d'* settled them in the dining room close to the open wall near the water.

"Harry?" Tess looked at him across the table. Her head was tilted so that her hair framed her face in blue-black waves. Her eyes that struck him as feline at some point seemed more like a terrier's now; quick, concerned, curious, and oddly predatory. "I really am sorry to have dragged you through this," she said. "Since we have been thrown together, we might as well make the most of it."

Exactly what does she mean by that?

"There's nothing I can do but wait," she continued. "I had a message from the gendarmerie this morning. They have apparently sent my husband's body to the morgue in Papeete but I am to stay here until Inspector Queequeg pronounces me innocent beyond any reasonable doubt."

"Innocent?"

"Of murder."

"Is that even open to question. You were with me."

"Precisely, and he wants to establish your innocence as well."

Your innocence, Harry? That might take a while.

"There's no reason we can't go diving or shopping," she said. "Whatever you'd like."

"I'm not much for shopping."

"We can just hang together. I'm quite upset, actually. I need the company."

So now it's a moral obligation to kill time with the bimbo.

Hardly a bimbo; and 'killing time' might be in questionable taste.

Like hanging together? I retreat.

And she did.

"So," Harry said. "Do I call you Mary or do I call you Tess?"

"Tess," she said and she offered no further explanation.

It was hardly like she was trying to hide behind a *nom de guerre*. He let the matter drop.

"So what do you think about Inspector Queequeg?" she asked.

"An interesting man."

"An interesting name. It's from *Moby-Dick*, isn't it?"

"I imagine it's an island name. Melville must have picked it up when he jumped ship in the Marquesas. Have you ever read *Typee*? It's a novel based on his experience there."

"I've never even read *Moby-Dick*," she confessed.

"I haven't either. Saw the movie."

"With Gregory Peck? It's a classic. I spent most of last night researching."

"Gregory Peck or movies in general?"

"Inspector Queequeg. It's always good to know your adversary."

Harry expressed surprise. "Is he an adversary?"

"Until we're proved innocent."

"That seems rather French," said Harry quite cheerfully. "Guilty until proven otherwise."

"I checked him out."

"You have Wi-Fi here?"

"This is the Muana Kea International, Harry. So pour us more coffee and settle back. Here's what I found. It doesn't tell us much but it accounts for his ferocious tattoo."

In the early seventies, when Theophil Queequeg was eight years old, he moved with his mother from Hiva Oa in the Marquesas Islands to Papeete on Tahiti. Teachers had informed her that he was an exceptional student but he needed more sophisticated instruction than they could offer. Leaving family and friends behind, they travelled for six days by freighter, sleeping on deck and eating fried foods from the small public galley on board. His mother set up a booth in the art nouveau market building in central Papeete, selling curios and handcrafts from her native island. Her business struggled but she managed to keep both of them fed and clothed until in Queequeg's last year at school she came down with influenza caught from a visiting tourist and died. By this time, he had become a favourite among his teachers and arrangements were made for him to attend university in Paris. Due to the high cost of travel through the vast reaches of Polynesia, he had never been back to his native village of Atuona on Hiva Oa, which he came to know in his years at the Sorbonne as the final resting place of Paul Gauguin.

Queequeg was a handsome young man with an exotic but familiar appearance much admired by the continental French. The many women in his life proved a major distraction and he struggled through to an undistinguished degree, after which he lingered for three years in the Latin Quarter, staying in a small flat on Rue Mouffetard, next to where Ernest Hemingway had lived in the early 1920s. Fleeing an irate husband, Theophil travelled to London where he lived for a year on Bloomsbury Square and spent his time doing penance of sorts in the British Library, which was still housed in the British Museum, before returning to France and joining the *Alliance Police Nationale* in Marseille, using his education to secure a position with the Intelligence and Investigations division.

For the next decade he was content. He worked hard, took advanced training, and excelled at his job. He married a woman from rural Provence and they had three children, twin girls and a boy. He seldom socialized with Polynesians, who made him uncomfortable since he hardly remembered Hiva Oa, and Tahiti was wrapped in the desolation he had felt on the death of his mother. He was often unfaithful to his wife but careful not to upset her by being blatant in doing so. He considered his life to be a modest but satisfying success.

On July 17th, 1997, he dropped his family at a public beach east of Marseille before heading in to his office where his job was to undermine an incomprehensible plot by Islamist zealots to murder schoolchildren. He was wading through intercepted documents when a call came in that there had been an incident in the area where he had left his family. Although he was not part of the tactical unit sent out to deal with the situation, he went along to the scene. Five children and three adults had been arbitrarily gunned down by a disaffected student from Toulon who in a final act of immeasurable cowardice fired into the gathering crowd, maiming an infant in its mother's arms before turning the gun on himself.

Queequeg desperately and methodically moved among the dead. When he found his family alive, he gathered them up and put them in a car. They didn't talk while he drove. His wife was silent from shock, his children wept quietly in the back.

Driving up a steep slope towards their home in the outlying region of Marseille, Queequeg watched as an oncoming truck careened down the hill out of control. He braked and swung to the side. The truck swerved and rolled, hitting Queequeg's car with full force. Both vehicles exploded on impact. Queequeg was thrown clear.

The other driver, Queequeg's wife, twin daughters, and son, disintegrated amidst the sound and the terrible fury. Queequeg rose to his feet. He observed beyond comprehension as the burning, bloody, shattered pieces of his world settled on the earth around him. He stood in that exact spot until medics administered a sedative and led him away.

When he was dismissed from the hospital, Queequeg visited his family's grave, then flew out with Air France to Papeete and caught an Air Tahiti Nui flight over to Hiva Oa. He arranged for a boat to Nuku Hiva and settled into a small cottage in the Taipivai valley where Herman Melville had survived the appetites of his neighbours a hundred and fifty years previously. During his sojourn on Nuku Hiva, he had his face tattooed in the most fierce of traditional Marquesian designs. After five years he took a boat back to Hiva Oa, visited the graves of Gauguin and Jacques Brel in Atuona, and flew over to Papeete where he joined the gendarmerie and was sent to Bora Bora in recognition of his experience in France.

Harry and Tess spent the day looking at black pearls in hotel shops within walking distance. The gendarme posted to keep watch seemed comfortable with their comings and goings and remained at the hotel. They ate lunch together. She had a nap in the afternoon while he read. They had dinner down the road at the Maitai Hotel. They chatted aimlessly but talked no further about Queequeg.

Harry did not know what to make of the parallels between the policeman's life and his own. He thought about how the Marquesian allowed his pain to show on the outside. Was the facial disfiguration a disguise or was it enhancement? Did it hide or distort what he actually felt? Did the evocation of his tragic heritage signify acceptance or defiance? Harry remembered what Cardinal Newman had said, that to say the same thing as your ancestors said, you may have to say something different.

And to say something different, you may have so say much the same.

He decided the scar tissue on Queequeg's face was symbolic, but could not fathom for what. The semiotics of Queequeg's tattoo were clearly a private affair.

Later in the evening, after he had left Tess at the Muana Kea, he walked back along the shore road to Fati's tattoo shop near the Maitai, collaborated on a Marquesian design to wrap around one of his ankles, and paid cash to have his bewilderment etched blue-black into his flesh, after which he limped back to Chez NoNo, wearing an emblem of the sorrows he shared with a man he hardly knew, and feeling pain for the apparent indifference to the death of her husband shown by the woman who had somehow insinuated her way into the shadows of his own private grief.

4 IN THE DEAD OF NIGHT

At first it might have seemed a dream, so gentle were the changes which signalled to Tess Saintsbury that she was not alone: a feathered movement of air disturbed the darkness, the temperature shifted from another human being in the room, the aroma of a middle-aged man was subtly invasive. Lying on top of the sheets, she opened her eyes and slowly raised her head. A dark figure shuffled through the shadows. She could hear him breathe. She adjusted her own breathing to his. She narrowed her eyes so the lamplight through the window didn't reflect and lying preternaturally still she watched his deliberate approach and waited.

When he was an arms-length away, she could see his hands. They were extended in front of him as if he were afraid of stumbling into something terrifying. She could feel body heat radiate from his closeness. The intruder leaned forward. Tess slammed one fist against the bridge of his nose. Twisting low she brought the other fist up sharply between his legs, grinding deep as he screamed and grasping the pulverized flesh she twisted and yanked until he collapsed across her naked body, quivering in pain.

She pushed him off.

The house telephone buzzed.

She turned on the lights, walked to her dive kit and pulled out a roll of silver duct tape. She taped the intruder's wrists, his ankles, his mouth, and dragged him into the bathroom. She stepped out and slipped on a t-shirt and boxer shorts and turned out the lights before the gendarme knocked at the door.

He was a young French national. His sunburned face gleamed from the light on the post by the causeway that connected the cottages to the main hotel.

"No," she told him. "No problem. Just a bad dream."

"Would you like someone to stay with you?"

"Thank you," she said. "I'm fine."

"I will be very close." (*Je serai très proche*, he said. He was speaking French.)

"*Bien sûr, merci,*" she responded, then added in English, "To keep me safe or to keep me confined?"

The crisp red skin on his face crinkled. "For safety, of course." He was apparently bilingual.

"If I need anything," she said, "I'll scream."

He retreated and she closed the door. After standing a few moments in the darkness, listening to his footsteps recede on the wooden causeway, she turned on her bedside lamp and walked back into the bathroom, which was illuminated only by light shining through the open door. She prodded her captive's groin with a bare foot. He groaned. She rolled him over so that he faced the wall. Then she sat on the toilet and peed, flushed, and went back to bed, lying on top of the sheets in her t-shirt and shorts. She switched off the table lamp and stared at the mottled darkness. There were sporadic involuntary groans coming from the bathroom.

She got up and retrieved a slender boxcutter from her dive gear. She stepped confidently through the darkness to the mini-fridge where she extracted a bag of ice cubes that had partially melted then refrozen into a mass. She carried the ice into the bathroom, switched on the light over the sink, and squatted beside the man on the floor. She tore the tape from his mouth and forced the handle of a plastic toothbrush between his teeth, then undid his pants. As she pulled them loose she tucked something hidden by his clothes—in the shape of a handgun—deeper into his pocket. She pushed the ice down inside the front of his underwear as far as it would go, while he stifled a shriek of pain, then she did up his pants, used the boxcutter to cut the tape loose on his wrists and, leaving the bathroom light on, she went back into the other room, shutting the door behind her. She tore off a fresh strip of duct tape and working by feel she folded a cardboard sleeve around the blade of the boxcutter and attached it against the small of her back, then returned to her bed.

After a few moments, she slept.

Before the breaking of dawn the bathroom door opened. Hunched stiffly over his pain, the man came out and moved stealthily towards the bed with the woman asleep on top of the sheets. Blood leaked from his nose. A torn strip of duct tape dragged from one ankle against the floor mats. The front of the man's pants was darkened with blood-smeared water stains. His face twitched with tremors of pain. The toothbrush was still clenched between his teeth. His eyes pierced the gloom, anticipating the slightest movement. He glanced at the tape on the bedside table. With a swift powerful lunge overriding his agonies and her violent response, he dropped his weight on top of her and pinioned her arms, spat out the toothbrush as he flipped her over, and bound her wrists tightly behind her back with duct tape.

He hauled her to her feet and withdrew a compact Smith & Wesson M&P Shield, 9 mm, from the front pocket of his soiled pants, wiping it clean on his shirt. He made a gesture to pistol-whip her, stopping a finger's breadth from her face, then he grimaced through a forced smile and motioned her towards the door. He didn't bother to tape her mouth.

Their two figures like silver spectres in the brightening light moved along the elevated docks between cottages with Tess in front. The young gendarme didn't notice them until they were almost in front of him. He stood up, perplexed by the presence of her companion, and draped his hand casually across the grip of his service pistol.

"*Bonjour, ça va?*" he said.

Tess searched his eyes, he smiled.

The other man stayed behind her.

"*Monsieur?*" the gendarme asked.

The other man stepped to the side. His weapon was pointed directly at the young Frenchman's heart. A brief explosion resonated like a dropped plate through the early morning air. The man slipped past Tess and caught the crumpling gendarme, his pale blue eyes still wide with astonishment, and dragged his body into the shadows. Then he turned to Tess and motioned for her to proceed through the deserted lobby to a blue sedan parked by the open pavilion across the lane. They got in and drove to the paved road and turned right, away from Viatape.

Her captor squirmed in his seat, trying to find a position to comfort his wounded testicles, then placed his Smith & Wesson in the coffee holder on the console between them. With her arms taped behind her back, Tess lurched against the seat belt; her awkward movements allowing her to tug the boxcutter loose from under her t-shirt. She clasped the cutter with the fingers of both hands, removed the cardboard sleeve, pressed the blade against the tape and cut her wrists free.

As the car swung around the lower end of the island and turned northeast, the rising sun glared in the driver's eyes. He had to squint to avoid Polynesians walking to work and tourist runners beating the heat. He didn't notice when Tess tumbled sideways and palmed his handgun. When they turned into a gravel drive beside an isolated rental cottage, he pulled the car to a stop and got out, walking around to her side as if he were still in charge.

She got out, holding the Smith & Wesson poised to fire.

"Okay, my friend," she said. "Let's meet your boss."

The man seemed more resigned than surprised that she had once again taken control. He shrugged. "He is not my boss."

"I imagine he has a gun trained on us right now so please, move to your left and stay in front of me. We'll go in together."

As he veered to his left a small calibre weapon shattered the air. Tess dove headlong into the shadows close to the house, out of the shooter's sightline, as her assailant reeled and crashed, shaking convulsively. His eyes reached hers and words bubbled as he tried to speak through the blood filling his mouth.

She nodded, aimed the Smith & Wesson at his head and pulled the trigger. His head snapped back and he was still.

Now her adversary in the house knew her exact location.

"You there," she said in a conversational voice. "Buddy out here is dead. Do you want to talk?"

"Not much to talk about."

"I think we should, just the same," she said.

She rose to her feet and stepped into the sunlight, exposing herself fully to the man who intended to kill her.

"Put down your weapon," he said.

She stepped closer and meticulously positioned the compact Smith & Wesson on the weathered window sill. He moved forward until he was framed in the open casement. She could make out his shadowy form among the interior shadows.

"I've been waiting for you," he said. His voice seemed familiar the way strangers sometimes are when their message is clearly expected.

"You didn't think he'd succeed?"

"Killing you? Probably not. But I knew if he didn't, he'd bring you back, or you would bring him."

"Fate," she said. "It was inevitable."

"Yes it was."

"Must you stay in the shadows?"

"I prefer anonymity."

"But I know who you are."

"I doubt that."

"I know who sent you."

"It does not matter."

"No, I suppose it doesn't," she said. As she spoke she moved imperceptibly closer, peering intently through the open window. She glanced down at the Smith & Wesson poised on the sill.

"There is no use prolonging this," she said. "Do you have any last words?"

"Me?"

He was momentarily flustered and in that fraction of a second she dropped from his sight below the sill while her hand flashed forward and grasped the gun that was aimed in his direction and her finger squeezed the trigger. He was dead before she hit the ground.

She listened as his body collapsed and she stood up, brushing herself off. She pushed the door open and walked into the shadows. Once inside she could see from the light through the window. The man was dressed like an American tourist, the same as his cohort lying in the dirt outside.

She searched the house and found nothing of interest. She wiped everything for prints as she went along, using a dish towel from beside the sink. Before leaving, she pressed the sharp serrated front sight of the second dead man's gun, a small Glock, to her cheek and jerked sharply, leaving a tear in her flesh and a smattering of blood on the barrel. She wiped her prints from the gun and dropped it beside his corpse, grasped a gold religious medallion and wrenched it free from a thin gold chain, which she left around his neck. She turned and walked out to the other dead man in the dirt. She placed the Smith & Wesson, wiped clean of her own prints, in his hand and yanked a similar medallion from a chain, retrieved the car keys from his pants pocket and wiped them clean on his floral shirt.

She drove to the end of the Matira Point road, chose a spot out of sight, swerved the car at slow speed and crashed into a cement road-marker before side-slipping to a stop in the ditch. She wiped her prints from the wheel and driver's door with tissues from a box in the console, leaned over and picked up her boxcutter from the floor on the passenger side and scraped the blade against the congealed blood on her cheek before dropping it back on the floor, got out of the car, started walking, then returned to retrieve the boxcutter and cut a small slash on the side of her neck, letting a few drops of blood fall onto the front of her t-shirt, wiped the handle clean of prints and dropped it again. She cleaned her prints from the outside handle of the driver's door, blew her nose on the tissue, tucked it under the elasticized top of her boxer shorts, and walked in bare feet beside the gravel laneway towards her hotel.

A cluster of gendarmes with Inspector Queequeg at the centre was waiting by the entrance. She collapsed in front of them and was carried to her cottage over the water and settled onto her bed, still in her t-shirt and boxers. She lay apparently exhausted with her eyes half-closed. They left her to rest before questioning. She was clutching two gold medallions in the palm of one hand. She stretched languidly, reached over and dropped the medallions into a bag on the floor by her bedside table and almost immediately fell into a deep and empty sleep.

5 THE THIRD MAN

HARRY RECLINED ON A CHAISE LONGUE IN THE FILIGREED shade of the towering palms between Chez NoNo and the beach, reading a tattered copy of *Le Compte de Monte-Cristo*. By struggling to read it in French, he absolved himself for wasting time on a frivolous classic. Karen insisted Alexandre Dumas wrote highly compelling social commentary. Harry thought he wrote pot-boilers. Karen insisted they were well-written, Harry argued she was no more fluent in French than he was, so how would she know. Karen declared they had stood the test of time. So, Harry countered, has *Fanny Hill*. My point exactly, she said, leaving him nothing to argue.

He missed those discussions. Closing his book without bothering to note where he'd left off, he drifted into bittersweet reverie. So many intellectuals took themselves seriously. Harry and Karen held ideas and facts in high esteem but thought thinking was fun and thinkers amusing, seldom more so than when they were uncritically solemn. Most philosophers were dead men but their ideas were as vital as the air Harry breathed and Karen studied culture, not to fix it in aspic but to live among the leaves of its endless renewal.

With the onshore breeze soothing his brow against the rising heat, Harry's mind wandered to the stone house on the Sanctuary Line where they used to sit in front of a split-maple fire after Matt and Lucy were asleep and chat aimlessly about great books and pop culture, movies, colleagues, the kids, and the evils of conservative politics.

He could hear the fire crackle, the wind moan in the eaves and rattle the double glazed windows. The scent of maple smoke played in his nostrils, mixed with the tropical odours of growth and decay all around him. He could hear Karen's laughter and giggles amidst the swishing of surf, and he tried to recall what he'd said that had made her so pointlessly happy.

That was it. They had been pointlessly happy, splendidly pointlessly happy.

Then he burned the house down.

His eyes flashed open.

Inspector Queequeg was leaning over him, his tattooed face in the shade so that he looked almost kindly, like a benevolent stranger regretful for intruding in another man's dreams.

"Dr. Lindstrom," he said, speaking in a conspiratorial whisper. "Your friend, Madam Tess, she has asked for you."

"What, where? Is she all right?"

"She is alive, yes."

Harry rose to his feet. *Le Compte de Monte-Cristo* fell on the sand.

"Someone tried to kill her last night. She escaped but she has a few injuries, a couple of cuts, nothing special."

Not special, but they tried to kill her.

"I will take you to her, she is at her hotel."

"I thought you had a guard posted."

"A Frenchman. He is dead."

Her guard was killed and she's okay?

"Anyone else," Harry asked.

"Yes, two, they were shot. We found their bodies on the other side of the island. There was a third. He temporarily got away. We have roadblocks, we are monitoring all boats and planes, he cannot go far. Not if he is alive."

"And if he's not?"

"He would be difficult to find. This island is small but a dead body is easy to bury and might never be discovered—except perhaps by an anthropologist a thousand years hence."

A novel image, Harry. Your policeman is a poet.

"There is no urgency, we will walk," said Inspector Queequeg and added, as if Harry might not know his way, "Her hotel is very close."

When they stepped into the laneway in front of Chez NoNo, Harry momentarily recoiled at the Polynesian's fearsome face in broad daylight. At the same time, Queequeg caught sight of the tattoo etched around Harry's right ankle. The skin was raw but the design was a striking rendering of a turtle overlaid by a manta with an elongated stinger wrapped around the foot, incorporating various abstractions of a tiki god's head straight on and in profile, surrounded by vegetative tendrils and swirls.

"Celtic?" he enquired. He did not smile but he was clearly amused.

Harry grinned sheepishly. "Cultural appropriation," he confessed. "It's Marquesian."

As if he wouldn't know!

Queequeg seemed pleased.

"I prefer to think you have honoured us, not stolen from us." A clipped British inflection gave his Gallic accent a slight air of condescension. "I am offended when the body is turned into a canvas for psycho-aesthetic expression. I am pleased when it is used as homage to an ancient tradition."

He's trying to say his own tattoo is more than skin graffiti.

Harry said, "I am redeemed by your eloquence."

"Redeemed."

"My parents' generation, my Aunt Beth especially, would have been appalled."

"And at my scarification as well?"

Scarification? Autobiography.

"No, she would have admired yours."

"I like your Aunt Beth."

It dawned on Harry, his aunt would have liked Queequeg. Because he was so difficult to read. Or was he too easy? He wondered if Queequeg's face represented a Manichean dichotomy or the reconciliation of opposites in a single design.

Harry, stop thinking.

"Come, you are worried about your friend, yes?" They were still standing in the laneway. "Can you walk or should I send for the car?"

Harry was in bare feet to avoid abrasion from flip flops or sandals.

"It's only a bit sore," he said. "I'm fine."

"I was thinking of the other foot."

Harry glanced down at the mutilated toes on his left foot. He had incurred irremediable damage from frostbite the previous year that in a minor way affected his gait but he hardly noticed. The scarring didn't impede his motion. It gave what he thought of as *character* to his walk.

"I'm fine," he repeated.

They progressed down the laneway side by side, the burly man with his face permanently in shadow, the lean and angular man with a compound limp. When they reached Tess Saintsbury's new cottage, a small cluster of people on the causeway outside stood back to let them enter, where they discovered a throng of hotel staff, medical personnel, aggressively curious fellow guests, and police.

"Everyone out," Queequeg declared. *"Dépêche-toi!"*

The room fell quiet as the crowd quickly dispersed.

Tess gave Queequeg a glancing smile, then gazed up at Harry.

She looks gorgeous, Harry.

She was lying on top of the bed, wearing a sheer white peignoir over a diaphanous pale blue nightgown, making her appear delicate and demure, with her feet tucked under a light cover and her voluminous black hair framing her face. She had applied makeup with care to look casual but enhance her huge eyes and elegant features. A small bandage adorned one cheek and a similar bandage ran vertically down the side of her neck.

"Hello, Harry," she said.

He moved close to the bed and took her hand.

"It's been quite an ordeal," she said.

He squeezed her hand.

"Sit here," she said. She slid over and patted the side of the bed.

"No," said Queequeg. "Sit over there, please."

Harry slouched into a chair within her line of vision. Her face showed strain but her eyes, when they focussed on his, were unflinching.

"We found the two men, as you said." Queequeg addressed Tess as if they were alone in the room. "Hawaiian shirts, both dead."

"Shot," she observed. It was not a question.

"Yes. The third man is missing," said Queequeg. "Can you describe him?"

"It was very confusing, I was frightened."

"Of course. Were you blindfolded?"

"I was told to keep my eyes shut."

"And you did?"

"For the car ride, yes. He held a knife to my throat, he cut my cheek, no the man in the cottage cut my cheek with his gun, the other man slashed my neck when I tried to escape. I could hear surf but I couldn't see the ocean when we got to the cottage. You found it, anyway. That's good. The third man was wearing shorts and a polo shirt. He was in charge, I think. I can't be sure."

"Did you get any names?"

"Holly, I think. An odd name for a man."

"Holy?"

"Holly. Like Christmas. Another was called Harry. Not our Harry, just Harry. The third was Calloway."

"Which one abducted you?"

"That would be Holly. The other two were waiting for us."

"But you tried to fight him off?"

She hesitated. "Yes, I did. Yes, I smashed my knee into his groin."

"You must have really connected. He seems to have pissed himself."

"He dumped ice down his pants for the pain."

"But first he subdued you."

"He had a gun."

"Then this Holly person drove you to the cottage."

"Yes."

"And Calloway shot Holly and Harry. Was there an argument?"

"No, Calloway and Holly shot each other."

"Both men showed powder residue on their hands but the Smith & Wesson was fired at very close range, yet the man holding it was a good twenty feet away. Isn't that strange?"

"Is it? I guess it is."

"Could the third man have shot the man inside and then placed the gun in the other man's hand."

"It's possible. I was inside on the floor. Calloway pistol whipped me—I think that's what it's called—and Harry swore at him, yes, there was a shot, then he dragged me outside.

"And then what?"

"What? Oh, Harry bundled me back into the car and we took off. When we crashed I scrambled to get out. He grabbed me, he cut me with a knife. I punched him and ran. He chased after me but he was a very heavy man and gave up and when I looked around he was gone."

"How heavy? You said you couldn't describe him."

"Corpulent, but with a kind face. Very sinister, a killer with a kind face."

"Is that what they wanted, to kill you?"

"They killed my husband."

"Did they say that?"

"No, they didn't have to, it seemed obvious."

"This corpulent man, he was obese, yes? Perhaps like myself?"

"Inspector, I would say you are more on the portly side. Not obese."

"Portly, that is good. A little plump. But he was fat, yes. Yet you say he was wearing shorts?"

"He was." She seemed lost in thought for a moment. "There is no accounting for bad taste," she said.

"Sometimes I wear shorts."

"I'm sure on you they look good."

"Yes, I am portly, not corpulent."

"Distinguished," she said.

She looked over at Harry. Harry looked away. She was performing and he had no desire to be part of the act.

Queequeg said, "There was a cot folded against a wall in your cottage where you stayed with your husband."

"There was."

"Is that where your husband slept?"

"I beg your pardon?"

"Did you sleep on the big bed or the little bed?"

"When?"

"Before he was murdered."

"I'm sorry," Harry intruded. "I don't see—" He didn't finish his sentence.

"Of course," said Queequeg. "Now these three men called each other by name?"

"Yes, I think so. Perhaps not. Perhaps I imagined they did."

"Then where did the names come from?'

"I can hear their voices in my head."

"Naming themselves?"

"No, I think maybe one was Paul. And there was Peter. The third man was Jude. You know, 'Hey Jude.'"

"The John Lennon song, yes."

"Paul McCartney, I think."

"You seem confused, Madame Saintsbury. Perhaps you should rest a little."

"I'm sure it was McCartney, but yes, perhaps I should. I would like Professor Lindstrom to stay with me."

"If you wish."

Inspector Queequeg left, closing the door softly behind him.

"So what was that all about?" said Harry, moving closer but ignoring her gestured invitation to sit on the bed.

"What was what all about? Thank you for coming to my rescue."

"I was only reading."

"What?"

"*The Count of Monte Cristo* in French."

"I mean, thanks for protecting my marital secrets. It really is none of his business where I sleep or with whom."

"It probably is. But I was talking about the games."

"Games? Harry, I've been through a lot, it seems surreal, it really does. I couldn't think of anything better to say. The man wanted answers. He's a cop, they always want answers."

"Your three abductors, I'm guessing Harry's last name is Lime, Calloway is a major, Holly's last name in Martins. I spent some time in Vienna in the spring. I'm surprised Queequeg hasn't seen the film."

"I was confused, Harry."

"Not too confused to describe Harry as Orson Welles."

"Orson Welles wasn't fat in *The Third Man*, at least not obese."

"Corpulent."

"A little pudgy around the edges."

"And then you switched from *film noir* to religion. I'm surprised you didn't say the third one was Mary."

"My name? Why?"

"I was thinking of the folk-singing trio, Peter, Paul and Mary?"

"Before my time," she said.

"Mine too," said Harry, remembering the kids playing *Puff the Magic Dragon* over and over *ad nauseam*.

"They were just names, Harry."

"Those men were trying to kill you."

"I know."

"Why did they shoot each other? Queequeg didn't really ask you that?"

"I don't know. He knew I don't know."

"And one got away?"

"Yes. I imagine he's far gone by now or in very deep hiding."

"Queequeg said it's a difficult island to hide on unless you're dead."

"Corpses aren't always easy to hide."

"You know that from experience, do you?"

"I just think sometimes the dead have an awkward way of turning up."

He couldn't be sure what she meant. Her eyes gave away nothing. It occurred to Harry that their situation was beyond surreal, whatever that was. Very postmodern.

"Come on, Harry, lie with me for a bit. I need to be hugged."

He hesitated. The look on her face reminded him of great film actors, Orson Welles among them. Without blinking, their eyes could change from kind to sinister, playful to cruel, amused to malevolent—windows to the soul, mirrors reflecting back on the observing self. Al Pacino, he thought, Meryl Streep, Kenneth Branagh, Colin Farrell. Comedic eyes revealing tragedy within. Tragic eyes, promising comedy to come. Surreal eyes.

He gently stretched out beside her, surprised at how small she was. (Karen was silent but not far away.) They lay very still, enjoined from movement that might be construed as sexual. After a while, as late afternoon dulled the light seeping through the closed curtains, sentiment gave way to rising desire and they snuggled closer. She looked up at him, their lips briefly touched.

Immediately, Harry rose to his feet. Tess turned away. She slid off the other side of the bed.

"Time to go for a walk," he declared.

"If that's what you'd like," she said.

She edged around past the end of the bed. Her peignoir shimmered as she moved, revealing her figure in sensuous pale blue planes. She said, "We need to finish our kiss."

She smiled, her eyes creased at the edges.

"For future reference," he said.

With lips open and moist she tilted her head and seemed to draw him to her, yet when the length of their bodies touched she did not initiate the kiss. She waited until his lips pressed hers before rising to him, at first gently, then briefly devouring, then suddenly she pulled away. They stood close for a long time, until pooling drops of perspiration became distracting and they separated shyly. Without saying anything she picked a few things from her dresser and wardrobe and walked into the bathroom to change.

She took his arm when they entered the lobby and informed the gendarme on guard they were going for a stroll before dinner. He asked them to wait while he checked with Inspector Queequeg, talked on his cell phone, then nodded congenial acquiescence, and they stepped out into the glow of dusk streaming past palm tree trunks and over the sand across the Matira Point lane.

They stopped in at Chez NoNo for Harry to pick up a pair of sandals. When he emerged from his grass cottage, she glanced down at his feet, appearing to notice his tattoo for the first time.

"When did you get that done? My God it looks sore."

"But beautiful, right?"

"They say it's all in the eyes of the beholder. Take off your sandal, let me admire it up close."

She squatted to examine his foot like it was a piece of found art and she was determining its worth. The lowering sun glinted off her diamond bracelet.

"It's getting late," he said, feeling self-conscious.

She rose and walked ahead of him into the laneway. Almost haphazardly, she choose to turn right and they walked through the narrowing light among shrubs and fences until they came to an opening near 'Chez Robert et Tina,' a modest pension at the tip of the point. Stepping carefully over the dead coral outcroppings into a dramatic display of crimson, orange, and yellow presaging the sun's collapse into the sea, they soon reached a small spit of sandy beach. He held her at arm's length, a little uneasy from mixed feelings of affection and betrayal. She appeared to be a figure in flames, but as an icon she was oddly askew. Her diamond bracelet glowed like hot embers, her dress in the twilight seemed colourless and opaque, her walking sandals inelegant, her leather handbag outsized and clumsy. Her voluptuous hair was subdued with a nondescript silver barrette. Her gaze in the unnatural light did not reflect back on Harry but seemed to look past him, trying to locate something offshore.

"Look," she said. "It's a trick of the light; you can see that sandy spur underwater, running out a good fifty metres or more."

He turned and followed her sightline but saw nothing unusual beyond a pale shimmering on the surface, stained by the lights of several resorts on the atoll a couple of kilometers away on the other side of the open lagoon.

"Stand here," she said. "There's a manta ray. You can just barely see it." She clambered up onto an elevation of coral. He stood in front of her. She grasped his shoulders for balance, then let go to move higher. Harry could not imagine being able to see a ray at depth in the diminishing light.

"Just give me a minute, Harry." Her voice receded. "I have to pee."

He gazed out over the lagoon. There was movement behind him, he tried not to listen. He heard a shuffling sound, then a rush of air like indrawn breath, followed by the muffled crack of a dead weight striking his skull.

6 HUAHINE

TESS SAINTSBURY GRASPED HARRY UNDER THE ARMPITS and shifted his body to clear ragged protrusions of coral as she lowered him onto the sand. She set to the side a fist-sized weighted pouch she had used as a bludgeon and withdrew a mesh sack from her leather handbag before dumping the rest of the bag's contents, including a high-powered underwater flashlight and a Suunto D9 diver computer. She placed the light inside the mesh sack and strapped the computer to her left wrist before sliding a fingernail sharply across the cut in her cheek, drawing blood. She pressed the empty handbag against her open flesh, then folded it carefully under Harry's head. Blood seeped from a wound at the base of his skull. She turned his head against his makeshift pillow to staunch the bleeding.

Standing straight, she untied the straps of her dress and let it drop, stepped out of it, and stuffed it into the sack. The light of a full moon had erased the fiery display of the setting sun as she picked up the canvas weight pouch and waded into the gentle surf, lifting her feet carefully over mounds of coral and the menacing spikes of sea urchins until she reached water up to her hips. She unzipped the canvas pouch and poured its contents of lead pellets into the water where they sank and merged with the sand. She removed the flashlight from the mesh sack, took off her shoes and tucked them in with her dress, along with the emptied pouch, and secured it with an extended drawstring around her waist. Wearing only her pale blue panties and bra, she began to swim the breast stroke, checking the compass on her computer twice and counting her kicks to seventy-five before stopping and shining her light down to the sea floor some forty feet below her. She propelled herself forward with a couple more kicks, took three deep breaths, and dived for the bottom.

Popping her ears as she descended, she slipped down through an eerie luminescence from the diffused light of the moon, but when she reached depth and turned her flashlight on, as she skimmed over the sand to a coral embankment, the world beyond its beam closed around her like a dark satin shroud. Grasping a broken outcropping of sheet coral, she projected the cone of light through the darkness in a searching arc. She swam to another outcropping and continued scanning. And a third time she swam and then scanned. Her chest began to spasm and her throat seized, the beam wavered, her fingers loosened. She kicked vigorously to hold her position, then released her grip, switched off the flashlight, and drifted free, slowly spiralling upwards. Suddenly she twisted, pulled masses of water towards her in a great sweeping embrace, and almost depleted she plunged down and down into a dark crevasse. She swam its length with her light on again and at the deepest narrowing dropped the light onto a patch of sand and reached into the darkest shadows, wrenching a two-tank rig of nitrox, with BCD and regulator attached, from its secured position under a coral overhang. She clasped the gear between her legs and twisted the valve counter-clockwise with one hand while grasping at the mouthpiece with the other, clasping it between her lips and teeth.

Heaving deeply as oxygen-enriched air flowed into her body, for several minutes she made no effort to do anything but breathe. When the small explosions of bubbles took on a syncopated rhythm, she reached deeper into the shadowed niche and pulled out a larger mesh bag and extracted a 5 ml wetsuit with a front zip. After considerable writhing, while holding the mouthpiece in place like a misplaced umbilicus, she snugged into the suit, then removed her silver barrette, dropping it in the sand, and combing her hair loose with her fingers she pulled on a black dive cap. She placed a mask over her face and blew it clear, slipped on a pair of super-efficient ScubaPro fins, and checked her gauges. She pulled a black rubber wristband from the large mesh bag and rolled it over her diamond bracelet, then slipped the weight pouches out of her BCD, one at a time, and dumped lead pellets into the sand until she achieved neutral buoyancy. She bundled the smaller mesh sack with her wet dress and shoes into the larger bag and stuffed it deep into a cleft at the back of the overhang, displacing a lobster who skittered through the ragged shaft of moonlight into deeper shadows. She picked up her flashlight, turned it off, and tucked it into her BCD. A green moray undulated past her in the glowing column of water as she slowly ascended.

Before breaking the surface she removed her mask to avoid reflection. She inflated her BCD enough to keep her head up and breathe fresh air. The figure of an injured man on the shore moved awkwardly towards a floodlight at the side of Robert and Tina's pension. Close around her, the water was a velvet blue, rippled with streaks of moonlight. She waited until Harry disappeared in the shadows and she sank back into the depths, putting on her mask and clearing as she descended. Below thirty feet, at just over one atmosphere of depth, she reoriented herself before swimming at a leisurely pace away from the shoreline.

Moonlight penetrating the overhead water allowed her to follow her route by dead reckoning as she glided over grasping shadows and wavering sandbars. Occasionally, when she flicked on her flashlight to check her gauges, or touched her compass light into brief confirmation of her direction, leering eyes indicated she was a figure of interest to curious tarpon and surly barracuda. Sometimes, when the coral mounded close, she caught the pale discs of shark eyes lazily observing her progress and the piercing gaze of green morays swinging into the gentle current. At one point she stopped to hover over a bucktoothed parrotfish asleep under a homespun blanket of protective mucus, recuperating from a day grinding coral into sand.

The enveloping translucent waters seemed her natural milieu and after nearly two hours of swimming, as the sea-bottom began to rise beneath her, she slowed even more to observe creatures and formations before surfacing. She came up close to a deserted beach on a low motu. When she emerged from the water, carrying her fins, she walked unsteadily, wavered, paused, and drew her strength upwards from her legs to her shoulders, recovered her balance, and strode into a cluster of palms. She began to shiver and stopped to strip off her wetsuit and shake out her thick black hair before finger-combing it into submission. She gazed back through the trees and across the broad lagoon. Extensive illumination surrounding the Muana Kea International drowned out the lesser lights on Matira Point but a single flashing beacon in their midst suggested a police vehicle or ambulance.

By the time she crossed to the ocean side of the motu and made her way through a tangle of scrub mangrove to a dugout canoe tucked away like a derelict among roots and branches, she had stopped shivering. Hauling the boat out into the open moonlight, she donned a green and blue pareu from a dry bag stowed under a seat, and dragged the boat to the water. She loaded her wetsuit, tanks, and gear into a large dive bag and placed it in the bottom as ballast, then climbed in and taking up a paddle wedged under the seat pushed off into the whispering surf.

Once clear of the shore swell and in open water, she shifted her dive equipment for balance. The canoe was tippy with the outrigger removed but she kept her weight low, kneeling on the bottom, and settled into perfect harmony with her craft and the surging sea.

For the next three hours she progressed away from Bora Bora, paddling a powerful j-stroke, which she modified to account for the swells. She kept her tiny vessel on due course for the islands of Tahaa and the more distant Ra'iatea, both islands circumscribed by the same coral atoll. At one point about half way, she stopped and removed two gold medallions from her dry bag and dropped them over the side. She watched as they swivelled and spun until they sank out of sight and then she resumed paddling.

When Tahaa loomed through the darkness in craggy silhouette, she slipped along the outer edge of the reef. The night was punctuated by a few lights in the village of Tapamu to the south and from a resort on a motu closer to the route she was taking. She shifted course for Huahine, still two hours distant.

In the darkness just before dawn, with the moon swallowed by the sea, she entered the placid lagoon surrounding Huahine Nui and hunched over for a few minutes, breathing deeply, before she rallied to beach her craft among a cluster of other canoes, which all had outriggers. Hers, as she walked away from the rising sunlight, seemed a broken discard.

After burying her nitrox tanks in a sandy hollow under the roots of a fallen tree, she hoisted the strap of her dive bag with the rest of her equipment and a small dry sack of toiletries, clothes, papers, and money onto her shoulder and turned towards the airstrip only a few hundred metres away. When she arrived at the small terminal, work crews were bustling about, their activity in contrast to the clusters of sleepy sun-wracked tourists awaiting departure. There was nothing about her to draw attention except a distracting tangle of black hair that seemed intentionally unkempt and mildly wanton.

Tess Saintsbury settled in for a leisurely breakfast in the airport cafeteria. As she sipped her second coffee she glanced down at her funky black wristband, toyed with it, then slid it off, revealing her diamond bracelet. She reached into the small dry sack that had become her purse and removed a cluster of silver bangles that she slid over the same wrist, disguising her treasure in a jangling display of costume jewellery.

After the morning plane from Tahiti arrived, she blended with arriving passengers and boarded a van for the Huahine Bali Hai where she checked in, handed her gear bag over to staff, and was escorted to a thatch-roofed bungalow on the edge of a pristine beach.

"Welcome back," said the Polynesian youth carrying her bag. "Will you be staying with us for longer this time, Miss MacPherson?"

"I think so, Henri. We'll see."

"And you will be diving, I expect." He spoke precise English.

"*Mais, bien sûr*," she said.

Henri was working to become a dive master for Huahine Divers. He lived at the hotel, where his mother was an employee especially valued for her proficiency in European languages.

"Would you like me to bring you some ice," Henri asked.

"*Non merci*, I think I'll just have a nap before dinner."

"For your cheek, do you want antiseptic."

She touched her fingers to her cheek.

"No," she said. "A small accident. It will be fine."

"Did you come this time from England? It is very far."

"I had a long journey, yes. Thank you, Henri."

He set her bag in the corner and left, smiling at her generous tip and the warmth that came through, despite her apparent exhaustion.

After closing the curtains, Tess stripped off her pareu, her underwear, and stepped into the small bathroom. She glanced at herself in the mirror and avoided the cliché of surveying her body. Clutching a mass of her tangled black hair she grimaced, picked out a pair of shears from her bag and poised to cut. Instead, she set the scissors down, had a shower with a thorough shampoo, towelled dry, and drew her damp hair back into a tight French roll. Her remarkably fine features stood proud against the revealed shape of her skull. Smiling to herself she went into the bed-sitting room and stretched out languidly on the bed with only the mosquito netting to cover her nakedness. Within minutes the woman who now called herself Teresa MacPherson was in a deep sleep.

7 VIATAPE

SUNLIGHT REFRACTING THROUGH A WINDOW RIPPLED ON the walls and ceiling. Harry seemed to be surfacing from deep underwater. He exhaled through pursed lips until his lungs were depleted. Someone spoke to him but the syllables collided and rushed past his ears. He closed his eyes tightly against pain, opened them again and looked for coherent shapes. To his right, an open doorway, to his left, a woman holding his hand, smiling, professional.

As he moved towards full consciousness, claustrophobia stifled his breathing. He gasped and the woman adjusted an oxygen mask over his face. Time jumped and images shot through his mind—manta rays swooping in front of the sun, pale unblinking eyes of a tiger shark, dinner plates throbbing with dead fish, unsmiling images of a woman with radiant black hair, of a drowned man staring through a shimmering column of water. He remembered the sounds of his cranial assault: the rush of a guillotine blade sliding downwards, the grating of a trapdoor released on the gallows, rifle bolts shifting before the onrush of bullets, the roar of tumultuous water.

His eyes darted to the side. The woman leaned closer. Her eyes were blue-green. She said, "You have a bad accident." Her English was awkward. "You rest. I tell them you be awake."

He watched her move away. Someone appeared close to his bedside and asked him questions. He wasn't aware that he answered. The person receded. He tried to lift his head but was immobilized by pain and carefully sank back against the pillow. It smelled of lavender. The woman who rearranged the pillow smelled of lavender. The room smelled of lavender, like the fields of southern France.

He woke up in a different place. He had been moved to a holding cell of some sort. An odour of disinfectant mingled with the acrid smell of urine and vomit and cigarettes and sweat. A recessed light saturated the fetid air with an unpleasant pall and pale shadows defined the emptiness of a room without furnishings except for the built-in cement bunk covered with a soiled grey blanket on which he was lying.

The closed door rattled. He realized that was what had awakened him. It rattled again. He struggled to sit up.

Fresh air flooded the room as a terrifying apparition appeared, balancing a metal tray. The apparition seemed primal, predatory, menacing, unnatural, yet somehow absurdly familiar and benign.

"Queequeg?" said Harry. His own voice surprised him.

"You are well, Harry. That is good."

Harry looked down at the tray then up at Inspector Queequeg.

"Thank you," he said.

Queequeg, who had never called him Harry before, backed out the door, leaving it open, and disappeared into the light.

Overriding the pain in the back of his skull, Harry devoured what was evidently his lunch, consisting of a brimming bowl of *café au lait*, crispy rolls with a chunk of nondescript cheese, a sliced banana with diced pineapple and papaya on a bed of romaine, no dressing, and a half litre of *vin de table rouge*.

He would have preferred a cold chardonnay. He would have preferred being on the beach in front of Chez NoNo. Or in his high-rise condo overlooking the Toronto harbour. Or being underwater out in the lagoon between the island and atoll, diving with Tess.

He looked around. The bare cement walls inspired a strangling sense of remorse. There was no tropical sunlight rippling on the ceiling. There was no window. The door was open. He was confused, he assumed he was still on Bora Bora. Nothing was certain.

Kafka.

He wondered where Karen was.

He ached to be with her, to talk about Kafka.

He rose to his feet slowly and carried his tray through the door into an office that opened onto the street. Queequeg was sitting at his desk with the clear golden side of his face in full light.

"Set the tray there, Dr. Lindstrom. And have a seat, please. You have been in the infirmary—a few stitches in the back of your head, they will dissolve, and probably there is no concussion."

"I was asleep."

"Well, you woke up. That was good. Then you were sedated."

"And now I'm here."

"You are of interest to police, now; not so much to doctors. You understand normally we are the most peaceful of islands."

"I'm sure," said Harry.

You notice once you're out of the cell, you're "Doctor" again.

So it seems. Where were you?

Sedated, Slate, cowering in your dreams.

"Madame Saintsbury," said Queequeg. "She is missing."

It made sense.

"What happened?"

"I thought perhaps you could tell me."

"No, I got hit on the head."

"By someone shorter than yourself, with a blunt instrument. Your skull was cracked open from the force. It was not cut."

"I was standing on a mound of coral. He could have been reaching up."

"He? The third man?"

"Who else?" said Harry.

"Where was Madame Saintsbury?"

"In the shadows."

"So, it was not dark?"

"Twilight."

"You heard nothing?"

"Nothing unexpected."

"The contents of her handbag were scattered, probably when she fell, but it is smeared with your blood. It seems she went down before you."

"Why didn't I hear anything? She would have put up a fight."

"Perhaps you forget. Your head, you know."

"Believe me, I know."

"It is not such a large wound. You were collateral damage. I would feel relieved if I were you, *monsieur le professeur*. You are alive."

"And her?"

"It is doubtful, yes."

Harry took a deep breath and exhaled slowly. He needed fresh air. Exhaust fumes wafted in from a passing car. He rose to his feet, a little unsteadily.

"May I go?" he said.

"I have seen *The Third Man*," said Queequeg. "I have read the novel by Graham Greene in English and French. It is better in the original, both are better than the movie."

For a moment, Harry was nonplussed. The residual effects of a severe blow to the head? Then he remembered.

"The names. Yes, I have no idea what she was up to."

"Considering the circumstances, it was an odd time to be playful. Perhaps she was flaunting authority."

Harry smiled inwardly. *Flouting!* It was the first real mistake he had heard Queequeg make.

"You are amused, Dr. Lindstrom. I *meant* flaunting, not flouting. Her own authority over mine. An expression, perhaps, of contempt."

He lived in the heart of literary London, remember.

"Perhaps it was nerves," Harry suggested.

"She does not strike me as a woman who would be nervous."

"Maybe she was testing to see if you'd get the joke."

"I did, but I chose to chuckle in private."

Harry missed mind games with Karen. He felt strangely nostalgic for common-room chatter.

"I'm quite exhausted," he said.

"Of course. You will be at the Chez NoNo, yes?"

"For another two weeks."

Harry hitched a ride back to Chez NoNo with one of the courtesy taxis island merchants provide to ferry wealthy hotel guests between pearl shops. No one had noticed he had been gone for two days. The woman in the tiny front office told him about the murders, assured him they were on the far side of the island. For him it was old news; for her, still very exciting. He shrugged. She declared what a fine day it promised to be. Most days on Bora Bora were fine, so Harry offered what he imagined was a congenial smile and moved on into the compound to his cottage, where he lowered himself gingerly onto bedclothes that smelled musty from not being used and rested his injured head on a scrunched up pillow before closing his eyes, but sleep would not come.

He thought about Tess and tried to resolve his conflicting impressions. She seemed naïve and yet worldly, vaguely wanton, wary, candid but not careless, haunted, self-reliant, and disarmingly clever. It was hard to imagine her dead, particularly when there was no corpse. Yet Harry knew better than to equate death with the presence or absence of earthly remains.

Karen's silver wedding band had been found but her body was never recovered. Locals in Algonquin Park were divided between two explanations. The force of the roiling water in Devils Cauldron had ground her into fragments, which merged with the natural detritus of the wilderness or her battered cadaver had drifted downriver into marshlands on the lower Anishnabi and become irretrievably lodged beneath floating islets of swamp vegetation. Either way, she was gone.

Harry gasped for breath as a deluge of images surged through his mind—the terror-stricken eyes of his children as they reached out to him in the whirling maelstrom, the thunderous turbulence as Karen vanished, the deafening, blinding, battering—until Harry alone was spewed from the tumult and floated downstream, coming to rest on a sandbar surrounded by eddies bobbing with shattered life jackets.

He had buried what remained of Lucy and Matt in a common urn and came to believe that Karen's ashes were mingled with theirs in the country cemetery on the Roman Line. They awaited his own to be added in due course.

An intrusive image of the old man's drenched stare brought him back to the present. Tess Saintsbury's unblinking eyes gazed at him from the darkest margins of his vision. His drowned brother Bobby whom he hardly remembered looked through him unseeing. He struggled against the terrors of sleep. A woman's voice intruded. He sat up abruptly and gazed in the direction of the door where the voice was coming from. At first he thought it was Karen summoning him back from the madness of memory, then he realized it was the day manager. She was announcing a visitor.

He glanced at his watch. It was morning. He'd slept through nearly a full day. He was famished but the dread that crept over him vanquished the pangs and all he craved was more sleep. He slashed water on his face, ran his fingers through his hair, and stroking his grizzled cheek he walked out to the front of Chez NoNo where Inspector Queequeg sat behind the wheel of his car.

Queequeg had maneuvered the police car around in the confined laneway to face away from Matira Point. He motioned to Harry to get in, then they drove a hundred car-lengths and rolled to a stop between the lush garden at the main entrance to the Muana Kea and the open pavilion across the lane.

They went into the bar, ordered coffees, and settled into a quiet corner.

Queequeg observed as if it were a matter of little consequence: "You did not know Madame Saintsbury's husband very well."

"No, we never met." He had already made this clear.

"But you saw him?"

"Coming in from the airport. I doubt he was aware I existed. As far as I could tell, he didn't know he existed himself."

"But you dated the woman you thought was his wife."

"We had dinner together."

"And went diving."

"We went diving separately."

"Why separately?"

"Because we had never met. We buddied up on the boat for our second dive."

"And the two of you got on well?"

"You know we did. And she invited me to dinner and I went and we enjoyed ourselves very much."

"Did that not strike you as unusual?"

"That we enjoyed ourselves?"

"That she left the man she was caring for on his own."

"Not particularly. I assumed she had made arrangements."

"And you went back to her hotel?"

"I was invited. She wanted me to meet him."

"But he was already dead."

"As it turned out."

"She was going to introduce you to a man who was not aware of his own existence?"

"Apparently," said Harry.

"And do you know who he was?"

"Not really. He was quite successful, I gather."

"Successful?"

"They travelled first class, she was half his age, very attractive, and she wore an expensive diamond bracelet."

"You are an expert on diamonds? Or on women who wear them?"

"I can recognize a fake."

Queequeg's silent response was tantamount to refuting his claim, which, on consideration, Harry realized was pretentious.

Eventually, the Inspector spoke up, as if the idea had just drifted into his mind, "Your friend is much like a character by Virginia Woolf," he said. "Tightly sprung, complex, lyrical, emotionally self-sufficient."

Harry was more interested in the allusion itself than its questionable accuracy.

"You read English novels, do you?" he asked.

"I lived for a year on Bloomsbury Square."

"Ah," said Harry.

Inspector Queequeg finished his coffee and upended the cup as if he were trying to shake something loose from the bottom. Quite suddenly, he rose from the table. Taking his cue, Harry stood up as well. Queequeg turned and walked out onto the wooden causeway leading to the scene of the original crime. He was fast for a big man.

When they entered the cottage Harry was surprised it had not been cleaned. The glass panel was closed but diffused daylight shone up through the water. He was startled when his portly companion stepped onto it, embedding himself in illumination refracted from the seabed below. Harry looked down, trying to break the illusion that Queequeg was floating, but myriad drowned eyes glowered up at him through a trick of the sunlight playing in the column of water. He felt queasy, he looked away and walked quickly into the bathroom. The eyes seemed to follow in his mind, gaping wide in terror and disbelief.

Avoiding himself in the mirror, he cracked open a bottle of room-temperature mineral water and took a long swig. He gazed around at the lavish fixtures. There were twin sinks and an elaborate Toto toilet that washed and air dried. There was a two person shower tiled in a free-form ceramic design with a raised lip across the floor to hold back the water, negating the need for a curtain. The expected bidet was absent. The Toto doubled for that. A huge used towel hung on a peg and a smaller towel lay across one of the sinks. Small shampoo and conditioner bottles and a partially used vial of body lotion were open on the vanity.

He went back into the main room.

"Sorry," he said.

Queequeg was still floating over the water.

"You seem shaken, are you all right? I'd think you would be accustomed to murder scenes."

"It was just images that flashed through my mind."

"Memory, imagination?"

"Mind tricks."

"The mind can be a terrible thing."

"Sometimes."

"Not always, yes," said Queequeg. "Or that would be madness."

With no explanation for why they were there, nor why they now departed, Queequeg led the way back to the bar and ordered two more coffees and a couple of croissants. He signed their bill, then turned to face Harry directly so that the opposing sides of his face were equally illuminated. In what Harry took to be a conspiratorial tone Queequeg asked, "What do you know about The Church Absolute?"

The question was so unexpected, it took Harry a moment to consider. "As far as I know they're neither," he said.

"Neither?"

"A church nor absolute."

"And how do you know this?"

"Just things I heard. I used to listen to my wife."

"And she was a gossip?"

"A literary and cultural theorist."

"So, *aussi une professeur,* Mrs. Lindstrom. But you say *used to.* She has quit her work? Or she is dead?"

"The latter. She was never Mrs. Lindstrom."

"But she was your wife, yes?"

"Her name was Karen Malone. Doctor, professor, just Karen, but never *Mrs.*"

"So, Professor Malone, she studied religion? But that is also the name of your detective partner, yes?"

"It's complicated."

"Not so much, she is dead. But she was also a scholar who studied The Church Absolute?"

"Not the theology, if you can call it that. She studied religious delusion."

"Faith, it is a quirk of human nature, yes?"

"Something like that."

"And did she regard all religions as delusional."

"She believed they all have a delusional component."

"Which is not always a bad thing to help us get through the night," said Queequeg, not smiling.

"Perhaps not," said Harry.

"You do not like religion?"

"Not really."

"Why?"

Nothing like a direct question to provoke an intemperate response.

Harry instead gave a measured answer. "I find it bewildering that intelligent people would choose superstition to override reason in denial of their fundamental human nature."

"We are fundamentally atheists, you think? I am like the philosopher Kierkegaard; I think perhaps between the violence of birth and the trauma of death, there is little room for pleasure but much for meaning. You are like the philosopher Nietzsche. Religion is a refuge from thinking."

"We are human, we are fundamentally rational."

"Then how do you account for The Church Absolute?"

"I don't know much about it. They're on the lunatic fringe. They trace their origins to somewhere in outer space. I take it this has something to do with your investigation."

"Yes, of course. You do not think The Church Absolute is a real religion?" Queequeg had the Gallic habit of asking a question that was also a statement of what the answer was expected to be, a rhetorical device that Harry found annoying because it limited his options to respond.

"No, I don't."

"But it is recognized in many countries, Dr. Lindstrom, including France. It is therefore a religion in French Polynesia and on Bora Bora, of course. Perhaps you think we are too tolerant. Is that possible?"

"Is it possible to be too tolerant? Of course. That's how outfits like The Church Absolute get ahead. They turn our fear of appearing intolerant against us. It is the worst legacy of humanism."

Harry, are you going to get drawn into this?

"We are desperate to appear open-minded," he continued. "Even when the theology on offer is patently absurd."

"Perhaps because it is so difficult to live with the unexplained?"

"So instead of living within the limits of our minds we explain what's beyond us by magic."

Harry, for God's sake.

"But they are Christian, are they not?" Queequeg seemed to be enjoying himself although he gave no overt indication of pleasure. "They do have a theology. They do believe in one God, in Jesus as prophet and martyr, in life after death. You just don't happen to agree with their doctrines."

"Throwing Jesus into your story does not make you a Christian, Inspector. They reduce him to a dead Jewish zealot, so of course they believe in him. He was a Jew. He was a zealot. He is dead. What's not to believe? And no, as I understand it, they do not believe in God as a separate being. As for the notion of life after death, they render it meaningless."

"An interesting trick."

"Death has no meaning if you are infinite and eternal already. They claim to originate as self-knowing aspects of the cosmic mind. If all goes according to plan, they will return to pure essence. They believe time and space are mathematical constructs to account for their temporary condition in a fallen world."

"We are all fallen, are we not?"

"You are a Catholic, I assume."

"I am indeed a survivor."

"I'm sorry,' said Harry. "How does this help your investigation?"

"We cannot live with the unexplained," Queequeg repeated and ordered a scotch on the rocks. Harry passed. He was feeling light headed from excess caffeine.

"What do you mean, Professor Lindstrom, when you say they believe that God is *not* 'a separate being?'"

"Could we move on to murder and abduction?"

"Soon, my friend. God is important."

Harry was beyond his level of comfort. He could chat about such things; he could not explain or defend them. "They offer believers the chance to *become* God," he said.

"To become angels, perhaps."

"To become *God*. At the ultimate level, if they can only just get there, they expect to merge with a limitless universal being and yet somehow maintain their personal awareness."

"That would seem a rather extreme paradox."

You ever hear of the Borg?

"If everything is a paradox, then nothing is a paradox," said Harry. "They're good at that kind of reasoning."

Now you've moved from 'Star Trek' to Beckett.

Samuel, I assume; not Thomas.

Have you any idea where this is going? Cops don't normally indulge in dialectical gossip while they're investigating a murder.

Apparently this one does.

After an awkward pause, Queequeg proceeded, "If The Church Absolute has beliefs, faith, and transcendent aspirations, it would seem to be a religion, just one you don't like."

"If you want it to be, it is," said Harry, looking around him then back at Queequeg. He had no reason to argue.

"Tell me," said Queequeg. "Do you know the name Pietro di Cosmos?"

"Yes," Harry said. "A science fiction writer, lousy prose style, fantastical plots. He wrote and directed a couple of horror films. That was all before he created The Church Absolute—I think as a bit of a joke, but it took off."

"A joke?"

"How could anyone with critical intelligence take it seriously?"

"Perhaps that is something he lacked."

Past tense, Harry.

"I'd say he was exceptionally intelligent," said Harry.

"But not critical?"

"Oh very, I think, but infinitely cynical. That allows him, *allowed* him, to exploit the fears and desires of the desperate and the gullible."

"Pietro di Cosmos became immeasurably rich. As head of a church, his wealth was literally beyond measure. He and his wives, they are very powerful. Did you know his wives were all called Mary?"

Harry let his eyes drift across the other man's features, but Queequeg's expression revealed nothing.

"I didn't know he was a polygamist," said Harry, feeling uncomfortable. "How many wives did he have?"

"Three. But one at a time, so far as we know. I have to ask you, Dr. Lindstrom, do you have any association with The Church Absolute, yourself?"

"I'd think it would be obvious I don't."

"Did you know Pietro di Cosmos was a pseudonym?"

"I'm guessing names are an unstable commodity in The Church. To change names is to shift power. All religions do it."

"He started life as William Alexander Saintsbury. Does that surprise you?"

"At this point, no," said Harry, although it did. "It appears you have a wealthy and devious corpse on your hands. And it does not surprise me that his latest Mary is Teresa-called-Tess."

"Or was. Did Madame Saintsbury ever talk about her religion?" Queequeg finished his scotch and ground the ice cubes between his teeth. It was an unpleasant sound.

"No," said Harry. "Are we finished here?"

"We are. You have been most informative."

"Why did you take me out to the cottage?"

"Curiosity."

"Yours or mine?"

"You did not seem like a man in a holy place."

"That's a relief."

"I had to check out the room one final time and sign off before the hotel can use it again."

"I bet there's a line-up."

"I believe there is."

Inspector Queequeg insisted on driving Harry back to Chez NoNo, which meant turning the police car around again on the narrow laneway and rolling one hundred car-lengths before pulling into the single parking spot in front and reversing the car into the lane facing away from Matira Point, at which juncture Harry climbed out.

"I will be in touch," said Queequeg through the open car window. "*Au revoir*," he called.

Harry shrugged and turned away. He had a lot to assimilate, a lot to reconsider.

8 THE CHURCH ABSOLUTE

FOR THE NEXT TEN DAYS HARRY TRIED TO RECOVER WHAT was left of his vacation. He dived several more times with Topdive but manta rays swooping through clouds of phytoplankton seemed strangely oppressive. The sight of staghorn coral formations and luminescent sponges shaped like sarcophagi and large enough to hold a corpse standing upright saddened him. He hiked overgrown trails to the heights of Mount Pahia and the shoulder of Mount Otemanu, but his exhaustion at the end of the day made him morose, swallowing the brief exhilaration he'd felt on being able to gaze out over the shimmering Pacific and see the twin islands of Tahaa and Ra'iatea looming in the sun-drenched air or catch a glimpse of the more distant Huahine almost invisible on the farthest horizon. Most evenings he walked up to the bar at the Muana Kea International and lingered over a couple of drinks, avoiding eye contact with guests and nursing his solitude. On the second or third night he switched from Hinano beer to Pernod over ice and at some point realized this signified a connection with Tess Saintsbury but he had grown fond of Pernod and continued to drink it, usually toying with the ice in his final glass until it melted to a milky residue, which he consumed as a chaser.

He thought about Tess. As usual, she aroused mixed feelings. He was repelled by her revealed identity but found himself grieving. He was sure if she turned up, dead or alive, island gossip would have reached him faster than a call from Queequeg. He wasn't so sure that he would learn as readily if her abductor were caught.

On the seventh day, he received a call from Inspector Queequeg, which he took in the Chez NoNo office. Queequeg was in Papeete. Forensic tests had revealed traces of Tess Saintsbury's blood beneath Harry's on the side of her handbag. Queequeg made an appointment for when he returned to bring Harry up to date on the investigation. He arrived three days later. They walked to the edge of the beach in front of the hotel and sat on a couple of chaises longues in the shade of the overhanging palms. The day manager, a large attractive woman in a loose pareu that threatened to fall open as she walked, brought them drinks of cool lemonade.

Setting a sheaf of notes on the sand, Queequeg turned to Harry and skipped the social preliminaries. "Madame Saintsbury tried to protect herself," he said. Almost as an afterthought he added, "She is alive, she is dead. Who knows?"

"Schrödinger's cat," said Harry.

"Since she cannot be both, alive and dead, until we know otherwise it is safe to assume she is neither."

"The paradox of the cat in a box is an incomplete analogy, Inspector," said Harry. "This is not a problem in Quantum mechanics."

Are you being pedantic, pretentious, or clever, Slade? It's sometimes hard to tell.

As if Queequeg had heard her, he clarified, "Rhetorical evasion unfortunately will not resolve a murder investigation."

"If there was a murder," said Harry.

"And that bit of circumlocution brings us back to Schrödinger," said Queequeg.

"Circular argument," said Harry. "It's not quite the same."

You cannot resist!

Harry looked out over the lagoon to the arc of the atoll, marvelling at how close it seemed in the midday light. A body had not turned up. The third man was still missing. Nothing had been resolved.

"There were traces of granulation in the blood smear on her handbag," said Queequeg.

"Scab tissue?"

"She held the bag in front of her face. She was trying to fight off her attacker. Since you heard nothing, he must have hit you first, then turned on her. Your blood pattern on the leather suggests the bag was subsequently folded and placed under your head. A small act of kindness but probably self-serving. He didn't want you bleeding to death."

"That was considerate."

"You were never meant to be part of the story. There was a particular scenario being played out that served the purposes of The Church Absolute. It included the murder of The Founder, the elimination of his wife, and the martyrdom of the assassins. It did not include you, for which you should be grateful."

The fate of Tess Saintsbury in the context of a religious conspiracy seemed comical, appalling, and despite evidence to the contrary, quite unlikely. Queequeg's confidence in what he called 'the scenario' certainly did not inspire gratitude. Harry had never been able to fathom being grateful for being spared when others were missing or dead.

"We talked to members of The Church both here and in Los Angeles," Queequeg explained. "Do you know, they are not surprised her body is missing. They take her disappearance as proof of her passing to another plane. They believe in corporeal transcendence under exceptional circumstances."

"The Assumption of Mary. It seems they borrow from Christianity when it's convenient. Did the other two wives also ascend?"

"One drowned at sea and was never recovered. The other was consumed in a fire and left behind only residual ash. There have been suspicions, of course."

"Assumptions of another kind."

Queequeg's eyes twinkled at Harry's quip, which had a surprisingly unnerving effect reinforced by his ominously bisected countenance.

"Charges were never laid. I talked several times to the daughter, Cassandra di Cosmos, in the States. She is convinced that her step-mother will never be found. On the basis of the daughter's conviction, Mary di Cosmos has been sanctified, beatified, venerated, canonized, and acclaimed as an Absolute saint, all in a matter of days. It's enough to make a doubter believe."

"Do they call her Saint Mary or Saint Tess?"

"They call her *Sister Celestial*. That is the highest status on offer."

"For which the price is not cash but your life."

"Something else they borrow from Christians, which they claim to be."

"If Mormons can co-opt Christ, why shouldn't they?"

"The founder came from a Christian background." Queequeg had clearly sought Harry out for the express purpose of sharing his revealed knowledge with someone he deemed a sympathetic intellectual peer. "Despite a lot of interplanetary hocus-pocus, they sell primarily to Christians desperate for a return to the supernatural."

Scepticism to match your own, Harry.

Harry thought of himself as a realist. "They must be disappointed the old man's body was recovered," he said.

"No, Pietro's body was a superfluous discard. He didn't merely transcend, he has moved on to a state of pure energy. He no longer had any use for it. His wife is a celestial human, but he has left humanity behind altogether."

Harry pictured the old man's gaping eyes and slack mouth, with blennies and wrasses nibbling at his face. There is no contingency that cannot be explained by the suspension of disbelief.

"He is the first to become God," said Queequeg. "He will prepare the way."

"You sound like you believe."

"God forbid. I believe they believe and that is what makes them disturbing. Harry, may I call you Harry, they think they have only to make the right moves and they will return to Eden."

"Sounds vaguely familiar."

"Ah, but it is not a garden paradise. Eden is a state of being where all become one but each is unique."

"And here I've been wasting my time reading *The Count of Monte Cristo*."

"The story of The Church Absolute makes fiction seem paltry. It is quite breathtaking in its audacity."

"A big lie sells better than a small fib."

"It is not so simple as a lie, Harry. It is a religious lie. When we delve into the arcane mysteries of The Church Absolute we find the usual drama of conflicting ideals, thwarted ambitions, internecine treachery, and, as you might expect where great sums of unregulated money are involved, murderous greed. In Church politics we find an explanation for the crimes on Bora Bora. Pietro di Cosmos was a sacrificed God. Mary di Cosmos was martyr, a victim."

"Most saints are."

Martyrs or victims?

"It turns out," Queequeg continued, "they were married for only a few weeks. She was a small-time fortune hunter who got caught up in something much bigger than she ever imagined. She has virtually no history, the sure sign of a grifter. She came from nowhere and has disappeared into an unmarked grave."

"A small price to pay for immortality." Harry did not believe she was dead. He did not believe she was small-time or a hustler.

"A large price if you're wrong," Queequeg responded.

"Yes it is. Are you sure they were actually married?"

"According to the di Cosmos daughter."

"She seemed all right with it?"

"She performed the ceremony. She supervised Teresa's instruction in the doctrines of The Church and officiated at the wedding. The Church Absolute is sanctioned to preside over births, marriages, deaths, and the financial tithes of their flock. Cassandra di Cosmos is an ordained minister."

"God help us."

"We can only hope. The daughter told me her father had his first stroke a year ago."

"So the old man was never poisoned? He was sick when Tess met him."

"The daughter said nothing about poison, nor did the L.A.P.D. Your friend married him after he'd had the first of several strokes, knowing he would never get better. As to why his daughter would go along with the marriage scam, she simply says that's what her father wanted. How she could be certain what he wanted, God only knows."

"It makes you wonder," said Harry.

"This all comes together when you find out about the dead men at the cottage. They were on a holy mission."

"Religious assassins?"

"Both were wearing gold chains around their necks. It seems adherents to The Church Absolute, after they reach a certain level of instruction, are awarded medallions engraved with a representation of the galaxy they came from."

Queequeg stopped and motioned to the concierge who sat in the shadows, watching them talk. She brought over a pitcher of cool lemonade and refilled their glasses.

"So you found their medallions?" Harry asked.

"No, only broken chains. The medallions have disappeared. Since nothing else was taken, I'm guessing they're more valuable as symbols than for the gold content."

"Once again, something missing is worth more than something found. And they depict a galaxy?"

"The Church says there are twelve thousand beings stranded among us, within us, who are refugees from a pinwheel galaxy one hundred million light years away."

"Oh come on, now."

"Mormons believe in extraterrestrial origins—we were spirits before we were flesh—although they're not so extreme as Scientologists who have our beginnings on the far side of the universe. We're dealing with the di Cosmos explanation for souls."

"Which is more than conventional Christianity is prepared to do."

"What? Explain the soul?"

"It's one of those things that is assumed to exist but no one tries to define it. A bit like the Holy Ghost. So tell me."

"Until Jesus came along, according to Pietro di Cosmos, these spirit beings so far from home had been reduced to mere cries in the perpetual night. But Jesus restored their awareness when he fasted in the wilderness. By defying temptation, he affirmed his humanity. Through him they became individuals on an earthly plane. However, when he was crucified, they were still without form. They were compelled to survive and forced to reside within passing human generations from one generation to the next until now. We were the only way they could achieve individual presence, Harry."

"They're spiritual parasites."

"So it seems. They leap from the corpse of one to the embryo of another."

"At conception or birth?"

"The Church Absolute opposes abortion, so I imagine conception."

"God help us, save us from God."

Harry was aware there were far more outlandish paradigms of religious credulity out there. As a philosopher, he had never bothered with them and Karen's interest had been from a behavioural perspective.

"You see," Queequeg continued, pleased or relieved to be sharing such arcane knowledge. "They cannot become *us*. However, if we can transcend from the celestial plane to become pure essence, we become *them*—self-knowing aspects of the infinite self. Ergo, immortal. All we need is a little help from The Church Absolute."

"Too many *howevers* and *buts*," said Harry. He didn't know whether to laugh or to cry. "Refugees from one hundred million light years away! They must have travelled exceptionally fast."

"Of course. Many times the speed of light."

"So Einstein was wrong," said Harry.

"According to the writings of Pietro di Cosmos, we are pretty much wrong about most things. Did you know his later books are called 'scriptures?'"

"How sad." Harry could think of no better word.

"You may borrow my notes. They will save you time researching yourself."

"I wasn't planning to make a study of The Church Absolute. Even less so, now."

"I would imagine a mind like yours will not rest without knowing whatever can be known."

"I promise you, beyond my personal involvement through Mrs. Saintsbury, I have no interest in Pietro di Cosmos or his ersatz religion."

"Well, just in case, I'll leave the notes, and there's a pamphlet from the official who flew in for the body. Read them if you wish. It doesn't matter. Drop them off or leave them here and I'll pick them up."

"The missionary assassins? Knowing they killed with conviction, what does that explain?"

"Ah yes, I got sidetracked. When I discovered the meaning of their neck-chains and their missing medallions, it all became clear."

"Really," said Harry.

"There are factions within The Church viciously at war with each other. Three of the rebel believers came to Bora Bora to eliminate The Founder and the most recent manifestation of his eternal wife."

"Making saints of their enemies."

"Saints being conveniently dead can be easily manipulated."

Harry was wavering towards accepting the Inspector's account. He believed a good story was one that convinced and a convincing story was one with all the details tucked into place.

"The mysterious third man eliminated the witnesses," Harry said. "You think after martyring his friends he returned to kill Tess, then slipped away?"

"No," said Queequeg. "It would be impossible to slip away. I believe he is also a martyr. He is no doubt buried with Madame Saintsbury."

Harry sipped his lemonade and tried not to imagine their bodies together like Heathcliff and Catherine in a state of advanced decomposition. "So there is another killer still out there?" he said.

"Ockham's Razor," said Queequeg. "The simplest answer is the right answer."

"Not always, but often," said Harry with the residual authority of a prematurely retired philosophy professor. Although he knew Queequeg's background, he was pleased to find a detective who would know about the principle of logistical parsimony in these remote islands, an island with no stoplights or traffic congestion, never mind murders or mayhem.

"In this case, Dr. Lindstrom, there are no competing hypotheses. The killer is a fourth man, he is a zealot in The Church Absolute, and he is no doubt one of *us*."

"A Polynesian?" said Harry. "Do you have many converts?"

"Many crave mystery, no matter how bizarre the dogmas and doctrines involved."

"Not only here," said Harry.

"Righteous Mormons, hard-sell Scientologists, frightened Children of The Church Absolute, their missionaries come to the islands and rake through the suffering souls for converts, as Catholics and mainstream protestants did in the past. And at least one of those converts to The Church Absolute was on Bora Bora, perhaps he still is, but how can we find him unless he confesses? He is safe, he is at home. In the eyes of his Church he is holy."

"But why kill the third man?"

"Housekeeping, Harry. To tie up all the loose ends. Make him a martyr as well, then the last killer goes to ground merely by staying at home."

"Housekeeping," Harry repeated. It was all disarmingly neat.

"*Bien sûr*, so it seems. We will keep our eyes open for Madame Saintsbury. There is little more we can do."

"And for the third man?"

"Yes."

"And for the fourth killer?"

"Every time I look at my fellow islanders, I will wonder."

"Of course."

"Harry, our investigation will remain open but it is essentially over."

Harry felt a chilling sense of relief.

After Inspector Queequeg left, Harry set the notes on di Cosmos aside and settled back into the copy of *Moby-Dick* he had started, having abandoned *Le Compte de Monte-Cristo*. For the next three days he did nothing but read. He became so absorbed in the adventures of Ishmael and the obsessions of Ahab that neither Tess Saintsbury nor Karen had a chance to penetrate his remaining hours, when he slept, ate, and wallowed in the darkness of Melville's voluptuous words.

On the morning of his last full day, although he had stayed up late reading Melville he rallied early enough to make the sumptuous buffet breakfast at the Hotel Maitai before the open-air dining room closed to get ready for lunch. Then he hitchhiked into Viatape and said his farewells at Topdive, ate fresh fruit from a vendor on the harbour square, and picked up a couple of postcards as souvenirs. He never carried a camera on the principle that most people took pictures to prove they'd been somewhere and he had no doubts where he'd been. Postcards were invariably better than his own compositions. Cameras interfered with seeing and distorted the memory with superficial representations, lacking sound, smells, or the frisson of actual experience. He took a cab back to Chez NoNo, had a brief nap, and dug his fins, snorkel, and mask out of his dive gear. He walked down to the beach for one last immersion in the shimmering blue-green lagoon.

When he had snorkelled along the coast to a point off the tip of Matira Point, he looked to the shore and recognized the sandy patch amidst coral outcroppings where he had last seen Tess before her abduction. Deep below him was the spur of sand she had pointed to in the twilight, saying she saw a solitary manta ray swimming over it, close to the surface. Taking in a full draught of air, Harry dived, levelled out at twenty feet, and surveyed what seemed like an elongated amphitheatre with infinitely complex growths of coral and sponges surrounding a golden field of sand, rippled gently from the surge and cross-checked with striations of sunlight from the waves overhead. He surfaced, nearly choked, discarded the snorkel, and dived again, this time trying to reach the bottom at the very limits of his capacity, forty feet down. He wanted to be there, to feel whatever it was that had caught her attention.

Something glittered in the sand of a small gully to the side. His lungs surged and his throat spasmed as he pulled desperately upwards, finally breaking into the air with a huge exhalation followed by a series of raucous deep breaths. When he recovered, he dived again, swimming directly to the glittering object in the crevasse, clasped it in his hand, and again pushed to the surface, this time rolling onto his back, utterly depleted, gasping for air until gradually his body relaxed. He turned and swam towards shore, grasping Tess's silver barrette in one hand.

Without his snorkel, he swam into the shallows, careful to avoid the sea urchins, then removed his fins and mask and walked up to the path that led him back on smooth earth beside the lane to Chez NoNo.

His first thought, the one that stayed with him as he walked, was that the man who ambushed them had thrown her barrette out into the water. Harry could see no earthly reason for doing that, considering he'd dumped her purse in the sand.

Sitting with a cool Hinano, gazing out at the atoll across the broad lagoon and running his fingers over the silver barrette, another idea came to him, one that seemed far-fetched but not impossible.

Surely, if she swam across, there was enough boat traffic even at night, she would risk being seen. There were police boats patrolling, pleasure craft lolling, fishing vessels coming and going.

He ran the fingers of his other hand over the side of his jaw. It was a common gesture of contemplation but this time he thought of the cut running down Tess's neck. It was a shallow vertical slash, not perpendicular. It would be almost impossible to be cut that way, unless you were holding the blade yourself.

Harry was disturbed by his thoughts. He retreated to his cottage and picked up the pamphlet and notes left by Queequeg. The pamphlet described The Church Absolute with a kind of breathless enthusiasm that made it seem a congenial variation of mainstream Christianity. There was nothing to suggest intergalactic travel or planes of invisible being. It seemed no more eccentric than the Latter Day Saints with their embarrassingly ersatz seventeenth-century scriptures and modest accounts of intercontinental teleportation taking Jesus from the outskirts of Jerusalem to Central America. Queequeg's notes, although cryptic and nearly illegible in places, were far more astonishing. The Inspector had peeled away layers of secrecy and deception through a variety of procedural methods to expose a cosmology that made Harry's head spin.

If this was the world Tess had been immersed in, that swallowed her up in an inexorable vortex of faith and corruption, then it was frightening and absurd in the extreme. Yet the story was one thing, the woman another. He did not lament, for he had come to believe she was not dead. She filled him with horror for the audacity of her deceptions, and with admiration, especially for all that he did not understand.

He scanned Queequeg's notes on the secretive backstory of The Church Absolute with a mixture of astonishment and incredulity. There was much repetition, using language that wavered between the quasi-scientific jargon of bad speculative fiction and the surging rhythms of liturgical cant, as if the original writer, whom Harry assumed was Pietro di Cosmos, was trying to connect on an esoteric and privileged level of discourse. Queequeg was quoting *verbatim* from tracts available only to the very devout, that is, to those with enough money to pay for the revelations, enough raw intelligence to comprehend them, and who were desperate enough to find them consoling.

Harry rifled through the notes until he found entries on The Founder and his originating self, William Alexander Saintsbury. There was little exceptional about him. He was a talented hack. Born in Wisconsin. Voted Republican. Flaunted several unearned degrees, two from Bob Jones University, another from Yale. About the first two wives there was little more than acknowledgement of their untimely deaths. About the third Mary, there was virtually nothing. Tess Saintsbury seemed to have materialized out of thin air. As Queequeg had observed, she had only been married a short while.

On his way to the airport the next morning Harry dropped off Queequeg's notes and the pamphlet at the gendarmerie in Viatape. Queequeg was out. Harry left a message, saying thanks and *au revoir*. Waiting for his flight from Bora Bora to Papeete, he felt curiously at peace. His final night had been restless. He didn't sleep until just before dawn and even then the alarming scenarios that intruded on his dreams left him exhausted and he rose earlier than needed to catch the van for the boat in Viatape. But once he was actually in transition, his perspective changed radically. Whatever fantasies he had had about Tess and The Church Absolute seemed strangely ephemeral. Loitering on the ferry dock at the terminal, he gazed across to the island. From the perspective of the airstrip atoll, Bora Bora was the archetypal model of a tropical paradise. He was stirred by the beginnings of the longing that would bring him back; he had no doubt that he would return.

He walked along the shore past the airstrip and looked out over the water. Even at sea-level he could see Ra'iatea looming on the horizon, a modest distance away by outrigger. The Polynesians were one of the greatest seafaring peoples in the world. He wondered if it would be possible to paddle open water like that in a Canadian canoe. He was startled when he thought he could hear moaning but it was only the sounds of the sea nudging the shore.

Returning to the terminal he ordered a drink. He had meant to have a beer but ordered Pernod. As he watched the ice melt in his glass he recalled the young Polynesian in the Muana Kea International, his name was Jean-Claude, he had asked Tess if she wanted more ice delivered to her cottage. She had her own fridge. The ice was for her husband. He soaked in cold baths once a day. Harry commented on her lifting William in and out of the tub.

There was a tiled shower, but no tub.

That's how she did it, Karen exclaimed.

It's over, Karen. We're on our way home.

Harry, the ice. It was all in the timing.

Feeling the peace he had welcomed begin to slip away, Harry envisioned Tess Saintsbury packing clumps of ice under the arm-rest and into the back-compartment of her husband's wheelchair. As graphically as if she were doing it in front of him, he could see her tie the old man in his chair and lower him into the water, hidden from view by the cottage walls, which extended down almost to high water level. He watched in his mind as she left to have dinner at Bloody Mary's.

And while you were at dinner, the ice melted.

There was nothing Saintsbury could do. He floated, then he sank.

Perhaps he didn't realize what was happening. That's what you told Inspector Queequeg.

Because the implications of consciousness are too horrific.

Sometimes they are.

He knew. We connected once, just for an instant, but that was enough to know there was somebody in there. He was more than a sack of bones with a pulse.

But you wish he was a mindless organism.

Yes.

You don't like to think of her as a cold-blooded killer.

It's not personal.

Of course it is, Harry. Everything is personal. Like when she split your skull open. That was personal.

I don't know she did that. I'm just guessing. There was no lasting damage.

She didn't hang around to find out.

No, she didn't.

So, where is she now?

Long gone, one way or another.

Wearing a diamond bracelet worth millions.

When his plane arrived in Papeete, Harry was agitated. He didn't know how the third man fit into his revised scenario, or if there was actually a fourth. There were too many loose ends, too much wilful delusion. Between flights, he did his best to empty his mind of anything baffling, threatening, sensual, or quasi-religious. He had one last Pernod over ice and thought about calling Queequeg but didn't.

9 TAHITI

THE WOMAN WHO CALLED HERSELF TERESA MACPHERSON remained on Huahine for three weeks, then she flew out to Tahiti. Her only socializing had been on a number of excursions with Huahine Divers, when she partnered with Henri as her eager protégé. Before she left the island, she recovered her buried tanks and presented them to her young companion, along with most of her gear, including her expensive D9 Suunto wrist-computer. He had been speechless with gratitude and with love.

On her last night she cut her hair short. She bleached it and coloured it honey blonde and lightened her eyebrows. In the morning, she switched her lipstick from scarlet to pink and put on a pareu printed with a profusion of blood-red hibiscus blossoms, worn long with a shot-silk blouse on top. The changes in her appearance puzzled her friend Henri when he came for her bag. He might have intended a farewell kiss on both cheeks at the shuttle van but instead took her hand for a moment in his and then backed away as if she were a stranger he had mistaken for someone else.

On the flight out, her plane touched down on Bora Bora before progressing to Tahiti. She remained expressionless when she saw Harry Lindstrom amble across the tarmac. She kept her gaze fixed on the world outside the window and sat perfectly still until he had edged past along the aisle to a seat in the rear. At Fa'aa, she entered the terminal before Harry disembarked and walked directly through the open air lobby to the taxi stand. By the time Harry had transferred his bags, she had arranged for her driver to pick up her luggage and was on the way to Papeete where she settled into a room at the shabby genteel Hotel le Mandarin on rue Colette.

For the next few days she kept to the bustling core of the city, lingering over breakfasts of *café au lait* in the sidewalk patios on the Boulevard Pomare overlooking the harbour, later having pick-up lunches in the art nouveau market surrounded by tables of fresh produce and tourist curios, and in the evenings eating at one of the innumerable food trucks parked between Boulevard Pomare and the water.

On Thursday, Teresa MacPherson made a local call on a public phone. After lunch, she booked a flight to Paris on Air France for the following Wednesday, paying with a credit card that identified her as Celestine du Maurier, then she caught a ferry over to Moorea where she had reserved a room at Motel Albert, across from the Moorea Bali Hai. She took most of her meals at the Bali Hai in an open pavilion overlooking the incomparably majestic Cook's Bay, eating alone. She was not bothered by other guests. Like many attractive people, she projected an aura of inviolable solitude.

On the Sunday evening a boy delivered a package to her door. She tipped him and unwrapped the package, removing a pair of surgical gloves and a pistol-shaped object shrouded in folds of blue cotton. The next morning she returned to the Hotel le Mandarin in Papeete and the following morning, wearing her silk blouse with the red pareu, she rented a small Renault to be dropped off at Faa'a Terminal later the same day.

She drove along the Tahiti shore road counter-clockwise past the airport and through three coastal villages before stopping for a small lunch, including a Pernod over ice, in the rambling village of Mataiea on the opposite side of the island. After lunch she doubled back a short distance and turned inland onto a ragged dirt road that rose steeply through a ravine extending down from the folds of Mount Orohena. She passed a few cottages along the way. Most of them were ramshackle but several were in good repair.

She slowed in front of one of the more substantial cottages. A signpost bearing the hand-lettered name, "Rochecoeur," identified the occupants. She edged the Renault higher up the slope until she found a widening where she could turn it around. She coasted back to a level spot on the shoulder just above the cottage and parked in the shade behind sparse shrubbery, allowing her to observe the cottage and the small clearing in front of it where three hens and a rooster picked lazily at the ground. A red wheelbarrow lolled on its side next to a worktable littered with carving tools. A couple of half-finished stone tiki sculptures sat to one side. The tools appeared to have been set down in a moment of distraction but not abandoned, as if the artisan had run out of energy or inspiration and was biding time, waiting for renewal. A lame cat hobbled out from under the house, reconsidered, and slipped back into the shadows.

After an hour, the cottage door swung open and a petite woman with long mouse-coloured hair emerged from the depths inside. She was wearing a faded cotton sundress but had nothing on her feet. Her hair was tied back with a colourless bit of frayed ribbon. She was a nondescript age; her face had been pretty but was lined and cross-hatched from smoking and sunlight. Her eyes appeared sleepless, the lids drooped at the sides. The pupils were unusually dark. She held an infant against her breast as she pushed two small children out into the yard. She said something to them. Their bland faces showed no emotion but as soon as the woman backed into the shadows and closed the door, they squatted down in the pebble-strewn dirt and started to play. The woman who now called herself Celestine du Maurier watched them. Little girls, two and maybe three-and-a-half, small for their age and untidy but not malnourished, they were soon lost in some incomprehensible fantasy and began to exchange pinched smiles, as if smiling were a secret language they shared only between themselves.

In mid-afternoon, as the sun crept through the glade of shadows, threatening to engulf the Renault, a man came trudging up the road and passed through the gate. The little girls ignored him. He paused to watch them play for a moment, said nothing, and entered the cottage.

Celestine waited another half hour, then withdrew surgical gloves from her purse and put them on and got out of her car, which by now was unbearably hot. She removed her damp silk blouse, hiked up her hibiscus pareu and re-tied it as a dress. She tossed the blouse into the back of the Renault on top of the carry-on bag she had picked up in the market and walked down to the Rochecoeur gate and through it into the yard. The girls stopped what they were doing and looked up but sat perfectly still, as if she might not see them if they did nothing to attract her attention.

Celestine walked to the door and placed her hand on the latch. There was no lock. In her other hand she held a compact Glock semi-automatic that she had withdrawn from the folds of blue cotton, which she stuffed back into her purse. She cocked the gun and slid the safety off, then depressed the latch and pushed open the door. She stepped inside and closed the door behind her.

The woman with mousey brown hair tied back with a frayed ribbon looked up. She was sitting at a grey Arborite table, bottle-feeding her baby. She glanced at her baby, she remained expressionless. The man standing by the sink moved his right hand towards a large knife on the counter. Celestine watched him. His fingers touched the knife but didn't close around the handle. Acknowledging the gun he turned and gazed out the window at the sun-dappled hillside sloping down to the cottage.

"What do you want?" said the woman in a tired voice. She spoke French out of habit, then repeated her question in English.

The man hissed something unintelligible.

Celestine glanced down at her gun.

"My children are here," said the woman.

"He will look after them," said Celestine. "I waited for him to come home."

The man turned slowly and faced Celestine. His English was awkward. "Cannot you leave us alone?"

Celestine du Maurier looked around her. There was no squalor. The cottage was orderly, but not immaculate. Lived in. Poor, not impoverished. A few clippings from French magazines were pinned to the walls. Several uninspired tiki sculptures sat heavily on the floor near the woven partition separating two cramped bedrooms from the living room-kitchen. There did not appear to be a bathroom. A single faucet hovered over the cast-cement sink.

"You should take the baby." Celestine addressed the man and pointed her gun towards the door.

The man looked at the woman. His pale features seemed permanently exhausted, apprehensive. The woman appeared resigned, a little annoyed.

"It is okay, Hugo. You take the boy and go with the girls. It will be fine."

She stood up and pushed her baby towards the man. For a moment, it seemed like the baby would be released in mid-air, then the man reached for him, leaned forward and kissed the woman on one cheek. He drew a snow-white gardenia from a wine-bottle vase and tucked it behind the woman's left ear. With the muzzle of the Glock following him, he stepped out through the door into the sunlight. Chickens scurried. The little girls were seized by the tension and moved close to their father and baby brother.

When the door closed, the Glock swung back to the woman.

"This will not give you satisfaction," she said.

"No," said Celestine.

"You did not know them."

"Not personally," said Celestine.

"I did," said the woman.

"Your sister," said Celestine. "Not the others."

"Will you be paid?" the woman asked.

"No," said Celestine.

"Then why do this? My children," she stopped.

Celestine sidled close to the kitchen counter and picked up the knife. It had flecks of melon stuck to the blade. She set down the Glock within reach and washed the blade clean, then picked up her gun and moved directly in front of the other woman.

"*Your children.*" Celestine repeated the woman's words, cutting them so precisely they fell through the air like a judgement.

"You do not know what I feel," said the woman. "You do not know me."

"No," Celestine agreed.

"It was my husband."

A shadow passed across Celestine's features. She breathed deeply, inhaling the rancid odour of cigarettes.

"My husband," repeated the woman. "Not Hugo. My husband."

"Yes?" said Celestine.

"It was not me."

"You watched."

"Sometimes."

"More than that."

"Sometimes."

"You took pictures. He took pictures of you."

The woman's mouth tightened.

"Yes," she said.

Celestine said: "Their bodies—" She stopped. Her words filled the room.

The woman with mouse-coloured hair turned away briefly, her features were in shadow, her eyes pale discs in the sliver of light seeping around the edge of the door.

Celestine said: "He will die in solitary confinement."

"Segregation," the woman clarified.

"Your lawyers withheld evidence. You served twelve years. Four years for each."

"Six. There was no charge for my sister; it was an act of God."

Celestine stared into the woman's eyes.

"I took no parole," said the woman. "I paid my debt."

"No," said Celestine.

"I am a mother now," the woman said.

"What about him?" Celestine gestured with the Glock towards the man outside. "Does he know?"

"That is why we are living here."

"Your children, when were you going to tell them?"

"Perhaps never."

"They will find out."

"Possibly."

"They will hate you."

"I am their mother."

Celestine's eyes momentarily narrowed.

"You are not any better," said the woman. "You with your gun. You like to kill."

"No," said Celestine. "I don't."

"It is not difficult," said the woman.

Celestine moved closer to her, exchanging the knife and the gun, one hand for the other. She pressed the knife tip against the worn cotton stretched across the woman's breasts, then let it slide down a few inches before thrusting the blade through the cloth into her torso below the rib cage, tilting and twisting the blade, lacerating the lungs in search of her heart. She watched light fade from the woman's eyes, then wrenched the knife upwards as the woman's dead weight collapsed on the blade.

She lowered the woman's body to the floor and extricated the knife, which she washed carefully in the kitchen sink. Wrapping the body in a sheet from the bed she carried it to a child's cot, where she laid it out taking care to cover the open wound. She rinsed her bangles and bracelet by holding her arm under the faucet and used two tea towels to wipe her gloved hands and blood-red dress, and to scrub the blood pooled on the floor, and threw them into a garbage canister under the cement sink. She picked up the white gardenia that had fallen to the floor and tucked it backwards behind the woman's ear so that the smears of blood on the petals were obscured.

When she opened the door, the man was clutching his children in the shade by the gate. Celestine brushed by them and walked up the road to her Renault.

She dropped the car off at Faa'a Terminal, removed her gloves and deposited them with her silk blouse and the unfired Glock wrapped in folds of blue cotton in a refuse bin. She had already removed the bullets, which she dropped into a different bin. She changed in a washroom and discarded her soiled red pareu, slipped on a black wig made from Polynesian hair, and had time for a Pernod over ice before boarding her flight to Los Angeles with only her carry-on bag. It was Tuesday evening. She was flying business class under the name of Teresa MacPherson. The Air France flight to Paris the following morning would have an empty seat in the Voyageur section, booked and paid for by Celestine du Maurier who would apparently have disappeared from the face of the earth. At about the same time, Teresa MacPherson would vanish from LAX and late Wednesday afternoon Jennifer Izett, travelling Tango Plus, would disembark from an Air Canada Airbus at Pearson International in Toronto.

Her sabbatical was almost over and it was time to prepare lectures for the coming term.

10 THE DISTILLERY DISTRICT

HARRY GAZED WITH SATISFACTION AT THE WALL OF BAD weather closing in over Lake Ontario. Much as he loved the tropics, especially the South Pacific, he was most at home in a temperate climate. He liked weather as a condition of life, not merely an amenable context. He liked the drama of seasons. He liked mud in the spring, kicking through leaves in the fall, the dry heat of summer. Mostly, as he now found himself observing the approaching storm from the comfort of his twenty-third story home with exhilarating apprehension, he liked winter. He liked snow, sleet, and slush, when infinite varieties of grey occasionally gave way to brilliant flashes of white upon white and shadows swallowed the light in their velvet folds of purple and blue.

It's been three months, Harry. You're confusing weather-watching with living.

I'm Canadian. They're inseparable.

You've been back since August.

I left a lot unresolved on Bora Bora.

It's not your business, Harry.

It is if I can't leave it behind.

She seems unreal from here.

Yes she does.

Then why are you thinking about her?

I'm not.

But he was. He thought about Tess Saintsbury a lot. She was a killer, he was almost sure of that. But ice melts; he had no proof. She was still alive. He had no proof of that either.

He switched on the radio.

Back on his blue linen sofa, he watched frozen rain begin pelting his balcony, covering the steel railings and cement with a thin layer of ice. In the background, the plummy voice of a newsreader threw the word *Tahiti* into the air but before Harry could grasp it she had gone on to another story.

When the news came up again at the top of the hour, Harry was still gazing past his grey curtains into the whirling opacity, but he caught the words *South Pacific* and *French Polynesia* and listened closely, wondering if The Church Absolute killings had finally captured the world's attention. Instead, there was a terse account of a mysterious murder on Tahiti several months previous. The story was of current interest on three counts: one, the police had just figured out the victim was a Canadian; two, she was a notorious sex-killer; and three, her victims had been in their teens and one of them was the killer's own sister. Just retribution, Harry thought. He didn't believe in capital punishment and abhorred the notion of vengeance, but there was something morally right about the woman's ignominious death at the hands of an anonymous assassin. She was survived by her ex-husband who was serving a life term in prison. She had served a relatively light sentence herself and then remarried and disappeared, it turned out, to Tahiti.

That must have been while we were still there.

I thought the story was going to be about the Saintsbury murders.

That's old news, Harry.

But important.

For whom? It's not like the Pope was knocked off by a team of Capuchin friars.

For believers in The Church Absolute, Pietro di Cosmos wasn't just heir to Saint Peter, he was Jesus, God, and the Holy Ghost. You'd think his death would have created a furor. I'm amazed at how completely The Church has contained the story.

They've made it a non-story.

But there must be a major reshuffling of power and authority.

As we speak. Are we speaking, Harry?

We're on good terms but, no, I'd say we're thinking.

Together?

More or less.

How very intimate.

He missed Karen more than he could express even to himself. That was the nature of grief. It resided in the infinite back corners of his mind where words couldn't reach.

Let's go for a walk, Harry. It's a good day for a stroll through the sleet. Late lunch in the Distillery District and an early night with a snifter of cognac and Moby-Dick. *No, you left Melville on Bora Bora. How about* Anna Karenina *or* Madame Bovary. *You like fallen women, apparently.*

Without thinking or saying anything, he got up and went into the bedroom where he dug his knee-length sheepskin from the back of the cupboard. It was still wrapped in dry-cleaning plastic from the previous spring and released the warm smell of smoke and wool when he opened it. In the front hall he found his light brown cashmere scarf that Karen had sewn for him with a single twist into a möbius loop and the black toque Miranda Quin had given him that belonged to her father. He couldn't find gloves but he laced up his Vasques hiking boots and stepped out into the hall where he waited for the elevator. It struck him with a vague sense of discomfort that his foray into the wildness outside was preceded by a descent of twenty-three stories in a steel box dangling on a cable.

Going out the main entrance, he stepped out into an icy blast, jammed his hands into his coat pockets, braced himself and walked on.

The worse the weather, the better. Bleak and bracing.

For the first time since he'd come back in late August, he felt he was where he belonged.

The Esplanade leading to the Distillery District was all but deserted. He skittered over the frozen sidewalk with shuffling movements, like a child on new skates. Cars crept through the weather but most pedestrians had retreated into the shops and walkways of the underground city spreading out from the bowels of Union Station. It was Saturday afternoon. Everyone else was home watching 'the game.'

Harry did not pay much attention to spectator sports. The idea of watching someone else play for pay seemed absurd, no matter how skilful they were.

When he had settled in at Rory's Chinese Emporium and Brew House, a rustic restaurant with steam-punk décor, he was surprised to have a cluster of noisy women seated at two pushed-together tables near his. The proprietors evidently placed the sparse gathering of customers close to create the impression of a crowd. The effect was the opposite. It made the emptiness seem more oppressive, which led the women to party in raucous defiance of the inclement weather and their enforced isolation.

Harry was facing away from them, looking towards an elderly couple who were almost certainly American tourists. How he knew that, he had no idea.

Bits and pieces of the women's conversation seemed to surround him. He glanced over his shoulder. They were mid-thirties, they were second wives, they were overly well-dressed, wearing excessive makeup for the middle of the day, and they projected the kind of boisterous self-confidence that had no relationship to personal achievement.

There were a dozen of them and they seemed to be holding a meeting of some sort to discuss an upcoming charity affair. Clearly, the organizational details were being looked after by professional event planners, so their comments were mostly about who should be invited, who shouldn't, who might snub their invitation, and who might be snubbed if they didn't receive one.

Harry ordered another beer and settled comfortably into his chair. There were worse ways to spend a storm-battered Saturday afternoon. The American couple had left, the waiters were in no hurry. Clearly, there was the expectation of a sizeable tip.

He listened without paying much attention. Then he caught the cadence of a familiar voice. He listened more carefully but the voice disappeared into the general hubbub. On the pretext of misplacing his serviette, he leaned forward and looked around and immediately caught the huge dark eyes of a striking redhead looking directly at him. He quickly turned away, feeling like a voyeur caught in the act. The eyes, the voice, were familiar, but it was a stranger's face. An eerie uncanny sense of dissociation swept over him.

The collective laughter became more strident. It seemed to be directed at him. Incipient paranoia made the décor oppressive. Copper pipes led nowhere, random cogs and flywheels, fake signage, faux windows, and stained-glass lampshades seemed suddenly unbearably self-consciously chic, twee, vulgar, alien. He signalled to the waiter and paid his bill, then rose to his feet. He had no choice but to face the women squarely in order to edge past their tables and escape. Most of them hardly noticed him. The redhead was missing.

He walked by, stopped, and went back, leaned down to address the woman closest to him who was dressed incongruously, appropriately, in a bright purple après-ski outfit.

"That woman who was here," he said. "The one with the red hair, I think I might know her."

"Good luck, Charlie. She's gone."

"What about me," shouted a woman with fortune cookie crumbs on her lips. "Do you know me?"

"Not yet," yelled another.

"No really," said Harry, embarrassed, annoyed, harassed.

"Jennifer Izett. She's the brains in this outfit."

Much laughter.

Harry left.

Despite the red-hair with appropriate makeup disguise, he knew who the familiar stranger was, who had slipped out after their eyes connected, and she was very much alive.

Back in his condo, Harry contemplated the yellow horizon and tried to assimilate the probability that Tess Saintsbury was more than a lingering illusion. She was in Toronto, she was Jennifer Izett. She was living a different life than he might ever have imagined.

The storm passed and darkness crept through his living room. He abruptly rose to his feet, retrieved his laptop from the bedroom, and turned on lights to drown the world outside in their reflected glare.

He tried several different spellings and came up with only one Jennifer Izett. He found her on the University of Toronto website. Faculty of Arts, Associate Professor, Department of Comparative Studies in Literature, Culture, and Religion. Her faculty page showed her with voluminous dark hair, brassy but stylish. Her credentials were impressive, with publications mainly in the area of ethical relativism, exploring the principle that truth and morality are determined by culture, society, and historical context.

There are no absolutes.

Ironic, isn't it?

That she works in an area closely associated with mine, or that she belongs to The Church Absolute?

I doubt she's maintained the connection.

With The Church? Are you absolutely sure?

No.

Well, if we're done amusing ourselves, what do we do? Are you going to get in touch? Are you going to turn her in? She's wearing a red wig. Do you think you'll become lovers? You're both spouseless at the moment.

It doesn't seem likely.

But you're perverse.

I'm in love.

With me?

Yes.

Lovely.

Harry decided on Monday to pay Jennifer Izett a visit. The ice had melted from the streets. He walked up University Avenue and clockwise around Queen's Park against the flow of traffic, turned left, and found her department squirreled away on the edge of King's College Circle. The departmental office was deserted. The corridor was empty. Despite the grand name, the Department of Comparative Studies in Literature, Culture, and Religion was clearly an academic backwater.

A safe haven for an outlaw scholar. Do you see they use the Oxford comma—Literature comma Culture comma and Religion. Semantic outlaws.

Refuge for a society maven.

Especially if she's faking it.

Which? Social status or scholarship?

On the door of her office several wry New Yorker cartoons vied for attention with a small brass plaque that declared: *Don't Be Disturbing.*

Succinct.

Very.

He knocked and when invited went in.

Tess rose to her feet and extended her hand across the desk.

"I'm not surprised to see you, Harry. I expected you sooner."

"I'm very surprised to see you. The last I heard you were dead."

"Queequeg. He leaps to conclusions. A dangerous thing for a cop. Sit down and let's catch up. And call me Jen."

"Did you kill him?"

"So much for the niceties. If I did, would I confess? Would it make any difference?"

"To me, not much. To William Alexander Saintsbury, a great deal. And to The Church Absolute, I'd think it'd be a game changer."

"Whether I killed him or whether he's dead?"

"If Sister Mary Celestial were found guilty of murder, the heavens might fall."

"Then it might be preferable if I'm not found."

"They don't know you're here?"

"It's better that way."

"For whom?"

"For everyone concerned. You're not going to tell them, are you?"

"This isn't hide-and-seek. We're talking about murder."

"Then let's talk about why Pietro di Cosmos had to die."

Harry kept waiting for Karen to whisper advice or outrage but all he could hear was a huge vacuum opening inside his skull.

That's the sound of moral equivocation, Harry. You're on your own with this one.

"Tell me," he said.

"It's lunch. I don't have a lecture until four. We'll go to the Faculty Club."

Harry had never been in the U of T Faculty Club. It was very sedately upscale, like a Bay Street gentlemen's warren that had let down the barriers to admit women and ethnic minorities but still maintained a polished décor. Original Group of Seven paintings garnished the pastel walls. There was a hushed ambience; furniture gathered in small clusters invited restrained conversation among men of the world.

Once they were seated in an obscured corner with drinks in hand, she turned to face him directly. "So now, Harry, tell me what makes you think I killed my husband?"

Harry looked around. No one could possibly have heard. He stared at her over the lip of his glass, trying to get the measure of this familiar stranger so at home in the heart of a rarefied academic enclave.

"He really was my husband, you know. We were legally married in the state of California."

"You seem to be adjusting to widowhood quite well."

"This?" She gestured around her. "I've been doing this for a few years. I had an associateship and tenure before I met William. I did not set out to catch a prophet, Harry. It just happened. You don't take me for a believer, do you?"

"I'd be relieved if you're not."

"More relieved than believing I'm innocent?"

"Something I seriously doubt."

"Well, how did I do it, Harry? I'd like to catch up on how clever I am."

Harry tinkled the ice against the inside of his glass and inhaled the peat bog aroma of Glenfiddich. He tinkled the glass again. She caught the allusion and smiled.

"Interesting," she said. "It might have been possible, but why bother? Surely there would have been easier ways."

"Apparently not. Not if you wanted to get the timing right."

"What about those thugs?" she asked with an ingenuous tilt of her head.

"What about them? Queequeg told me they were emissaries of The Church."

"There to eliminate my husband."

"Or protect him."

"From me?"

"They failed."

"So they ended up killing each other," she said.

"Except for the Orson Welles's stand-in."

"Did he die as well?"

"A martyr," said Harry.

"Someone killed him? Really? Well, it wasn't me."

"No, you were long gone."

"Was I? Now how did I do that?"

It struck Harry as foolish to suggest she swam and then paddled.

Unless you're right.

You've been following this, sailor. Good to have you on board.

She's amusing herself. You're no threat, Harry. You have a convoluted theory at best. Remember the talk with Queequeg about Ockham's Razor and the principle of logistical parsimony. The simplest explanation is likely the best. There's nothing simple about conning a Canadian detective and a Polynesian cop, overpowering a cadre of religious zealots, paddling the open ocean, swimming underwater out to the atoll, after whacking your buddy unconscious.

That's it, that's how she got away.

Of course.

You didn't think of it before.

It's as far to swim underwater as above.

She's a strong swimmer and no one could see her.

She must have had scuba gear stowed in the water out past the point. The silver barrette in the crevasse, remember?

"Harry?"

"Sorry, I was just thinking about your diving skills."

"And?"

"You disappeared."

"And?"

"I'm betting the third man was after you."

"Why?"

"Because you killed God."

"Why would I want to do that, Harry? Why bother?"

"Because you were paid."

"Money is never enough."

No, he thought, I don't suppose it is. The pathology of a hired assassin was bound to be complex. But he had pretty much decided that's what she was. A paid assassin with a perfect cover.

"You were going to tell me why he had to die."

"Someone actually did try to poison him last year. They kept it from the police. He never fully recovered. A man called Tom Severence took over church operations. William's daughter Cassandra was frantic. Severence is a very bad man. Worse than William. William was cynical about others but delusional enough to believe in himself."

"As a God?"

"As a writer."

"A lesser god."

"If you wish. Do you realize they have a paid-up membership of nearly ten million? People were being fleeced of their life savings when Cassandra tried to take over."

"By poisoning her father?"

"Believe it or not, Harry, she is a good woman. It was difficult for her and as it turned out, beyond her particular talents."

"Leaving the old man more dead than alive."

"Which unfortunately made him a convenient commodity for his successor who claimed for them both the status of transcendent beings."

"Transcendent?"

"Gods too modest to claim to be Gods. As William slipped closer towards oblivion, humility seemed superfluous and his living remains became more like the Holy Ghost, the object of mystical veneration. This made him useful to reinforce the venal authority of Tom Severence who was busily completing the Founder's mission, pitching fear of death as the door to eternity, for which only The Church had the keys."

"Sounds medieval but not unfamiliar."

"Would you like dessert or just coffee?"

Relieved, Harry indicated that he'd prefer coffee. He watched her while it was being poured, trying to discern evidence of a normal human inside the disguise, for he felt sure her icy demeanour was a cover for something deeper, warmer, more compassionate and humane.

"So the daughter hired you to close the door," he said.

"She contacted me."

"At the Playboy Mansion."

"At the Celebrity Mansion of The Church Absolute. They use it to recruit high-profile undereducated movie stars. I was an invited guest."

"Invited by her, I assume. And at that point he was still 'razor sharp?'"

"No, Harry. He wasn't. We never actually consummated, if I may use such a word, we never actually consummated a full conversation."

"I find that a bit of a relief. And how did she know where to find you?"

"It's a small world close to the centre."

"The centre?"

"Of the wheels within wheels."

"What wheels?"

"The wheels of the Gods that grind slowly."

"You're not answering, are you?"

"I'm not."

"Were the thugs working for Severence?"

"They were."

"To protect your husband."

"They failed."

"And the third man, the Orson Welles figure?'

"Very elusive."

"He didn't exist, did he?"

She smiled.

"Nor the fourth?"

"What fourth? That must have been Inspector Queequeg's invention."

"I liked him," said Harry.

"Queequeg?"

"You liked him too."

"I've heard he has joined The Church."

"Nonsense!" said Harry. "Impossible." He could not imagine something so bizarre or extreme.

"On good authority, Harry. I keep apprised of Church activities."

"Why, for God's sake?"

"Not for God, I assure you." Her smile turned in upon itself. She waited for Harry to pick a different tack for their conversation to follow.

"What about your acting career?"

"It didn't amount to much."

"Were you ever in a movie?"

"Not actually, but if I had been I would have been very good."

"No doubt."

"You should have seen through the cover right there, Harry."

"Meaning?"

"Do you think I'd confess to being third rate?"

"I should have known better. What about your classy companions at lunch yesterday? Where do they fit into the scheme of your life, such as it is?"

"The ladies' killing circle."

"What do they kill?"

"Time, Harry. They're career wives, every one."

"Except you."

"Except me. And one of them's a killer herself."

"What are you up to, Tess?"

"Jennifer."

"What are you up to, Jennifer?"

"Murder. They are wives of white-collar hoodlums. Did you see the one wearing the purple après-ski outfit, she's happily married to the most powerful drug boss in the entire country, Silvio Pomposello. She's bad news, herself, and I intend to kill them both."

"Literally?"

"Dead."

That night, Harry dined alone. He walked from the campus across Bloor to the top of Jarvis and down past the Saint Lawrence Market to The Esplanade, cutting east into the Distillery District as dusk turned to darkness, and sat at a table in the corner of Rory's Chinese Emporium, flanked by copper boilers and gear wheels painted matte black. At nine-thirty, slightly drunk, he walked home.

11 RETRIBUTION

YOU NEED TO TALK TO SOMEONE ALIVE, HARRY. YOU NEED to work this through with more than the ghost of your own desperation— you know, a living breathing human being who doesn't just think your contrary thoughts and feel your contrary feelings.

Harry poured himself a second coffee and sat in the armchair that allowed him to see the Klimts still hanging out of reach from direct sunlight on his southwestern wall. The Kiss and The Forces of Evil, each disturbingly sensuous although The Kiss inspired loneliness while The Forces of Evil aroused something more like the fascination, the intrigue, of horror and dread. He looked across at Blackwood's etching on his northerly wall displaying the implacable glee of a whale hovering beneath a fiery ship and diminutive dory set against the frigid nighttime sky.

"Karen?" He spoke out loud.

I'm here, Harry. I'll stay around for awhile, but let's face it, once you know the elephant in the room is an illusion, it's never an elephant again. It's just smoke and mirrors. Distorted perceptions, wishful thinking.

That's harsh.

Sorry, Harry. That's life. You have it, I don't.

Harry tried to focus on the Klimts. They were originals, bizarre souvenirs of a recent case. He decided he'd book a flight for later in the week and take them back to Vienna. That's where they belonged. Madalena Strauss, his client, had left them in his trust but he didn't trust himself. She had perished and the pictures, modelled by her great grandmother, were uncanny portraits of the woman he knew, the woman whose moral commitment, so different from his own, was unconditional, unwavering, and deadly. He loved the Klimts but was disturbed by what they conveyed.

He was inclined to keep them.

Madalena had died for what she believed in, and nearly killed Harry in the process.

The sooner he returned them the better.

If he tried to send them back, he would be caught up in vicious red tape. They were worth millions and their ownership was open to question. If he delivered them directly to the Belvedere Palace, they would likely be absorbed into the Österreichische Galerie with a modest reward and no questions asked.

Harry, you're evading the issues at hand. It won't work, you know, turning to Madalena. If you need help, what about the morally compromised Hannah Arnason in Stockholm? At least she's alive and as far as we know she's still your friend. Or what about your old buddy and erstwhile lover Miranda—or is she too much a cop?

Harry went for a long walk through the grey November morning and ended up cold and damp near Police Headquarters on College Street. The flowing water in the small granite stream outside the building had been turned off for the winter. The building looked bleak and forbidding. Miranda Quin, Superintendent of the Homicide Division, would welcome him as a confidante. He nearly went in but instead had a coffee at Tim Hortons on the corner opposite Starbucks.

How, he wondered, had women become such a defining part of his life? Karen, of course. She would always be there, no matter how deeply sublimated, but Hannah Arnason, whose capacity for moral compromise had seriously threatened his survival on a case in Sweden the previous year, and Madalena Straus, whose commitment to moral absolutes had nearly got him killed last spring in Austria, and Tess Saintsbury, whom he now had to think of as Jennifer Izett, whose moral compass was totally askew, these women collectively mirrored the formlessness of his own moral centre, which, following the accident at the Devil's Cauldron, had shattered and refused to coalesce. He was a moral man but not righteous. In spite of his history as an intellectual concerned with such things, his own morality was entirely intuitive.

He could feel Karen ache for him, sharing his confusion but unable to help.

This much he knew: Jennifer Izett was an associate professor at the University of Toronto whose specialty was moral relativism. This meant that she was not pathological—she could justify anything with a good argument. She was also quite possibly a killer for hire who had devised an elaborate plot to murder Pietro di Cosmos and alter the future course of The Church Absolute. Why else the elaborate hoax of her disappearance? Part of her deal with Cassandra di Cosmos must have been to walk away from the crime undiscovered, and with no claims on the estate. Her payment: a diamond bracelet. The justification: Pietro di Cosmos was evil, he was sick, he needed to die.

Fair enough. His own daughter wanted him dead. And she, by Jennifer's account, was an exceptionally good person.

But now, Jennifer Izett was positioning herself to kill a gangster, a drug lord responsible for heinous crimes and untold misery. Morally justifiable murder? No, Harry argued with himself, murder is indefensible. Yet what really bothered him was his lack of outrage.

He was curious to know how she might do it.

He ordered a double-double to go and dropped it unopened in a garbage container when he got down to Wellington Street. It had warmed his hands and he felt reassured by ordering an iconic drink with more sugar than he'd normally consume in a week.

Three days later he walked into the Café Central on Herrengasse in old Vienna and took a table among slender columns soaring beneath the high vaulted ceilings. It was noon and the pianist was playing Mozart's Piano Concerto No. 21 in C Major. Harry ordered *mélange* coffee, thinking for a fleeting moment of the double-double he had thrown away. He ordered *kaiserschmarrn.* He decided to treat himself after the overnight flight, then he would settle into a room at the Kressler Hotel and in the morning turn up at the Belvedere Palace with the offer of his impossibly rare Klimts.

He didn't plan to negotiate. He was counting on the good graces of the Austrian authorities, but he had paid nothing for the pictures and while their authenticity spoke for itself he couldn't guarantee their provenance. His client, their owner, Madalena Strauss, had died intestate. Although Harry knew where it was, her body was never recovered.

There was a possibility he would not make a cent out of the deal but it would still be a relief to relinquish responsibility for treasures that a thousand years hence would still be coveted and deeply admired.

He shuffled his foot beneath the table to make contact with his suitcase. He hadn't wanted the hassle of declaring the paintings at customs so he had stowed the paintings with his clothes and trusted the airline to keep them safe. He didn't bother with insurance because their worth was incalculable. He simply held his breath for eight hours and, as it turned out, that was sufficient.

After devouring an entire order of *kaiserschmarrn*, the succulent chopped pancake, which in the recent past he had shared with Madalena and nearly two decades before with Karen, he reluctantly left the Café Central and made his way to the Kressler, where he settled into a luxuriously decadent room on the fourth floor, looking out in the same direction as when he had witnessed the suicide of two Canadian lawyers who, in the process, murdered their newly acquired son.

Too much history, he decided! He closed the curtains, shutting in the darkness. He hoisted his bag onto the bed and switched on a single lamp with a plum coloured shade before he undid the locks and zippers, drawing underwear, socks, shirts, three sweaters, and two pairs of pants carefully to the side. He had packed more clothes than he needed to keep the Klimts safe. He was only staying for a couple of days. Much as he liked Vienna, if he had to endure the damp chill of November, we would prefer doing it in his high-rise condo overlooking Toronto harbour.

He reached deeper among his clothes, feeling the hard bottom and sides of the suitcase. The paintings were gone, the original undocumented invaluable exquisite inspired paintings by Gustav Klimt were missing.

Harry turned on the chandelier, which set the room alight and he pulled open the drapes, which muted the glare. He turned his suitcase upside down on the bed. There were no paintings. They were truly gone. He was incredulous. He moved frantically around the room, as if he might discover a thief hiding in the corners. He irrationally checked the bathroom, the closets, even the dresser drawers. Then he sat in a plush burgundy armchair and shook; his heart pounding against the walls of his chest, his breath rushing over clenched teeth, the bones of his skull throbbing against their surrounding envelope of impossibly tight skin.

There was no record of him bringing the Klimts into Austria. There was no record they had ever been painted.

He had taken them off the wall in his apartment. He had wrapped them in his suitcase. He had carried the bag to the airport and checked it in, and in Vienna he had picked it up and carried it to the Café Central, then along Herrengasse to the Kressler Hotel, and he had walked side by side with the porter who carried it to his room.

Who could have taken them, who even knew they existed?

He checked his bag and his clothes carefully to be sure they were his, that there hadn't been a switch, then he changed and went downstairs to the salon where he ordered a double scotch on the rocks and sat waiting, half-heartedly expecting Lena Strauss to walk around the corner smartly turned out under her corona of copper-red hair and smile her soul-searing smile and tell him everything was all right, that she had the paintings, she'd recovered them, and he could relax and go home. Except, he knew Madalena was dead.

Oh my God he wanted to go home.

She was dead in the shaft of an abandoned salt mine near Salzburg. He knew that, she had died in his arms. Still, Harry waited. Through the afternoon and evening and into the night. When the salon closed he went upstairs and sprawled on his bed, famished but with no appetite, exhausted but stark wide awake.

Harry liked to understand.

He was puzzled by his own moral equivocation in response to his suspicions about Jennifer Izett, but that was abstract. This was concrete. He was utterly bewildered by what had happened to the Klimts.

After breakfast he walked through Michaelerplatz and along Herrengasse, past the Café Central where despite his hunger he couldn't face up to the celebratory intimations of *kaiserschmarrn*, and finally arrived in front of the stolid Polizeizentaralkommando building, which even in daylight appeared to be closed.

He walked in and asked for Frau Detektiv Honsberger.

She appeared as Harry remembered her, with striking blue hair, this time a little closer to chartreuse, wearing pearls, and with a silver tooth that glared when she smiled.

"So," she said after she seated him with her formidable oak desk between them. She pressed the fingertips of both hands together and listened as he explained that two priceless paintings that had belonged to her friend Madalena had disappeared. She was no longer even attempting to smile. "You let Lena down very much. It is good for you she is dead."

"You don't believe they're genuine Klimts, do you?"

"If Madalena Strauss said they are Klimts, they are Klimts. If she said they are pictures of Madalena Strauss painted before she was born, then that is what happened. And if they are gone, they are gone. At least they are back in Austria, yes. You go, have a visit, eat *weinerschnitzel*, drink beer. You have brought the paintings home. That is very good. Otherwise, you are a large disappointment, Herr Doctor Professor Lindstrom. *Auf Wiedersehen, auf Weidersehen*. Is good to see you this last time again."

With that, she got up from behind her oak desk and escorted Harry to a door, which she closed abruptly behind him, leaving him in an anteroom with little option but to step out into the street.

Back in Toronto, Harry called Miranda Quin at Police Headquarters.

"Well, for God's sake, Harry. Why didn't you get in touch before this? When did you get back from Tahiti?"

"Quite a while ago." He felt like she was waiting for an explanation. "Sorry, I've been a bit of a recluse."

"The weather?"

"Yeah, the weather."

They were nursing soy milk lattes at Starbucks down the street from her office on College. Soy was her newest quirk, she was going vegan, and variants of soy had displaced most of the staples in her diet, including eggs and milk, meat, fish, and fowl.

"I feel great for it, Harry, my breath is sweet as lilacs in May, and I'm going to live to be one hundred and five. Menopause is murder but this is my chance to start over. Now what the hell is happening? You look bloody terrible."

"I'm just off the plane from Vienna, actually. I haven't been home yet."

"Vienna, for God's sake. There must be a story there."

"There is, but that's not why I'm here."

"Oh, come on."

"You know the Klimts I got from Madalena Strauss?"

The corners of her eyes crinkled in a gentle suppressed smile.

"I took them back to Austria."

"And?"

"And nothing. That's where they should be."

"Okay. I can tell when you're lying, but okay. So, back to the South Pacific—tell me, I'm booked off for the day, I've got time."

Harry reached over the table and took her hand briefly in his. He needed the touch of her skin, the feel of her heartbeat. He had known her since he was in his early teens, when she was staff and he was a kid at Camp Anishnabi in Algonquin Park. Ten years later, after she had left the RCMP and was starting in with the Toronto Police Service, they had been lovers. Then he had gone back to Cambridge to finish his doctorate, she partnered with David Morgan in Homicide, and they went their separate ways until she heard of his accident on the news and had helped him re-establish as a private investigator. She understood he needed to leave the academic life behind. She understood he needed to live with his guilt and his anguish, without being cured or consoled as the shrinks and well-meaning counsellors wanted. She understood him better than anyone. Karen teased him about her but accepted her special place in his life.

Harry told Miranda everything he could remember about Tess and her dead husband and her current manifestation as Jennifer Izett. He told her about The Church Absolute and Queequeg and about threats to the lives of the Pomposellos.

The details came burbling out. It was like a child recounting a nightmare to an indulgent parent. Miranda asked encouraging questions. He repeated himself with variations. She noted contradictions. He untangled the knots. Mostly she listened. Finally, he stopped.

"I'll contact Inspector Queequeg if you'd like. I talked to him briefly last August. He called to check out your credentials. You didn't know? Well, he did.

"And I'll check out your Professor Izett. But I'm thinking whatever her reasons for dissembling, and then disappearing, if she's as good as you say she is, she'll have it all covered—assuming she's not wanted for murder. You say Queequeg figures The Church assassins tried to abduct her, then did it again. Somehow she survived, she juggled identities. Lots of people do that. Have you checked out her academic credentials?"

"Yeah, *bona fide*. Yale for her doctorate. I didn't go back earlier than that. Two years lecturing at Boston College, then U of T. Solid publications. Strictly legit."

"So as I see it, the key to the entire venture is how she disappeared."

"And why."

"Okay, Harry. All she has to do is say she doesn't know. She just turned up back in Toronto. It's a blur. She doesn't deny she was married to the guy, that she took the name Mary di Cosmos. She'll say she must have got beat up pretty badly the same time you got hit over the head. The ice explanation for the death of her husband isn't going to hold water, so to speak. What you've got is—a missing woman reappears and that's about it. Cause for celebration, although from what you tell me some of her Church compatriots might not be happy. Beyond that, there's nowhere to go. I'd forget about it, Harry. I really would."

"What about Silvio Pomposello? I think that's the guy she says she's going to kill next."

"Can't do much until he's dead. Lots of people fantasize about murder. It's not a crime—sometimes it's therapeutic. Let it go, Harry. Avoid her if she upsets you so much. If you can."

Harry walked down Yonge Street, grinding his teeth. He had expected more.

Like what, Harry?

That was the first time he'd heard Karen's voice in days. She'd been silent through the entire Vienna affair.

I stayed at home, Slate.

I needed you, Sailor. I really did.

That's the problem, my love. You need me too much. Especially now, with Tess aka Jennifer Izett. This one's for you to sort out. Miranda's wrong, that's all I'll say. You need to stick with it. And good luck.

By the time he reached home it was dusk. As soon as the elevator stopped on the twenty-third floor, he heard the opening bar of Beethoven's Fifth waft through the door. His phone was ringing. He used a landline mostly for business. He had few enough friends, he had no need for a cell phone. Without bothering to turn on a light, he picked up. It was Miranda. She started in without saying hello.

"When did you leave Tahiti, Harry?"

"Mid-August."

"The date?"

"The 17th, I think."

"Okay, just checking. Carol Rochecoeur died a week later."

"Who's Carol Rochecoeur?"

"She was Carol Brancuso."

"Oh God, evil incarnate. Yeah, I heard somebody got to her. Word didn't come through until a few weeks ago."

"Last week."

"You don't suppose I was involved?"

"Of course not, but I wondered if your high I.Q. buddy was."

Harry thought it was a reasonable conjecture but said nothing.

"Harry."

"Yes?"

"I'm sorry I'm not more help."

"That's okay."

"I know you find this woman attractive."

"Compelling."

"And you find her morally intriguing."

"Scary as hell."

"For good reason, Harry. Trust yourself. Stay away."

Trust yourself. Pursue.

"I will," he said. Gazing around the darkening room, his eyes came to rest on the closest Klimt, a detail from The Forces of Evil, the picture of a pale woman who looked exactly like Madalena Strauss with clearly defined features and an amazing corona of copper red hair, head bent forward against her knee, with her chin pushed slightly askew, looking upward and to the side with an unrelenting, glamorous, and whimsical gaze promising intimacy, affection, passion, not as sin or vice but as the enthralling allure of forbidden virtue.

"Harry, I love you. Take good care."

He stared at the Klimts in the shadows on the wall with a northern exposure.

"Thanks," he said. And after he hung up, he added, "I love you, too."

He flicked on the overhead lights. The lost Klimts were safe on the wall. He smiled with horror on the edge of hysteria and sank into his teak and leather armchair. He closed his eyes, held his breath, breathed, and opened them again. The Klimts were still there.

12 **THE GARAGE**

DECEMBER 24TH, CHRISTMAS EVE. CHERUBIM AND SERAPHIM adorned with glitter were poised amidst garlands of fresh-cut cedar draped over the mantle of a cavernous fireplace carved from solid chunks of blue-grey Carrara marble imported from Tuscany. The electric flames in the grate flickered in vain competition with the glittering radiance of the two-story artificial Christmas tree festooned with skein upon skein of dancing white lights. On a mahogany side table, a crudely hand-carved wooden crèche depicted the tiny infant Jesus in a Bethlehem manger surrounded by cotton batting snow in swirling drifts. Above the nativity scene was a shelf holding a plaster virgin with weeping eyes, her tears made of tiny pendant diamonds. Jennifer Izett stood beside the table, very much a presence in her emerald silk dress but out of everyone's way.

Silvio Pomposello signalled a waiter to take her a fresh drink. Dom Perignon and orange juice. She smiled at her host, tilting her glass in his direction but setting it down when he turned away. It seemed she didn't have the heart to drink a mimosa made from adulterated Dom. She pulled back into the dining room and then slipped out to the kitchen, which was crowded with service people who ignored her. She poured herself a small tumbler of undefiled Dom and then stepped through into the narrow pantry and taking cigarettes from her purse made a show of exiting through an outer door into the garage for a smoke.

As soon as she closed the door behind her, she set her glass down and lit a cigarette, then replaced the pack in her purse. She set the smouldering cigarette on the first of three wooden steps leading down to the cement floor at ground level where there were four cars: a pink Cadillac, identical red and green Ferarri 458 mid-engine Spiders, and a custom gun-metal blue Bentley with a disguised armour-plate body and bulletproof glass. Silvio Pomposello was famous for driving himself. He kept a chauffeur-mechanic on call for his wife and to service his cars but he was known to take pride in not wasting money on a driver for himself. He never drove the Ferarris. They were strictly for the pleasure of ownership. He drove his

Bentley, parked it himself, and never employed a bodyguard. The Bentley was impregnable, it was reputed to be his point of least vulnerability. He never parked where he was not certain of his own safety.

Jennifer touched each car in turn, triggering no alarms, then checked the elaborate security system on the garage doors and windows. She noted a redundant surveillance camera on the far wall, and without approaching it she could see that it was covered in dust and likely defunct. She removed an electronic device the size of a cell phone from her purse and keyed in some numbers. She pressed a button and the doors of the Bentley clicked open. She glanced over at the burning cigarette on the stoop. It was half-way done, she had five more minutes. She climbed into the Bentley and pressed her electronic device. The doors locked. She pushed other buttons, keyed in other numbers. Pressed again and the car started with a barely perceptible purring. She immediately shut it off. She got out of the car, clicked to relock, and dashed to the stoop where she picked up her cigarette and flicked off the long ash just as the door opened from the pantry.

She took in a deep mouthful of smoke and slowly released it as a waiter came out with a case of empty Dom Perignon bottles. The waiter glanced at Jennifer but was too well domesticated to make eye contact. He picked up her tumbler of champagne and handed it to her, nodded without making eye contact, and retreated into the pantry. She blew out the rest of the smoke in a grey-white cloud. She hadn't inhaled. She drank the champagne. It was still *pétillant* and dry as a razor. By the time she passed back through the kitchen, the waiter she had encountered was gone. When she resumed her position beside the crèche on the mahogany side-table, he appeared with a fresh mimosa. She took the adulterated drink and ignored him. She drank it in one draft, and catching the eye of her hostess, dressed in a purple jumpsuit, she nodded her thanks for the invitation, signalled she'd call by waggling an extended thumb and little finger, and walked to the front door where a young woman in a black and white uniform had already selected her coat and scarf from the closet and helped her put them on before she embraced the December chill, which was as cold in Rosedale as anywhere else in the city.

On December 28th, Jennifer Izett rose late and combed out her unruly black hair before donning a red wig that changed her appearance remarkably, softening her cheekbones and giving more well-defined proportions to her nose and lips while strengthening her chin and lowering her brow. The changes were subtle. She was still exceptionally attractive, but to the casual observer she would hardly be recognizable. Yet her colleagues hadn't noticed. When she came back from the summer break, several were momentarily puzzled but accepted that they had not remembered her as she actually was. Her students never noticed, at all. The red wig was very expensive, made from real human hair, and seemed to define who she was.

After breakfast at Tim Hortons she took a cross-town streetcar to Jarvis and walked down almost to Front Street, where she entered a nondescript flophouse and asked for John. A woman behind the desk with sparse hair, missing front teeth, and a cloudy eye, looked her over carefully.

"There's no John here, lady."

"John Munro."

"Oh, that John. Yeah. He's in 221."

Jennifer walked up a narrow staircase and down a creaking corridor that smelled of cat piss and French fries and approached 221. Someone had scrawled the letter B in black marker beside the number on the door.

"Come in," a voice called out before she could knock. "It's you," he said. "Sit down." John Munro was dressed in grungy boxer shorts and a sweatshirt that might have originally been white. He pointed to the bed, then continued picking away at the disembowelled laptop on the table in front of him. He hummed as he worked. The room was sweltering. She pulled her coat off her shoulders and waited. Finally, he sat back in his chair and addressed her directly.

"So, how did it work?"

"Perfectly," she said. She took the small electronic device from her purse and handed it to him.

"What model?"

"Bentley."

"I know it's a Bentley."

"A 2012 Mulsanne."

"Good. But you just turned it on, right? You took control. Now you need to temporarily disable it and impose an alternate system. You don't want to just override it, you've got to disengage the built-in electronic system completely, and then turn it back on when you're done. That's what you want, right?"

"That's what I want."

"And don't forget to override the garage doors. They're on a separate system. I'll mark the console clearly so you can't miss the right button. Okay?"

"Okay."

"Come back in a week. Bring money."

"How much."

"The usual."

"Ten thousand."

"That'll do. Let yourself out."

On January 3rd, Gina Pomposello picked Jennifer up in her pink Cadillac and drove her to the Rosedale house. Silvio wasn't home. They changed into matching Lululemon yoga gear and worked out on the treadmill and the elliptical trainer, hydrating periodically from an ice cold bottle of leftover Dom Perignon. Afterwards they switched up to weights but by then their resolve had eked away and they retired to the sauna, which had already been turned on.

"So what were you doing in the garage?" Gina asked. She seemed on edge.

"When? Oh, I was having a smoke."

"You don't smoke."

"I try not to but I do when I'm nervous."

"Nervous?"

"Strangers. From worlds I can't even begin to understand. One cigarette. It was warm out there and I didn't think anyone would notice."

"Silvio's got cameras everywhere. He noticed. What were you doing with the cars?"

"Is this an interrogation?"

"Yeah, like I give a shit. No, it is not an interrogation. Silvio just wants to know. He doesn't like people being where he doesn't expect them to be."

"The waiter squealed on me, right?"

"Yeah. And they caught you on tape."

"How many cameras are in the bloody garage? It looks like Fort Knox in there. Nobody could ever get in."

"Nobody could from the outside. Two cameras, maybe. Who pays attention?"

"Unless they're worried they might be attacked."

"Silvio isn't worried. He's not afraid of anybody, anything, anywhere, no how. He's just cautious. It's part of the job."

"You've got a major security system." Jennifer indicated the control panel against the gymnasium wall.

"Yeah, well it's only on when we're at home. When we're out, why bother? There's not a thief working this part of town who doesn't know Silvio Pomposello lives here."

"So you're afraid of assassination but not robbery."

"I told you. Silvio's afraid of nobody. If we both go out, we leave it off so the housekeeper can get in. She can reset it if she leaves before we get back just by a flick of the switch. There's a two minute delay to let her off the property, or for us to punch in the code, like before the sirens start wailing."

"Lucky I didn't set it off in the garage, I just slipped out for a smoke. I admired the Maseratis."

"Ferraris, they're Ferraris."

"Beautiful cars."

"Not as expensive as you might think. Silvio's careful with money."

"He's very successful at what he does."

"He is. He works hard, he doesn't do drugs. He's generous to a fault."

"Drugs?"

"You know Goddamn well what he does. There are suckers and creeps and perverts and streetscum who pay him good money. And he takes it, that's what he does. You don't want to cross Silvio Pomposello. How come you started the car?"

"It wasn't locked. I've never been in a Bentley before, I just wanted to hear it run."

"You can't hardly hear it at all. He fired my driver."

"Really? Why?"

"For leaving the Bentley unlocked."

"That's unfortunate."

"Yeah, with the keys in."

"The keys?"

"Yeah, so it seems. He gave him a few raps in the head for being so careless, you know."

"Yeah, tell Silvio I'm sorry. It won't happen again."

"Better it not."

"Gotcha."

"Let's crack open another Dom."

"Can't. Got to lecture tonight."

"Just a snort. We don't have to kill the bottle."

"Just one."

They stepped out of the sauna and Gina went upstairs for a fresh bottle. Jennifer turned on the shower and withdrew a length of wire from her gym bag, along with her towel, which she draped casually over her shoulder. She walked into the main workout room and quickly attached the wire to circumvent the alarm on the exterior door leading up to the hot tub on the deck outside. She tucked the extra bit of wire out of sight behind the purple drapes and was back in the shower before Gina reappeared with an open bottle frothing over at the brim.

"No more Dom, we'll have to settle for Veuve Clicquot."

"I can manage," said Jennifer. "A draft of the old widow, just the right thing."

When it was time to go, Gina called Jennifer a taxi. Jennifer went directly to her office. She didn't have a lecture. She read for a couple of hours and went home.

On January 7th, a sharp knock on Jennifer Izett's office door announced an unfamiliar visitor. A man of about thirty with short hair and a dark complexion stepped into the room and closed the door behind him.

He was wearing a t-shirt under a leather jacket.

"Sit down," he said.

"It's my office, thank you. I'll stand."

He moved rapidly around her large oak desk and crowded against her, forcing her into the chair.

She swivelled away from him and straightened a pile of papers. He moved back to the other side of the desk.

"You're not too good at this," she said.

"Don't have to be. You're not much of a threat."

"My office hours are posted outside. You need an appointment."

"Listen," he said. "Mr. Pomposello isn't happy."

"I'm sorry about that. What seems to be his problem?"

"You, lady. You were out with his cars the night before Christmas."

"I was, I was having a smoke."

"Mr. Pomposello doesn't allow smoking in his garage."

"I didn't know that. I'll try to remember."

"Mr. Pomposello doesn't allow smoking on his property."

"You mean on the property where he lives. He owns a lot of properties."

"Smart-ass."

"Thank you."

Jennifer rose to her feet. Her visitor stayed still. She moved around the desk until she was directly in front of him. She looked up into his eyes. He was a big man.

"I don't think you understand," she said. "I was a guest in the Pomposello house. I wanted a cigarette. It was bitterly cold outside. The heated garage seemed like a good place to smoke."

"It's you who don't understand, lady. You don't smoke in the Pomposello house. So, there's a key missing."

"For the car?"

"The Bentley. You started the car, so what did you do with the key?"

"There wasn't a key. It's electronic ignition. Must have been a control fob stashed close by. I just pressed the starter button. Didn't expect it start. Pressed it again. It stopped. Simple."

"How do you know all that? Mrs. P. told me there was a key."

"Mrs. P. is mistaken. I know all that, as you say, because it started. And stopped."

The big man leaned forward. Since she didn't move, he placed one hand squarely on her desk to keep from tumbling against her. With the other, he touched her cheek, regaining the initiative. "Very nice," he said. "Nice skin. Delicate."

"Thank you," she responded, ignoring the threat, glancing demurely downwards before driving a stainless steel letter-opener through the back of his hand, embedding it deeply into the top of her desk. She stepped back just out of his reach.

He stared at her with wide-eyed astonishment.

"Holy mother of Jesus," he said, his voice shaking with pain. "Holy Mary, mother of God."

"I've been called worse," she said. "Don't move, it's excruciating I imagine. Stay very still. Sharp point, dull blade. We've broken a few small bones and cut through strands of cartilage. Not much blood but a lot of damage. Stay still, we'll have to think what to do next."

Her visitor's face had taken on an ashen pallor.

"Now then." She moved around her desk and reached into a drawer and pulled out a snub-nosed revolver, a black Smith & Wesson Bodyguard .38 Special with a faux wood grip. She tripped the safety slide and moved back in front of her visitor. He stood tall against the pain, defiant but wary. With a single quick movement she wrenched the letter-opener free and tossed it into the trash pail by the door. In the same flourish of movement she pushed the gun against his neck under his chin, pushed upwards hard so that he rose on his toes, then she relaxed and backed away. He stood very still, waiting.

"Here's what I'm going to do," she said. "I'm going to kill you."

"Lady?"

"Professor. Or Doctor, if you'd prefer."

"Please."

"What? You have children, yes, I can tell by the fear in your eyes. I'm going to kill your children too. Then I will have a talk with Silvio Pomposello."

"Mr. Pomposello—"

"Is the scum of the earth, yes. Yes?"

He nodded assent.

"We agree. Now there is one possible out. Do you have money in the bank? Did you hear me, do you have money in the bank?"

"Yes."

"Yes what?"

"Yes I have money, whatever you want."

"You go and get your money. Then you leave Toronto. In three months you send for your kid. Your kids. Pomposello won't be happy, but we don't care, do we? No, we don't care."

"Mr. Pomposello—"

"You let me worry about Silvio Pomposello. You go out to Vancouver, no don't tell me, go wherever, go back to school, you're well spoken, you'll get in as a mature student, get a student loan, go to UBC. You can do better than this."

"You've got to be kidding."

"And quit smoking."

"I, you."

"I'm not a smoker. I wouldn't want you to think I'm a smoker. There are things going down you don't understand. You need to go very far away. And if I so much as hear your name again, ever, I will kill you."

"You don't know my name."

"I will by tonight. Gina Pomposello is one of my closest friends. Now get the hell out of here. Take some Kleenex; don't bleed on the floor."

"It's Tony Muratori," he said.

After he left, she picked the stainless steel letter opener out of the garbage, wiped the blade clean, and deposited it in her top drawer along with the revolver.

Before she left for the day, she removed the gun from the drawer again and dropped it into her purse.

At 4:45 am, before dawn the next morning, Jennifer Izett rose from her bed, listened to the weather forecast, which promised extreme cold but no snow, and prepared for work. When she was ready she stepped out into the frigid air, shuddered, and drew her coat tight, clutching her large handbag against her chest as she walked to the subway. She caught an early train to the Rosedale stop. There was no one on the open air platform when she got off. She walked four blocks northwest until she came to a new grey brick fortress set back from the street, one of those monstrosities built on adjoining properties where two or more vintage houses had been demolished to make way. The four-car garage was set on an oblique angle to the street so that passersby could see it as a mark of wealth, while it pretended to be discreet. That was the aura of the entire house, ostentatiously discreet. New money.

While the sun was not yet up, the air was filled with light that shimmered from lamp standards placed artfully among ancient trees along the footpath—nothing so mean as a cement sidewalk. Jennifer glanced around, then stepped into the shadows of shrubbery planted full grown and made her way through the diffuse gloom around to the back of the house, being careful to avoid the beams of motion sensors placed at intervals along the way.

The hot tub was covered but radiated a fine mist in the cold still air. She slipped by and pressed close to a door leading down to the basement gymnasium. The door opened to a pick with only a brief hesitation. She stepped inside, wiped her feet on the broadloom, took out her revolver with the safety off, and made her way directly upstairs through the kitchen and pantry into the garage.

She spotted the other camera tucked in the rafters and standing on a plastic chair she draped an opaque muslin cloth over the lens. She settled in a dark corner and waited, crouching behind a stack of boxes filled with used clothing marked for pickup by the Diabetes Association.

At 7:30 she could hear voices in the kitchen. She tucked her Smith & Wesson back in her bag. At 8:15, the door from the pantry opened.

Silvio and Gina Pomposello were quarrelling. Jennifer remained hidden until they were both in the Bentley, then she stepped forward, moving directly in front of the car. She held her small electronic device in one hand. She flipped the switch for the garage door override. She smiled.

The Pomposellos were startled. Gina looked momentarily pleased, then confused, then frightened. She smiled back. Silvio looked furious.

Jennifer clicked her new device and highjacked the Bentley's entire electronic system. The car doors simultaneously locked. Pomposello turned the ignition on and off, trying to connect power to open them again. He whacked his fist on the dashboard. Jennifer turned on the air conditioner intake and started the car. Pomposello tried in vain to turn the engine off. He reached up and switched the garage door opener but it was disconnected. He tried to jam the car into reverse but the transmission was locked in the starting position and wouldn't shift out of neutral. He leaned on the horn but nothing happened.

The Bentley is so well built than no sounds emerged from inside as Silvio and Gina Pomposello thrashed about trying to escape. At one point, he struck his wife across the mouth to extinguish a silent scream. She slapped him and scraped her nails down the side of his face. Four brilliant streaks of blood flowed red and smeared across his cheek as he wiped at them with his hand.

Jennifer pulled out a compact mask with a tube running down to a small compressed-air cylinder inside her handbag. She reached in and turned on the valve and sealed the mask against her face. The air in the garage began taking on the colour of pale blue smoke from the exceptionally low exhaust emissions. The atmosphere inside the car turned hazy. The carbon monoxide buildup itself was clear, odourless, and tasteless, and Jennifer could only be sure of its presence when she saw the Pomposellos display signs of confusion and began clutching at their heads to stifle the pain.

She turned off the car engine. After a few moments, while the couple sat perfectly still, staring expressionlessly at Jennifer in her mask, she released the window on the driver's side so that it rolled down a couple of inches.

"You need a moment to grasp what is happening," she said, holding her mask away from her face.

Gina Pomposello rasped out Jennifer's name as a plea.

Jennifer took a deep breath of compressed air and removed her mask. She said, as if the words had been prepared in advance: "Gina, you are amused by suffering. You laugh at the addicts and derelicts. You joke about them as gossip." She took a deep breath of clean air. "Silvio, the extermination of lives is a serious business. You don't laugh at all. Not now and now not ever."

Her smile was beatific.

She put the mask back on. She started the engine again and moved to the far end of the garage. As she manipulated her electronics console, the window began scrolling up. Silvio jammed a pair of sunglasses into the open space and the window smashed them but stopped. He poked his fingers through the crack and pulled until the fingernails burst with blood along the edges. He banged on the bulletproof glass with his fists and the bones of his fingers twisted at strange angles as they pushed through his bloodied flesh. He seemed to collapse into himself when his powerful body gave way to nausea and convulsions. Gina's lips turned cherry-red. She reached over and held his mangled hands in her own. Her laboured breathing began to subside. She reached up and touched the marks where her nails had scraped flesh from his face.

Jennifer extracted her revolver beside the compressed-air cylinder in her handbag and slid the safety back on. The repulsive sounds of dying seeped through the crack in the car window. She waited. When the Pomposellos succumbed she reactivated the garage door opener and turned the car off, disengaged her electronic remote and restored the car's own system, climbed onto the plastic chair and removed the muslin cover from the surveillance camera, keeping out of its field of vision as she mounted the steps into the house and opened the door, then turned around and started the engine again. She left the car running, stepped through, closed the door, and walked into the pantry, through the kitchen, along the hallway, and down into the gymnasium. She reset the master security system so alarms would go off when the housekeeper arrived, and she reconnected the alarm wire for the exterior door out to the deck. She slipped through into freezing air.

The snow was so cold she left no tracks as she walked out to the footpath and turned south. A block away she passed the Pomposello's Filipino housekeeper heading in the other direction, hunched against the cold and paying no notice. Jennifer slowed until the piercing wail of the alarm shattered the calm of the early morning. By the time she had gone two more blocks she could hear approaching sirens. Her boots squeaked in the cold snow. She was just another early riser on her way to work or the spa, a woman carrying a large handbag, in no hurry despite the bitter temperature. She would be home soon for a leisurely breakfast before heading out to the university. It was the first day classes resumed after the Christmas break. Students would be lined up at her door for what she and her colleagues called 'office hours,' from 10:30 to noon.

13 FEAR

A SECRETARY FROM POLICE HEADQUARTERS CALLED AND asked Harry to come in. Superintendent Quin wanted to interview him. Would 11:15 be appropriate? It would be and was. When Miranda saw him through the glass wall of her office she motioned him to enter. She looked gravely serious. Her former partner, David Morgan, didn't get up from the sofa. The situation from his perspective obviously wasn't as solemn.

Morgan and Harry greeted each other warmly, embarrassed that neither had been in touch.

"I told you I couldn't do anything about your buddy from Bora Bora," Miranda said before the men could start to talk about diving, which was their principle shared interest. "Now maybe I can."

"Are you going to tell me Silvio Pomposello is dead?"

She seemed surprised.

"What else?" he said.

"And his wife."

"You've arrested Jennifer Izett?"

"It's not as easy as that, Harry." Miranda spoke as the Superintendent of Homicide, not his mentor and friend.

"She told you she'd kill him," said Morgan, shifting forward on the sofa. "She said she'd kill them both." Morgan rose to his feet. "Look, Harry, she's a professor at prestige-U. Cultural studies, for goodness sake. We need witnesses. Did anyone hear her tell you she planned to bump off the most powerful hoodlum on the continent?"

"Morgan, don't exaggerate." Miranda reverted from being his boss to being his long-time partner.

"In Canada, then. Okay, in Toronto. The most powerful untouchable hoodlum in Toronto and environs."

"Morgan, no one says *environs* out loud," said Miranda. "That's one of those words we write but don't say."

"Like piping."

"What?"

"Piping hot, no one says *piping* hot."

"What about *risible,* what about *derisory.* They only appear in English papers like *The Guardian.*"

Harry listened and watched the two of them flutter like moths near a flame, flitting and darting and spiralling closer. They were legendary for their discursive wit as they circled a case before closing in.

Bad metaphor, Harry. Flames burn, moths die.

Bitchy and terse, but still a relief to have Karen close. He didn't respond.

"Can't say I care much about the murders themselves," said Morgan. "How it was done is interesting, though."

"How?" said Harry.

"Death by Mulsanne."

"Sounds nasty."

"It's not a poison, it's a Bentley."

"A car?"

"Top-of-the-line."

"Crashed?" Harry asked. He wasn't bothered by the Pomposello murders either. Sympathy was too rare and precious to squander on the insatiably degenerate. He was, in fact, strangely exhilarated and curious to hear more about how she had done it. He had no doubt that she had.

"They were inside the car," said Morgan. "They never made it out of the garage. We're on our way to take a look. We'd like you to come along."

"Please," said Miranda, as if he were hesitating, which he was not.

Harry and Morgan talked diving on the way up to the Pomposello house. Harry described the squadron of manta rays swooping overhead in the Bora Bora lagoon and the close encounter with a large tiger shark and the devastation being done to the coral by infestations of crown of thorns starfish. He talked about Tess. Not about Jennifer and certainly not about Mary di Cosmos. Tess Saintsbury was someone he knew, Jennifer was someone he had no desire to know, and Mary was the figment of a diabolical imagination who could never be known.

Silvio and Gina Pomposello were still in the car. The police first on the scene had called a Bentley dealer to come and spring the locks. Such was the intimidating power of luxury that they didn't just try to break in a window. When the doors had been unlocked, no one opened them or went near the bodies. They were waiting for Morgan, the senior detective assigned to the case. Such was the power of authority and the fear of screwing up a high profile murder investigation, especially one involving a very wealthy thug with connections to the highest society and the most powerful politicos in the city.

Peering through the tinted bulletproof glass at the rictus of anticipated death distorting their features, which were ruddy as if a mortician had already applied unnaturally lifelike cosmetics, Harry felt a twinge of horror, not for their demise but for the squalid ugliness of their passing. As the doors of the car swung open, he had a better view and felt sick. Never had he seen the look of fear so boldly displayed, an emotion that connected to the depth of his being and his own private terrors and unassuaged dread. These too, he thought, were humans like me.

No, Harry, they weren't.

Harry examined the ripped flesh on Silvio's cheek. The gashes were still livid, surrounded by smears of dried blood that made them seem fresh. There was a nasty bruise across Gina's jaw and a trickle of blood had dried on her lower lip. The eyes of both corpses were distended wide, their mouths gaped open, their limbs were entangled so that as rigor mortis had begun to set in they had to be pried from each other's arms.

Harry turned away. He watched Morgan from a distance and admired the man's apparent indifference to death. He didn't envy it.

"You never get used to it," said Morgan.

"Is that what happened to Miranda?"

"She got a promotion."

"Is that why she took it."

"Harry, there's always the fear you'll be scarred so badly your soul turns stiff."

"Your soul?"

"Figure of speech. Come on, let's get out of here."

In the car, Morgan talked about what he'd seen. "The engine was left running. The door from the house into the garage was slightly ajar, setting off the alarm. He didn't want the indignity of not being found. It looks like they'd had a knock-down quarrel. Seems like maybe she wasn't ready to die."

"So you think he did it?"

"Your friend may claim the credit but my money's on murder-suicide. Running a mob operation is hard on the nerves. Some guys break from the pressure. Do you know, they have the second highest suicide rate, after dentists, I think. Or vets."

"Vets, they get to hang around with animals."

"Military vets. War vets, not veterinarians."

Both men laughed, breaking the tension.

Domestic violence was ugly. Morgan was comfortable with his work, Harry knew that, but murder among people who had loved each other and lost that love was distressing. He wasn't sure how Morgan coped.

Morgan often unnerved people by apparently knowing their thoughts. He said, "You never get used to it, Harry. Not ever."

"So, is that it? You're going with a marital spat."

"The forensics people move in next. They'll dust for prints. They'll vet the place from top to bottom. But the pressure's on—Pomposello's colleagues want it to be a mishap, nothing more. They don't like family quarrels and they don't want to believe their top people are vulnerable. They don't want news, just a good obituary."

"Surely they can't pressure Miranda?"

"Not directly. But you'll find most of the news reports will fall into line: tragic accident takes the lives of prominent philanthropists, Silvio Pomposello and his wife, Gina. Please send donations to your charity of choice."

"Accident?"

"From a gas leak."

"Philanthropists?"

"Very generous. Running the gamut from the elite arts, you know, ballet and opera, to homes for the wretched."

"Gas leak?"

"No one wants to blame a Bentley. They don't malfunction."

"She's done it, then."

"Well, if she did, she's amazing."

"You can't admire a killer, Morgan."

"Only the ones I've never heard of. *You* admire her."

"She scares the hell out of me. She strikes fear into the depths of my soul—figure of speech."

"Great basis for a relationship."

Morgan smiled. He dropped Harry off in front of his condo building on the waterfront.

Jennifer Izett was waiting in the lobby.

Without her red wig and with her black hair brushed into waves, with her impossibly dark eyes and ingenuous smile, it was the woman Harry knew from Bora Bora, the woman he had kissed, the woman who remained an enigma and continued to engage him with deep ambivalence for her moral commitment and murderous ways, it was without question the woman he knew as Tess Saintsbury. She was wearing a smart blue suit and when she stood to greet Harry she picked up a sleek duffle coat lying on the sofa beside her and a blue leather purse large enough to hold a Smith & Wesson revolver.

"Harry, I need to talk to you." She seemed determined but not distressed.

"I'm surprised you're waiting down here. I would have assumed you have access."

"To your flat? Why would you think that? You have a double dead bolt."

"And you know that, how?"

"Good point. Can we go up?"

Once in his condo, she walked straight to the Klimts, standing first in front of The Kiss and then moving to The Forces of Evil. She stood with her back to the room until the ice in the drink Harry offered her clinked against the glass. She turned and took the drink, sniffed and smiled broadly. "I do love Pernod," she said. "I never drink it in Canada, only in the tropics, especially the French territories. Don't you miss Tahiti?"

"I spent very little time on the island itself."

"Yes, you remained on Bora Bora. I moved around."

"There was a time," he said, glancing wistfully out over the harbour, "when I did too. Where'd you mostly stay?"

"Mostly? Different places. Huahine. I like Huahine."

"How did she find you?"

"Cassandra? In the beginning? I told you."

"You evaded, you talked about wheels within wheels."

"She got in touch. I didn't offer."

"You're on LinkedIn or did she Google?"

"She heard. I am discreet but not unknown."

"Why Bora Bora?"

"Because Pietro had been there many times in the past so going again wouldn't arouse suspicion. I'd been to the islands before. It was a good place to do my work out of the limelight."

"Your work?"

"You know what I mean. It played to my skills. Canoeing, diving, meeting a handsome stranger with eyes like amber and steel grey hair and no excess fat. I hate fat almost as much as smoking."

"You picked me by where I placed on the body-mass index?"

"No, for your eyes. Sorry if that's deflating."

"I can live with it. Why marry him?"

"So we could travel alone. No nurses, no bodyguards. I hadn't expected the thugs."

"But you turned them to your advantage."

"Only temporarily."

"The Pomposellos are dead."

"So I understand."

"You can't just go around killing people."

"Why not? Especially if they deserve it."

"Does anyone deserve to die?"

"We all do, eventually."

"Before their time?"

"Premature death is an oxymoron. Whenever it happens, it's time."

"Even if you make it happen."

"Yes, Harry. Unequivocally yes. Sometimes it is a moral necessity."

"Gina Pomposello? Her crime was to marry a bad man."

"Silvio was a pestilence. Do you know how much misery drugs cause, have you any idea? But Gina died her own death, for her own crimes, and she knew it."

"Did you kill them?"

"Possibly."

"What crimes?"

"She murdered a former student of mine, a very promising young woman."

Harry had not been expecting that kind of specific justification.

"Explain?"

"Shall we sit down? Please."

Harry waited. She seemed wary. She opened her purse and withdrew the Smith & Wesson Bodyguard .38 Special. She wasn't brandishing it like a weapon but held it across the open palm of her hand. Harry made a show of not flinching. She set the gun down on the coffee table.

"I've brought you this, Harry. It's loaded, the safety is on. I know you don't carry a weapon but you might need one. Your world is about to get a lot smaller and much more dangerous."

"Because of what you're going to tell me?"

"Where should I start?"

She rose from the sofa and walked over to the glass door opening onto his balcony. She rested her hand on the door, then turned around quickly.

"You should keep this door locked. Otherwise dead-bolts are a waste of money."

"It was you, wasn't it?"

"It was."

"Why?"

"I know you will return them eventually but she wanted you to have them. They're yours for a lifetime. I'm especially fond of this one." She tilted her head towards The Forces of Evil. "She is raw and wanton and demure and genteel. How could you not fall in love with her?"

"It's a painting." Harry felt uneasily that Tess was describing herself, perhaps without knowing it. "How?" he asked.

"It's very straightforward. I abseiled."

"Abseiled?"

"Rappelled. Down and back up. You packed, you slept. I removed them and stacked them in the back of your front hall cupboard."

"They never were in Austria."

"Not this time. They weren't out of your home."

"Why?"

"Because I could."

"That's all you'll tell me?"

"That's all for now. Perhaps I just wanted to capture your attention. We have more important things to deal with."

"Like the Pomposellos?"

"No, they're dead and gone."

"I hope you didn't leave any prints?"

"Of course I did."

"You want to get caught?"

"I was there for a Christmas party, I went out for a smoke. They caught me on a surveillance camera that has since become untrustworthy. Remember, I was one of Gina's best friends. My prints are all over the place."

"And Gina Pomposello killed your student—"

"Who came from Sudbury, who was studying psychology, who dated a young neighbour of the Pomposellos. Silvio took a shine to her."

"A shine?"

"He lusted for her, is that more explicit? Silvio generally got what he wanted but this time he was careless. He fucked her in his own bed, the bed he shared with Gina. Gina caught them. Gina was enraged. She violated my student with a champagne bottle. Right there, she opened the bottle and jammed it into her vagina and watched the girl writhe as the bubbles flowed, and she laughed. And Silvio watched."

"How could you know this?"

"Because Gina told me. We got drunk, she told me Dom Perignon gave the best head that money could buy. But you had to be careful. Too deep, too tight, it could rupture your guts. Which it did, my student haemorrhaged, she bled to death. Gina told me in detail. Her story strengthened the bond between us. Silvio made the girl's body disappear. She apparently dropped out of university and was living the high life in Thailand. I knew that wasn't true."

"Your student, did she have a name?"

"Teresa MacPherson."

"Was your name MacPherson?"

"Not really."

"So she wasn't your sister, and not a relative? Was she a lover?"

"We weren't related. Harry. Pick up the gun, get used to it."

"You could have gone to the police."

"Good luck with that. Look, Harry. The woman was evil. Do you believe people can be evil? She'd make you a believer. In high school she literally bullied another girl to death, then after the kid swallowed bleach and died, Gina posted cartoons on the bulletin boards about the social benefits of suicide. After she married Pomposello she donated money to fight suicide among kids and laughed at the irony with her friends. Pick up the gun."

"I don't use guns."

"Pick it up."

"Why, what's this all about?"

"What I've been telling you is just a preamble. You and I are about to be hunted down and, if our enemies have their way, we will be murdered."

She smiled. Her dark eyes sank deeper into her skull as the afternoon sun passed behind a storm cloud hanging over the islands. Harry picked up the revolver contemplatively. He turned it over in his hands and set it down again. It felt no bigger than a toy but it was surprisingly heavy and he had no doubt it could kill. He felt the dread, the fear, the excitement, rising within him. His amber eyes narrowed, his mouth hardened, and he smiled in return.

14 THE RAPTURE

AN AURA OF FOREBODING DESCENDED OVER THE TWO OF them sitting in the afternoon gloom. He seemed to have known this woman across from him all his life and yet he didn't know her at all. She was like the part of him deep inside where surprises come from, when he would find himself mystified by his own inexplicable thoughts.

He started to speak but she interrupted before the words came out.

"Did you know Cassandra di Cosmos is dead?" she asked. "Have you been following Church politics?"

"If anything I've been avoiding The Church Absolute. Are you suggesting her death was political?"

"She died from a seizure. Probably a tincture of aconite root. Wolf's bane, the buttercup family."

"That's what she used to poison her father."

"But her adversaries got the dosage right. Now Tom Severence is totally in charge."

"And they're after you?"

"They're after *us*, Harry. As far as the Holy Gathering knows, you helped me escape. Executioners are closing in on us as we speak. It's not a big leap from mindless zealot to suicide martyr or killer assassin. Toronto has a sizeable congregation to draw from."

"And they know you're still around?"

"No longer among the ascended—that was Cassandra's inspired contribution. At the time it seemed like an excellent plan. Heaven's a good place to hide. But now the Holy Gathering knows I'm alive and they're desperate to see me vanish from the face of the earth."

"You've done it before."

"This time for real."

Harry wasn't sure how things had changed. He needed perspective, he needed to understand.

"What is the Holy Gathering?"

"They run the show, like the Sacred College of Cardinals in Rome. Severence is their newly elected Pope. They struck William's corpse on the forehead three times with a silver hammer and demanded, 'William Alexander Saintsbury, are you dead?'"

"I take it he didn't answer."

"Dead Popes seldom do. Did you know that's what actually happens when a pope dies, a cardinal knocks on his head and asks if he's gone? The Absolutes loathe Catholicism but they love the rituals. It makes everything bizarre seem familiar. So, they elected Severence as Pietro's successor: *Annuntio vobis gaudium magnum. Habemus Papam. Eminentissimum ac Reverendissimum Dominum, Dominum Princeps Rector.*"

"So they skipped Pope Joan," said Harry.

"Joan?"

"The only female pope—as far as we know."

"Only men can succeed The Founder. Cassandra was the regent. It was awkward while she was alive but now that she's gone, the take-over is complete. Like most Western religions, they have a visceral fear of women."

"Including you."

"Especially me. They're afraid I'll bring their whole scheme crashing down."

"You talk like it's a specific event."

"It is, Harry. And immeasurably evil. But you and I can stop it."

"Maybe you. I'm not religious." The more anxiety she revealed the more compelled he felt to assuage his own fears if not hers by being wry, dismissive, professorial.

"What do you know about the Rapture, Harry?"

"It comes from the medieval Latin word for rape."

"Seriously, what do you know about Christian eschatology?"

"Quasi-philosophical rantings about the end of days, the last of humanity, the Great Tribulation and the Second Coming, when the fallen shall perish forever and Christ will resurrect the redeemed from their graves."

"You know the Book of Revelation?"

"I live in a world condemned for millennia by its utter nonsensical hysteria."

"Well, Pietro di Cosmos declared the Rapture is imminent but he added a few refinements. First of all, he cut Jesus out of the equation. He made himself the agent of redemption. He qualified immortality as the personal experience of becoming an intrinsic part of God."

"If the Trinity can offer three gods in one, why not? Seems reasonable."

"Conventional Christian dogma doesn't take eternal life so literally."

"If it isn't literal," said Harry, "what the hell does it mean? The 'resurrection of the body and life everlasting.' If that's only figurative then what's it stand for?"

"That's where theologians slip into abstraction, talking about perpetual grace, divine essence, eternal ecstasy."

"Heaven as a prolonged non-physical orgasm. No wonder they have such hang-ups about sex in the here-and-now."

"Harry, I'm not trying to engage in religious intercourse."

"Oh." He thought he heard Karen admonish him, *be quiet*. He had no desire to quip.

"Stay with me, the worst is yet to come."

"I'm listening. I'm trying to follow."

"Pietro's original idea was an elaborate enticement to squeeze cash from converts. A select few would be chosen by the depth of their pockets and promised a short-cut to eternity. The whole thing horrified Cassandra. She tried to make him recant. And then, well, you know, she tried to set things right and she failed. But Tom Severence put a specific date on the Rapture. He turned the spiritual extortion practiced by so many religions into an outright scam. He turned my disappearance on Bora Bora to his advantage by declaring that I would be there to welcome the incoming dead."

"On the celestial plane."

"So, if I turn up alive I will bring the scheme crumbling down and destroy him."

"You're still talking in riddles. What bloody scheme?"

"Mass suicide."

"Oh God."

"Remember Jim Jones and the Peoples Temple? Over 900 died from a cyanide Valium cocktail, served up in a sugar drink. Do you remember Joseph Kibvetere's Movement for the Restoration of the Ten Commandments of God? More than a thousand died by self-immolation. What about Marshall Applewhite and his UFO conspiracy? Thirty-nine dead from a mixture of Phenobarbital and applesauce with a vodka chaser.

Remember Luc Jouret from Switzerland and his Canadian acolyte, Joseph Di Mambray? A total of 74 dead by various causes. And so it goes. Do you remember, Harry?"

"It's hard to forget. They all string together like a serial nightmare."

"Suicide is the loneliest act. Yet time and again people gather to kill themselves. Harry, religion is one way to deal with the horrors of the human condition, self-annihilation is another. Put them together and you have a death cult, where the consolation for being human is to deny that you are. Take this to its logical extreme: the sooner you die, the better."

"Most of us don't, though, we cling desperately to every last second." Harry felt simultaneously contemplative and anguished. "That is the divine paradox, isn't it? *Great is the promise of death, yet we choose to endure.*"

"Who said that?"

"I did."

"You sounded like you were quoting."

He sometimes does.

"Most people choose life," she continued. "Because of a lack of specifics. Jews are hazy on immortality and don't embrace death. Christianity venerates a perpetually dying God, it is a death cult, but heaven is so amorphous believers willingly wait their turn. Islam offers more details, but mostly too trivial for all except zealots to try jumping the queue. Religions who strive for nirvana seek death while remaining alive. And so it goes. But, Harry, when a visionary, a charlatan, a psychopath comes along and offers particulars, the more outlandish the better, the most fearful and lonely among us can't seem to resist. There is so much death, Harry. So much, and it's going to happen again. This time on a massive scale."

"How massive?"

"Twelve thousand."

"Good God!"

"Severence has conceived an enterprise that is huge and yet paradoxically modest. Twelve thousand from a congregation of millions are chosen to join me on the celestial plane. Twelve is the symbolic number of totality in the Book of Revelation, multiplied by one thousand, as determined by The Founder. The select few, who are many, are required to assign their worldly goods to The Church in preparation for their bodily ascent. I am the proof that ascension will happen. I have gone ahead. I will be there to greet them in the presence of my husband, who has passed into pure essence that is known as God. You can see, Harry, if I were to turn up back on this brutish planet, the disappointment would be catastrophic and the new Leader would have to relinquish the riches assigned to him by the Holy Gathering."

"How can they hunt you down without admitting you exist?"

"Ah, but I'm not me. I am the devil in earthly disguise."

"The Devil Incarnate; making your elimination a holy mission."

"And yours too, I'm afraid."

Harry got clean glasses from the cupboard, polished them, and brought out his best scotch, a bottle of Bruichladdich Octomore, which he poured neat and savoured the peat smoke aroma while he carried them over and gave one to Tess before sitting opposite in his teak and leather armchair. They wordlessly tipped their glasses to each other, swirled the amber liquid gently, and sipped.

"So that there can be no turning back, the select twelve thousand must die at the same moment in earthly time. February 6th of this year, as it turns out."

"A memorable day. That's my birthday," said Harry. "Why then?"

"If death is not synchronized, the collective will might collapse," she said. "It's not as if they're doing it for a cause, not like the thousands of Jews who died by self-slaughter at Masada. To embrace death when there is no alternative is depraved but inspired defiance. The one thing Absolutists have in common with each other and the man whose machinations will destroy them is cowardly self-interest. The fanatic's commitment is superficial at best."

"And the date?"

"Arbitrary, of relatively minor significance apart from your nativity. Severence chose it to honour the day William Alexander Saintsbury took on his new name and declared The Church Absolute to exist."

"Some famous people died on their own birthdays. Shakespeare, Raphael, Ingrid Bergman."

"Shakespeare is arguable. You forgot Moses and Mohammed. And as for you, Harry, don't count on it. You'll be lucky to live that long."

"So you say."

"He needs you wiped from the face of the earth because you're the one irrefutable link between Tess Saintsbury and Jennifer Izett. You're proof Mary di Cosmos is no longer dead. Our deaths may be different categories,

Harry—it may not be an act of religious devotion to kill you—but you're proof Severence has no direct connection with God, without which he cannot survive the Rapture."

"He's not planning to die?"

"Not yet. But he will, of course."

"He concedes that, does he?"

"He intends martyring himself by staying behind to take care of earthly affairs. In due course, he will join the celestials on a plane where time no longer exists. Then, simultaneously, the Rapture will take us into itself and we will become essence together."

"You sound like you almost want to believe it."

"We are the Borg, elevated to a spiritual plane. A rather charming idea. Unfortunately, celestial transmogrification is preceded by the suicides of twelve thousand lost and miserable souls whose worlds are destroyed in their wake."

"And who leave behind their collective wealth."

"Somewhere over a billion dollars, all legally willed or assigned to The Church Absolute. Take a deep breath, Harry. Drink your scotch and admire your Klimts."

Harry glanced at the darkened hallway leading to the dead-bolt door. He looked back at Tess Saintsbury who uncrossed her legs and flashing a length of thigh settled comfortably against the cushions. She curled her legs under her and smoothing the skirt of her suit, apparently savouring the moment when only a brief moment before she had been palpably anxious.

"Queequeg," she said, and at first Harry thought she was about to reminisce. "Our erstwhile friend, he put it all together, or as much as was necessary, when he discovered the two thugs were not on Bora Bora to kill my husband but to protect him."

"How did he know that?"

"He figured out they were emissaries of The Church."

"So he told me."

"Ah, but it wasn't until he connected with Severence that he discovered they were on the island as bodyguards."

"And that you were on Cassandra's side. And that there was no third man."

"Which he realized meant they didn't kill me."

"But Severence had already elevated you to celestial wonderland."

"Where he was desperate to have me remain."

"By the way, Queequeg knew you made up the names."

"Graham Greene made them up."

"Greene wrote the book, the film wasn't the same."

"They never are." She simulated a protracted yawn.

The relaxed atmosphere persisted as they talked through the remainder of the afternoon. By the time the sun disappeared, the effects of three premium scotches and a Pernod had made them both very mellow. Several times Harry tried to sort out his strong attraction to this woman he thought of as Tess, whatever her name actually was and what brutal crimes she might have committed. It wasn't that the ambivalence of his response was something he struggled to ignore; it was that it didn't seem to matter. She was not pathological. Her crimes were not arbitrary. They were morally defensible. Some might almost be considered altruistic. She was not especially mercenary. She had taken the diamond bracelet as a reasonable payment, or he assumed she had, and placed no further demands on The Church Absolute for ridding it of its monstrous leader, without whom Cassandra had hoped it would fall. Tess was not an adrenalin junky. The thrill was too much sublimated by her skills and efficiency. But she was, to use Karen's expression, the most female of females and in spite of all reasons to the contrary, he found her enchanting.

Like a cobra, Harry.

He was surprised at how retiring Karen had been. He was disappointed and relieved at the same time.

"You want pizza?" he asked. "We can call for takeout."

"Let's eat Far Eastern."

They settled on Chinese and when it arrived Harry buzzed the delivery person in through the lobby security door, then he stepped out in the hall and down the short corridor, with his hand on the Smith & Wesson tucked into the back of his pants. The boy was surprised when Harry emerged from the shadows behind him to pay.

"Tell me about the paintings," Harry asked once the egg rolls had quelled his stomach and he began to feel hungry.

"I told you, I rappelled from the roof."

"Abseiled, rappelled. Okay, but how did you know I was going to take them back to Vienna."

"Harry, you lead a pretty boring life but I've been following it closely."

"How closely?"

"Very, since we got back from Tahiti."

"You got back a week later, didn't you?"

"I stayed over for a bit, yes. I had something I had to do."

"Doesn't it bother you?"

"You mean the kids, the new husband?"

"Yeah."

"No, Harry, it doesn't bother me. They're better off without her."

"Maybe. God, you're efficient."

"Thank you. At what?"

"At getting me sidetracked. How closely have you been monitoring my life?"

"Like I said, close enough to know it's not very exciting."

"Sometimes it is." He could feel anger mounting at the obvious violations. "You tapped my phone."

"Very primitive, but yes."

"And my laptop." She waited as he processed the implications. "You knew what I Googled, you read my emails."

"And was pleased you don't troll chat rooms or porn sites."

"You expect me to be angry, I can see that. But I'm not. I'm just disappointed. I thought you had more class."

She swung around to face him. They were standing at the kitchen island. Her face expressed fury. Her eyes flared obsidian, her chin quivered. She reached out and pressed an index finger against his chest.

"Don't you dare patronize me, Harry Lindstrom. You got to keep your beloved paintings! What the hell more do you bloody well want?"

His supercilious attitude collapsed. Harry realized the Klimts were her way of saying *thank you, thanks for standing by me;* of saying, *sorry, I'm sorry for all I put you through.* They were the treasured legacy from a dead woman, and special for that, but they were also a truly precious gift from the woman boring a dent into his chest.

As he gently reached out to put his arms around her, she dropped her own arms to her sides. He drew her close until the lengths of their bodies touched. He leaned a little away, so their pelvises pressed and their thighs strained through their clothes, and he took her face between his hands and he kissed her. She wrapped her arms around him and they kissed pressed together, and when they finally pulled apart they wordlessly walked into the bedroom and switched on the lamps on their own sides of the bed so they could see each other as they removed their clothes and clambered over to meet in the centre.

And, somewhere deep inside Harry's mind, Karen wept.

15 THE CANADIAN CANOE MUSEUM

HARRY DRANK HIS MORNING COFFEE AND GAZED OUT over the harbour while Tess slept peacefully in the next room. He felt inexplicably lonely. It helped that assassins were after them. It was a welcome distraction.

Slate, death is the ultimate distraction.

He jumped inside his own skin; he assumed she had left him.

I'm not jealous, Harry. I'm dead. If I can assimilate that, I'm okay with a ghostly threesome now and then. It's only sex. With a moral degenerate, at that.

Or a determined idealist.

Don't argue.

Sailor, I—

You love me and always will. Now focus on surviving.

He could hear Tess moving in the background. He poured her a coffee and took it into the bedroom. She was in the shower so he set it on the bedside table. He had already washed up and shaved and dressed to go out, although he wasn't sure where they would go. He went back into the kitchen and poured his second coffee of the day.

She came out after a while, dripping, stark naked, without so much as a towel, and moved lazily around the living room, occupying space like a prize cat. He watched her ignoring him. She poured herself a coffee—she hadn't seen the one he left for her on the night table—and disappeared with it back into the bedroom.

After a surprisingly short time she emerged completely dressed, with full makeup, wearing yesterday's clothes but looking fresh and immaculate.

"No underwear," she said. "I left it in the hamper in the bathroom."

"Oh," said Harry.

She rinsed her empty cup in the sink.

"Where to from here." She seemed to be making an existential statement rather than asking an answerless question.

"Breakfast," said Harry. "Then we'd better check in with the police."

"And explain my husband's death, or should we give them a rundown of Church activities over the past few months, none of which we can prove?"

"So, lets hit the road for awhile."

"Harry, they won't stop until we're eliminated. There's nowhere to go."

"What do you suggest?"

"Well, with ten million people on six continents looking for us and a good number of those who would like to see us dead, I'd say our best bet is to fake our own deaths and disappear."

"Are you serious?"

"Possibly."

"Death isn't the answer to everything, Tess."

"You like calling me Tess. Can I call you Angel?"

"No." Angel Clare, of course. From Thomas Hardy.

"No, death isn't the answer to everything. Our own weren't even on my hit list. Have you read *Tess of the d' Urbervilles*? Spoiler: she's hanged in the end."

"My God, do you have a hit list?"

"I always remember the line, *thy damnation slumbereth not.*"

"Tess, do you have a hit list?"

"Just a few names pencilled in."

They talked while Harry slow cooked steel cut oats into a thick porridge.

She could take compassionate leave for having lost her closest friend under tragic circumstances. Silvio Pomposello had served on several advisory committees of the University. Harry would call Miranda Quin and explain he was heading over to the Gatineau Hills north of Ottawa to cross-country ski for an indeterminate length of time. No one else would be concerned by his absence, so long as his bills were paid. They decided to rent a car in a fictitious name for which she happened to have a license. He could make a single withdrawal at an automatic teller without laying a trail. It wasn't really necessary, since she had cash in her purse, almost forty thousand, as it turned out.

Harry had a friend from his camping days who worked as a curator at the Canadian Canoe Museum in Peterborough. He had visited her once for a tour but otherwise hadn't spent time with her in twenty years. She was totally laid back and irrepressibly adventurous. She would put them up for a few days with no questions asked. She knew he was a widower and she wouldn't be surprised to see him turn up with a woman, especially an experienced canoeist.

Harry packed a bag while Tess cleaned the dishes, including the cup she retrieved from the bedroom. They each made a few strategic calls. He looked up a number in his address book and punched it in, then hung up before anyone answered. Dropping in unannounced didn't seem like such a good idea, but calling from a tapped phone seemed even worse. He put on his knee-length sheepskin, his black toque, and the möbius loop Karen had made for him from a long cashmere scarf. He helped Tess with her duffel coat and after listening carefully they stepped out into an empty hallway.

When they emerged from the elevator into the lobby they looked determinedly nonchalant. As they pushed through the outer door, however, Harry glanced back. Two men with winter coats bundled up to their chins, although they were in the warmth on the far side of the lobby, were trying to ignore them. As soon as Harry and Tess stepped out into the cold, the two men followed.

"Harry, walk, don't run. We'll go to the car rental place at the Royal York, next to the one you usually use. Don't worry about those guys for now. They won't touch us in the open. They're brainwashed zealots but they're not stupid."

"You hope. How do you know where I rent cars? I don't very often."

"But when you do, you go to the same place. How else will we get to visit your friend."

"What friend?"

"The friend you didn't call. You'd better let him know we're on the way. You can call from the rental office."

"Her."

"Who?"

"My friend, it's a her."

"Oh God."

"Just a friend. We weren't lovers."

"It's possible."

They stopped in at a lingerie shop in the Royal York and Tess bought some sky-blue underwear, which she put on in the change room. The two men following them stayed close by in the marble foyer and resumed the chase as soon as they left.

At the car rental office, they decided to rent in Harry's name since the clerk addressed him as Mr. Lindstrom when they went in. Harry didn't recognize her but she apparently worked part-time for both establishments. Harry called the Canoe Museum from the car rental office and without giving details explained he and Tess were in trouble, he'd fill her in when they got there. His friend lived by herself in the country near Lakefield. She agreed to stay at the Museum until they arrived. She had to work late, so no hurry, no worries, it was a discreet place to connect.

It hadn't occurred to Harry not to drive straight to Peterborough. It was less than two hours away. But Tess had insisted they drive north to Muskoka first, to leave a credit card trail; and his friend had clearly picked up the aura of intrigue and insisted they arrive around midnight. Harry knew of a good place to have dinner, the Deerhurst Resort near Huntsville. It would be crowded with Nordic skiers. If they hadn't lost their pursuers by then, it would be easy enough to slip out and cut cross-country down through Haliburton and Lindsay. Peterborough was not the most likely of destinations for people on the run.

By the time they got to Bracebridge, they felt quite sure they weren't being followed and decided to dine at The Riverside Inn, which was more to their liking, especially after the Deerhurst had been tarted up for the G7 debacle of 2010 when a billion dollars was blown in a few days of grandstanding by a pathetically insecure Canadian government.

They talked into the evening about politics and avoided mentioning The Church Absolute, which both of them felt bore discomfiting similarities to the federal Conservative party presently in power.

When they arrived in Peterborough, they turned off Monaghan for the parking lot at the Canadian Canoe Museum and rolled the car into the shadows beside a storage shed. The outside of the Museum was brightly illuminated but it was surrounded by a vast gloomy expanse of gravel beyond the range of the lights. They walked swiftly across the open area to a side door that his friend had left unlocked, slipped into the darkness, and pulled the door closed behind them.

Emergency exit signs allowed them to see their way up the service stairs to a corridor eerily aglow with the monitor lights from dormant computers and printers and other devices. At the end of the corridor a lamp was on in a large corner office where his friend had said she'd wait for them, no matter how late they arrived. But the air was unnaturally still.

When they reached the door, stealth turned to shock as they stepped into the luminous glow surrounding the body of Harry's friend slumped over her desk. Without checking, he knew she was dead.

She had been shot through the forehead. It had been a professional job but not by a natural-born killer. Consideration had been shown for how her body was meant to be discovered, as if death had overtaken her by surprise. He felt waves of pity and fear sweep through his body. He turned to Tess and in a redundant gesture with a finger to his lips indicated they should be quiet.

They listened.

There were only the sounds of a cavernous old building. Air pushed gently through vents, carrying the purring whirl of a furnace fan buried deep in the bowels of the vast hidden infrastructure. It was like the building was breathing, but breathing so cautiously it might have been mimicking death.

With nothing they could do for his friend, Harry led Tess through an open doorway into the exhibition hall, which was divided into myriad display areas and exhibits on two floors, with a grand staircase beside a water course with the water turned off. Emergency nightlights and exit signs glowed in profusion. The entire vast area opened into a cacophony of shades and shadows and elongated tentacles of darkness with narrow striations of light. They moved cautiously, soundlessly, through reconstructions of a trapper's cabin, an artisan's shop, and a voyageur camp, stopping dead still every few paces among antiquated tools, stooks of sweetgrass, and stretched animal skins, to listen for anyone else, until they came into a section with canoes poised on racks and stands, scattered artfully askew for maximum exposure, casting terrifying sinuous shadows that threatened to open up caverns beneath their feet or reach out and entwine their limbs.

They stopped between a huge redwood dugout and a featherlight birchbark prototype for the modern recreational craft, and they listened. They heard something move, a switch snap, a hum, then suddenly they grasped at each other as a tumbling rush of water resonated through the quiet air before it settled into a burbling flow. Someone had turned on the recirculating stream. Someone armed with a small calibre gun. They heard footsteps on the stairs beside the water course. Harry grabbed at Tess's hand and led her through the mottled darkness around to the other side of the canoe displays, past the kayaks, many of them skeletons grasping at the dim light as they passed. They ducked into a reconstructed wigwam.

Tess seemed amenable to Harry having assumed leadership but Harry balked at what he had done. There were a couple of storage boxes in the wigwam but nowhere to hide. He drew Tess close, peered out, saw no one, and darted with her across to a work room set a few feet below floor level for demonstrating woodcraft skills. He pushed her under a bench near the back behind a half-finished stack of paddles and moved forward against the raised floor, crouching beneath a wood railing.

The flowing water might have been intended to conceal footsteps or simply to terrify, but it helped to isolate and enhance the approaching shuffle of shoes across the plank floors.

The assassin stood just above Harry, peering into the dimness. Suddenly, there was a terrible sound as he vaulted over the rail and with two steps stood directly in front of the lattice of shadows concealing Tess. Harry leapt to his feet. A gun exploded. Harry was momentarily blinded by the flash. He froze as their would-be killer crumpled onto the floor.

Tess crawled out as the stack of paddles clattered. Her Smith & Wesson was still in her hand. The air smelled of gun smoke. She blew across the barrel with a hint of melodrama and lowered the gun back into the recesses of her purse.

"Let's hope there's only one," said Harry in a low voice.

"There's another," she whispered. "If he's smart, he'll recognize the gunshot wasn't his buddy's. He'll wait for us to step into the open. What on earth were you thinking, hiding us in a wigwam? It's made of bark, for God's sake."

Harry shrugged.

"Sorry about your friend," she added. "For what it's worth, it was a clean kill."

"Really."

"One shot, quick. She didn't suffer, she probably didn't know what was happening, she looked up and bang, that was it."

"That was it," said Harry. There was nothing more he could think of to say.

"They tracked your call from the Hertz office."

It wasn't Hertz, but it didn't matter.

Harry hauled the dead man out to an open space between work benches. He had a morbid irrational dread that somehow the body wouldn't be found.

He retrieved the man's handgun from the floor and tucked it under his own belt. He didn't like guns but he liked even less being stalked by a gunman.

"Okay," he whispered.

They moved cautiously back through the kayaks stacked out of reach on display. Desiccated skin coverings stretched over bone and driftwood ribs lashed together with sinew. He tried to erase the image from his mind. A display of Inuit carvings caught his attention, especially the huge whalebone vertebra carved with faces on both sides, one with a broad grin, the other scowling. He thought of Queequeg and smiled in spite of himself. There was no way that man had converted to The Church Absolute. It was inconceivable.

They moved like wraiths down the steps. As they skirted the edge of the broad landing, Tess bumped into the kayak Adam Van Koeverden had raced to gold in the Athens Olympics. Harry grabbed the boat with his hand to steady it and immediately pulled away, burned by visceral guilt for violating rules never to touch the displays.

They continued down to the ground floor. There was no alternative. The service stairs were closed in—it would be certain disaster to be caught going down that way. They were better out in the open, where the gunman couldn't get close without being seen. The farther down they went, however, the more confined the spaces, the easier for him to hide. They passed around the side of the stairs in front of a showcase featuring Pierre Trudeau's fringed and beaded buckskin jacket. Harry detested affectations of native dress but Trudeau had fairly earned his as a gift, either for his canoeing prowess or because he'd been Prime Minister. They moved past the representation of a Bill Mason campsite, complete with red canoe and a half-finished painting. They slipped past a mock-up of a trip shed and still no sign of their executioner. If they could get through the trading post with its hands-on displays and into the adjoining classroom, they might be able to make it out the back door to the parking lot.

Nothing concentrates the mind like imminent disaster, or so Harry understood. Yet his mind skipped around like a firefly evading the moonlight. He looked over at Tess. Her face in the dappled light was serene but clutched in her hand with a finger on the trigger was a loaded gun. She frightened him in some ways more than the killer hidden in the shadows. She made him fear himself.

He motioned for her to wait and he stepped into the Hudson's Bay Post reconstruction, so authentic that he might have travelled through time. The smells of tanned skins and old wood, of tallow and tar and gunmetal and traps, drew part of his mind into a world that far preceded his own recollections and yet were as real as memory. In another part of his mind, he listened. He could hear his breath rushing through his nostrils, he could hear Tess breathing behind him. He held his breath, he could hear someone else breathing.

He glanced around. He could tell by the tilt of her head and the absence of light in the recesses of her eyes that Tess was staring directly at him. He was shocked when she stepped forward and spoke.

"Why don't you come out now?" she said. "What if the Holy Gathering is wrong, my friend? You know who I am, you cannot kill me. Without me you will be banished from the presence of God. Come out, now, stand before me, we will enter the Rapture together. Come out, my friend."

She spoke softly, but with such poise and conviction that Harry could almost imagine she was celestial. He knew she was not, he knew she killed people. She was righteous perhaps but exceptionally lethal.

In the silence after she stopped speaking, he wished the man hunting them wouldn't respond, he wished their misguided assassin would just slip away. There were enough dead already.

Sounds of shuffling emerged from behind the factor's counter and a middle-aged man rose to his feet. He looked very ordinary. He held a new Glock in one hand but rested it on the boards in front of him. Harry could make out his broad features but couldn't see his expression. Tess turned on the lights. The man was smiling.

Tess walked over and stood in front of him.

His eyes filled with tears.

He released his gun and let his hands drop to his sides. Tess fired a bullet into his left temple. His head snapped away. She reached out and pulled him forward. He collapsed across a stack of dried beaver skins. A slight trickle of blood ran down the front of the counter and pooled on the floor.

16 THE DEVIL'S CAULDRON

THEY DROVE EAST THROUGH THE NIGHT AND WHEN THE
sun was bright on the horizon they stopped for a Tim Hortons breakfast
and then turned north. Arriving on the outskirts of Killaloe, near the
eastern entrance to Algonquin Park, they rented a small cabin before
doubling back into town for clothes for Tess and supplies to last them
a week. More supplies would have attracted attention. Fewer, and
they'd become daily familiars in the local stores.

Settling into the cabin, they read paperback novels piled in the
kitchenette next to the plates and quickly lost track of current events and
the larger world. Before long they were lovers again and developed a close
friendship based almost entirely on shared present moments, although
occasionally each revealed something of the past that brought them closer
and made them more vulnerable. Harry was surprised when one morning
he woke up and she was gone.

The car was still parked in front of the cabin and covered in snow.
She had arranged for someone in Killaloe to pick her up. There was no
note.

Five days later, she returned. A taxi brought her out from town with a
backpack, winter camping gear, and backcountry Nordic ski equipment,
which the driver carried around to the closed-in back porch and stacked
next to the woodpile.

"I thought you had left," said Harry, looking up from his book.

"You're still here."

"That's heartwarming," he said.

"I brought some supplies."

"Good, we're running low."

They didn't talk anymore until after dinner, which they cooked
together.

"You would have tried to stop me," she said.

"Maybe, maybe not."

"I had a taxi drop me off in the Park. The driver picked me up this afternoon. You would have tried to stop me, Harry."

"I probably would have." He felt the anxiety rising.

"The falls are frozen over, Harry. It's breathtaking, awesome. There's like, it's a frozen carapace of ridges and folds—but you can hear water thundering beneath the ice. Absolute stillness on the surface; violence surging below."

Describes some people I know, Harry. Karen had settled deep in his mind while Tess was away. He was surprised to hear her, now.

"I followed the river down through the marsh," Tess continued.

"Why, why on earth did you go to that place, why did you do that?"

"I needed to."

"It's my story, not yours." He was angry. "It's not your life, Tess."

"I can see why they call it the Devil's Cauldron."

Was she taunting him or trying to connect?

"The river run is sublimely beautiful this time of year," she said. "Away from the falls, the silence overwhelms. The snow, the ice, the cedars, the spruce, the towering pines."

"Good, you've done an inventory, now let it drop."

"I'd like to take you there."

"No fucking way."

"Maybe someday."

He lowered a clenched fist slowly onto the table, restraining the violence he felt surging within.

The weight of Karen's absence he had assigned to his being with Tess, and the comfort of her presence to his solitude. Now he realized her mutable nature was a response to geography. The Park extends half way across the province and because they had approached from a different direction than he had in the past he had not consciously paid attention to their proximity to the Anishnabi River and the place where Karen had died. Where Karen and Matt and Lucy had died.

"I'm glad you're back," he said.

"Me too, Harry. I'm tired. We'll talk in the morning."

In the morning, they talked more than they ever had about the past, about places they had been, especially in England where they had both lived, especially about London, where they had both stayed at the splendidly eccentric Hazlitt's Hotel in Soho amidst an eclectic miscellany of antiques and collectibles, in rooms scattered among narrow corridors, cranky staircases, and Kafkaesque parlours. They talked about British novels. Both liked Jane Austin and the Brontë sisters, especially the neglected Anne, although Harry insisted he liked later novelists like Hardy and Conrad while Tess preferred the subversive forbearance of Mrs. Gaskell and the earlier gothic mysteries of Ann Radcliffe and, of course, Mary Shelley.

As the morning wore on, she suddenly turned their talk to an account of herself, speaking almost as if she were fiction.

Jennifer Izett was born to a single mother in the same small Ontario city called Preston where Harry's family had in more prosperous times owned a foundry and made cast iron stoves. When she was three months old she was molested. At nine she challenged one of her innumerable step-fathers and he took her outside in her nightdress and beat her about the head, finally forcing her face-down in the snow with his boot until he got cold and went back in, leaving her too weak to move. She must have, eventually, because she survived, although paleness on her right ear showed evidence of frostbite. The next morning there was a grotesque pattern of blood in the snow, as if a stray dog had massacred a rabbit. At twelve, she was expelled from Preston High School at the end of her first full month in attendance. She bit the principal. She was sent to a reformatory where she spent three months in a cell by herself, permitted to talk only to a matron who treated her kindly. The matron's name was Jennifer Izett. She didn't remember her own mother's name, she chose not to remember.

She was released from the reformatory when she was fourteen and, living in a foster home as Jennifer Izett, she completed secondary school. She was abused by her foster father but chose to endure the abuse and intervened between him and his natural daughters who resented her favoured status. She was groped repeatedly through her teens by the elderly Anglican priest at the church her foster family attended but turned his pathetic ministrations to her advantage by getting an exemplary recommendation to attend the Royal Military College in Kingston.

From there she went to McGill for an MA, then on to Yale where she earned a Ph.D. before taking an interim job teaching at Boston College and then moving to a tenure-stream post at Toronto.

Harry had checked out the last part, but he wondered how much of the rest was either prevarication or outright untruth. She wasn't a pathological liar who believed her own lies. She only fabricated alternative realities if there was a strategic advantage. He wondered what advantage could be gained from misleading him now. Sympathy? Outrage? Acceptance?

On Bora Bora she had told him she grew up American, in a military family. Now she was Canadian. She had been Tess, then Jennifer. But Jennifer was a borrowed name. It was as if she had no name of her own. He imagined if she grew up in what had once been called Preston she would have known it amalgamated with Hespeler, Galt, and the hamlet of Blair in the early seventies as the city of Cambridge. It wasn't Preston anymore. Or was it, in the minds of its residents? He wondered what else was open to question?

Was she intentionally merging her own story with his? Miranda came from the same part of the country. Was this strange woman with her elusive mercurial capricious and unpredictable identities struggling to give herself authenticity, to make herself real? Or was she trying to escape who she was?

He didn't challenge her. It was feasible that he and Miranda and Jennifer Izett, Tess Saintsbury, or whoever she was, originated in the same region of the country, in the same part of the province, the same county, even the same flatlands along the Grand River. Given the courses of their convergent lives, it was a reasonable possibility. He gazed at her with a mixture of fear and affection. She was a person who made coincidences happen. He shuddered.

If the story of infant abuse was true, it was unbearably horrifying, although she could only have learned about it from hearsay. If it wasn't true, it was unbearably grotesque to claim it had happened. The beating in the snow seemed authentic, although sometimes lies can smack of authenticity through more details than memory can possibly convey.

Before lunch they went out for a walk. The snow ruts on the road had frozen into solid ridges and made the going treacherous. After a half hour they turned back.

"I bought skis for you too, you know. They're in the back porch with mine," she announced, quite pleased with herself.

"I'm not going up there." He stated emphatically, knowing exactly where this was leading.

"Why the hell not, Harry? Nature didn't kill them." Large snowflakes hovered in the air, which had warmed since they left the cabin. "It was bad judgement, call it whatever, the earth stays the same."

"So you're laying blame."

"Assigning responsibility. You were there, you might have prevented it from happening. But you didn't. You didn't, Harry, so forgive yourself and move on."

"Jesus, you're tough."

"No Harry, I'm not. I just know how to live with what cannot be changed."

"And how to change what can't be endured."

"Sometimes, when I can."

"Did that shit really happen to you?"

"My childhood? Yeah, childhood happened. Not quite like that, but it happened. It's kind of an extended metaphor for what I really went though."

"Tell me, Tess."

"Let's have beans and toast for lunch."

They went in and ate lunch, then Tess poured them each a tumbler of cognac and they sat close to the cast iron stove and she began to tell her story.

"Let's start with the present," she said. "I'm the invention of my own will and desire."

He started to say something but she held up her hand: "Listen," she said. "You are who you want to be. That's very different from accepting who you are. Do you understand?"

Harry stoked the fire and settled back with his scotch. She waited, then took a stiff drink and started to speak. "I grew up in the village of Blair, which remained a distinct hamlet after the amalgamation because it was separated across the river flats from the rest of Cambridge. My father was an insurance agent who had a small office in the front room. My mother was his office manager. I told you we were an American military family. That was my cover in The Church. I did go to fake-Indian canoe camp in Haliburton. I went on serious canoe trips. My parents never took a vacation. I said I was an only child. I had a sister who died when I was four and she was three years older. She drowned in a small lake at the south end of the village. We called it Wilson's Pond. Between the Wars the owner prospered cutting ice in the winter and storing it in a huge insulated shed to sell during the summers in Preston. Business dwindled over the next generation and by the early eighties there were occasional calls from ice sculptors and winter festivals but the market for ice had pretty much disappeared so no one was surprised when one day the shed burned to the ground. It was an old double-clad barn with sawdust stuffed between the walls. That last winter, a skeleton crew was still cutting blocks of ice, even though most of it would melt where it sat the following summer. It was like a farmer gathering hay after he'd been forced to sell his livestock. Just habit that had once meant survival. My sister and her friends were inside the shed. In a village, you have friends of all ages. Most of them were older than her. It was cold, they was sheltering from the weather, removing their skates, none of them were smoking, they knew it was far too dangerous. Someone deliberately set the fire—no one knows for sure. The boys in their hockey sweaters jumped to the ground from the stacked ice covered in layers of straw through the open door at the front. My sister and some other girls scrambled onto the loading slide leading down to the channel of water cut into the ice surface out to the centre of the pond. The older girls climbed down, all but Sarah, she slid, and when she hit the water she struggled and slipped under the ice at the side of the channel. The other girls had already started running. They were terrified. They knew they would be blamed for the fire. They ran helter-skelter back into the village to their own separate homes. My sister's name was Sarah, police divers dragged her body out of the pond during the night, working under portable floodlights. She had drifted out to the open water beside the snow-cleared area where we skated. Some older boys played hockey in the extra light and were there when they found her. My parents were there, too, and I was there. It's one of my first memories, the boys in Maple Leafs sweaters, a few girls watching from the snow banks, the divers in alien drysuits, my parents distraught. I don't remember Sarah at all. But I remember she didn't have boots on and one sock was missing. It turned up the next spring when the village kids were swimming. I was watching them. They wouldn't let me swim. I was still too young. They gave me the sock to take home."

Because his own brother had drowned when Harry was seven, not in Blair but in Trois-Rivières, he again had the eerie feeling she was co-opting his own story, either through an uncanny coincidence or with some malignant unfathomable intent. Since Bobby's death had been assimilated into his own personality, it was no longer a tragedy but simply a dramatic episode in his childhood narrative. He was inclined to believe the coincidence was one of those strange modalities that draws people with comparable experience together.

"I don't remember anything else before that," she continued. "It was like I was born at four, surrounded by sorrow, as if I had no beginning of my own. We never talked about Sarah. We never talked about the past. There were rules and that was the prime directive. The past didn't exist."

Harry smiled wistfully at her allusion to Star Trek.

"There must have been a funeral but I wasn't allowed. Does that sound strange? I didn't even know where Sarah was buried until I was in high school and searched out her grave, but by then we had nothing in common. She was forever seven and I was fourteen.

"In my recollections of primary school, the years slide together. I was always the same. I wasn't unpopular. I had friends at school. But at home the three of us lived separate lives, each of my parents and I. We didn't touch, we didn't talk, we didn't mourn. We just filled space, we filled in the time.

"In grade nine, where we had to be bussed over to Preston, an English teacher called Mr. Robertson nicknamed me Black-Eyed Susan and the name stuck. He was the first adult I remember who knew I was a separate person, not just one of a cluster of kids or a knot in the family tree. I did well in English and had him again in grade ten. When he was killed before Christmas that year, for the first time in my life I grieved. I didn't even know his first name. He was always, even now, Mr. Robertson. He died in a car accident.

"I wish I could tell you something about my parents, but I can't. They were ordinary and detached, not even exemplary at being dull. I can hardly remember them."

"They're not alive?"

"No. In grade eleven I went out for the cheerleading squad. I have no idea why. I made it as a substitute, which meant I had to practice and went to the home games, but never away. In grade twelve, I catapulted to head cheerleader. I had an identity. Short skirts, cartwheels, hair bobbed, boobs and legs and lips on display. And then it was over. I left high school a virgin. I wasn't invited to the formal, what we'd taken to calling The Prom in emulation of our American cousins. Black-Eyed Susan had moved into full blossom. The boys were intimidated, I was indifferent. Not to sex, I'd tried it on my own. But I was indifferent to being liked. I didn't care. That made me alluring, apparently, even awesome, but apparently scary as hell.

"Sounds pretty uninspired, doesn't it? For the most part, it was. My parents died when I was in grade twelve. That was the only outstanding event that year, apart from missing The Prom. We lived in an older house on the main Blair Road, in the centre of the village. My parents did enough business collecting insurance premiums from succeeding generations of clients that they managed to get by, living frugally, which is what they preferred. They watched television. I studied in my room. Then my mother hanged herself in the basement.

"One day in February I came home and she wasn't at her desk. I could hear the washing machine whirring in the basement, even though it was a weekday. So I went down the rickety wooden steps and there she was, hanging from one of the joists with my father's extra belt around her neck. She looked ghastly, her eyes bulged, and her tongue had been bitten almost off and lolled between her teeth with her jaw pulled askew. Her hair was done neatly and she wore a Sunday dress. I think the washing machine running empty was to attract my attention so she wouldn't be there too long. My father might not have noticed.

"I didn't scream. I climbed back up the wooden stairs and touched my father's shoulder. He looked at me in shock. I had never intentionally touched him before. He rose to his feet, stacked a few papers neatly, and followed me down into the basement. He didn't seem surprised. He stood in front of my mother and stared, looking up at her contorted face, then he reached out and brushed a wisp of spider's web from the front of her dress.

"He told me to go upstairs and phone for help.

"I could hear scraping of wood on cement, ominous thuds, and a clatter. I assumed he was lifting her down, but when I returned to the basement after unlocking the front door—we always kept the doors locked even when we were at home—he had carefully arranged a wooden chair beside my mother's body and he had stepped up on the chair and secured an electric extension cord over the adjoining joist and tied it around his neck and kicked out the chair, hanging himself beside her.

"He kicked and twitched, but resistance at this point was pretty much futile and he soon began twisting around, turning slowly, facing my mother, facing me, with his mouth emitting inhuman gagging noises, and he strained to keep his eyes from rolling back as he looked into mine. I watched, I didn't try to intervene, but when the life went out of his eyes and he gave a final spastic shudder, I realized perhaps he had been pleading for help. Or perhaps asking forgiveness. Or, more likely, just letting me know he was finally free."

Harry caught the second Star Trek reference, which somehow seemed the contemporary equivalent of a Biblical allusion, especially coming from a professor of comparative studies.

"Social Services arranged for me to board near the school with the Wake family, an appropriate name for people taking in someone defined by bereavement in everyone's mind. Their two older daughters went to The Prom and I stayed at home to babysit Madeleine, the youngest, while the parents attended as chaperones. I think actually I scared the hell out of boys my own age, having been so closely associated with death. The Wakes were a happy family and embraced me with compassion, which I didn't know how to handle. When I went off to university, I never returned for a visit.

"In the yearbook I'm identified as 'Black-Eyed Susan, living proof that beauty is the loneliest virtue.' It was meant as a cryptic joke.

"I attended the Royal Military College and did well, worked part-time in the library, refused all invitations to date or socialize, and moved on to McGill for a Masters degree."

"Do you want a refill?" said Harry. He could see she was getting tired.

"I'm a little drunk, already. Why not?"

He poured a couple of inches of scotch into both tumblers and sat back. She needed to tell him the rest.

"I've always been good in languages," she continued. "In Montreal I lived among Francophone Québécois. I avoided my English-speaking classmates as much as I could. And very quickly, I learned how easy it was to lead separate and parallel lives. I was Black-Eyed Susan, the philosophical scholar, and I was Susan Montaigne, the demure sales-clerk at an unknown shop in Old Montreal."

"I knew you had degrees before Yale but I didn't track your records. You re-named yourself after a Renaissance essayist."

"Michel de Montaigne, the father of modern scepticism. I wish. But I wasn't yet there as a sceptic. Montaigne was my birth name, although my parents spelled it without an 'i,' which may or may not be significant. They were the only Montagnes in our part of Ontario as far as I know. Huguenot background, Anglicans to the core. My mother's family was from Belfast. They were probably Spanish if you went back far enough. Black Irish. That's where I get my dark hair and anaemic complexion."

Like alabaster, alabaster and obsidian; hardly anaemic. Harry was beginning to relax, feeling the worst parts of her story were over, when suddenly she was back to her student days in Montreal.

"I met a wonderful boy, a neighbour in Saint Henri where I lived. He was beautiful and simple and kind. We became lovers, he was my first. When he discovered I wasn't a clerk in a store, he laughed, and didn't ask what I really did. We didn't talk much about anything, really. We just kind of hung out when I wasn't at McGill. The only strange thing about him was his fear of menstruation, but I didn't know much about the rituals of romance so I let it go. It seemed every month that he was angry at me. I thought it was delayed PMS or whatever. My fault. It had to be. Now, don't turn away, Harry. This is part of my story."

"Talk about it all you want."

"It?"

"You know."

"Harry, Harry, Harry."

He wasn't disturbed by talking about such things. He and Karen had been comfortable with bodily functions. He was concerned with how her strange little revelation could be relevant.

"Roger had a motorcycle, an old Harley." She pronounced his name *Rogé* and his bike *Arlee*, the same ways he must have. "One gorgeous spring day just before my graduation, we took a spin up to Mont Tremblant. Coming back down Highway 15, outside of Boisbriand we slowed for a traffic accident. Some kids in a van were heading home from a hockey tournament. Their van had rolled. There was hockey equipment scattered all over. We slowed, but the car beside us pulled ahead, swerved, and smashed through scattered equipment on the pavement. Splintered hockey sticks, goalie pads, uniforms, skates, filled the air and we had no option but to barrel through the maelstrom of flying debris. I clutched Roger tightly, my hands closed around him under his rib cage, my fingers dug through his jacket into his flesh. My right hand suddenly felt like it had been whacked with a hammer. We got through, he slowed to a stop at the side of the highway. He didn't move, we were both in shock. I couldn't feel my hand. It was impaled by a shattered hockey stick that had smashed completely through his rib cage. The Harley teetered and fell and my hand was ripped free when I tumbled away. Roger sprawled sideways on his back, twisted around the shaft running through his body, wriggling in spasms of pain, then he lay deathly still. I crawled to him before anyone reached us. He was conscious. He whispered in a clear voice, *je t'aime, mon Christ Jesus, je t'aime. Pas de sang, jamais.* The last word he spoke was *jamais*, never."

"He died there."

"No, helicopters were on the way for the other accident, the hockey kids were shaken up, we were airlifted to a Montreal hospital. They stitched up my hand. There's still a dent and a scar. I was bruised but back on my feet in an hour. And Roger, he lay on a gurney on the edge of unconsciousness. He had a card in his wallet prohibiting blood transfusions. He'd told me no blood, never. Then his parents arrived by taxi. I had no legal status. They declared no transfusion, they were Jehovah's Witnesses—by the 1945 order of God Almighty blood was ordained as a sacred commodity, vile if exposed to air, evil if shared. No red cells, white cells, platelets, or plasma could be ingested in any way."

"And you didn't know?"

"No sex during menstruation, disgust at my periods, of course I should have, but we didn't talk religion, we didn't talk bodily functions, we hardly talked. And then I watched him die. They couldn't pull the spear from his side without him bleeding to death in a great gushing surge but they couldn't leave it in him, of course. His ribs were shattered and his lung was pierced right through. So there he was, lying in the corridor of a hospital with a hockey stick protruding from his gut, gurgling and gasping while a debate raged around him about medicine, law, and God's holy ordinance.

"I pleaded with his family, I listened, I cried, I raged, I cajoled, I argued, I threatened. Nothing worked. His father would not allow him to *eat* blood, as they called it. There wasn't time to get lawyers involved. His father quoted Genesis, Leviticus, Acts, and the Watchtower Society. The Jehovah's Witness Hospital Liaison Committee tried, very meekly, to intervene to avoid controversial publicity, but they refused to compromise true believers. The hospital authorities were Catholic. They meekly submitted. They didn't want to appear intolerant. Roger died.

"In the foul name of a false fucking God, in the name of tolerance for the intolerable, in the name of religion, he died."

"I'm sorry," said Harry.

"Me too, Harry. You lost your family through an error in judgement. I lost Roger by an act of sheer ignorance. You can forgive yourself. I told you, you must. But I cannot forgive the madness of religion. Something snapped while I sat with his hand, his dear dead hand, in my own. Or something connected. It's much the same thing.

"My life changed. I dropped Susan Montaigne and became someone else and went to Yale, where I was diligent and developed physical skills to balance the rigours of cerebral development. I did a lot of scuba diving and abseiling and martial arts and I learned more about guns and things that blow up, stuff I'd been introduced to in military college. And of course I made contacts. There isn't a so-called civilized country in the world where I can't track down an Ivy League grad with sleazy connections and righteous presumptions."

"You became who you are."

"More or less."

"And who is Jennifer Izett if she wasn't a reform-school matron?"

"I took the name by deed poll before I went down to New Haven. Fresh beginnings, you know. It was actually my mother's name."

"What about the story of being tromped into the snow? You have scarring from frostbite."

"I was nine. I was angry, I lay down in a snowbank and refused to go in for dinner or when it was bedtime. I was a very stubborn child, Harry. And remember, my parents were very damaged. I got hypothermia. When I went to the door after the lights were turned out, it was locked. I had to knock. My mother answered. She seemed surprised to see me. I was disoriented and shaking. I didn't know my own name. She put me to bed. I don't remember what I was angry about."

Harry looked at her eyes, she was looking away. They glistened with flames as he opened the stove door and shoved in a piece of split maple, then they turned black when he closed it again. She looked up, pushed her hair away from her face and offered a wan smile as if there was someone else in the room.

17 A SKI IN THE PARK

"Jehovah's Witnesses believe that as of October 1914 the end-times have already begun. Mormon's believe God is an anthropoid who lives on a planet called Kolob and men who dress like Quakers live on the far side of the moon. Astronomers at the University named after the Mormon prophet Brigham Young track Kolob with the latest scientific equipment and the President of The Church of Jesus Christ of Latter-day Saints, who subscribe to notions of magic spectacles, sacred underwear, and converting the dead, has literal conversations with God, presumably in English laced with seventeenth century semantic anachronisms. Scientologists believe an anthroprogenitor by the name of Xenu banished followers to Earth from the planet Teegeeack and then attempted to destroy them. Some United Church congregations believe God may not be a divine being at all or have agency in the world but still is worth praising. Unitarian Universalists believe anything they want. Absolutists believe we are inhabited by self-knowing aspects of the cosmic mind who migrated from the planet Philon following an intergalactic war. Catholics adore holy relics and appallingly mundane plaster statues. Hindus believe in a deity with extra arms and the head of an elephant. Moslems mete out death by stoning for crimes of blasphemy. They sometimes blame women for being raped and occasionally they stone the victims of rape to death. They abhor women, they all abhor women. Without exception, they all fear women and deny them equivalent status to males with external genitalia. Such contemptible crap is beyond comprehension, were it not accepted by millions upon millions. You think sacred cows are absurd. Try magical underwear and communing with Jesus by drinking his blood."

Harry held up his hand as a gesture of surrender. It felt like she was holding him responsible for the religious foibles of the species. He had nothing to argue. He did not share her contempt, nor her bitterness, nor did he condemn what he took as the instinctive impulse of his fellow humans to explain what the mind could not comprehend through ritual and magic.

His antipathy to religion had always been personal, not political. He found faith sometimes to be a ludicrous and sometimes dangerous mystery, a quirky facet of the human adventure that was sometimes responsible for a great deal of good.

That's where he and Karen had diverged. Don't you think people can be virtuous without threats of damnation or the promise of glory, she'd argue. And then they'd get into discussions of good and bad, virtue and evil, right and wrong, dichotomies of ethics and morality where they essentially agreed but could rouse up a fiery discussion, which usually concluded being very good being bad together in bed.

Tess was different. Religion was not a matter of opinions and arguments. It was the face of the enemy, as real as Satan for those who believed. For Harry, with Nietzsche in mind, it was the refuge of those not wanting to know what is true.

They went to bed, both on edge. Harry lay awake. He could smell the sweet smoky aroma of split maple burning in the stove, the same aura that had nurtured winter discussions in the farmhouse on the Granton Road. He was tired of arguing with God, he didn't want to fight anymore.

Tess shook his arm. He woke with a start.

"Be quiet," she whispered. "There's someone coming."

They could hear the rumble and crunch of winter tires rolling over tracks in the frozen snow, getting closer, then fading in ominous silence.

"Harry, they're here," she said, peering through a gap in the blue gingham curtains. "They're just sitting there. Ah, they're having a smoke. Two of them. Don't they know smoking is deadly? Get dressed. I'm betting they're waiting for killer reinforcements. If there's a gun battle, we'll lose. We need to get out of here while we can."

She moved about in the dark with quiet assurance, getting their gear ready and helping Harry into his warmest clothes and sheepskin coat. When he reached for his winter boots, she pushed them aside and handed him an old pair of high-cut ski boots from under a bench in the kitchen area by the back door.

"Put these on, they'll fit."

Headlights flashing outside drew her back to the front window.

"Another two cars have just pulled in. They're getting out and gathering courage. My God, it's a lynch mob with guns. They're filled with holy fervour and bound for glory if they can murder us—so let's get the hell out of here."

She put on her quilted blue jacket and hoisted a heavy pack onto her back. She passed a smaller one over to Harry. Running a hand along a shelf by the door, she grabbed two pairs of ancient sunglasses and a small canvas packet that appeared to be a fishing kit, which she tucked into a side pocket of Harry's pack. She knocked a tin box to the floor, creating a muffled rattle as it spilled out its meagre contents of medicinal ointments, bandages and aspirins, which she scooped back in before pushing the box into the pocket on the other side of Harry's pack.

"You never know," she explained

They slipped out the back door into the closed-in porch. She reached among the shadows beside the stacked chords of split maple and pulled out skis and poles, handing a set to Harry and dropping the other pair on the snow outside, where she adjusted the harnesses and kicked and shuffled in place while Harry made his own secure. The shadow of the cabin loomed in a ghostly silhouette outlined by the shafts of light penetrating the bush from the headlights of the cars out front.

Tess led the way, moving into the darkness. Once they broke free of the glare from the headlights they skied hard for half an hour in the silver light of the quarter moon and stopped only when glancing behind them from a high rise of ground to see an orange glare of the burning cabin punched into the night.

"No shots. I'm guessing they think we're still in there," said Tess.

"How many Absolutists do you think there are around here?"

"Don't blame Killaloe, Harry. I imagine they've known about us for a couple of days and brought in backup from away."

There was a fine dusting of snow in the air. The green wax she had pre-applied to their skis was perfect and they had been gliding along the surface, leaving barely a trail behind them.

"Okay," she said. "We've got a good head start but when they don't find our charred remains, you can count on snowmobiles chasing in hot pursuit. I'd say they won't start until noon and by then our tracks should be snowed over. They'll have to fan out to find us."

"Have you any bloody idea where we're going?"

"Sure, follow me."

Harry tugged at her sleeve.

"Where, Tess? We're in this together."

"Sorry," she said. "I'm used to travelling on my own. See the pole star up there, the brightest star in Ursa Major, no, there, the end of the handle in the Little Dipper. The other stars wheel around but it stays constant. We're taking our course from that, but heading about twenty degrees to the west."

"Why?"

"Because that's where we want to go."

She pushed off and started down a long gradual incline, coasting until they reached a frozen lake where they seemed unaccountably vulnerable and traversed as quickly as possible. When they got to the far side, she waited for Harry to catch up, then offered a terse explanation.

"Dead reckoning, Harry. Point to point in the same direction. Connecting the dots."

She moved on before he had time to query further where they were going.

The air became exceedingly cold and dark before turning pale as the sun forced its way into view above the eastern horizon. The meagre rays of grey and yellow burnished their cheeks with a shallow warmth and they stopped on a rise of land and drank from the bottle she had packed. He was surprised to taste cognac. She caught his expression and offered, "It's to stop the water from freezing. And because it tastes good. Here, take these." She handed him one of the pairs of sunglasses. "Let's move."

She pressed on. Harry followed. They skied another nine hours, pausing a few times for water with dense clumps of sourdough bread she had made, and handfuls of raisins, until they came over a ridge and descended into a canyon where she selected a site to set up camp.

"Be careful," she said when they stepped off their skis. "You can see by the glare on the surface of the snow where it's crusty enough to hold your weight. Step to the side and you'll be in up to your chin. And there you'll stay. I'm too tired to dig you out."

He was relieved by her admission of exhaustion. His legs quivered as he tentatively took a few steps. *The wet noodle effect,* Karen used to call it. He steadied himself on his poles, trying to locate his feet. Earlier in the day his toes had been viciously painful but now it felt like he was manoeuvring on formless stumps. Disorientation from frostbite was aggravated by the bleariness of his vision when he looked down. His eyes were snow-burnt and wind-seared despite the sunglasses.

Excruciating pain coursed through his entire body as blood flowed back into his toes while he helped scoop out a shallow depression in the snow for the tent. His left foot was the worst, where he had lost flesh down to the first joint on several toes in a previous encounter with extreme cold. (Hanging from his twenty-third story balcony overlooking Toronto Harbour, he remembered vividly.) He limped and kept moving. Tess kept moving. Not frantically, but with focussed determination. She knew exactly what she was doing and Harry accepted that their survival depended on her keen set of mind and awesome skills.

She withdrew a small North Face tent from her voluminous pack, along with a modest kitchen kit consisting of a pot, a single-element naphtha stove, two cups, two plates, and two spoons. After pitching their tent in the depression, they pushed snow up against the lower walls and started a small fire in front of it with dried cedar twigs over a mound of birchbark. After the fire flared into life they added a few broken branches of dead pine. The smoke surrounded them in the still air and they breathed in the blue-grey fumes for the illusion of warmth while they toasted their hands against the flames. Then Tess opened a small plastic-lined canvas bag of savoury oats she had prepared at the cabin and using the naphtha stove she heated water for the oats, turmeric, chipotle, and sun-dried tomatoes, and they ate well. She rinsed the pot with granular snow and put it back on the flickering blue flame with more snow to melt for tea. Together they heaped snow higher against the tent to the point where the walls began to sag inwards, then she lifted her pack inside and clambered after it, calling for Harry to hand her a cup of tea before zipping the door.

Harry lingered over his own cup of hot black tea by the fire. His sweat-drenched clothes steamed as he tried vainly to dry them without scorching himself or turning to flame.

"Come in here, Harry. Wipe off your snow on the way."

He dampened the fire and crawled in, leaving his boots in the confined vestibule. There was one sleeping bag. She was in it. She sat up, reached over, and propped a flashlight in the corner against her bunched up blue coat. She helped him remove his left sock, which was encrusted with dead skin and dried blood. While she worked antibiotic ointment into the mutilated flesh on his toes, Harry leaned away and stifled a scream that would have shattered the night had he let it emerge. He leaned forward. She was naked, totally unabashed in the frozen air and piercing illumination. Her breasts, through his pain, moved like snub-nosed somnolent creatures of unbearable beauty.

"There you go," she said at last, spreading her blue coat over top of the sleeping bag and slipping back down into the warmth, shuddering violently, then lying sensuously inert. "There's only one bag so climb in, it's the only way to keep warm. Naked, Harry, completely. Skin to skin, flesh to flesh, survival strategy."

She shivered again as she held the bag open for him after he had spread his damp clothes out on the tent floor, and he slithered down beside her with clumsy modesty.

"No moving," she admonished. "We've got to stay on top of the sleeping mat. The cold comes from the bottom up. Stay still, if we sweat we'll freeze to death."

They were nose to nose. He had been too self-conscious to slide past with his bottom in her face. He could feel her toes against his shins, their thighs flexed, pressing tightly, and as they adjusted for comfort his erection bent awkwardly between them. Her breasts burned into his chest. Their hearts pumped against each other. She tucked her head down on his shoulder. He pushed her hair away from his mouth and nose but inhaled its smoky aroma and felt it wisping across his eyes, catching in his eyebrows and lashes. His toes throbbed gently; the pain was largely subsumed by restrained passion.

"Where are we?" he whispered.

"We're alive. We're in the Baron River Canyon."

"I hope you're right."

Does it make any difference, Harry?

"Trust me," said Tess.

Thinking about the correlation between hope and trust, he drifted into a deep sleep and was aroused, literally, when she slithered up the length of his body and emerged from their sleeping bag, quickly dressed, and exited the tent. A short time later, he could smell woodsmoke and soon joined her for bread, jam, and coffee.

They huddled close to the fire, trying to turn their sweat-frozen clothes to a clammy pliable warmth, then striking camp and setting out before the sun had broken free of the trees on the southern bank of the canyon.

When they paused for a break after three hours of skiing, Tess cautioned Harry to stay quiet. She listened, turning her head this way and that, tilting, adjusting, until she could pinpoint the direction of a distant snowmobile.

"They're after us, Harry."

"It could be anyone out for a spin or a trek."

She pointed behind them.

"Not coming from there. They've got a real woodsman, he's following the shadows we've left in our wake. Our tracks are obscured but there are broken twigs, bent grass stalks, anomalies in the surface of the snow."

"How many?"

"Two, the tracker, he's local, and one more."

"How long?"

"Twenty minutes, let's move."

"We're not going to outrun them."

"To the trees, there, where the rocks converge."

They stopped when they got part way through a narrow passage of rocks, flanked by a few cedars. She swung her pack around onto the snow and retrieved the fishing gear from the pocket in Harry's pack, then motioned him to ski straight head. She removed from the fishing packet a coil of 80-pound test copper trolling wire wrapped around a shank of wood. Fifty feet on, Harry stopped on a rise in the land. He held his head high and listened. The snowmobiles were getting perilously close. He watched as Tess methodically removed her mitts, took off her skis, and walked gingerly over the hard snow, careful not to break through the surface, and tied an end of the copper wire around a cedar at breast height. She maneuvered across the narrow gully and attached the other end of the copper wire at the same height to another cedar, drawing the wire taunt.

The snowmobiles were in sight across the small open plain where the land slanted gently towards them.

Harry's heart pounded as he watched her tuck the fishing packet back into her jacket, adjust her pack, put her skis back on, and pull her mitts over numbed fingers.

She looked around at the snowmobiles. They were close enough Harry could make out the sky reflected on their helmet visors. She skied towards him, passed him, and motioned for him to follow. By her pace she made it clear it was only to simulate panicked flight.

Harry heard the roar and surge of engines shatter the wilderness as the snowmobiles entered the narrowed gorge. The air shook, then suddenly the whirring scream of an engine without traction pierced the air, and was immediately swallowed in a thunderous crash.

Harry and Tess stopped. They looked back. One machine had slammed into the rocks. The driver lay sprawled on the snow, blood shooting from his neck. His disembodied head, still inside his helmet, lay quivering at the base of a cedar. The other machine had crashed into the first. The driver staggered to his feet, stunned, bleeding.

Tess pushed away from Harry and reversed her direction and glided down the incline to within an arm's length of the man still standing. She removed her skis and stepped past him on the hard snow. He seemed confused and ignored her. She retrieved her copper wire, then picked up the severed head inside the helmet and dropped it on the smouldering machinery before she approached the survivor from behind and led him close to the wreckage where she kicked his knees out from under him and as he collapsed she pushed him forward with enough force the leaking gasoline from the machines spilled, ignited, flared, and while she walked away exploded into a fiery mass.

She didn't look back as she moved up beside Harry.

"He would have called for help," she said.

They skied on for another five hours and came to a lane that had drifted over and followed it for awhile to a clearing beside a large open lake. Off to the side there was an awkward pile of snow. Tess removed her skis and walked over to it, then backed away as if she had discovered something unpleasant and pointed to the other side of the clearing.

"Let's set up over there for the night," she said.

He hadn't spoken since the episode in the gully. She seemed to have moved on. He wondered if she felt anything at all. In a way, it didn't matter. She had saved their lives. He wanted her to be bothered by the decapitation of one religious zealot, the immolation of another, yet he didn't want her to suffer remorse. He didn't want her to suffer.

"Looks good," he said.

They ate savoury porridge in the dark, cooked over the naphtha burner. Tess was afraid an open fire might attract attention. They were on an unplowed laneway but within snowmobile reach of several communities. Harry was so exhausted, he trusted her judgement and didn't pay much attention. After they drank the last of their tea, she tried to dress his wounded toes but the antibacterial ointment had run out and the best she could do was re-bandage them and let him precede her into the sleeping bag so that she did all the wriggling and squirming. He fell asleep easily despite the pain, which had become a more generalized throbbing ache along his entire left leg.

When daylight brightened the inside of the tent, Harry stirred into consciousness. Tess had got up for a pee sometime in the night, he'd fallen back into a deep and exhausted sleep. He didn't notice she hadn't returned. After he dressed in his stiff and clammy clothes he went outside and saw that her skis and poles were missing. It was a dull day and the air was filled with fine misty snow. He judged it would be safe to start a small fire while he tried to assimilate his aching muscles and joints into the semblance of a functioning human being. He lit the naphtha stove and cooked up the last of their savoury oatmeal, of which he ate half, saving the rest for Tess, or for later if she didn't return.

He kicked a severed stump free and rolled it close to the fire, then he removed his left ski boot and sock and immersed his foot in the cedar smoke, roasting his toes as close to the flames as he could.

He thought about Karen but she seemed very distant. He thought about Tess. He still didn't know why, of all her names, that was his preference. Where he was sitting he could gaze out over the lake but the air was filled with infinite shades of white, some moving gently and some eerily still. He couldn't make out a horizon.

He reused the tea bag from dinner and sipped the insipid hot liquid slowly to make it last. He looked around over one shoulder and surveyed the mound Tess had seemed interested in. A few chunks of snow had slipped away, revealing patches of a blue tarpaulin. Looking back out into the imponderable whiteness he lost himself in aimless rumination.

After a while his thoughts coalesced into horror as he realized for the first time in days that the lives of twelve thousand people hung in the balance. What balance? He and Tess were fleeing for their lives. But if they appeared, if she appeared, the suicide scheme would collapse. So where in hell had she gone?

He'd decided to wait until midday and if she didn't reappear he would backtrack along the snowed-in lane. Sooner or later, the lane would become a ploughed road, the road a highway, and along the highway he would find people.

And if he did, they might kill him.

If he didn't, then he would die of exposure.

When the day seemed its brightest although there was no sun in the sky, his watch insisted it was noon. He put on his matted sock and his seared ski boot, throttled the fire down to smouldering embers, and walked over to the shoreline. There were faint tracks from her skis. He looked out into the dazzling whiteness. With an absolute absence of details, there was no horizon. He turned and looked back at their campsite.

An orange sign, near what under the snow and ice would be the takeout point for canoeists, read: "Long Pine Lake: Camping by Permit Only." Of course, *Long Pine Lake*. Where else would she take him? This was the place where he and Karen and the kids had scheduled a shuttle car to pick them up after their trip. This is where the tangled remnants of Matt and Lucy's bodies, recovered from the Devil's Cauldron, had been transferred from rescue boats to vehicles to carry them to the morgue at the Petawawa military base. This is where Harry refused to leave in an ambulance until he was given a sedative and told that Karen's body might never be recovered, that it was pulverized by the force of the falls or had washed downriver and was irretrievably lodged under the vast floating marsh on the far side of the lake.

Harry walked slowly up to the fire and stirred the coals. He crumpled a wad of birchbark and gathered sticks broken from dead trees and built up the flames, then sat as close as he could endure the heat and smoke and he waited.

He waited.

When night fell, he climbed into the sleeping bag naked and in the morning he dressed again in his still damp clothes and rekindled the fire and sat in the smoke, which was the warmest place and squinted and stared out into the white abyss and waited.

At midday, a colourless speck appeared in the whiteness and defined the horizon and slowly the speck became a black dot and then lightened to blue as it grew with no perceptible motion and moved down from the horizon and enlarged until it took on the form of a human on skis, faltering occasionally until she was close and he could be sure it was her.

"I thought you had gone," he called out, his voice cracking.

"You're still here." Was that a question, a statement of fact, or an explanation?

"Yeah, I am," he said.

He rose awkwardly to his feet, hobbled close to her, and kneeling he undid the ski bindings, which resisted because they were frozen almost solid, indicating she had skied mostly on the level, probably along the lake surface, and very slowly, because she had travelled a long distance, not flexing her feet. He helped her over to share his log by the fire.

"I brought some tea and popcorn and a first-aid kit," she said. "It's all in my pocket."

"Popcorn?"

"Frozen."

"Welcome back," he said.

18 THE TRADING POST

IN THE MORNING THEY MADE LOVE. WITH THE SLEEPING BAG unzipped and open to the cold, wrapped in a splendid miasma of sweat and exhaustion, they made passionate unrestrained love. Afterwards, they whispered endearments so intimate no one else could have imagined their meaning, and cradled in each other's arms until the intense warmth between them in contrast to the frigid air bathing their exposed surfaces forced them to rise and break camp.

When they were packed up and ready to leave, Tess walked over to the mound of snow and reaching down she grasped an edge of blue tarpaulin and tugged. It resisted, then slid away under the weight of its covering, revealing a rusted-out four-wheel drive Subaru with inflated winter tires. Obviously in running condition.

"So, here we are, Harry."

"You knew about this."

"I thought we might need it."

"That's why we came here?"

"One of the reasons." She dug into her jacket pocket and pulled out a worn shot-silk bandana in a brown paisley pattern. She shook it free of creases and handed it to Harry. "I thought you might want this."

It was Karen's.

His first impulse was to recoil but he reached out and took it.

"Where?" he said.

"There's a small cabin off the lake to the north. I saw it last week so I went back."

"But the last time you didn't go in."

"No, I knew we'd be here again."

"For the car?"

"Yes, and while you were asleep I revisited the place. It's much farther than I remembered. The door wasn't locked. Nobody locks doors in case travellers need to get in. There was virtually nothing, except popcorn and tea. I don't know what I expected but when I was leaving I found the scarf on a peg by the door. I thought it might belong to you. It does, doesn't it?"

"It was my wife's."

"The cabin belongs to a local recluse, he must have found it in the river."

"A recluse?"

"He works for the trading post outside the park boundary during the winters. That's where I bought my gear and the car. During the rest of the year from early spring to late fall he lives in the cabin. I semi-met him. We didn't talk but I saw him through a shed door repairing canoes. He knew I was looking at him and kept his back to me as much as he could."

"So what did you think you'd find at his cabin?"

"I was looking for your wife, Harry. For evidence to prove she is dead. The scarf was the only thing."

Harry was dumbfounded. Why would she do that? To set him free. But why?

He tucked Karen's bandana in his jacket pocket and cleared snow from around the wheels of the car before loading their gear in the back.

She drove.

The car plunged against the snow and pushed forward, bucked and skidded and spun, inching its way along the lane until at last they broke through a high embankment of ploughed frozen slush onto an open road, where she turned east.

After a while, she raised a question about the place furthest from his mind at the moment. "You once asked me why Bora Bora? So now I want to know: for you, why Bora Bora? It's one of the most famous destinations in the world and one of the most romantic. But it's also one of the most remote and probably among the most expensive."

Harry gazed out the window, watching the drifted snow and mounded screeds of ploughed ice along the side of the road. "We got there by accident," he said. "A combination of serendipity and desperation."

"Your life is defined by accidents." She blanched, which suggested she had not meant to be cruel but Harry was deluged by the sudden image of water as it pulverized rocks and bones and the blood-red Kevlar canoe. Then, in an instant, the chaos subsided and the muffled roar of tires over patches of snow filled him with recollections of a tropical freighter working its way among the islands of French Polynesia—he and Karen had travelled steerage on what amounted to a belated honeymoon, sleeping on deck, sharing their space between lifeboats and hatchways and plastic-wrapped bags with Polynesian families heading home from Tahiti, sitting up on hard wooden benches in the tiny cafeteria and being driven into the open by the penetrating odours of boiling cooking oil, watching a curious rat by starlight on deck as it watched them watching him, dropping in on the soaring twin islands of Huahine Nui and Huahine Iti, and vanilla-scented Tahaa, and at last disembarking on fabled Ra'iatea for a few days, sleeping in an open bandshell the first morning until a small restaurant opened across the park. After *café au lait* with *croissant aux noisettes* and succulent sliced *pamplemousse* picked locally, they were led up a hidden stairs into a charmingly eccentric hotel. Later, they toured ancient sites of celebration and devotion.

"Sounds very romantic," Tess said when he paused, caught up in his memories. They were so vivid, he had not been aware he was talking.

"We went down to the wharf the last morning on Ra'iatea," he continued. "An hour before departure. And we watched our freighter disappearing over the horizon. The Captain had apparently decided to leave early."

"On island time, as they say."

"We were marooned. I was frantic, Karen was ecstatic. Our compromise was to go out for a big breakfast at the waterfront café. A waitress told us she had family connections on Bora Bora. We protested that we weren't interested in a *Vanity Fair* destination and couldn't afford it, anyway. Turns out her cousin could get us into Chez NoNo. We didn't have a choice since Bora Bora was the only way for us to get back to Papeete—we were due to fly out at the end of the week. So we spent a few idyllic days in paradise and fell in love all over again."

"With the island? With each other?"

"Both." He paused to savour the memories. "We returned once. It was good, but revisiting an old haunt isn't the same as discovering a new one."

"And then you went back on your own last summer."

"And then I went back."

"Whatever you were looking for wasn't there."

"No, it wasn't."

"And it never will be, Harry."

"I know that. Why are we having this conversation?"

"Because in my own way I'm in love with you, Harry."

After half an hour they pulled into an ESSO station and both went in where the proprietors served them hot coffees and toasted cinnamon-raisin bagels.

This was the trading post where Tess had bought the old Subaru, the same outfitter that had ferried their Volvo wagon to the takeout on his final canoe trip with his family. It was under new management, a middle-aged couple, but still called 'Virgil's Outfitting Emporium.' Virgil had retired to a nursing home in Renfrew and died.

Curiously, when they asked about local news, no mention was made of the dead snowmobilers or the fire down near Killaloe. The woman chattered amiably, mostly about the weather. Her husband didn't smile or say very much. Neither showed any curiosity about their dirty and dishevelled appearance and unusual arrival from the direction of the Park. There wasn't much activity in there at this time of year and no through traffic at all. A few snowmobilers, a few old timers, but no trappers or hunters, not legally—it was a provincial preserve.

"You want to wash up?" the woman observed, nodding in the direction of the washroom.

They took turns in the single washroom, bathing in the sink and changing to rustic tourist garb that was on sale in the store.

When Harry emerged in his new get-up. Tess was on the store computer.

"Do they have satellite?" he asked.

"We've got everything here," said the woman.

"Just checking road conditions," said Tess. "Apart from the scruffy beard, you look great."

Harry glanced at the proprietor, whose face was garnished with a week's growth of untrimmed beard like his own. On the other man, it looked inevitable.

"You want to get that foot looked after," said the woman. She hadn't noticed Harry's limp until after he cleaned up.

"I will, thanks."

As they were climbing into the car, Harry asked Tess about the hired man. He wanted to speak to him about the bandana, he wanted to connect.

"Over there." She pointed to a low wooden shed beside some rickety canoe racks set back from the store.

Harry got out of the car and walked over to the shed and looked in. The lights were on but no one was around. He called through to the living quarters but no one came out. He went back into the store.

"Old George, he comes and he goes," the proprietor said. "If he's not there, I suspect he and his missus slipped out for a walk in the woods."

"A walk?"

"On snowshoes. You wouldn't find them on skis. They're not the sort."

I wonder what sort that is, Harry wondered. "He's married, is he?"

"Like as not he isn't, but that don't mean they're not as thick as two thieves in a woodpile, though God knows they never speak to each other and sure not a word to the two of us," he said. "Come spring break-up and they'll be gone, but they're hard workers when they're here and that is a fact."

"Thanks," said Harry and made for the door.

"I only been here three years, retired from the town." Harry wondered which local community qualified as *the town*. "George's been around from day one. He was born in that cabin the far side of Long Pine Lake. Quite a character, he and his missus, two peas in a pod."

Harry opened the door.

"He's a river man, he pulled more bodies outta the water than you could shake a stick at."

Harry closed the door behind him.

Tess waited patiently behind the wheel. Harry clambered into the passenger seat.

"What was that all about?" she asked.

"Don't know. His wife was out back so he figured he could squeeze out his daily quota of words in one burst. He verged on loquacity."

"That's a new one," she said. "Quite magniloquent."

Tess pulled the Subaru up the slight incline to the highway. Off to the right two figures appeared like wraiths at the edge of the woods opening onto the Trading Post compound. Both were bundled in warm parkas. They were on snowshoes and stepped lightly, side by side, over the packed snow into the clearing. Harry waved. The man waved. The woman dipped her shoulder in salutation but her sleeve was tucked into her pocket. Her face was in shadow behind a halo of wolf fur trim on her parka hood. He couldn't see the man's face at all.

He warmed at the sight. They were obviously engaged with each other, yet the way they moved they took in the world around them with the casual proprietary air of born woodsmen. A blur of envy passed through Harry and he looked away, almost as if his emotions were an invasion of privacy. When he looked back, as Tess pulled onto the highway, the couple had disappeared into the shadows.

They drove south, for the first hour in silence, then both started to talk at once. They agreed that on the whole, they'd had an adventure. Winter camping, with a warm dry change of clothing, was something to look forward to, provided they survived the Rapture. Tess suggested they should try canoeing but Harry didn't respond. Tess changed the subject. "The end of the world's looming up and it's not going to be pretty," she said.

There were a thousand religious fanatics ready to exterminate them. There were twelve thousand zealots madly raising money to buy their way out of the mortal condition into which they were born. There was a church hierarchy poised to collect their fare and bank it offshore before basking in the glow of illimitable wealth. There were the crimes Tess had committed and the consequences that might catch up with her or drag her down.

Down into what? Despair? It didn't seem likely. Everything she had done that Harry knew about or imagined, from decapitation of a backwoods assassin to the extermination of a drug lord and his odious wife, to the slow drowning of her malevolent husband, and possibly the cold blooded murder of an unrepentant sexual predator, everything could be justified in moral equations that pitted righteousness against evil. He feared and admired her for what he saw of his own inner desires made manifest. If life was precious, then it should be fiercely relentlessly mercilessly remorselessly defended. She did what he only dreamed should be done.

"We do have a problem," he agreed. "How does it work?"

"How does what work?"

"Armageddon. The Apocalypse."

"The Apocalypse. There's no Armageddon. The battle of good and evil is over. Evil prevailed. There's only the final barrier; that's all that's left."

"The final barrier. Death."

"Which one may transcend—there is a website explaining it all."

"Accessible, I imagine, only by the Chosen who have paid a hefty access fee."

"A minimum of one hundred thousand per person."

"My God, Tess. That's unrealistic. How many people have that kind of money?"

"Two hundred thousand for a couple. Think about it, Harry. They sell their house, or borrow against it, confident they'll never have to repay. Many have enthusiastically donated a lot more. They won't need property or investments on the celestial plane."

"Or when they're stone cold dead."

"Where they won't complain if it turns out they're wrong."

"And the money all goes to Tom Severence."

"Well over a billion. Including donations, more like a billion and a half. Mostly in the Cayman Islands. Have you ever been there. The diving is fantastic."

He ignored the invitation to stray into a more congenial area of conversation.

"On February 6th," he noted. "My birthday. The Chosen will gather around their computers and die."

"At midnight, when the day opens."

"It's always confusing, isn't it, which day midnight belongs to, the one just ended or the one coming up. What about friends and relatives?"

"The Church has decreed that only those who have paid can experience the Rapture. Others will die off over time until no one is left and they will be physically resurrected on the celestial plane, but the Rapture itself is reserved for the chosen who will become self-knowing aspects of the cosmic mind, the essence itself. They will become God."

"It's all quite tricky though not as extreme as the Jehovah's Witnesses or the Mormons, perhaps."

"Or Scientology," she said. "They're equally manufactured constructs of minds benumbed or inspired by the fear of mortality. So was Christianity, so was Islam."

"My wife used to write about religion restraining mob violence through dogma and doctrine. A cynic might argue the more radical versions of religion in fact do the reverse. They channel violence by suppressing restraints. I mean how else do you account for Taliban executions of teenage feminists, rape victims, and blasphemers?"

"Welcome to the world of The Church Absolute."

"Okay, here's what I don't get. If they consider themselves trapped in the time continuum, aren't they on some level immortal already?"

"Don't confuse Pietro's beings from the planet Philon with their hosts on Earth. We're talking about humans born into this world who are inhabited by spiritual visitors. At the Rapture, host and residing spirit merge. The Philonian resumes immortality, the human attains it. I mean, where do souls come from in conventional Christianity, Harry? They have a beginning but no end—a logical impossibility for which Pietro tried to account."

"A little awkwardly, perhaps."

"Since only twelve thousand qualify, yes. When he was still William Alexander Saintsbury he conflated the Book of Revelation with his own fanciful sense of a significant nonsensical number. Tom Severence introduced the venal twist. With The Founder ascended, The Church could now determine who was a host on track for immortality and who wasn't."

"As selected by the believer's ability to pay. And the rest, what happens to them?"

"If they're sufficiently devout, they make it as far as the celestial plane."

"And that's it?"

"Isn't that enough? They are physically resurrected and outside the boundaries of time. They get to be their best selves forever."

"And the chosen become God."

"If they ascend during the Rapture."

"Die?"

"Die."

"How?"

"They won't if we can stop them."

"But if they do, how will they do it?"

"A potion of sedatives and poison. It should be painless. Packets have been mailed out already, with some still to go for the last minute converts. I doubt Severence would leave anyone out, even if he secretly breaks past the holy limit of twelve thousand. A buck is a buck."

"And why does God and the universal Essence of Everything need money?"

"Why do Popes need golden vestments and mitres embroidered with pearls? Why do evangelicals need new-age cathedrals, why do mullah's own oil wells and rabbis drive cars?"

"Seriously, don't some people on the verge of self-annihilation question the entry fee to cosmic ascension, especially when the leader chooses to stay behind?"

"Severence has declared the millions who remain will be cared for. To oversee all this, the Leader has volunteered to martyr himself by missing the Rapture this time around. He will stay to clean up the worldly affairs of The Church Absolute, after which he will ascend in his own good time, body and all."

"But arrive at the same moment!"

"Because time doesn't exist on the celestial plane. That was William's brilliant contrivance to account for the unaccountable."

"So the Rapture will be on hold until Severence gets there but nobody will notice. And then he becomes just like you."

"Like Sister Mary Celestial, yes. Like me, he will achieve physical immortality but also as an immortal body he will partake in the absolute essence of God. The best of all possible worlds shall be his."

"Does he believe that?"

"It's hard to say. William pretty much convinced himself. I'm not sure Severence is so gullible. Like the leaders of most religions, he is a practical man."

"One who believes in neither retribution nor redemption," said Harry.

"How do you figure?"

"If he did, he'd be terrified of whatever comes next."

"I'm sure it's enough for now that he's already half way to heaven. He's moved to an impregnable estate in England. The new headquarters for The Church Absolute is in the Cotswold Hills."

Harry knew the Cotswolds west of Oxford as a warren of impossibly quaint villages with compound names: Stow-on-the-Wold, Wakefield-super-Vale, Moreton-in-Marsh, Bourton-on-the-Water, Upper and Lower Slaughter.

"Why there?"

"Why not? England is a country where intolerance is considered quite gauche. It's a pleasant place to be and he's a new-age computer guy, he can be anywhere. Why not the heart of Anglo-Saxon neo-Christendom?"

"I would have thought Los Angeles was safe."

"England is safer. Gloucestershire is safer yet. The Cotswolds are infectiously beautiful. Wakefield Hall is safest of all."

They drove down from Smith's Falls to Kingston in silence. They had been through enough they were comfortable together without words. When she pulled into a parking space at Tim Hortons near the Wolfe Island ferry terminal, she leaned forward in her seat and turned to face him. "I've been thinking, with me out of the way there's no need for you to be murdered. Don't take offence but your death might be incidental to the whole scheme of things in an Absolute universe. If I'm gone they'll probably ignore you."

"*Probably* is not reassuring."

"You need to lie low. I need to die all over again. I mean, any god worth his wings could reappear on the road to Jerusalem, but who would die a second death I wonder, except, perhaps, me."

"Tess, let's not forget, you're not really a god."

"That's a relief," she said and got out of the car.

Inside Tim Hortons they both headed straight for the washrooms.

"Shall I order you a coffee?" he asked.

"No, I'm okay," she said, before both of them slipped behind closed doors.

When Harry came out, he stood in line. When she didn't join him, he ordered a coffee and a toasted cinnamon-raisin bagel for himself and took a seat by the window where he could look out at the evening and see the ferry approaching through the channel in the ice, and beyond, the lights of Wolfe Island village. He had only been over there once, a long time ago.

Anxiety mounted as time passed and Tess didn't emerge from the washroom. He finished his coffee and walked over to the glass door at the front. He scanned the line of cars, looking for the Subaru. It wasn't there. Perhaps she had gone for gas. He stepped out into the bitter cold. He could see the gas pumps at the nearby service station. No Subaru.

He knew she was gone. This time for good.

Bewildered by what he should do next, perplexed by why she would leave, he felt strangely like crying.

Tough guys don't cry, Slate. Catch a train or a bus.

Karen!

Who else? It's time to go home.

19 **OLD MONTREAL**

DURING THE NEXT TWO WEEKS, HARRY MOSTLY STAYED home. He only went out to shop for food and proceeded warily, assuming an assassin lurked down every aisle in the Saint Lawrence Market, behind every shadow of each passing streetcar or truck. He stayed out of the subway and walked among crowds. It eventually occurred to him the Absolutists might not be so considerate with Tess as he assumed they would be with him. They would attack her no matter how many innocent people stood between them. It wouldn't matter who died if she could be eliminated as the only impediment to the Celestial hereafter. If she were alive, she was the Devil Incarnate. Dead, she was the gateway to heaven.

He read the papers assiduously, surfed Google and Yahoo looking for references to Tess, or anything anomalous in connection with The Church Absolute and its leader, Tom Severence, who with condescending forbearance had allowed the name of Pietro di Cosmos II to be conferred upon him by the Holy Gathering of his peers.

Harry placed Karen's folded paisley bandana, along with her dented silver wedding band, in the fine piece of antique Japanese lacquer-ware they had picked up in a flea market in England. He thought of her quite often but she seldom spoke to him anymore. Words were displaced by images of their lives together. Occasionally, glimpses of Matt and Lucy slipped in but nostalgia was displacing sorrow.

He called the car rental company and explained he had had a skiing accident and that their car was parked near a burnt out cabin outside the town of Killaloe. No problem. They would pick it up, cover most of the expenses with insurance, and inform him if there were additional costs.

He changed the dressing on his frost-bitten toes every day, paring away the chunks of dead flesh and keeping the wounds clean. Even after they healed enough that he could walk without pain, he had a slight limp. He retrieved a beechwood cane from his locker in the basement and polished it with tung oil to bring out the fine ancient grain. He polished the metal band separating the wood from the tightly curved handle made from the horn of a water buffalo and added a rubber tip over the brass capsule on the bottom, which he had a shoemaker replace to extend the length. The cane was still a little short for proper use but when his Aunt Beth had used it, it was a little long. After a few days practice, he found that by leaning slightly away from his injured foot he could move quite comfortably.

And with such jaunty élan. From Bogart to Astaire with a wave of your wand.

Karen!

But that was all she said.

He missed their conversations. He grieved for the fading memories, rather than the lost times themselves, which seemed increasingly unreal.

On the day after January gave up the ghost and February arrived on little cat feet, as someone once said, Harry picked up an oblique reference to Tess in an offbeat story about murder in Old Montreal. Police were mystified, the press was intrigued: a man's body had been just been discovered, garrotted, in a stone building in an upstairs room locked from the inside with bars on the windows and no instrument or weapon was found at the scene.

No mention was made of a suspect or motive. The address, while given as near the corners of Poiccart and Morel, was not precise, and yet the location was identified as the proprietor's office above a specialty bookstore. The victim's name was Georges Manfred. The police inspector in charge was Leon Gonsalez.

Near the conclusion of the story, it was noted that Monsieur Manfred had recently disposed of his entire estate and was living in the walk-up office. The correspondent did not say who alerted the police but implied that the death had been recent as no one had complained of odours, nor had there been complaints recorded in previous days of violent disturbances that might have presaged or accompanied an unseemly death.

Given the flawless nature of the crime, the lack of public grief for the victim, and the fact of his having recently cashed in his fortune, such as it was, Harry felt certain the bookstore had been a front for the dissemination of tracts for The Church Absolute. He felt equally certain that Tess had killed the proprietor in her quest to expose the evils of the Rapture. He had no doubt the murder was righteous, but there was pathos in his reading of the crime. What had Tess achieved with the death of one man?

Driving sleet stung his eyes as he progressed along a deserted Yonge Street but Harry preferred to walk outside rather than in the shelter of the Eaton Centre, named for a store that no longer existed. He picked up two soy lattes from Starbucks, one for Miranda and one for himself, walked them down College with his cane draped over his arm and waited in the elevator at Police Headquarters until someone came in and pressed the button to the appropriate floor. She saw him coming, awkwardly grasping the coffees with hands swathed in layers of leather and wool. She smiled.

"So how was the skiing?" she asked, taking her coffee and gesturing for him to sit. "Accident or affectation?" she asked, noting the cane.

"A little of both," he said, offering no further explanation as he sprawled, exhausted, on her leather sofa. It took a moment before he remembered he had led her to believe he had been skiing in the Gatineau hills.

He didn't know how much to tell her. She was a little bit older, a whole lot more sophisticated in police procedures, and had pretty much assimilated his tales of Bora Bora as the exercise of an active imagination. As for his suspicions about Jennifer Izett's involvement in the deaths of Silvio and Gina Pomposello, they had fizzled and faded. The Pomposellos were upstanding citizens and insidiously corrupt. They had officially died by misadventure.

He proceeded cautiously, simply suggesting he was interested in a killing in Montreal and needed her help.

He told her about the locked-room murder. She phoned Inspector Leon Gonsalez who explained that frankly they were baffled. She asked if he'd mind if her independent associate were to look into things in relation to a case he was working on. No problem, Gonsalez said, and so it went. Harry was on the train to Montreal by mid-afternoon.

After a restless night at *Le Reine Élizabeth*, paradoxically located on the boulevard named after the separatist, Rene Levesque, and after breakfast in *La Ville Souterraine,* the underground city, Harry walked over to the police station on Rue Sainte Elisabeth and connected with Inspector Gonsalez who briefed him on the way to the murder scene. The police were baffled and the press knew they were baffled, which made a good story. It also made it hard to conceal the presence of a private investigator from Toronto. When they arrived at the bookstore a very chilled crowd of reporters, photographers, cameramen, TV correspondents, and freelance bloggers were waiting, some of them outraged at the *foreign* incursion, others thrilled by the apparent humiliation of Inspector Gonsalez.

"I thought you might want to look around down here, first," said the policeman, who seemed resigned to the fuss outside. "It's hardly twenty-four hours since the body was discovered. I'm not sure how they knew you'd be coming."

"I didn't tell them," said Harry.

He found Gonsalez to be an affable sort, with hair cropped so short his head might have been shaved, a thick walrus moustache, and eyes droopy and moist like an aging bloodhound.

"You know about this Church Absolute, Harry?"

"A little."

"Your colleague, Superintendent Quin, she says you know a lot."

Harry thought he could detect a hint of Spanish beneath the precise English, spoken by a man who lived and worked in French. Harry was essentially unilingual. He was not musical and had no facility with languages. He envied those who did. He could read French and a little German, and loved the sonorous evasive sounds of Chinese. And sometimes he imagined he spoke Spanish and Italian but didn't.

Harry leaned on his cane and looked around the shop. There had been a lot of water damage and many of the books were lying about in frozen clumps. The pipes upstairs had burst and flooded the building, allowing water to seep out under both doors before it froze in waves like hardened lava. While most of the books, as far as Harry could make out from their soiled covers, were tracts and pamphlets relating to The Church Absolute, there were also alcoves jammed with science fiction and fantasy and a surprising number of mysteries and other esoterica that might equally corrupt the minds of impressionable readers.

Sardonic humour, Harry? Or are you beginning to doubt your chosen field?

Only doubting those who write about murder or read about it for pleasure.

Come on, Harry, how did she do it?

"Nothing here, no clues," he said, speaking simultaneously to himself, to Karen, and to Inspector Gonsalez. "There's only one entrance to the second floor, is there?"

"To the *first* floor, yes. We must go outside," the policeman responded, compounding the cultural divergence that unifies Canada.

On the landing, Harry noticed an emergency exit leading out to the back.

"It goes nowhere," said Gonsalez. "This door, the broken one, was locked from inside."

Harry glanced down to see if there would have been space below the door to slide a key through, before the police shattered the frame breaking in. He glanced at Gonsalez.

"No, Harry. The door was pulled tight from the outside and locked with iron bolts inside."

Harry slid the bolts back and forth in their tracks, surprised at how easily they moved. He checked for bits of string or thread that might have been used to slide them from outside, then realized the door would have been set too securely in the frame to permit such a manoeuvre.

Chalk marks showed where the body had been found in the centre of the room. Harry's imagination filled in the outline. He shuddered—he often found what he imagined more disturbing than the bodies themselves, no matter how badly brutalized or touchingly serene. The mind is a terrible thing.

Gonsalez observed his reaction.

"He was not a good man, Harry. Mr. Georges Manfred beat his youngest daughter so badly she is brain-damaged. We suspect he raped both his girls but he was not charged. His wife wouldn't testify, the girls were too young to speak up. He served time for abusing his wife. I don't condone murder but if someone had to die it might as well have been him."

Harry looked down at the chalk marks again. He noticed a broken elastic band on the floor amidst dustballs and unidentifiable detritus. Gonsalez explained the throat and neck had been severed to the bone. "The cut went deeply into the seventh cervical vertebra but there was no particular intention to decapitate him, I think, or he would have been headless."

Gonsalez chuckled. Harry grimaced appropriately. The two men had established a macabre rapport.

"So as the news reports said he was garrotted," Harry observed.

"It was a clean kill. The cut through the surface flesh was precise. The garrotte seems to have torn through at a rough angle but the groove in the bone is again quite precise. The killer was no doubt a sadist."

"How so?"

"To have been so precise."

"Or practical, perhaps."

"My turn, Harry. How so?"

"The wounds may have been inflicted that way through necessity."

"A curious term in a murder. *Through necessity*. Do you wish to examine the body? We can go to the morgue, if you'd like."

"No need," said Harry. "Your descriptive analysis of the wounds is enough."

"But you do not think the killer is a sadist. Garrotting is an intimate procedure, Harry. Very hands-on."

"Up close and personal," Harry admitted, covering his concession with a trite turn of phrase. "But then why not just hands, why use a weapon or instrument?"

"Lack of confidence, perhaps? Lack of strength? Some call it the Spanish death. The garrotte was used for executions in Spain until 1978. The killer was Spanish, perhaps. Possibly a ritual execution—but there are no other signs of a ceremonial rite. It was certainly not a crime of passion."

"Perhaps it was," said Harry.

Inspector Gonsalez looked at him sharply. "Are you going somewhere with that?"

"No, I'm just thinking out loud."

"In French we call that 'having a conversation.'"

"Sorry. It just seems passion doesn't have to be spontaneous or reckless or stupid. Controlled passion can be lethal." He was thinking of Tess, he was thinking of the corrupt machinations of The Church Absolute.

"Perhaps you are right, but only a sadist could show such restraint. Unless, he were a ghost. I do not know much about ghosts—but you see, Harry, we have come full circle. Our killer was pathologically precise, unearthly elusive, and exceptionally brutal. A rope might have been used to strangle the victim, but this was done with a very strong wire. When the wire sliced through the carotid arteries, they would have spurted like geysers, drenching the killer. Yet the blood spatters and smears were consistent with the presence of only one person in the room. It appears the victim was alone. There were a few gouges in his throat, as if he had vainly clutched at the wire. There was flesh under his nails, apparently his own. He appears to have tumbled forward from a kneeling position."

"Praying, perhaps."

"Do these Absolutist people believe in God, I wonder?"

"They certainly believe in death."

"What do you mean, Harry?"

But Harry wasn't inclined to explain.

"Please," said Gonsalez. "Look around. We have finished with the crime scene. You may touch anything you want. There were no fingerprints apart from the victim's. There was no evidence of a struggle. And trust me, Harry, there are no hidden passages or secret trap doors. He was alone. He seems to have simply kneeled in the middle of the room and allowed himself to be executed."

"Then he wasn't alone."

"But no one else was here. Even Houdini could not have bolted the door from the outside."

"Houdini, perhaps. He's dead; he could have slipped through the keyhole." Harry walked not to the door but to the casement windows. "These were open, were they?"

"Wide open, Harry. But test those bars. They are solid. They are much too close for even the littlest person to pass between them. Not even a child could do that. And we are on the first floor."

"Or second," said Harry. "It's a matter of perspective."

Harry touched his fingers gingerly to the bars, testing to see if they would stick to the frozen metal. They did. He pulled off a layer of skin, freeing them. He put on his leather gloves and ran his hands along the bars, tugging firmly every now and then, feeling for concealed cuts, telltale imperfections, outright fakery. The bars were solid. He checked around the casement, looking for panels that might come loose. The building was ancient and it was rundown, but structurally solid.

He checked the kitchenette, thumping the walls in the back of the cupboards. He scanned the ceiling. There were cracks in the plaster but no geometrical seams suggesting an opening. Access to the crawl space above was through a removable panel out over the landing. The wood floor was solid. There were no rugs to hide a trapdoor. The boards were of an indeterminate softwood, wide and worn so deeply the knots formed mounds on the unpolished surface. They had been washed through the generations but no one had swept or vacuumed in recent times. He pushed at a dustball, his shoe left a scuffmark in the dirt. He checked the bathroom, the walls, the floor, the ceiling. Gonsalez chewed on the lower edge of his walrus moustache and watched with amusement. He was not critical, but he was confident that the mystery of the locked room would not be resolved, at least not by a private investigator from Ontario.

Harry turned his attention back to the door. There were two large sliding bolts and they were intact. The iron fittings set into the frame to hold them had shattered the wood when the police broke in. The hinges were solid. There was no way they could have been dismantled and reassembled from outside on the landing. He checked the huge cast iron lock with its brass knob and brass slide bolt. It was a magnificent old thing and had not been tampered with. He squatted in front of it and peered through the keyhole. He blew into it, holding a tissue on the far side. A few strands of white lint floated through. He brushed his hand over the lock. It looked tarnished. He folded the tissue carefully around the bits of lint and dabbed it against the iron. It came away with flecks of dull red. Rust, probably. He folded the tissue to contain the flecks and handed it to Inspector Gonsalez.

"Might be something," he said. "She didn't leave us much to go on."

"She?"

"Just a gut feeling."

How very arch. You know it's her because you know it's her. And you're not about to tell your new best friend. There's too much at stake to blow the whistle. Right, Slate?

She wanted to create a small-scale crime that would attract big attention.

Well, she's done that!

A crime that's morally defensible.

There's no such thing, not when murder's the outcome.

"Let's get out of here," said Harry. "Can I buy you a drink?"

"Several."

They pushed through the media crowd shivering in the afternoon cold and climbed into a squad car. Harry was curiously content.

20 THE LOCKED ROOM

TESS SAINTSBURY PARKED IN A PUBLIC GARAGE IN OLD Montreal. She locked the car and made her solitary way through interlocking pools of radiance cast on the drifted snow by archaic streetlights. She hunched into her quilted blue jacket, with her gloved hands deep in her pockets, carrying a small bag on a strap over her shoulder. It was bitterly cold and she walked rapidly, arriving eventually at the locked door of a nondescript building with a sign designating it an otherwise nameless *Hôtel*. She was buzzed in.

The man behind the counter looked up and was surprised. Although her coat was shabby and she appeared tired and dishevelled, he could tell by her face and the casual elegance of her posture that she was not his usual type of guest.

They spoke in French.

"Are you alone?" he asked.

"Yes, one room for four nights, maybe five."

"Name?"

"Evelyn Wallace."

"Cash only."

She counted out two hundreds and a fifty dollar bill. He gave her the key.

"Five nights, then. Room two thirty-four, first floor, turn right."

"Is there a back door?"

"For fires only, down there."

"Good night," she said.

"Pleasant dreams, Evelyn."

He returned to his small TV and she disappeared up the stairs. It was a brief encounter. He would never see her again but it didn't matter.

For the next few days she used the fire exit at the back and ate in greasy spoons, avoiding the fashionable restaurants of Old Montreal dotted along cobblestone streets and brick-paved lanes mounded with frozen snow. She bought clothes in local thrift shops, but with her sense of style looked as if she had shopped in the trendy boutiques. Most of the time she spent in her room, armed with an iPad she had picked up in the east end, monitoring the far flung activities of her adversaries.

In the afternoon of the third day she entered the bookshop down from her hotel wearing an outsized knitted ski hat with a droopy peak that cast the upper part of her face in deep shadow.

"Monsieur Manfred, Georges Manfred?" she inquired of the man who appeared to be the proprietor. There was no one else in the shop.

"Can I help you?" He seemed a wary man with close knit brows, thin lips, and bottle-cap glasses exaggerating eyes so squinted his pupils were bands of darkness. "Would you like a book?"

"Yes, certainly," she said.

"Any one in particular, mademoiselle?"

"You choose."

He did not seem surprised by her request. "Of course," he said. "Perhaps this would be what you are looking for." He placed a copy of *Absolute Absolution* by Pietro di Cosmos on the glass showcase and slid it across to her. "Do you know this book?" he asked.

"I do," she said.

"There are only a few copies left," he said. "Very few."

"How much?"

"Very inexpensive, considering."

"Considering what?"

"Ah, mademoiselle, you know or you would not be in my store."

"And you are the banker."

"I am a poor bookseller."

"A bookseller, yes. Poor? If so, by choice."

"In the book, it is explained, such choices we make are small acts of courage. I am a brave man."

"In the face of life and all its travails."

"In the face of death, mademoiselle. You are one of us, yes?"

"How much time is left?"

"Ten days, mademoiselle."

"I will think about it."

"To think is to fall, mademoiselle. To think is to fail. To act is to rise."

"I will remember that. Good-day."

She left, closing the door behind her, and embraced the stinging cold. She took a few deep breathes, shivered, and walked around the block, entering *Hôtel* from the back, having, when she first went out, unobtrusively taped the lock to provide access from the outside. From the inside, by law it had to open freely in case of a fire and after she had made minor repairs to the push-bar mechanism, it did.

The rest of the day she researched Monsieur Georges Manfred. He had recently sold his semi-detached house in Notre-Dame-de-Grâce, which had been registered at the time of purchase in accordance with Napoleonic law in his name only. The entire proceeds he had transferred to an account in the Cayman Islands. At present, his wife and five children were living in a subsidized flat and surviving on welfare. After abandoning his family he had moved into his office, which consisted of one room with a desk and a sophisticated computer system, two metal chairs, and a foldup metal cot feigning as a sofa. Partitioned off to the side was a kitchenette with a hot plate, a kettle, and a small fridge, and in one corner a two-piece cold water bathroom. He had sold the office building, with the title to be transferred to the new owners on February 7th.

She found that he had a brief but odious criminal record and had served time for domestic violence. She hacked into email, which suggested he had molested his daughters. She tracked through a series of sites and accounts until she confirmed her earlier supposition that he was indeed a banker for The Church and had moved in excess of one hundred million dollars out of Canada over the last several months, mostly to the same numbered account in the Caymans.

He was a banker but he had not the patience to be a beneficiary. His personal preparations, barbarous in their execution, affirmed his choice to ascend with the Rapture and wait for others to follow. Presumably, these would include his discarded family, although after the infamy of collective suicide and the misery of desertion, it was possible his wife would take up a different religion. Selective annihilation through mass hysteria might pall in the interminable years to come, especially when the alternative was to join a vile misanthrope for eternity.

That same night, the coldest night of the year, Tess gathered a few things together and slipped out the back door into the windy night.

She walked quickly along to the bookshop and picked open the sturdy door to the side that led up an interior flight of stairs to the office. The air smelled musty, with a hint of cat piss from strays that had occasionally crept in out of the elements. The bare stone walls felt damp to the touch and emitted a slight sulphuric odour. The wood beams and steps gave off the acrid smell of stale tobacco as she slid her feet carefully from one tread to the next.

At the top step she turned right on the narrow landing, then right again to face the door. She tested it quietly. She paused to slip on kid gloves, then she knocked.

"Hello," she called.

"What! What!"

She had woken him. He was safe behind a thick bolted door but startled to find someone, a woman's voice, had penetrated this far into his miserable sanctuary. "Georges," she said, speaking in clear tones to dispel the notion of a ghost or a fiend in the night. "Georges, I have brought your money."

"The woman today in my shop, is it you, mademoiselle?"

"You know who I am, Georges, you have already reported your suspicions to the Holy Gathering."

"Yes. I have talked to Pietro himself. By computer. He says you are the Devil."

"But you, dear Georges, you know better than that. I am Mary."

"You have come back." His voice was getting closer.

"I have brought money."

"How much?"

"As much as it takes, as much as we need. Even for your family."

There was a long silence.

"Or, Georges, if you choose to resist the Rapture, I give you my blessing. You can live like a rich man beyond your wildest dreams. I know you buy lottery tickets, I know you dream, and when you die you will ascend with the Chosen to become your perfect self. You will become God."

Shuffling sounds on the floor were followed by the sharp whisper of iron bolts sliding and the door swung open.

"Saint Mary Celestial."

"My poor Georges," she said and brandished her Smith & Wesson revolver so that it gleamed from the ambient streetlight shining through the windows.

"You do not need a gun," he said, more confused than frightened.

She moved a metal chair into a direct line between the windows and door, then commanded him with a wave of her gun to sit. She placed his arms behind his back, had him lean forward, and taking a strong elastic band from her pocket she secured his thumbs together.

Reaching into her bag, she took out the canvas fishing packet from Killaloe and removed the shank of wood wrapped with heavy-test copper trolling wire.

She wrapped the wire around his neck in a single loop, being careful not to cut into his flesh or restrict his breathing. She walked one end of the wire over to the door and pushed it through the keyhole of the large cast iron lock with a brass knob and sliding brass mechanism that no longer worked. The other strand she kept in a firm grasp as she sat down at his computer behind him.

"Now, then," she said. "I need you to give me access to your Cayman account."

"I can't do that, of course."

"Oh, but you must. Otherwise I will kill you right here, right now, you will miss the Rapture, Georges. You will simply die and that will be the end of it."

"No," he protested. "Please. You cannot."

"But I can," she said, giving the copper wire a sharp tug. "Of course I can."

Within minutes, she had transferred over one hundred million dollars into a Cayman account registered to a consortium consisting of Evelyn Wallace, Tess Saintsbury, Jennifer Izett, Teresa MacPherson, Celestine du Maurier, and Harry Lindstrom, to be accessed by any one of, or combination of, the above. She also had him provide access to parallel accounts in the name of Tom Severence, which she would deal with later.

"Thank you," she said.

Keeping the copper wire taunt but not tight, she walked the loose end over to the casement and opened both windows wide. A blast of cold air surged into the room; the thermostat was downstairs in the bookshop. She tucked the wire around one of the sturdy iron bars, careful not to tear her latex gloves, and kinked the wire slightly to hold it at a height so it crossed in a horizontal line over to Monsieur Manfred's neck and beyond to the large ancient keyhole in the door. She led the loose end back across the room behind Monsieur Manfred and parallel to the first, and pushed the end likewise through the open keyhole.

She removed a white silk bandana from her jacket pocket and tied it close to the door, firmly around the shorter strand of wire.

"Now then, Georges, I need you to do as I say. Stand up. Carefully, now." She removed the chair and placed it against the wall, near the partition marking off the toilet area and the kitchenette. She raised his shirt collar to keep the wire away from his neck while she directed him to move with her to the door, adjusting the strands to keep them taunt. She reached around and drew the wires through the keyhole, then reached back and adjusted his collar so the wire noose was against his flesh. "Georges, I am going to go out. I want you to shut the door after me. I need you to bolt the door. Your hands are secured so you will have to use your head—don't look puzzled, Georges, use your chin. The bolts will slide easily, you have kept them in good repair."

He gestured with a confused nod of appreciation for the compliment.

"Then I need you to shuffle back very slowly very carefully into the centre of the room. You don't want to hurt yourself. When you get there, where the chair was, I want you to kneel. I will know when you are kneeling. Then I need you to stay very still, Georges. That is all there is to it, you stay very still. I will do everything else."

She adjusted the wire to rest tightly against the flesh of his neck, stepped out onto the landing and carefully pulled the door shut. She could hear him slide the bolts into place and as she paid out one wire and drew in the other she felt him manoeuvre across the filthy bare wood floor until he was equidistant from the locked door and the open windows. She felt the copper wires go momentarily slack as he kneeled and she drew in the extra wire until both were snug again, in parallel lines.

She slipped heavy welder's gloves on over her kid gloves.

"Are you all right, Georges?" she called.

"Yes," he said. "I am okay."

"Good."

She wrapped both strands of wire around her gloved hands and leaned against the weight on the other end. Using a slight sawing motion she increased the pressure. She heard him gag. She knew he must have snapped the elastic band restraint. She felt his fingers grasp at the wire and tear into his throat. The ululation of despair that pierced the thick wood door at last gave way to a deathly silence. The tension on the wires increased in a liquid convulsion and then they went slack. She began to tighten her purchase when the wires suddenly snapped taut and yanked her off balance in a shattering tremor as copper tore through oesophageal tissue and sinewy flesh, slamming her against the outside of the door.

From inside came a terrible thrashing clatter of a body pitching forward. Then, again, there was silence within. She unwrapped the wire that had cut deeply into her gloves and looked down at her trembling hands. Her breath rasped in her windpipe. There were no other sounds but the whisper of vibrating wires and the wind moaning in the crawl space above the ceiling over her head.

She reached into her bag and removed a bottle of Québécoise cider, which she opened and proceeded to drink as she slouched down on the unheated landing and made herself comfortable. The cider was slightly sweet but it was comforting on a dry throat. She took out a bag of salted peanuts and consumed them as well. The ambient heat radiating from the store below was negated by the cold penetrating the locked door from the open window in the office. She wrapped her coat close around herself and drew her legs up into its folds and dozed.

Just before dawn she roused herself and facing the door she tugged at the end of the wire that still had tension. The other strand was limp but she drew it in until both were tight, then with a slight sawing motion she tugged back and forth until the wire slid easily in either direction. She stopped and tied a tiny fishhook from her kit on the end that she knew went directly to the open window and slipped it through the keyhole. Slowly she drew the more sluggish wire as it passed around the vertebral bone without binding on the half-frozen flesh, drawing the loose wire over the bar in the window in its wake. As she drew the strand of taut wire through the keyhole she felt it being cleansed of bloodied detritus by the knot of fine white silk pressed against the iron lock. Finally the hook tugged at thick tissue around the neck, then popped away, vibrated for a moment as loose wire slid free, and caught hold of the silk. Once the silk poked through the keyhole she twisted it straight as it wrapped around the hook and it came easily through into her hands.

She wrapped the copper wire around the shank of wood and put her gear together in the fishing packet, took off her welding gloves, which were grooved from the wire, and her kid glove liners, put of knitted wool mittens and picked up her empty bottle and peanut wrapper and tucked them into her bag. Descending the stairs she walked out into the ice-cold air that whistled through her nostrils as she hurried along. She glanced back only once to see the windows of the office above the old stone bookshop ajar, inviting the weather indoors where it had frozen the dead flesh of her victim and would cause the pipes to freeze and burst, in due course alerting the world to the fate of Monsieur Georges Manfred, prop., Canadian banker for the Holy Gathering of The Church Absolute.

She had rather hoped to see the pleasantly nondescript man on the night desk before checking out, but when she entered *Hôtel* he was hunched over his desk behind the counter, sound asleep, and she saw no need to disturb him. She would rest for a few hours, go up to *La Ville Souterraine* under *Le Reine Élizabeth* and buy new clothes and luggage, and walk through to Central Station where she would board a train for New York City and go directly to JFK to catch her overnight flight to London. By the time Harry Lindstrom caught up with her activities, Professor Currer Bell would be ensconced amidst the inimitably gracious confines of Hazlitt's Hotel on Frith Street just to the south of Soho Square.

21 HAZLITT'S HOTEL

THE FIRST THING HARRY DID WHEN HE GOT BACK FROM Montreal was arrange to meet Miranda Quin for dinner. He called her when he landed at Pearson after trying to sort out a few things on the flight. Leon Gonsalez had caught him before he checked out of *Le Reine Élizabeth* to tell him that the red flecks in the tissue were not rust but human blood, the victim's own, and the white fibres in the keyhole were silk. He also found a confusing message on line, confirming his status as the fiduciary trustee for a numbered offshore account.

He and Miranda met at The Little Italian. Her choice. He would have preferred Rory's Chinese Emporium and Brew House just down the lane, an establishment that shared the same outer walls of industrial red brick. He walked over from his Harbourfront condo along The Esplanade, which in fine weather bustled with kids playing, players performing, loiterers gossiping, strollers strolling, and was now as bleak as the Barrens. Entering the architecturally demarcated Distillery District, the lengths of his various shadows converged across brick and stone surfaces of nineteenth century warehouses and factories and offices nestled helter-skelter along cobbled laneways, with antiqued casements broadcasting the warm glow of innumerable eateries and shops and modern services within their walls.

Miranda was waiting.

"A colleague dropped me off," she explained. "You look like the abominable snowman."

"I feel like him, too," said Harry, taking off his sheepskin coat, tucking her father's toque into the pocket and wrapping his möbius cashmere scarf around the hook, before hooking his cane on the back of his chair and sitting across from her, with a diminutive candle flickering between them.

"You can get claws for those things, you know." It took him a moment to realize she was talking about his Aunt Beth's walking stick. His great aunt had never used a claw on the tip, so it hadn't occurred to him as an option.

"How was Montreal? How did you like Leon Gonsalez?"

"Good, and very much."

"Did you know he didn't speak a word of English until he went to McGill?"

"Just Spanish?"

"Just French. He doesn't speak Spanish at all. You assumed, because of the name."

"I did. I'd swear I heard an accent."

"You can't tell 'Silent Night' from 'O Canada.' You don't have an ear for auracular nuance, Harry."

"There's no such word as *auracular*."

"There should be. So, tell me, did you solve the locked-room murder?"

"Not yet, but I know who did it. It's too clever to be anyone else."

"You admire strange talents."

"I do. Let's order, eat, have a few drinks, then I'll fill you in on the end of the world as we know it."

Later, sipping postprandial glasses of Sambuca Molinari, each with three coffee beans floating ceremoniously on the surface, Harry shifted the conversation to murder.

"I'm sure it was Tess."

"Tess?"

"Jennifer Izett. When I was off skiing in the Gatineau, I wasn't. I was with her."

"Are they mutually exclusive, skiing and hanging out with a killer girlfriend?"

"Miranda, listen. And let me finish before you shift into (a) witty, (b) disparaging, or (c) professional mode."

"I'll try."

And she did.

He explained the Rapture scam. She listened intently, taking one break to go to the washroom, and then she sat back, ordered a double scotch on the rocks for both of them, and asked questions. Satisfied that she knew as much as he was able or willing to reveal, she finished her drink and rose to her feet.

"Where are you going?" he asked, dumbfounded.

"Home."

"You didn't believe any of it, did you?"

"On the contrary, I believe the whole story. I'm tired, it was exhausting, I'm going to bed. And by the way, not to put too fine a point on it, you have a very dangerous girlfriend."

"Please stay," he said, trying not to sound plaintive.

"Okay." She sat down. "That was just a dramatic gesture. But I wanted to make a point, Harry. There's nothing I can do, there's nothing anyone can do. People believe in the Rapture, in eschatological termination, in the End of the World. In a civilized society we remain tolerant. At all costs, we remain tolerant, because *intolerance* is the one thing we cannot, we will not, we must not abide. And if the end does come, well, then we will buckle down to post-Apocalyptic analysis, but by then, of course, who gives a damn?"

He was incredulous, he was angry. "Mass suicide, you can't just dismiss it."

"The exhortation of suicide is murder, once the suicides occur. Until then, it's a scream in the dark."

"The scam?"

"What scam? Churches collect money. Christianity is the largest capitalist entity in history. The Pope wears gold."

"The outrageous confabulations?"

"Believers believe. The Mormon's think God is six-foot-two and lives on the planet Kolob, and they nearly got their man into the White House and may yet. Who knows? Scientologists think we're infested by spiritual parasites from the planet Teegeeack. Catholics believe communion means swallowing the actual blood of their Lord and chewing on his actual flesh, and they agree with Moslems who feel women are innately provocative and men irrepressibly licentious. Some Islamists think blaspheming the prophet is a motive for murder and mayhem, and Absolutists believe death is salvation. Trust me, if your mass suicide occurs, I will be on the task force to figure out how it happened, who is responsible, and how it could have been prevented. Meanwhile, good luck to you and your girlfriend. From what you've told me, if anyone can shift the flow of history, it's Sister Mary, the Devil Incarnate, or, as you know her, ravishing Tess."

"Did I ever say *ravishing*?"

"Every time you opened your mouth."

He found her quip irritating, invasive, demeaning. He felt depleted by her bureaucratic response to his revelations. He was angry, frustrated, and confused. Clearly, the moral thing for him to do was to act. Ethically it was not advisable. It was the right thing to do, joining Tess. It was wrong to condone her tactics.

"Just why did you need to go to Montreal, Harry?"

"To be sure it was her."

"And now you're sure, even though the crime is unsolved?"

Harry nodded in the affirmative. He was already well on the way to working out how she'd done it. To say so would be a betrayal. After receiving his notice from the Caymans, he thought he understood *why*. She had somehow made him too valuable to kill, and both of them too much of a threat to ignore. She could not hunt Tom Severence down. She would have been murdered on sight by zealots but by devising the high profile murder of one of his bankers, she had signalled him, as well as Harry, that she was out there and dangerous. She had set herself up as a lure to draw Severence into the open. She was counting on Harry to lead him within reach.

"Sorry but I have to go," he said, rising to his feet. "Always good to see you. I'm walking. I'll call you a cab at the door."

He strode out into the night, forgetting the cab, and marched precariously through slippery slush for home, ruminating wildly about the tyranny of profligate tolerance, almost frantic to book the first possible flight to Heathrow. He was certain she would be in London.

Before noon the next day he checked into Hazlitt's Hotel in the heart of Soho.

"You are the Canadian gentleman, we have been expecting you." The clerk was a middle-aged German who spoke English with precision enough to make even the most English of English seem unspeakably colonial. "Your name is Mr. Ellis Bell, I believe. Your cousin has arranged for your room adjoining her own."

Harry was trying to piece this together when the clerk leaned forward over the counter and unaccountably said: "Nudge-nudge, wink-wink."

Harry blushed, not at the lascivious implications but embarrassed by the awkwardness of sharing Monty Python with a stranger. With his pale colouring, the blood rose easily to his cheeks, sometimes undermining his otherwise austere expression. He offered a John Cleese look of disdain and feared he appeared like Eric Idle about to sing, "Always look on the bright side!"

"If you would just sign here," said the clerk. "Would you like assistance with your bag or is the cane an acquired accoutrement?"

"I'll manage," said Harry. He scrawled an indecipherable signature and took his key.

"Teresa Cornelys," said the Clerk.

"I'm sorry?" said Harry, who had not yet adjusted to being Ellis Bell.

"Your cousin, Miss Currer Bell, has taken the Teresa Cornelys Suite."

"I see, thank you."

"She was a famous courtesan."

"My cousin?"

"Mademoiselle Cornelys. We refer to such people in the French. Would you like breakfast sent to your room? Or lunch, if you would prefer?"

"No thank you, I ate on the plane. Is Miss Bell in at the moment?"

"She asked that you join her in the usual place."

He pronounced the word *usual* with a sibilant stress on the 's,' as if it were a term with unmentionable connotations borrowed from a lesser language.

"The usual?" said Harry, reproducing the sound as best he could. "Of course."

He turned away from the counter and admired the intimate antique décor, with requisite glass encased bookshelves. He walked through and around, over gently sloped floors, passing wondrously crooked staircases poised every which way like an Escher drawing, until he came to his room, named after a beheaded sixteenth-century dandy. He noted the small sign on the door next to his declaring it the suite honouring Mlle Teresa Cornelys. He knocked, then tried the door. It was locked.

His own room was perfect. The walls were painted in deep Farrow and Ball hues to enhance the presence of an eighteenth century four-poster bed and an enchanting assortment of antique dressers, a wardrobe, and tables. The lamps were bordello eccentric, with heavy shades. The bathroom had an original Thomas Crapper toilet with a chain covered in a plush velvet cord leading down from a water box overhead. The sinks and bath were free-standing porcelain sculptural artefacts and the floor was an exquisite mosaic.

While he washed up, Harry tried to recall what she would have regarded as a *usual* haunt. In their conversations leaning close to the cast-iron stove during the long evenings in the Killaloe cabin, they often toured London together in words and images, searching out places that evoked mutual affection. Hazlitt's Hotel was a favourite, with its charmingly eccentric absurdities. The Embankment in front of the statue of Boadicea, or Boudicca, the fierce and bloodthirsty warrior queen, came to mind. Too exposed, too obvious. The poet's corner in Westminster Abbey? Too esoteric, too obviously subtle. And the clerk had implied lunch. One good spot was The Bunch of Grapes on Brompton Road. Just down from that was the second story coffee shop in Georgio Armani and, going the other way, the cafeteria at Harrods. There was the incomparable dining room in the Tate Gallery, and there was The Cheshire Cheese, an historic pub down a tiny passage off Fleet Street.

The Cheshire Cheese would be it. Intimate but public, famous but discreet. A perfect place to meet, surreptitiously exposed. They wanted to be followed, they needed to be seen as evasive.

Harry stopped inside the doorway of The Cheshire Cheese for a moment, letting his eyes adjust to the subdued illumination, then stepped forward and peered around to the left into the small main room and as he expected, saw Tess sitting in a corner. Behind her were dark portraits of a scowling Samuel Johnson and at right angles a benign Charles Dickens—cohorts where they had both often dined, although separated in life by a full generation. He moved over the dark uneven wood floor and around her chair and slid onto the bench, placing his cane carefully in the corner within sight so he wouldn't forget it.

"Harry," she greeted him as if he had just returned from the washroom. "You must try the braised pheasant."

"I'll have the steak and kidney pudding. This is the only place in the world where I can stomach offal."

"Were you followed?"

"I think so. Yes, I'm sure." Over by the door, a man looking self-consciously inconspicuous under the low ceiling turned away and crossed into the bar.

"I like your walking stick. Is it permanent?"

"Is anything? It's good to see you."

"Sorry I left you in a bit of a lurch."

"No lurch. I was home before midnight. I gather you had an appointment in Samara."

"Mr. Manfred had an appointment in Samara. I was merely the vehicle to get him there."

Harry shuddered but took heart as he recognized her clinical detachment might save twelve thousand miserable lives.

"It was the copper fishing line, wasn't it? And the keyhole."

"It was."

"He was kneeling. Was he praying or pleading?"

"He was just kneeling."

"And he did not resist?"

"He was secured."

"There were no ropes or manacles."

"There was an elastic band."

"Ah, the elastic. And silk, you used a piece of silk to clean the wire when you pulled it through."

She nodded.

"You had to let his body freeze so the wire would slide around his vertebrae."

"Let's talk about us, Harry."

"Why am I here?"

"In England? I needed you and you came."

"Why?"

"Well, I'm not inside your head or your heart but I'd say you thought I wanted your help."

"And how could you be certain I'd find you in London?"

"You did, didn't you?"

"Yes."

"That's how I was certain. You recognized what we were doing and here you are."

"And what are we doing?"

"We're going to eat lunch. I've already ordered you pheasant. It's famous. I hope you don't mind."

Her face was awash in yellowish shadows cast by the sconces on walls discoloured from the Great Fire of 1666. The ceiling, which had once been white, was low but rather than pressing down it seemed to lift weightlessly above them, although the waitress unconsciously stooped as she brought their plates heaping with braised foul, bacon, celery, and new potatoes. The savoury aroma wafted around them and they ate in silence, consuming pints of cider to aid digestion. When they finished, Tess sat back against her chair and said,

"We are both immensely desirable in certain quarters."

He smiled.

She became eerily serious, leaned forward into the flickering light of a forlorn candle in the centre of their table, and whispered. "You, for access to their money. Me, for access to the hereafter. You're safe for the time being, Harry, but don't get complacent. Whether the Rapture falls, fails, or fades away, they'll use whatever coercion it takes to make you sign off on the Cayman fund. The trick is, as soon as I'm gone, you need to turn your authority over to public trustees and walk away, before Severence and his acolytes can put you to the rack."

Harry listened. It seemed like she was describing a parallel universe that precisely mirrored his own without touching it directly. He gazed around at the palpable ambience of the Cheshire Cheese and thought about parallel realities and other times.

"And what about you?" he said.

"They want me dead, they want me alive. It is a dilemma. The assassination of Monsieur Georges Manfred changed everything. After the flamboyantly inexplicable signature murder of a revered banker of The Church Absolute, Tom Severence is torn between desperately wanting me dead so I can resume my part in the story to greet twelve thousand arrivals on the celestial plane and wanting to capture me alive to prove he can subdue, suppress, or otherwise stifle, the Devil Incarnate, and then have me exterminated as a measure of his own omnipotence."

"What you call your signature crime led me here and his minions followed."

"I could never have got here in the open. I travelled so deeply underground, I'm lucky I wasn't buried alive. But once here, I needed them to know where I am."

"Why, Tess? What can you possibly do to dissuade mindless zealots from irrational acts? Fanatics cannot be reasoned with, argued with, coerced, compelled, cajoled or otherwise convinced of their folly."

"But they can easily be fooled! They can be exposed to the truth. We'll see."

"Severence needs you alive to prove you're actually dead. But he also needs you dead to prove you're alive. Am I missing anything?"

"Interesting, isn't it?"

"So you're sitting here exposing yourself to capture."

"I am."

"Unless you catch him first."

"I had you lead them to me so Pietro the Second and I can catch each other."

"And it had to be here?"

"It had to be in England. Wherever he is or has been in the world, madly drumming up business, he will finish things off right here. Since I don't know precisely where in England, I have to play games."

"Games?"

"Cat and mouse. Let them think they've caught me, let them think I've escaped. Caught me, escaped, caught me, escaped. Until it's too late."

"You really think you can do this?"

"The lives of twelve thousand stupid lost souls depend on it. But your bit is done for now."

"How so?"

"You exposed me, now I want you out of the way. I need you to go home."

"I've just arrived."

"And we have had a very good lunch. We'll go back to Hazlitt's and fuck until dawn. Then it's over."

She was not being flippant or intentionally provocative, nor was she expressing indifference, merely acknowledgement that they were, of course, lovers. But this time, in these circumstances, she wanted to be on her own. She looked poignant and sultry. She did not smile.

"I stay, Harry. You leave."

"You can't do this by yourself," he protested.

"I must. Don't you see, I really must. There is no other way. I'm sorry to leave you behind to pick up the pieces."

"You don't have any idea what to do next. The bloody end of the world is at hand and you're eating lunch." He mustered as much scorn as he could.

"You're angry. Good, that will make what's coming easier to deal with. You're right, Harry. I don't know exactly what's next. Severence has declared the Rapture will occur where and when the eternal and the infinite meet. He loves riddles. I hate them. Where the eternal and the infinite meet! He will be there to lead his people through, although he will lead from the rear. Martyrdom for Pietro the Second will be *not to die* when death is the course of salvation."

"From sin and guilt?"

"From mortality and the human condition. And I must be there with him."

"You're scaring me, Tess."

"I am a frightening person, Harry. Surely you know that by now."

The waitress came over and cleared their dishes. She chatted for a while. She was from Australia, with her next stop Aspen Colorado for a month of skiing. They ordered spotted dick for dessert, in part to share the unspoken joke of its name.

"I thought you liked riddles," he said in a conciliatory tone.

"Puzzles. Riddles have trick answers. There's no ambiguity about puzzles."

"So I'm puzzled," he said. "Where have you been? It's been nearly a week since you left Montreal."

"Amsterdam, mostly."

"To sell your diamond bracelet?"

"There's nowhere better. And I love the bizarre juxtaposition of Van Goghs and Rembrandts and I like eating *ristofel.*"

"Where else?"

"You don't ask a lady her personal secrets."

"Were you travelling in England?"

"I wasn't travelling, Harry."

"You went to Holland because you needed money. But you opened an account in the Cayman Islands in my name."

"And in mine. The password is secret."

"So I've discovered. Then how do I get in?"

"The password, it's the word 'secret.'"

"More original than using your birthday."

"Or yours. It doesn't have to be original. If I'm not around, you're the only one who has access."

"To what exactly?"

"A fortune. For the time being it's your life insurance. There will be more. Much much more. I used access provided by the late Monsieur Manfred to override The Church accounts worldwide. You will become the sole trustee for all their assets when Tom Severence dies. You will have access to everything."

Harry sucked in his breath so deeply he whistled.

Her dark eyes gleamed in the flickering candlelight. "Any man who refuses to cash in two original paintings by Gustav Klimt is not going to abscond with funds extorted on the promise of interminable bliss."

"Well then, Tess. Since I seem to have a vested interest in the outcome of your clash with The Church, I figure I'll stay around for awhile. We're in this together."

She lowered her voice: "This is a struggle to the death, Harry. You are not suited to the work. You have never killed anyone. You're no longer in this at all."

"I am and I have."

"No, you have not. We've talked about this. You are absolved."

"By the God I do not accept?"

"By me, that's enough." Again, she did not smile.

"And you're not a killer," he protested under his breath.

"I am, Harry. Think of me as a soldier. I kill, that's what I do. And I will kill again when I have to. You remember I told you about my sister?"

"Sarah. She died under the ice."

"And my parents. They hanged themselves. That was their response to intolerable sorrow."

He could feel her heartbeat like a fire in an empty room.

"I know what I'm doing," she said.

He was at a loss for words; he felt desperate.

She pushed her unfinished dessert away. It might have been midday outside but in the gloomy charm of the Cheshire Cheese it seemed like a pleasantly perennial twilight.

"Harry, do you remember I told you about getting hypothermia and frostbite?"

"When you were nine and being inordinately stubborn with your parents."

"It wasn't about my parents, it was about God. The night before I had refused to say prayers at bedtime. The quarrel went on through the next day. Punishments just made me bolder. Finally, I buried myself in a snowdrift. I did it myself, Harry. It wasn't my parents, it was just me having an argument with God."

"You were refusing to say your prayers?"

"A gentle and soporific and grotesquely barbaric prayer.

Now I lay me down to sleep
I pray the Lord my soul to keep
If I should die before I wake
I pray the Lord my soul to take

"I was nine years old! I was just beginning to learn about death, mostly from television, where it was totally ephemeral, and from roadkill, where it was gruesome, irrefutable, and horrifically mundane. I had to live with death, they said. I understood that, I still do. But they explained I was guilty of original sin and wanted me to venerate a pathetic impoverished tormented eye-rolling daydreaming delusional drifter from ignorant times who embraced an instrument of hideous torture so that he could suffer instead of me for things I didn't do. *For things I didn't even do!* I felt sorry for Jesus the way you feel sorry for a run-over dachshund but since he was also a Holy Spirit my sympathy went only so far. He was an immortal after all and since he was simultaneously God the Father of everything, and therefore in charge of his own demise, and I was an incipient feminist with almost no control of my life at all. I wasn't about to negotiate my death with him in any of his forms just before going to sleep."

"And so you froze your bloody ear."

"Mary conceived through the ear, if the annunciation account is to be believed."

"How very unpleasant."

"If you want unpleasant, how about the vampire song?" She started to sing in a sepulchral barely audible drone, pausing here and there as she edited and abridged:

Sons of God: Hear His Holy word,
Gather round the table of the Lord
Eat His Body, drink His Blood
And we will sing a song of love
Da da da, dadah dadadah,
Eat his body, drink his blood,
Da da, dadah dadadah,
And we will live forever.

"Even at nine I didn't believe in vampires. Do you remember that?"

He didn't. Scraping the last of the custard from his plate as she mumbled about being washed in the blood of the Lamb, Harry shifted their conversation to something less oppressive and was surprised that her gratified response was immediate.

"Why Currer Bell?" he asked.

"Why not?"

"You know I travelled here under my own name don't you?"

"The change at Hazlitt's will confuse them. The fakery smacks of authenticity."

"Where does the name Tess come from, did you name yourself after Teresa Cornelys?"

"The beheaded courtesan?"

"You're staying in her suite. I read the hotel brochure. She wasn't beheaded. The Duke of something-or-another was, a few hundred years earlier."

"It wasn't her suite, they just borrowed her name."

"As did you."

"I told you, it was my mother's."

"Izett. Not Tess. Her name was Jennifer Izett."

"Then I named myself after Boadicea."

"Whose first name was Teresa?"

"It might have been."

"Okay," he conceded.

"Thank you."

"I like your disguise."

"Hair extensions."

"Tess?"

"Believe it or not it was the name I was born with."

"For Teresa."

"Just Tess."

"What about Susan Montaigne?"

"Montagne with no 'i.' No, I prefer Tess, don't you?"

She smiled and her face lit up. Her hair flared out in voluptuous Polynesian waves like a Pre-Raphaelite rendering of Salome. The yellowish taciturn portraits of Johnson and Dickens were poised on the walls behind them, looking on with indifference.

22 'A DREADFUL DARKNESS CLOSES IN'

THEY HEADED BACK TO HAZLITT'S BY MID-AFTERNOON, walking along Fleet Street, around Saint Clements Church standing squarely in the middle of the road, along the Strand and up through Covent Garden, over and across Charing Cross Road, down Shaftsbury and up Frith, circumventing the tourist throngs in Leicester Square. Jetlag had caught up with Harry. They decided to go to the Teresa Cornelys Suite, call for room service, and load him up on caffeine. But the clerk who buzzed them through the main door called out to inform them they had a visitor. He spoke with disarming precision. The English, Harry thought, are not so well suited to the hospitality trade as foreigners unbound by constrictions of class, unencumbered by accents many visitors find quaint but impenetrable.

"He gives his name as Acton Bell. I do not believe he is another cousin."

"Oh really?"

"No, he is French."

"One can have French cousins, *Monsieur*." She said this quite sharply.

"Pardon, je ne réalisais pas que vous êtes français, vous-même."

"Bien sûr. Only on my mother's side. Where is this cousin of mine?"

"He is in his room. I believe he is asleep. He had a very long flight. Would you like me to ring him?"

Harry turned obliquely away from the counter and whispered, "Were you expecting another cousin?"

"No, do not wake him," she said to the clerk. "No," she said to Harry. "You were my first choice."

Slightly bewildered, Harry followed her along the maze of corridors and stairs, past bookshelves stacked with leather tomes and paperbacks, past marble busts and age-darkened paintings and gilt-encrusted mirrors on wood-panelled walls to their rooms.

"Perhaps I should have a quick nap," he said, pausing at his own door while she opened hers.

"If you wish," she said.

Before Harry could recant, she disappeared into the vestibule of the Teresa Cornelys Suite and drew the door closed behind her.

Harry sprawled on top of his bedspread. He caught himself feeling happy and giving in to the pleasant confusion he drifted off. Time passed and a light knocking drew him reluctantly out of a deep sleep. It was still daylight but with closed drapes the room was the violet colour of evening shade in fresh fallen snow. At first he didn't have any idea where he was, although he knew it was Tess at the door. He was clambering out of a four-poster bed. Hazlitt's, of course.

He switched on a lamp and hobbled to the door. He pulled it open, hardly looking up. Looming in the chartreuse shadows was the face of a monster, leaning forward with an amiable grin.

"Queequeg!" he exclaimed, reeling within, not sure if he was wake or asleep.

"*Monsieur le professeur, ça va?*"

"It's you, Inspector, my other cousin."

"It is I, *moi-même*. I inquired under your name, as instructed by Superintendent Miranda Quin, and since you were not here I scanned the register. I am a policeman, no? And then I signed in as the third Bell, *Monsieur* Acton. May I enter?"

"Please, of course. Let me splash water on my face. Have a seat, take the Louis Quatorze." Harry swept his hand grandly past an opulent chair.

"Regency, I believe. More refined."

"It is good to see you," said Harry with a wry smile. As he spoke he recalled the rumour that Theophil Queequeg had become an adherent of The Church Absolute. "You're not here to murder me, are you?"

"If I was, as they say, you would already be dead."

"That's a relief."

Harry was giddy as he tried to assimilate the unlikelihood of Queequeg as a presence at Hazlitt's Hotel. "Have you talked to Tess?" he asked.

"Madame Saintsbury? Not yet. You first, I thought, and then we will talk together. Cousins, we will catch up on family affairs."

"How did you know?"

"I am a reader of great literature, Harry. Acton and Ellis and Currer Bell were the pen names, of course, used by the Brontë sisters. I know the author of *Jane Eyre* was Currer. I'm not actually sure whether I am named after the author of *Wuthering Heights* or *The Tenant of Wildfell Hall*. I would prefer the latter. Anne was an ardent feminist. We are *simpatico*."

"And you are an astonishing mystery," Harry declared. "As much as I'd like to talk books, I need to know why in God's name you are here."

"God, books, and mystery. That sums it up, I think."

"Are you stoned, Queequeg?"

"I flew in from Tahiti. It is a very long flight."

"Of course," said Harry. "Let me get Tess and we'll talk."

Harry knocked on the great panelled door with 'Teresa Cornelys' inscribed on a brass plate. He tried the door. It was unlocked. He went in. There was no sign of Tess.

There was no indication she had ever been there. The soap and lotion bottles were unopened. The toilet tissue was folded over at the end. The towels were arranged with clinical precision, the pillows and bedspread were undisturbed. He went to the front desk and checked with the clerk, who had not seen her leave, nor had he heard a commotion. She might have left unnoticed, he said, since the Georgian front door was out of his line of vision from the reception desk, but after some consideration, he decided she had never been there in the first place.

"We just came in," said Harry. He looked at his watch. "Two hours ago."

"I was not working two hours ago." He met Harry's frenzied agitation with unflappable calm. "Perhaps you are mistaken, sir."

"About what, for God's sake?"

"There is no need for obscenity."

"Profanity."

"I beg your pardon sir, profanity it is. As for Professor Bell, I am at a loss. At Hazlitt's, we are not accustomed to losing our clients."

The clerk glanced up and looked away. Harry heard shuffling noises off to his side and turned to find Queequeg had followed him into the lobby or parlour or whatever they called it. The Polynesian handed Harry his cane.

"What is it, Harry?"

"I seem to have lost Tess again."

"It has happened before, yes."

"Many times, but this time it's serious."

"I believe her abduction on Bora Bora was serious as well. She seems rather a blithe spirit, doesn't she? She comes and goes as she pleases."

"Are we sure it was her choice?"

"Well," said Queequeg. "If she were abducted there would have been a terrible ruckus, *n'est pas*?"

"Unless she wanted to be abducted," said Harry.

"Then there would have been evidence of her having settled into the room. You know, luggage, clothes, toiletries, et al. I peaked in on the way down. No sign of a struggle, no sign of a guest. She went of her own accord."

"Or not," said Harry. He returned his attention to the clerk: "This morning you told me she was in the Teresa Cornelys Suite. I saw her go in, she had a key."

"That was not me, sir. The lady was registered but she never turned up. She could not have had the key, it is here."

"You gave me a message to meet her, surely you remember? At the 'usual place,' you said."

"I have no idea what usual place that would be, sir. London has many *unusual* places, but *usual* places, well that would be a list of limited interest, wouldn't it? It was some other fellow, perhaps, who told you that."

"Can I get in touch with the other fellow, then."

"What other fellow, sir?"

"The German we talked to when we came back from lunch. He checked in Monsieur Queequeg."

"I am German, he is Austrian." The clerk seemed to notice Queequeg for the first time. He surveyed Queequeg's dramatically bifurcated countenance like he was assessing a lesser work by Picasso; two faces in one and neither of them pleased him. "I do not know Mr. Queequeg, sir. If you mean Mr. Acton Bell, whom I presume is from one of the more remote *départments* of the French Republic, he stands beside you."

You do presume *and you mean* who, *not* whom.

A reassuring voice, rarely heard.

"Where can I reach the other clerk?" Harry demanded.

"Unfortunately, my colleague has been called home to Vienna on an urgent family matter. That is why I am here, six hours before my shift must begin."

Harry and Queequeg adjourned through a long narrow corridor into a small library and sat facing each other in front of the fire, like two gentlemen squaring off across an imaginary board to enjoin a deadly game of chess.

"Please call me Theo," said Queequeg. "In England I am not an inspector of police. I am a visitor but I am quite at home. I once resided in Bloomsbury Square, twenty minutes from here. For a year, a lifetime ago."

Harry noted the Inspector's English had taken a more British turn but paradoxically with a more pronounced continental inflection.

"I lived in Cambridge. Also a lifetime ago."

"Yes, I know."

"What else do you know? You were talking to Miranda Quin. Perhaps we can save some time if you explain."

"When I first called her, it was about you as the third man in Madame Saintsbury's abduction."

"There was no abduction and there was no third man, not me, not Orson Welles, not Harry Lime, no one. She didn't just make up his name, he didn't exist. Tess worked on her own."

"So I now understand. Please, we must confer. I know you are anxious to rush off and rescue her but that is a complex matter. She does not want to be rescued. So, I will explain, yes. Then you will explain. Then we will go." Then he rather inexplicably added, "old chap."

"I'm listening."

"Well, first of all, I put two unrelated murders together. What they had in common, they were both unresolved."

"Her husband's and—?"

"It was international news for a day or two. A Canadian woman on Tahiti who was summarily executed by one Celestine du Maurier, who subsequently disappeared from the face of the earth. That was my proof that Tess Saintsbury was alive. She had a record of vanishing. I attempted to track her down as Mary di Pietro but The Church blocked all possible avenues of discovery. Whatever her past, it was erased. So I joined The Church."

"Just like that? You joined The Church Absolute. So that part is true."

"It is. I am quite a quick study and very curious, but I was driven by pity and fear. My interest shifted from forensics to the personal. I rapidly rose within reach of the top. When the di Cosmos daughter was murdered, I was already an esteemed and invaluable native convert, sufficiently exotic to attract other indigenous seekers, and relatively wealthy from years of good pay with limited expenses. Valued enough to be invited under the utmost shroud of secrecy to partake in the Rapture. When it was explained, I was shocked, of course, but not surprised. Religion never surprises.

"Following the death of the daughter, Cassandra di Cosmos, I learned from her intimates about Madame Saintsbury, who I realized had perhaps not assumed celestial status as she was vaunted to do, and I discovered her connection with an obscure professor in Toronto. When I heard about the audaciously insoluble murder of the bookseller-banker in Montreal, I knew immediately it must have been Madame Saintsbury, or Jennifer Izett, and contacted Superintendent Quin to try and reach you. She told me you had already been to Montreal, confirming my suspicions, and we assumed you were now in England."

"How could she have known that? I didn't tell her."

"It's where The Church Mothership is moored, it's where their headquarters is based. I am a policeman, Harry. I put two and two together and came up with twenty-two. Miss Quin told me Hazlitt's was your favourite hotel in London. I surmised that's where you would make your base and where I would find Tess Saintsbury. You are both sufficiently eccentric for such an inspired choice. I knew, of course, that Tom Severence, aka Pietro di Cosmos the Second, my spiritual leader, had moved to the Cotswolds in Gloucestershire after the opportune passing of Cassandra di Cosmos and his own elevation. I have followed Madame Saintsbury's career long enough to know what she is planning to do."

"You're not going to arrest her." This was a statement, not a question.

"No, I am going to help her."

"Really?"

"Really."

"You and I are going to help her," said Harry.

"Yes. Good. For now, we relax. I have already bought tickets for us to leave Paddington Station at 8:05 pm. It is only now approaching 6:30 pm."

"For the Cotswolds, I assume?"

"Via Oxford, yes. We will visit Mr. Pietro di Cosmos number two at Wakefield Hall."

"And what if Tess is not there?"

"You seem to have forgotten our priorities, Harry. It is hoped she will be available, but what is important is for us to reach di Cosmos. We must put a stop to his apocalyptic insanity."

"Without Tess, it may not be easy."

"We are resourceful men, we will manage."

"But we have limits about how far we can go to achieve our ends and she does not."

"You mean she will kill, if necessary."

"And even as a cop, you probably won't, nor will I."

"And you admire that in your friend."

"I envy her freedom of conscience."

"That is the definition of a psychopath, Harry: 'freedom of conscience.'"

"No," said Harry. "Freedom *from* conscience is psychopathic. She has a conscience, trust me, she has. In some ways she is the most moral person I have ever encountered. But her conscience guides her, it doesn't control her."

"Do you think your appreciation of her moral flexibility has something to do with your own history?"

"Don't mistake flexibility with being facile. She's thoughtful. She does what she does because she thinks it is right, not because she feels it is right. Her tendentious actions don't mirror her inner turmoil, they resolve it. She is a woman strangely at peace with herself. So, yes, my own history, as you call it, is eased by her example. And how the hell do you know about my history?"

"Mostly, the same way you probably know about mine. Research. And a few insights from Superintendent Quin who speaks about you with somewhat baffling affection and a great deal of clinical candour. We have both suffered terrible losses, Harry. Our families perished by the arbitrary whim of an indifferent universe and we both struggle against the dreadful darkness of their end by confronting death in our daily work. We both live in the shadow of sorrow. We have both contemplated suicide as a means to conquer mortality by casting it aside. But we endure. Why? Because we must. I have marked my flesh to signify that, while I face life and embrace it, I also face death and accept it as well. You, I believe you do the same. Because you must. And Tess, she accepts life and embraces death. Because she must. And she does so with more passion and flair and conviction and resolve than both of us together."

"So here we are."

"But there is only a little time. Now we must hurry, yes."

"This is the antepenultimate day."

Queequeg looked at him and offered a wry smile.

"More like one day left, not two. Midnight that begins February 6th, not that ends it," said Queequeg. "Midnight, Greenwich Mean Time."

"And people all over the world are rejoicing at the prospect of death."

"Yes, Harry. *A dreadful darkness closes in.* Anne Brontë wrote that a few weeks after Emily died, not long before she died herself. It rakes like fingernails across the soul." The opposing sides of his face converged in an expression of inconsolable sadness. "The next line expresses her bewilderment, and the next, her tortured relationship with God. She was twenty-nine."

Death, thought Harry, no matter how distant, is personal.

23 WAKEFIELD HALL

AS THEY STEPPED OUT ONTO FRITH STREET, HARRY WAS NOT thinking about the Brontë sisters but about the Irish writer, Iris Murdoch. To avoid panic or despair he tried to focus on Murdoch and her penchant for cumulative adjectives as they walked through the yellowish gauzy bone-chilling luminescent beguiling London twilight. Thoughts about language and literature clamoured to crowd out of his mind the apprehension he felt for Tess and his increasing horror at the realization that the deaths of twelve thousand desperate gullible dangerous self-obsessed inordinately unimaginative adherents to a fanatical enclave deemed in many parts of the world an authentic religion, were with every passing moment less a heinous abstract possibility and more an inexorable fact.

They had devised no plan but walked side by side down Frith Street, the stout man with his cruelly inscribed face and his aggressive stride, the lean muscular man, leaning on a cane, proceeding with single-minded resolve towards their common but indeterminate goal. They descended underground at the Leister Square station on Charing Cross Road and caught the Northern Line to Warren Street, then the Circle Line to the Paddington terminal where they emerged near the platform for the train to Oxford, with a transfer to Moreton-in-Marsh, at which point they intended to travel by taxi to the village of Wakefield-super-Vale poised over a plunging fold in the Cotswold landscape.

They chose a car on the evening express, which was nearly empty until they reached Reading when a handful of noisy louts stormed into the far end, determined to keep their drunken revels going all the way home. One of them noticed Queequeg.

"Good Christ," he shouted down the length of the car. "Laddies and Gennemen, would you look at that!"

"Oi, oi," called out another. "Where you come from, darlin'?"

"Bradford," declared one of his mates and they all laughed uproariously.

"Having your friend for dinner, are we?" the first one exclaimed. "Oxford, Oxford, raw raw raw," he shrieked.

Amidst the mishmash of racist obscenities, Queequeg sat stoic and silent. One of the louts began beating a drum rhythm on the back of a seat. Harry stood up and walked past the few other passengers towards them, five young men and a woman.

"So what's it to you, mate?" The loudest one challenged Harry. He tried to rise from his seat but sprawled backwards when the train lurched, then recovered himself and approached uncomfortably close. "You got a problem, then?"

Harry wanted to be clever or witty or cutting. Wryly sardonic, cruelly droll. Nothing. He was angry and embarrassed.

"So who's your friend when he's not pretending to be human?"

"I mean he's not human, is he?" said the girl in a shrill drunken hiss.

"He's a bloody brute."

"Freak."

"Foreigner."

"Muslim."

"Nig."

Suddenly they went quiet. Queequeg had approached immediately behind Harry and gently pushed his way past. He was a huge man and his terrifying face was fully illuminated. He moved forward. The bully backed away. The girl started to say something. Someone told her to shut up.

"You are young and stupid," Queequeg said in his soft voice with the Gallic inflection. "It is sad, you will not be young very long but you will always be stupid. My friend and I are enjoying a pleasant conversation. You will be very quiet, please."

He seemed to grow bigger and more fierce as he spoke.

"And if you are not silent, my other friend will mediate the differences between us." As he spoke he reached into the folds of his jacket and withdrew a Smith & Wesson revolver. He flicked off the safety. The Oxford students recoiled. They stared at his face, it was the face of a monster. He smiled and they shrank into their separate selves like horrified children.

"Not a word," he said. "I have never eaten an Englishman myself—my grandparents said British sailors had little nutrition and tasted like rancid lard. For my ancestors' sake I will shoot you if you do not remain quiet, and then you will be dead, right here, on this train, just like that. And I will devour you, and pick my teeth with your bones."

He spun the cylinder of the gun, clicked the safety back on, and slid it into his jacket pocket.

"Good night, children, good night," he said, as if he were quoting someone profound.

Turning, he nudged Harry and they walked back up the aisle to their seats, accompanied by the applause of their small scattering of fellow passengers.

"That was a distraction," he said as they resumed their places.

"Where'd you get the bloody gun?" Harry asked. Nothing Queequeg did could surprise him.

"I am a policeman, Harry. Given what we are up against, I could not afford to get so close to the action without one."

"Do you suppose Tess has one too?"

"Your question is a tautology. To ask it is to prove it is true."

"Of course she does," Harry said. "If that's what she wants."

Queequeg was quiet for awhile, then he asked, "Antepenultimate?"

"Pardon?"

"You said antepenultimate back at Hazlitt's."

"I always wanted to work it into a conversation where it made sense."

"You miss the lecture hall, don't you?"

"Sometimes."

"Intellectuals are expected to play with language."

"Private detectives, not so much."

A conductor approached them from the far end of the car. He asked politely about the gun. Wearing a uniform he had been taken as a figure of authority by the rowdy Oxford ruffians who quietly lodged a complaint.

"A gun, yes, of course," said Queequeg. "I am on an urgent assignment." He showed the official his credentials, which had no validity at all in a British jurisdiction but the man seemed satisfied, chuckled, and departed. The Oxford kids no longer even pretended to be swaggering. They cowered and lined up anxiously when the train pulled into Oxford, debarking before it came to a full stop, then yelling obscenities as they raced to the exit, all except the girl who walked away on her own, rather forlorn.

Harry and Queequeg waited for the slow train from London on its way west to Moreton-in-Marsh. It had left Paddington an hour and a half before theirs but due to the quirky exigencies of British Rail it was now fifteen minutes behind.

In Moreton they stopped in at the Royal Hart for a late supper in front of the open fire, sitting under ubiquitous pictures of horses and dogs in the company of horsey-looking types and dog-fanciers, several of whom had their actual canine companions sprawled on the stone floor at their feet, and then they had the clerk at the desk arrange for a taxi. On the narrow steep roads to Wakefield-super-Vale, the driver talked incessantly and they ignored him until he asked for the exact destination and when they said Wakefield Hall he turned very solemn.

"I don't know as you want to go there gentlemen."

"Why is that?" asked Queequeg. Harry was fascinated by the driver's apparent disinterest in Queequeg's appearance. An English yeoman can be infuriatingly self-possessed, he thought; wonderfully, maddeningly, sure of his own place in the world.

"A person hears rumours, you know. That's where those Scientologists have their commando school. They're going to take over everything. It didn't work out for Adolph, it won't work out for them. Just saying, for what it's worth."

"I think Wakefield Hall is actually an administrative centre for The Church Absolute," said Harry.

"That's right, gov. Abso-bloody-lutely. The administrative centre. They've turned the tennis courts into a landing pad for space ships from their home planet. They say it's a basketball pitch, that's what they say. Maybe not Scientologists but there's talk around The Twisted Anchor that says they'll be killing themselves, and not just there. Better'n taking over, I s'pose. If it's them versus us, let it be them. Mormons, they are, the lot of them."

"You've heard there's going to be a mass suicide, have you?" said Harry, leaning forward in his seat to be heard over the hum of the tires.

"It's common knowledge for those who know it, gov. What you going to do? If they want to create a fuss, like when they burned down those twin towers and blowed up the tube in London, you can't stop them until it's all over. You know what I mean? They're death cults. It's death and sex, just like the Catholics, the Romans, it always is. They're not Hairy Krishnas; they don't have the purple robes."

"Saffron yellow," said Harry.

"What do you know about the death cults?" Queequeg demanded in an urgent tone that transformed their chatter into an interrogation. The headlights of the car behind them glared off the mirror, highlighting the grotesquery of Queequeg's face.

"They say it's the end of the world tomorrow. They're making their final arrangements. I expect you'll want to stay clear."

"On the contrary," said Queequeg. "We wouldn't miss it for anything."

"Are you two gentlemen part of the cults? Like, religious believers. I can respect that, I mean, each to his own, gov. My own brother-in-law belongs to these guys, only he didn't have sufficient funds enough so he won't be dying tonight. Or tomorrow night, I guess it is, since it's pretty much tomorrow already. They call it the Rupture but I expect he'll be down at The Twisted Anchor like he always is." He held his wrist up to the dashboard lights to read his watch. "Yessir, it's already tomorrow and the world hasn't ended as yet so far as we know. The missus will tell me for sure when I get home."

The driver dropped them off, pointing to a call box on a gatepost and offering the admonition to avoid the Rupture if they were inclined to survive. As the taillights flashed and disappeared around a bend, they turned in the icy gloom to confront a huge iron gate that blocked access to a private road leading through sheep-shorn lawns covered in frost, between rows of ancient oaks and past frost-rimed manicured gardens, to a large country house of ochre Cotswold limestone with erratic rooflines and smoke wisping skyward from four separate chimney stacks, and the two men without speaking shared the absurdity of their own amusement at the driver's existential aplomb, given the unknown fate of Tess somewhere within, either as a prisoner, a saboteur, or possibly a corpse, not to mention the fate of twelve thousand lives hanging in the balance while they had not yet formulated a plan.

Harry shuddered, gazing into the depths of the gothic scene before them.

"I don't suppose we ring the call box?"

Queequeg ignored him and stepped into the dark bushes to the side of the gate pillars and proceeded to climb over the high yellow stone wall. For such a large man he was uncommonly agile. Harry leaned his cane in the shadows and clambered after him. He realized he was giddy from lack of sleep and apprehension—not fear. He was not afraid, he was anxious, and he realized he was leaning emotionally on Queequeg, who must have been even more jet-lagged and equally as uneasy but maintained a professional decorum that gave Harry the gravity necessary to focus on what they were trying to do.

As there seemed no alternative and since their presence was likely already known from hidden surveillance cameras, they walked side by side up the road, the burly man with half his face in permanent shadow, the lean resolute man limping beside him. The road was made of stone bricks laid in an intricate pattern to resemble a series of Union Jacks, but which, it occurred to Harry without inspiring amusement, was yellow.

In the dull pool of illumination near the massive front door, Queequeg removed his Smith & Wesson from its holster under his jacket and flicked off the safety. He returned the gun to its sequestered place as the door opened before they had knocked.

A tall thin man with a cadaverous complexion, wearing a thin gold necklace from which was suspended an inscribed golden medallion, with thin eyebrows and a fringe of colourless hair opened the door, squinted at them, and asked what they wanted, as if they might have been door-to-door proselytes for a competing religion.

"We're here to see Pietro di Cosmos II," said Queequeg, moving into the light of the large foyer, with Harry beside him, forcing the sallow functionary to take several steps back.

"Ah, yes, I will tell him you are here, Mr. Queequeg."

Harry did a double take. Lurch, here, knows Queequeg. What the Hell was going on?

"Queequeg?"

"Harry."

"Theophil!" Another tall lean man with perfect posture and a raffish smile, dressed impeccably in an Armani suit and wearing a silk ascot but mercifully no jewellery, called out to Harry's companion. "Theophil Queequeg, it is so very good to meet you at last. And this is Professor Lindstrom? How are you Harry?"

"Mr. Severence, I presume."

"I am Thomas called Pietro, as they say."

Harry turned to Queequeg; shocked, incredulous, baffled, deeply disappointed, enraged. He said, as if they were alone in the room, "My friend, my good friend Theophil, you two-faced bastard, you delivered me up on a platter?"

"I did, I suppose."

"My God," said Harry. "I have been a fool, haven't I?"

"You have been, and you're not the first. If you'll excuse me, I'm tired, I think I'll just go to my room. Your Holiness?"

"Of course."

Harry glared at Severence: his captor, Queequeg's host.

"Where's Tess?"

"A good question, Professor. You should retire, of course, Theophil. You will need to be rested. Tomorrow is rapidly closing in."

"Like the 'dreadful darkness,'" snapped Harry, glowering at Queequeq who flipped a medallion on a gold necklace from under his shirt so it gleamed in the artificial light and smiled in return.

"'What shall it profit a man, if he gains the whole world—'" said Harry.

"'...pay one for another, that ye may be healed. The prayer of a righteous man availeth much.' *Book of Job*. You may have turned from God, Harry, but the words are still there, if not precisely as quoted."

"They're like shadows of a ghost with nothing to cast them," said Harry.

"I'm glad to see you two have such esoteric rapport," said Pietro di Cosmos. "I rather wish you were on our side, Dr. Lindstrom."

"Sometimes it is easier to understand a monster than his maker," said Harry. He glowered at Severence. "You don't really interest me." He turned back to Queequeg. "Do you get to die?" he demanded as the big Polynesian followed the cadaverous man called Benson and moved towards the marble staircase in front of them. "Or just to wallow in the wealth left behind."

"The latter, Harry. I've seen too much of death already. Good night, my friend. Perhaps I will see you in the morning."

Harry watched silently as Queequeg ascended the staircase, huge and hunched over like a beast in a fantasy, and when the Marquesian looked back the intricately tattooed side of his face projected sheer monstrous evil. As Tom Severence tilted his head slightly in Harry's direction, indicating where he wished Harry to move, his face by contrast was flawless in the way that only the most expensive of treatments can manage. The creases around his eyes gave an indication of how old he was, in middling years, but otherwise he might have been ageless. When he smiled his teeth were excessively perfect and his shock of silver hair gave the impression of being not so much brushed as arranged. In his dark blue evening suit and white shirt with the paisley ascot, he looked like the epitome of gracious benevolence, the personification of goodness and enlightenment, the agent of expiation and redemption, the bringer of hope and transcendence.

Harry entered the embracing gloom of a large library with Tom Severence moving forward to indicate in front of a grate-fire two leather wing-backed chairs facing each other, one of which Harry was to sit in while he sat in the other.

"So," said Severence. "Let the interrogation begin. Would you like a drink?" He got up and walked to an ancient sideboard and poured them both stiff drinks of Bruichladdich Octomore. The peat smoke aroma filled the room. "A good scotch," he said. "I prefer Cutty Sark, myself. As an American I'd rather have bourbon. I suppose you prefer Canadian rye whiskey."

"No," said Harry.

"Ah, Professor Lindstrom, you must not sulk. You feel betrayed by your friends, of course. Dr. Izett has disappeared. I assure you I don't know where she has got to. If you do, it would be advisable to tell me. And Mr. Queequeg has given you up in a most foul and unforgivable way. He is a monster, indeed. I am perhaps your only friend left."

Harry took a long slow drink of scotch and for want of a coaster held the glass in his hand instead of placing it down on the table between them.

"I have a few questions," said Severence. "But first, you have something of mine. It would be most impolite not to return it."

"The money?"

"Ah, yes, how crass, the money. Your friend seems to have set you up with sole authority to redistribute much of my funds in the event of her own demise, which I assure you is imminent. Or of mine, which I assure you is not."

"And if I don't wish to give it up?"

"Is money worth dying for, Harry? No matter how much?"

"It seems worth killing for, no matter how many."

"I intend to kill no one. A few of my followers choose to die. Some of my people, Lord knows, not me, have provided the means."

"They will be tracked down."

"No matter. If they seize the opportunity to die along with the others, as is their right, their duty, and their privilege, they cannot be held accountable."

"You can be. Charles Manson was convicted of murder and he was at home when his victims died."

"I have better lawyers, excellent connections, more money."

"Not from me. You won't get the money from me."

"Then your death is also imminent. Or worse, I shall have you so exquisitely tortured you would throw your own mother onto the flames."

"Too late, she was cremated."

"And your children, were they cremated?"

"Fuck you."

"And your wife, Karen?"

"What about her?"

"Do you believe she is ashes as well, or fish pellets, perhaps. Ah, you flinch. I know much about you Harry. Your dead are your weakness. And your wife, is she dead, can you be sure? It is too horrible, not knowing, is it not?"

Karen was dead, he had her ring, he talked to her ghost, his kids were dead. Their ashes were buried. How could his dead be used against him? Like a sharp stick prodding an open sore.

Severence leaned forward and handed Harry a framed photograph. Matt and Lucy. Harry's stomach heaved upwards against his lungs, he struggled to breathe, his heart jerked in a series of spasmodic explosions.

He struggled to speak. "Take your damned money. Let them live."

"They are dead already, are they not?"

"I mean the twelve thousand!"

"Without their ascension, there is no money, or at least it would soon be rescinded. I'm afraid you will have to cooperate."

"Not while Tess is alive. You need our signatures together."

"Yes, that is true. She is the Antichrist in our little scenario."

"Making you Christ, I presume? Even William Saintsbury didn't aspire so high."

"And William is dead. His widow lives, like most of us, under a number of guises. Call her what you will, she is my adversary. She threatens to bring down The Church Absolute. She is the embodiment of Lucifer, the Lord Satan made flesh, the Devil Incarnate." Severence stopped, he seemed to recognize that Harry had provoked him into ranting. "It is necessary, Professor Lindstrom, if she appears on this planet, that she be cast in that light. If she has fled into oblivion, that is good, but I imagine she is at this very moment scheming about how to bring an end to the Rapture and, of course, to me."

"Unless you have captured her already and are keeping her hidden until after the madness to pit us against each other. But trust me, her commitment wouldn't waver at seeing me tortured."

"Ah, if I had her I would happily test your premise. I do not, or at this very moment we would be busy in a darker part of my castle. *She* might not break to save you, Harry, but *you* would break to save her. You would sign, she would die. My funds would be, as they say, unencumbered."

"And what if you don't catch her, what if I don't break?"

"Catch her we will. She cannot remain in hiding, not if there's a chance she could extinguish the Rapture. And as for breaking, I guarantee that you will. Emotional arithmetic, Harry. You did *not* save your wife, therefore you *will* save your friend. It is a simple equation."

"Twelve thousand lives versus one."

"Two small children, you let them die. And your wife, you let her go."

"You know nothing about her, about us."

"Your beloved Karen."

"Fuck you."

"Yes, perhaps, but meanwhile, I think you should spend some time on your own, contemplating the end." He picked up a small silver bell and gave it a brisk shake. The thin man with the cadaverous face appeared from a side door hidden among the vast display of books and waited for instructions.

"Good night, Harry. I trust you will sleep well."

Harry was led to a comfortable room furnished in much the manner of the suites at Hazlitt's Hotel in Soho. Left on his own, he explored and found the windows barred, the doors locked, and escape impossible. In the bathroom, there were all the toiletry accoutrements he could need and flannel pyjamas in his size.

It occurred to him that he could flood the toilet and force them to open the door, but then what? Or he might start a fire, but he might immolate or suffocate before anyone responded. He could break the window glass and shout into the empty night, but the bars would prevent his escape and he would likely die of frostbite or hypothermia. He had a hot shower, a late-night shave because it made him feel better, slipped on the warm pyjamas, and crawled under linen sheets, pulled up the goosedown duvet, and fell abruptly into a dark and dreamless sleep.

24 THE END OF THE WORLD

HARRY WOKE IN THE GRIP OF TERROR. IT IMPALED HIS innards with shards of unbearable pain. He could not think straight or comprehend his own feelings. His friend Queequeg had betrayed him, his friend Tess had abandoned him. He desperately wanted to hear Karen's voice but she had faded into sorrowful oblivion. In the vacuum she left behind, he could hear Friedrich Nietzsche extolling over and over, to live is to suffer, to endure is to find meaning in the suffering. But there was no meaning in all of this, only emotion. He was desperately alone and vulnerable, yet as he came back into himself he felt rage, not fear, righteous determination to raise hell in The Church Absolute, horror that he might be able to do nothing, dizzying confidence that he could.

A soft knock on the door preceded the entry of the cadaverous Benson who set down a breakfast tray on a oak side table and drew open the thick velvet drapes, letting a brilliant cascade of sunlight flood into the room. Harry squinted, looking at his watch. It was almost noon.

"His Holiness left instructions you are to be well fed. If you would like anything more, please ring. There is a bell by the bed and I will be outside the door. If you try to escape, I have been instructed in the name of Sister Celestial to shoot you dead and I am carrying this weapon for that purpose." He flourished a snub-nosed pistol. "It is an English breakfast, of course. Fried tomatoes, blood pudding, two eggs poached to a chalky consistency, and cold toast saturated with gelled butter. I hope you enjoy." The cadaverous man giggled and withdrew from the room, locking the door behind him.

Harry ate what he could and dressed. He stood at the window. The sun had burned off the frost and the green of the lawns and the gardens glistened. He watched various minions moving about the estate. Some poked with rakes at frozen mounds of dry leaves, some wore flack-jackets with AK-47s strapped across their backs, a few wore business suits. Just as he started to turn away, a flurry outside drew his attention. A Rolls Royce Phantom Coupé the colour of polished ebony pulled up beneath his window. A small entourage moved from the house to the opened door with Tom Severence at the centre. He shook hands all around, beamed an infectious smile, and slid his well-dressed carefully maintained body into the leather and walnut interior. The door closed, the chauffeur got in, and the car rolled gently around the drive and down the lane, disappearing from Harry's view beneath clouds of soft dead oak leaves still clinging to their places in the sky.

Harry was puzzled. Clearly Severence, or Pietro di Cosmos II, was leaving on a journey of significant import to be bid such an elaborate farewell by his staff.

Harry waited until his breakfast tray was taken away, then holding an antique boot-horn that had been resting against the fireplace he paced the room, examining the ancient oak floorboards, even looking under the rugs, until he found a narrow crack sufficiently wide to jam the silver end of the horn between them. He prodded this way and that until a board came loose. He removed a slat from under his mattress and used it to pry the board free. He lifted several more boards until there was a gap wide enough to lean through between joists and reach the underside of the ceiling of the room below.

He had calculated that he was directly over the library, which he knew was Severence's *sanctum sanctorum* and not likely to be entered if the owner were absent. Lowering himself feet-down between two hand-hewn joists, he touched his shoes to the plaster and lathe, then bent his legs up and plunged his feet forcefully against the ceiling. He could hear crumbling plaster but the lathe strapping held. He cocked his legs and plunged again. More crumbling. The third time, sections of lathe gave way and slabs of plaster plummeted onto the fine Heriz carpet below, leaving Harry dangling through, his feet still eight or ten feet from the floor.

He released his grip from a joist, hung by one hand as he cleared shattered wood and plaster with the other to enlarge the hole, then released his hold and tumbled through, landing on the floor with a crash that left him sprawling amidst the debris. Rising unsteadily to his feet, he stared straight into the eyes of Queequeg who sat a leather wingback with his Smith & Wesson revolver in his hand, watching with a benevolent grin.

"So far, so good," said Queequeg.

Harry wiped plaster dust from his eyes and glared, then noticed the other man's finger was not on the trigger. "Have you seen my cane?" Harry asked with feigned nonchalance.

"Good to connect again, Harry. You know we're still on the same side, don't you?" Queequeg's smile faded and his grim countenance grew mournful. "I seem to have been locked into this elegant room. Your escape is ingenious but as in *Le Compte de Monte-Cristo* you have gone from one prisoner's cell to another. And my weapon has been decommissioned. They removed most of the bullets but left one in the chamber, giving me the suicide option. They didn't expect you to drop in but it could do for both of us, I suppose, if we stand very close."

Wit under extreme duress is the sign of a truly brave and brilliant man. Or not. "If I can break into your cell, we can break out. What about the windows?"

"Locked and barred."

"So why you? I thought they believed you were one of theirs."

"I seem to have disabused them of the notion, my friend, when I tried to execute the boss."

"His Holiness?"

"I shot him three times. Turns out, he sleeps in a different room each night. There are twenty-seven bedrooms in this place, and someone else sleeps as a decoy in all but a few. I killed the wrong man."

"He's left, you know. I watched from my window." Harry gestured to the hole in the ceiling.

"He has to come back," said Queequeg. "It's in the script, the master text. We will need to be ready."

"And how can we do that?"

"Not sure just yet. Perhaps we pray."

"No" said Harry emphatically. "We don't give up."

"Don't be tiresome. Sometimes a euphemism is also a metaphor. We focus, we contemplate our options."

"Sorry."

"And don't be Presbyterian. Is there anyone who says *sorry* more than a Presbyterian Canadian? God save us. Where's Tess? You don't think they got her at Hazlitt's?"

"The room was too orderly. I saw her go in. She slipped out on her own."

"What about the missing German?"

Harry had to think for a moment, then realized Queequeg meant the Austrian clerk who had gone off to Vienna.

"Maybe he really had urgent family business, especially if he were an Absolutist, or, more likely, Tess paid him off or threatened him. She needed complete invisibility."

"Which meant going without us?"

"You are far from invisible," said Harry.

"And you blend in like a hockey player on a cricket pitch."

"Have you seen my cane?"

"Actually, I have. It's in the corner. Someone must have brought it in from the gate."

Harry walked over to the darkest corner of the room and retrieved his cane. He rubbed the silver band against his sleeve and admired the shine.

"You're sure he's not got her already?" said Queequeg.

"Absolutely not, or we'd know it."

"You think so?"

"If she was close by, he would be dead."

"You have a great deal of confidence in her."

"I do."

"Then where is she? Where did he go?"

"They're both in London," said Harry. "He's not coming back."

"Explain?"

"We have come to the wrong place, Theo. We came to Wakefield Hall to get Severence. She is waiting in London for him to come to her."

"How do you figure that, my friend?"

"I just did," he responded. "What time is it?"

"Going on to three-thirty."

"There isn't much time left. We've got to get there."

"Where, Harry, where are you talking about? You must explain. I need to understand if we are to do this together."

"You were willing to sacrifice my life."

"Yes, yes, it was a means to get in and it almost worked. And you are alive, you have descended from the Heavens, now explain."

"'Where the eternal and the infinite meet.'"

"What eternal, what infinite?"

"There's only one of each. Severence told her that was where he would be for the Rapture, directing the entire show."

"What the hell are you talking about?"

"The prime meridian, O degrees latitude, 360 degrees, it's all the same thing. Infinity. And at the stroke of midnight, the precise theoretical instant between one day and the next, there is no time, it collapses, there is only forever. It is the eternal moment. It's a puzzle, don't you see?"

"I do, actually."

"The Mothership of The Church Absolute is moored directly off the old tea clipper, the Cutty Sark, in Greenwich on the Thames, right smack on the prime meridian. That's where Tess will be waiting, that's where Severence will be going."

"Are you sure?"

"No. I've never enjoyed puzzles."

The burly man with the bisected face stared at Harry with a mixture of incredulity and admiration. Harry stared back with affection and regret. He was a philosopher manqué, burdened by his imagined inability to convert the cerebral to action. He toyed with his cane.

Theophil Queequeg rose in a cumbersome mass to his feet. Only then did Harry realize he'd been beaten, probably with blows to the kidneys. There was a thin strand of blood around his neck where The Church medallion had been ripped away before he was locked into the Severence library with a single bullet and a welter of books to provide him an ironically humane exit. Severence was not without a sense of humour.

"You have given me an idea, Harry. If you can break through a ceiling, together we can walk through the walls. Such barriers are merely conventions, n'est ce pas?"

He pushed on the door. It was solid oak. He reached behind the books on one side of the door, tapped lightly, then reached through on the other side and tapped again.

"Here," he said. He handed Harry a stack of leather-bound books. "Put them over there. We do not want to cause damage to such wonderful things."

Together, they emptied rows of books and removed shelves until there was a space on the bare wall roughly the shape of a small door.

Queequeg looked around and spotted a pair of sturdy wrought-iron fire tongs. He brought them to the wall, cocked his arms, and jammed the tongs with explosive force into the plaster. Harry pulled slabs away. Queequeg kept prodding and poking until he had broken through between two studs and forced holes through the plaster and lathe on the far side of the wall. Queequeg kicked out the last few pieces and stepped through with Harry following close behind.

They were met by several Church functionaries who seemed not in the least alarmed by their unorthodox entry into the grand foyer and only a little interested. A man with an expressionless face confronted them with an AK-47. Queequeg levelled his revolver at the man's head and fired. The man's body collapsed to the floor. Queequeg slowly waved his Smith & Wesson across the room. The others simply dropped their weapons and walked away. Harry picked up a couple of assault rifles but exchanged them for two heavy coats from a cloakroom on the way to the garage where they commandeered a 1930 Rolls Royce Phantom II open roadster with a body of solid copper burnished to perfection. They drove down the driveway. No one made a move to stop them. When they reached the yellow stone wall, the iron gates were open. They pulled out onto the main road and were on their way in their open car through Swindon to London on the M4. It was now just past 6:00 pm and a few stars were struggling to pick their way through the bone-chilling darkness.

In a stretch of open fields before the villages and estates closed in on the highway, their car coughed and came to a halt.

They walked to a roadside call box. Queequeg returned to the car, which still radiated a modicum of engine heat into the open interior, while Harry called and was eventually connected with a Rolls Royce representative.

"I'm sorry, sir," said an officious voice of indeterminate gender, addressing Harry as if he were a lord of the realm despite his subversive accent. "Rolls Royce automobiles as you know do not break down."

"But ours has," he protested.

"Perhaps you are out of petrol."

"Full tank."

"Gasoline?"

"Full tank."

"Do you have the top securely fastened?"

"We couldn't get it up."

"Perhaps you are frozen."

"We bloody well are, but that wouldn't make the car stop, would it?"

"It might, sir. You have told me the model. Can you give me your name?"

"It's not registered in my name."

"Are you the chauffeur?"

"No, I'm not the bloody chauffeur."

"Have you stolen the car, sir?"

"Yes, of course."

"Well, that explains it, sir. The legal owner has installed a mechanism to bring the car to a halt after fifty miles without the appropriate password. Do you have the password, sir?"

"There's no bloody computer," Harry protested. "It's a 1930s car."

"There is a computer, sir. I assure you. I am checking my records. Is the car clad in copper?"

"Yes, it is."

"Pure copper?"

"How the hell should I—yes, it is."

"It belongs to a religious organization. It needs a password. How could you steal from a religious organization, sir?"

"Thanks for your help," said Harry. "We'll just muddle on."

"I think you should return the automobile to its God-given owners sir. That would be the right thing to do."

"Thank you for your help."

"Thank you for calling sir."

Harry returned to Queequeg who seemed diminutive huddled inside his coat and otherworldly, peering up at him with his bifurcated face strangely illuminated from below by the purple dashboard lights. "We need a password," he said.

"You're not serious?"

"Apparently I am," said Harry. "The monster needs coaxing."

"Then let us coax," said Queequeg.

The onboard computer was in plain view, disguised as part of a retrofitted mobile phone console.

"Try punching in God," said Harry.

"I think not, old chap. Try Rapture."

Harry punched in Rapture, then Cosmos, then Severence. An ignition light flashed. They started and drove on to a country pub where they stopped for a quick bite and warmed themselves by an open fire. As soon as they started up again, Harry driving, they settled down into their stolen coats with the sleeves pulled over their hands, and nearly froze until they hit urban congestion, which slowed them down and warmed them with the cold light shining from street lamps and through frosted windows.

At 10:45 they hit a roadblock along the south bank of the Thames as they came into Greenwich.

A policeman informed them there was a commotion ahead of some sort and when Harry refused to be re-routed after Queequeg showed the bobby his credentials, he was motioned to a parking spot on a lane by a pub called the Jolly Miller. He cut through the lane and down side streets until he reached the A2, then circled Greenwich Park and cut back along the edge of the Old Royal Naval College until he found a gap off Hamilton Road where he left the Rolls parked illegally. They walked rapidly down to within sight of the Cutty Sark, guided by floodlights raking the sky. It must have seemed like a replay of the Blitz, Harry thought, then wondered if there was anyone alive old enough to remember.

"It looks like she made it," said Harry.

"You're sure this is her? It's a big day for The Church—it may just be devotional showmanship, if you'll excuse the oxymoron."

"I think Severence would have preferred mass hysteria to be private."

"Which is equally paradoxical, Harry. Look, look out on the water."

They had come around a corner and cut across a bizarre dry dock structure meant to create the illusion that the Cutty Sark was at sea while simultaneously allowing tourists to walk around her below the waterline. Between her spars and ropes he could see the rigging of another tall ship with furled sails moored less than a hundred feet offshore, facing prow-on into a ripping tidal current. It was the *Teegeeack*, Mothership of The Church Absolute. The entire vessel was illuminated with searchlights streaming from the shore. Harry glanced at Queequeg who had moved out of the shadows into the glare. Despite the Polynesian designs in bold strokes of gold leaf where the name was inscribed on the transom and aft of the figurehead, he realized his Marquesian friend must know she was named in homage to the foundation planet, Teegeeack, in L. Ron Hubbard's madly inspired mythic origins of Scientology. William Alexander Saintsbury as Pietro di Cosmos, the Founder of The Church Absolute and lately the personage himself of their multivariate and indivisible God, was brilliantly eclectic in his borrowings. Harry was reminded that the Rapture, with all its horrors and outrageous intentions, was the Founder's idea—the man Tess had married and murdered.

The two men moved closer through the gathered throng to the edge of the wharf when a collective murmur drew their attention to movement high in the Mothership's rigging. A pair of diminutive figures had emerged into the glare from a swarm of shadows close to the foremast and lowered themselves down from the crow's-nest platform onto the main foresail yard before easing themselves farther down onto a footrope strung underneath. The first, an awkward figure edging tentatively forward and the other moving with the grace and assurance of an aerial gymnast. The two of them grasped the spar at waist level and edged away from the mast until the first reached a vertical jackstay joining the end of the yardarm to the one above it. He hesitated, then climbed in slow motion back onto the spar itself. She followed, reaching up for balance and grasping a curiously knotted rope hanging down from the spar overhead. She grasped another hanging rope and placed its gaping noose over the man's head and drew it snug. He let go of the jackstay and grasped at the rope shank above the back of his neck. She settled the noose she had been holding for balance around her own head and appeared to draw it tight against the nape of her neck.

They had edged well beyond the deck and stood high over thin layers of scrim ice and patches of black open water gleaming like a shattered mirror far below them. Limned by the floodlights against the yellowish brown urban sky, like a night-time landscape by Turner, they were two precise figures caught in the centre of subliminal stillness.

Harry had to force himself to breathe. He felt the profound urge to swim out but Queequeg grasped his arm in an iron grip.

"Don't be absurd, Harry. There's nothing you could do. We are witnesses. That's all we can be. That's all we can do."

Without taking his eyes off Tess, Harry slumped into himself, shivering from the cold and from impotent rage. People around them were watching close-ups on laptops and smartphones. Someone, somehow, was reporting on the scene, using a telephoto lens, and the reception was excellent, the details precise.

"Let me see," he demanded and a young couple, seeing Queequeg loom monstrously behind him, relinquished their screen.

"Just for a moment," the young woman said.

Harry and Queequeg held the machine close in their own shadows to cut the glare.

"Do you see that?" said Harry. "The nooses. The ropes holding them steady, they're hangman's knots."

"Inevitably," said Queequeg.

"Let us see," said the girl. "They're religious nutters. We need to see."

"Thank you," said Queequeg and handed her their machine. "Very kind."

Harry turned to Queequeg and gazed into his eyes. "They're going to hang," he said. "They're going to fall. They'll drown under the ice."

"Yes," said Queequeg, "I think they are. Perhaps we should leave."

As Queequeg led him away from the edge, Harry looked back. The floodlights were no longer sweeping the sky. Their beams had converged on the two small figures balanced precariously over the ebbing flow of the Thames with only nooses to keep them from falling. He wanted to call out to her. She would never hear him over the rumble of the throng.

They approached a police van. Queequeg talked to someone and they were invited in. No one wanted to offend a French gendarme with such a ferociously formidable presence. They hardly noticed Harry at all.

Suddenly, Harry became aware of Tess's voice. She and Severence were both wired for sound. Harry crowded closer to the monitor. Her voice cut out.

"Can't get it," said a technician. "It's blocked."

"The hell," said another. "We just heard her."

"Mate," said another, "We're the lady's backup. She's reaching out to her people and we're waving flags to get their attention."

Harry could see Tess was talking. It was 11:57 pm. He watched her lips move, thought he could see her eyes flash. She tossed her head several times, keeping her black hair from her face. He could have sworn she smiled. She was poised on the spar with her fingers hardly touching the rope around her neck hanging down from above.

She turned to look at the man.

She reached out and adjusted his noose, then drew her own snug. Severence clutched his rope, trying to coil it around his frozen fingers, trying vainly to pull it away from his throat.

Something slipped from her hand. It glistened in the floodlights as it fell. There was a violent explosion as it hit the scrim ice. For a moment the tremors echoed, smoke and flames billowed briefly and were squelched by the sprayed water and particles of blasted ice.

Harry watched her speak silently into the night, looking straight ahead, and then she paused, as if listening. The crowd who had been excited, even festive, fell deathly quiet.

Astute observers in London well know, the first bong of Big Ben on the hour comes a fraction of a second before the other bells of the city join in and can be heard on a clear cold evening as far away as the shores of Greenwich. Everyone was listening. Suddenly the silence exploded with a dull thunderous clang, pursued by clarion chimes and reverberations as the sky on the prime meridian filled with the clamorous sounds of midnight.

Harry stared at the police monitor, he seemed to have stepped out of time. As he watched her face, his emotions filled in details obscured and distorted by the electronic image. He knew he was where the infinite and eternal converge and he felt utterly empty, depleted, no longer himself.

Bells and chimes still shook the air as Tess leaned forward, commanding the attention of Severence who appeared terrified but somehow hopeful, as if their performance was over, and he could soon stand down. Tess herself looked beatific in the dazzling light against the angry dark yellowish sky. Her black hair lifted away from her face in the ice cold breeze. Her deep eyes opened wide and she smiled. Then gently, carefully, she reached out to Severence, took his hand, tilted her head as if sniffing the sea breeze, and together they stepped into the air.

Their bodies plummeted forward, for an instant he clutched at his rope, they both jerked upright as the nooses twisted their necks straight, their arms flailed, and for a moment they dandled like puppets. The man's body swayed foolishly in the bitter cold breeze. Beside him a single rope snapped and the woman plunged through the dazzling air down against shattering ice and disappeared into the dark murky waters of the Thames. Searchlights swept the surface, revealing bleak swirling reflections, holes torn into shreds of darkness as the water and ice twisted slowly in the current.

Harry turned away and walked out into the night. When Queequeg caught up to him, he was quietly weeping.

"She stopped it, Harry."

His huge friend draped an arm over Harry's shoulders. Harry looked up. Queequeg's eyes glistened against the darkness of his own skin, of the night, of the world.

Tess, Harry thought. Words failed him. He wanted Karen for comfort, she was gone.

Tess, her name rolled like distant thunder. She was gone.

25 STITCH IN TIME

TESS SAINTSBURY TURNED AWAY FROM HARRY AS HE lingered at the door of his room. She used a master key to open the Theresa Cornelys Suite and stepped into the small vestibule, closed the door, and leaned for a few minutes with her forehead against the painted molding of the frame before quietly slipping back into the hall. She followed the charming concatenation of stairways and corridors to an outside exit at the back of the conjoined buildings, which opened onto an obscured lane. She hurried down the lane to Frith Street, well below Hazlitt's main entrance, turned and walked rapidly to Old Compton Street, across to Wardour, then down and across to Coventry, which led into Piccadilly Circus. She stopped inside the lobby of the Ripley's Believe It or Not! museum where she had a clear view up Shaftsbury Avenue and over to the midwinter diehards loitering under the statue of Eros. When she was sure she hadn't been followed she moved quickly through a single lane of traffic and descended into the labyrinthine caverns of the Piccadilly Circus tube station.

She got off at Knightsbridge and left through the Harrods exit, walked along Brompton Road and down into Beaufort Gardens, a street with a tree-lined boulevard down the centre. She took the left side and walked to a small hotel near the end. When she stopped to pick up her key at the desk, the concierge informed her that a number of parcels had been delivered and he had taken the liberty of putting them in her room. She thanked him and ascended the stairs that had been annoyingly narrowed when an elevator was installed.

"Good night Miss Montagne," he called after her. He pronounced it *mon-tan*.

"Good night, Mr. Shimkovitz," she called back. "Thanks for your help." She paused. "If I have to leave early, bill my card and forward my receipt to Toronto."

"Of course, Miss Montagne, good night."

Mr. Shimkovitz turned off the lights over the desk. It was dark outside although it was still early evening. The hotel's few other occupants were permanent guests with keys of their own.

In her small suite of rooms on the third floor, Tess placed the new deliveries beside myriad other packages in discrete anonymous piles on the spare bed. She moved a large black empty tuba case up onto the bed she'd been using.

After standing back and doing a mental inventory, she unwrapped everything. She hoisted a large cylinder of oxygen-enriched air into the empty tuba case and assembled first and second stage scuba regulators onto a buoyancy vest, which she packed in, along with a folded black drysuit, some black Scubapro fins, a low profile black mask, and a couple of weight pouches. She thought better of the weights and placed the pouches into the bottom of a large nondescript handbag. She picked up a small heavy box labelled magnets, checked the contents, walked to the radiator below the window overlooking Beaufort Gardens, set the box against the radiator and flicked a toggle switch. The magnet box clanked against the iron and when she yanked hard she couldn't break contact. She flicked the switch off and returned the box to her workspace on the bed, secured it in a small waterproof bag with straps, making sure she could access the toggle through the rubberized material, and lowered the unit into her handbag. She scrunched up a set of long thermal underwear and pushed it into the space beside the magnet.

She sat down on the edge of her bed and picked up a bundle of 3/8" 3-strand manila hemp rope. She measured out two pieces to precise lengths, and with practised expertise she manipulated the end of one into a hangman's noose with exactly thirteen coils, the number reputed to snap the neck rather than strangle through slippage. Then she tied the other piece, which was slightly longer with the same number of coils, the traditional thirteen, but before drawing the knot tight she inserted a small steel blade against the straight length and kinked the coils around it so that the weight of a falling object would sever the hemp if applied precisely on a perpendicular bias.

She placed the two nooses in a small dry sack and set it in her handbag, along with a snub-nosed baby Glock pistol, which she removed from a discreetly festive bag labelled Fortnum and Mason and marked 'fragile.' She stripped the wrapping from a small box bearing an Amsterdam shipping label and removed an ornate silver lipstick and a thick matching compact. She twisted the top off the lipstick tube and sniffed, then dropped it into a metallic bronze clutch purse. She slid a broad elastic band over the compact and placed it in the purse, along with a disposable cell phone. She gathered up a few other things, including a pair of soft-soled slippers and a seasonally inappropriate pair of metallic bronze high-heeled strappy sandals along with a down-filled crushable vest reduced to the size of a teacup, and placed them with the purse in a different dry bag, which she sealed and also put in her large handbag.

Tess sat down at a small table and using the hotel stationary she penned a note to Harry. She paused several times to make sure of her words, and signed off With Love, Tess. She sealed the envelop, addressed it to his condo in Toronto, and affixed a stamp, which had been laid by for the purpose.

She walked into the bathroom and removed her new Suunto dive computer from her toiletry kit, set it on the vanity, and took off her Raymond Weil watch, which she left with a note for Mr. Shimkovitz, expressing her thanks.

She showered and put on expensive sheer underwear and black pearl studs in her ears, then a form-hugging 3 ml neoprene bodysuit with three-quarter arms and legs, followed by loose-fitting Caren Shen pants in a pleated synthetic and a matching soft-shouldered free-form jacket, both with a striking iridescent copper sheen.

She contemplatively rubbed her fingers over the faded scar on the back of her right hand and secured her dive computer high on her other wrist so it did not show beneath the folds of her jacket sleeve, hoisted her heavy handbag onto her shoulder, and rolled her tuba case out to the elevator, which she took to the first floor and exited the building without attracting attention.

On Brompton Road she hailed a taxi to the South Bank, the Wibbly Wobbly pub on Rainbow Quay. The cabbie helped her load and unload the tuba case. She asked him to mail her letter to Harry and tipped him generously. In the shadows by a jetty she slipped on her thermal underwear over her Caren Shen outfit and sealed up her drysuit, assembled her dive gear, attaching low pressure hoses to her suit and her BCD, adjusted her weights and attached the electromagnetic unit securely. She gathered her dry bags in a large net bag, then sat on the jetty to put on her fins and mask and kicking a jagged opening in the shore ice she dropped down into the black water and disappeared.

She remained a body's length below the surface, breathing in a slow deliberate rhythm, and with gloved hands clasped loosely in front of her, propelled herself with unhurried strokes of her fins. She was able to follow the lights along the quay, counting off the bridges and overpasses and boats moored at the edge. It was 8:15 pm by the time she swam out into the Thames. The tide was just beginning to ebb but the current was powerful enough to sweep her out away from the shore and she let herself drift in its grasp until it thrust her shoreward again where the river swung down into Greenwich before it veered to the north. As the icy waters carried her along, the city lights flared above her in greens and oranges and purples in a panoply of ghoulish and gothic discolouration.

Judging her free-floating progress by depth and direction in the sheer black water, which from the surface had a sheen like crushed foil, as she anticipated she was soon sweeping past a vast curved hull that had to be the *Teegeeack*, the Mothership of The Church Absolute. She kicked powerfully against the flow that dragged her downriver while feeling for the toggle on the magnet and with a wild series of thrusts she lunged forward and slapped the magnet against the steel plate of the rudder, and hung on, heaving for breath.

The ship was a restored square rigger with a teak hull clad in an alloy of copper and zinc, but with steel and iron around the steering mechanism. Although equipped with powerful auxiliary engines, she was a wind machine to the core, deep hulled and as sleek as the Cutty Sark in dry-dock close by. She was also the communications centre of the entire Church Absolute establishment, easily sailed out of jurisdictional limits, undetected by the sound of engines if necessary. Her electronics were *avant-garde* in the literal sense. Her security systems made her virtually impregnable.

Tess slipped out of her BCD harness and taking a final deep breath before leaving her dive gear attached securely to the rudder plate she swam to the surface with her dry bags, kicking vigorously to propel herself into the lee of the stern. She dropped her fins, mask, and computer into the depths, then hauled herself up onto the deck using the elaborate wood brightwork on the transom and taffrail for handholds. The sounds of the *Teegeeack*'s staff and crew indicated they were gathered along the port side, vigilant against intruders arriving in boats from the shore. A few looked occasionally to starboard but the river was wide and swollen with ice chunks and as the ebb-tide increased it was turbulent. There were pings now and then echoing through the ship of alarms set off by ice hitting the hull. No one was on watch in the bow or the stern, since invaders would necessarily approach off the beam.

Tess scooted into a shadowy alcove where she made a neat pile of her remaining gear. She removed the manila ropes from their bag, opened the nooses sufficiently to drape them over her shoulder, and crept through the shadows on the shadowy starboard side to the foremast ratlines and still in her black drysuit she climbed to the fore lower topsail yard, where she edged along the footrope past the foremast over to the outer end of the spar above the security people gathered on the port side below. Supporting herself against the vertical jackstay running between the outermost ends of the yards, she tied her two ropes securely and dropped the nooses to within reach of the larger foresail yardarm.

Returning in the darkness to the alcove near the stern, she peeled off her drysuit and thermal underwear, dropped them overboard, donned her high heeled sandals, and tucked her snub-nose Glock 26 under her waistband, doing up the jacket to conceal the bulge. She removed the bronze coloured clutch purse from the dry bag, which she discarded, sprayed on a touch of lavender perfume, shook out her hair, and stepped into the open. She walked forward towards the light, heels clacking on the teak deck, until someone noticed her and shouted. Others shouted, there was much scurrying about, with AK-47s covering her from every aspect.

She stood still. She had to sneeze but resisted. Severence appeared.

"Tom," she said.

"Mary. I've been expecting you. And still, I am surprised. You look lovely, how did you do it?"

"Good taste. And money."

"How did you get on board?"

"Walked on water. It's easier if it's frozen."

Seeming unable to resist, Severence looked out to the open water on either side of the ship.

"You invariably surprise by doing the impossible," he said. "Which is predictable, of course. It becomes tedious after awhile."

"I will try to be less obvious in future, Tom. Or would you prefer I call you Pietro since I am here to deal with you as the head of The Church?"

"To *deal* with me? How quaint. You have enough bullets aimed at your body to turn it into a collapsible sieve."

"But of course you can't shoot me, Tom. I am Sister Mary Celestial. I have died at least once already. This time it's your turn."

A few audible gasps, followed by murmurs of wonder and confusion emerged from the henchmen and acolytes surrounding them. Devotees had been conditioned to the point of paranoia, but their fears had not been refined. They knew dangers from outside were ranged against them, but from whom exactly and towards whom precisely they were uncertain. And she was not an outsider; she was one of them.

"Shall we go in out of the cold?" Severence said. "Please, this way, you have not seen the old scow since she's been done over."

They stepped through a heavily carved doorway and abruptly the world transformed. Outside, the ship was a model of meticulous restoration, as had been directed by her husband, the original Pietro di Cosmos. Inside, it was now self-consciously postmodern, with sheer surfaces of pale wood panels and stainless steel, soft furnishings and sleek fabrics, muted luminescence and an unnatural absence of shadows. The iridescent copper sheen of her pleated pants and flowing free-form jacket, her bronzed purse and shoes, her black hair and the black pearl studs in her ears, her deep lipstick and dark eyes transformed the entire interior into a staged background, as if it were set up by an artistic director for a photo shoot.

"Wait," said Severence. He nodded towards a large middle-aged man and a chunky young woman. "You two, search her."

"You," said Tess, indicating the pudgy young woman.

"No, you," said Severence to the man, who proceeded to run his hands over her body with brutal intimacy. The man grimaced when he produced the snub-nosed Glock but indicated no awareness of the neoprene bodysuit under her clothes.

"Well, you caught me," said Tess derisively.

"Mary, Mary, Mary. Did you really think you could traipse in here and shoot me, just like that?"

"I'd prefer Tess. I have a very close friend who likes me as Tess. That's my preferred name."

"You will be Mary a bit longer. You are here and you will be useful. I am so glad you found me—you solved my little riddle."

"It was a puzzle not a riddle, and yes I did."

"Well in any case. Come, I want to show you the most amazing things."

He led her through a series of doors and they came out in an electronics room of startling complexity, aglow with myriad planes of metallic colours and glaring glass screens.

"It's the new era," he said with a sweeping gesture to take in the entire room, including keyboard operators, their equipment, even the security people. "From here I can reach the world."

"A modest undertaking. Especially tonight of all nights."

"Indeed, dear Mary. Especially tonight. Now, what I need you to do is sit over here. We will send out our image to the world, you and me. Pietro di Cosmos II with Mary the Devil Incarnate as my prisoner, rebuked, chastened, subdued."

Tess stood squarely confronting him, glowering. Several guards backed away, as if they found what was coming distasteful.

Severence moved closer. She stood motionless. Suddenly, he lashed out with his fist and caught her a severe blow across the jaw. She lurched back but managed to stand her ground. The next blow was a vicious slap against her right cheek that swept across her nose, cutting deep on the bridge with his pontifical ring. She teetered on her bronzed heels but remained on her feet. The third blow was a fist squarely between her eyes. It shattered her nose before tearing the skin as it deflected to the side. Her purse dropped to the floor, disgorging its contents as she twisted around on herself and collapsed.

"Now then, clean her up but just a little, she must be recognizable," he said to the pudgy young woman. "Sit her there. It is good, Mary, for our followers see that you have been vanquished."

"May I have my things?" Tess asked in a barely audible voice as the man who had groped her assisted her into a chair.

Severence kicked her compact and lipstick towards her purse. When the young woman picked up the purse he looked inside but saw only a pair of soft slippers. Mary reached out for the silver compact and lipstick. Without asking she slipped the top off the lipstick and dabbed at her lower lip, which she then pursed against the upper to spread the blood-red smear. She smacked her lips in a curious display of satisfaction.

"Now, Tom," she said, cutting her words abruptly and forcing a smile.

"Yes, Mary?" His lean body loomed over her, his worsted wool suit, a smoky grey pinstripe, with a satin waistcoat of the same colour and a white shirt and an Ivy League tie, declaring a deceptively austere and sinister worldliness.

"Do not do this."

"This? What? Come now, Mary!"

"This thing. You have their money. Why don't you just disappear?"

"Ah if only it were so easy." He leaned down and whispered. "Your husband and I have been too successful. You see that, don't you? Our devoted followers are spread all over this Earth. They would find me, they would punish me for not being God. And of course, there's no guarantee you would give me back my money—I assume that is what you are getting at with your sad little negotiation."

"You realize I have locked you out of all your accounts. My friend has sole access."

"I will remind him. He is presently my guest at Wakefield Hall, he and his grotesquely Manichaean friend with two faces."

"Inspector Theophil Queequeg, he is here too? Poor Tom. He was your follower for such a brief time."

"He is a confused primitive, a savage of irritating consequence. It is your friend Harry we need to discuss."

"Really?"

"Yes, really. You see, after your death," he lowered his voice, "and the deaths of the chosen twelve thousand at midnight, I will go back to my Cotswold sanctuary and encourage your friend Professor Lindstrom to forfeit his claims on my money. I can be very persuasive. Very very persuasive, if need be."

Tess was toying with the ornate lipstick container, running her thumb over the antiqued swirls of silver.

"Midnight?" she said. "When do you plan to start broadcasting to your sacrificial lambs out there so eager to die?"

"Soon, they are waiting already. With the flip of a switch I intend to deliver the sermon of my life. Of their lives, if you'd rather. It will be inspired, I assure you."

"Then we had better proceed."

"I will decide that."

"No," said Mary. She looked over to the open doorway and around the room, which itself was like an imagined interior of a giant computer with all the arcane workings exposed. She looked at a clock on a screen; she had dumped her Suunto dive computer into the Thames. It was 9:30 pm.

"I will decide," she said. She wheeled around on her chair and flung the lipstick with all her might against the wood panelled wall outside the door. There was an immediate explosion that shattered into flames and smoke and people screamed and ran, but there was no damage in the computer room. She rose to her feet. Severence had fallen to the floor. She reached a hand out to help him up, then pushed him down in a chair. The guards in the room were recovering their equilibrium but confused. None made a move to restrain Tess nor to help Severence.

She held out her silver compact, peeled off the elastic band, then with a flourishing gesture she invited the others to listen. She opened the compact. As the mirror came into view, there was a click. Despite the chaos in the corridor with people rushing about trying to extinguish fires and assist the injured the click resounded through the room. The compact closed against a spring and she slid the elastic back into place so it wouldn't burst open.

"That sound was the triggering mechanism," she explained. "This is a much bigger bomb. If it goes off the pristine interior of your entire Mothership will have to be washed down just to scrape off our guts. If the case opens, the bomb goes off. Now watch carefully, Tom."

She slid the elastic off the compact and over her wrist, holding the hinged sides closed between her fingers.

"Now, then," she said. "If your people were to shoot me, in my death throes I would release my grip and bang, we're all in little charred pieces very dead, do you understand?"

"It won't work," he declared with bravado.

"I believe it will. Now, let us inform the press, the police, and fire up the computers to connect with your victims. And let us encourage the press to use telephoto shots we can share. Oh, and we must be wired for sound. Then, in a while, you and I will go for a stroll." She pointed straight up.

It was 9:45 pm.

By 11:15 pm helicopters hovered overhead, floodlights and searchlight beams scoured the sky and the water, everyone looking for evidence of the publicly enacted murder-suicide promised aboard the *Teegeeak*, Mothership of The Church Absolute.

"It's time," she said.

Holding her silver compact in one hand, with her other on the scruff of Tom Severence's suit, Tess guided him through the smouldering rubble in the ship's central corridor and out into the bracing antique atmosphere of the open deck. She paused to remove her heeled sandals and slide on her slippers, then walked him to the ratlines on the starboard side of the foremast, away from the shore lights but illuminated by the erratic dazzle of lights from the police helicopters. Media choppers, used mostly for weather and traffic, had apparently been banned from the airspace between the ship and the near shore of the Thames. The far shore was hardly discernable through the low rising mist in the distance.

Tess moved the elastic down over the compact so that she could use both hands for climbing, then urged Severence to precede her upwards on the ratlines until they reached the crow's-nest.

At 11:30 pm Tess did a soundcheck to make sure their broadcast voices would reach the throng of prospective dead, the horde still champing to die at the midnight hour. She instructed the I.T. people below decks to begin transmission. She looked down at her smartphone and saw that the news media were broadcasting live, which meant their telephoto shots were being streamed through The Church computer network simultaneously to all parts of the world. She knew the I.T. people would deliver, believing either that she was the incarnation of the devil or a saint of The Church; either way not to be ignored. It would not occur to them that the life of Pietro di Cosmos II might hang in the balance. He was, for the time being, immortal.

He seemed much of the same mind, for he moved ahead of Tess with an apparent air of resigned contempt.

"Just do as I say," she intoned in a quietly commanding voice, adding a paraphrase from Max Ehrmann's hackneyed *Desiderata*: "Things will turn out as they should."

"It is what it is," he shrugged, as if to slough off with an equally banal cliché any illusions she might have had that she was in control.

He hesitated, however, seeming to reconsider his errant confidence when she ordered him to descend off the crow's-nest platform into the glare of searchlights on the onshore side and urged him across the footrope draped beneath the fore mainsail yardarm. Half way along, he turned back towards her:

"Turn the sound off, Mary, I want to talk."

His quavering voice undermined his struggle to condescend. She nodded that she had done so. There were only the two of them in the dazzling glare.

"If you explode your bomb, you will die too."

"I know."

"Can we come to a compromise?"

"We can."

"I knew it, you're not ready for death. Neither of us is. It goes against nature."

"What about the chosen twelve thousand?" she asked.

"We all die sooner or later."

"Your Holy Gathering will be rich and the others will be dead? So much for the Rapture."

"Fuck the Rapture."

"The sound is still on, Pietro di Cosmos. Your people have heard you."

"Cunt!"

"An improvement from the Devil Incarnate."

It seemed as if the air filled with a roar but it was only the wind over the Thames for a moment drowning out the sounds of the helicopters and crowd.

"Move along, Tom, or I'll finish this here."

She flourished the silver compact as a powerful talisman forcing her adversary into submission, like garlic or a crucifix in the face of a vampire. And yet from an onlooker's perspective, it seemed like nothing more than perhaps a religious medallion whose magic she was offering to share.

As they edged out over the water, she spoke into the dazzling light, saying in a clear voice, "My beloved friends. The obscenity of his doubt affirms the humanity of Pietro di Cosmos II." She paused to gaze down into the searchlights on shore. "I take him now as a man, not a god, to die in your place." She paused again. "We honour you for your courage to live. Reclaim what is yours, my friends, where the infinite and eternal converge. Do not reach for the Rapture. Death will come in its time. Let the universe unfold as it may. The Church Absolute is no more."

With a seemingly whimsical and yet authoritative 'Amen,' she turned off the sound connection and urged Severence forward to the end of the narrow yardarm where he grasped the port jackstay running vertically from the topsail yard and hoisted himself up to balance precariously on the fore mainsail spar and she followed beside him. He seemed unnerved by the audacity of her scheme, incredulous that she had carried it so far.

She arranged the nooses around their necks and drew them tight. He looked at her with a mixture of hope and despair. He reached up to clutch the rope with icy fingers, trying to stop from swaying, trying to ease it away from his flesh. Tess grasped her own rope hanging from the topsail spar lightly, without losing grip of her compact while delicately and deliberately positioning the knot more firmly against the nape of her neck.

With her free hand she reached out and took his. Her fingers were warm. She unclenched the fingers of her other hand and let the silver compact fall through the air. It tumbled and smashed against the black scrim ice close to the hull and exploded in a vicious eruption of water and ice.

Before the reverberations subsided, Tess spoke a few words, tilted her head back and stepped off the spar, drawing Tom Severence with her. They seemed to hover briefly before falling a full body length when Tess's hand was torn from his as he jerked upwards, then as their heads yanked around on their necks Severence dangled in swaying repose while Tess shuddered abruptly and plummeted through the glistening air smashing through ice disappearing into the roiling black water.

The frigid Thames brought Tess to her senses as she plunged deep under the hull of the Mothership, twisted away from the light and started to ascend on the offshore side, lifted a little by the tiny air bubbles in her neoprene wetsuit as she fought against the swirling current. Her left shoulder had nearly wrenched out of its socket and made one arm useless as she struggled with vigorous kicks towards the stern, on the verge of passing out from the pain in the nape of her neck where she had borne the main force of the noose until the severing of the hemp against the embedded steel blade, which was fleetingly delayed by the dead weight of Severence whose hand pulled her upwards as his neck broke their initial fall. Almost overwhelmed by from oxygen depletion, she grasped at her scuba gear as the current swept her past, caught hold with stiff fingers, secured her icy grip, and switched off the toggle, releasing the magnets and allowing her to drift free as she drew in deep gulps of enriched air.

Tumbling through the water with neutral buoyancy so she neither sank nor ascended, she clung to her dive gear, not bothering to try putting it on as she passed under pans of ice and fragments of light from the shore. Her fingers started to go numb and she began to slip away from the weighted tank and BCD. She released her hold and surfaced and swam desperately for shore.

Wading through mud that sucked her slippers from her feet, she staggered into a gloomy pool of light near a lone lamp standard, stripped off her still smart-looking Caren Shen pantsuit, unpacked her crushed down vest from its small dry bag, carefully worked off the remains of the coiled noose with the embedded steel blade, pulled the vest on over the wet neoprene and zipped it up, then jogged barefoot through the Old Royal Naval College grounds to a small rental car parked on Hamilton Road. Inside the car, she changed into dry clothes and sat for a moment, catching her breath, before she pulled out of the parking space. As she did, she couldn't help notice a vintage Rolls Royce Roadster with a body of solid copper burnished to perfection. It was illegally parked, straddled across the prime meridian.

26 THE LAST ENEMY

FROM HIS VANTAGE OVERLOOKING LAKE ONTARIO, HIGH ON the southern edge of the Toronto skyline, Harry couldn't see the city at all. With his first coffee of the day in hand and still dressed in flannel pyjamas he stood on the twenty-third floor gazing at space and weather and the endless inland sea as it merged with the lowering sky into an amorphous, oppressive, and unnatural wall closing in from the south. The off-shore islands, already partially erased by accumulations of snow, were fading from sight and the jagged edges of ice pans in the harbour were softening in a gauzy buffer of yellowish air. He might have been the last man in the world.

He turned away and stared at the Klimts standing proud on the wall, declaring lives of their own. They envisioned Madalena Strauss in gold leaf and fine strokes as evil and goodness, and he couldn't be sure in the artist's voluptuous renderings which was meant to be which. An overwhelming sense of loss and isolation crept over him and he sat down abruptly on his teak and leather armchair, legs sprawled in front. He sighed.

Abruptly, he stood up again. Being morose was one thing, sighing was another.

I will be sad, he thought. I refuse to be pathetic.

He looked to the Blackwood etching across from the Klimts. The huge smiling whale was a force of nature. The fate of the humans in the ice-strewn sea was irrelevant. With deliberate strides, Harry walked across his antique tribal carpet into the bedroom, turning his back on the whale and on the Klimts, which reminded him of Tess Saintsbury who reminded him of the amoral enchantment of Hannah Arnason when he was trapped with her in a burial tomb off the coast of Sweden, who reminded him of Karen.

He dressed warmly, he intended to go out. He wasn't sure where, but he couldn't allow himself to stay in through the coming storm. He refused to indulge anymore in the comfort of morbid maunderings. In the week since he'd been back from England he had consumed inordinate quantities of scotch and avoided contacting anyone he knew. He talked to strangers whose function enabled him to get through the day: clerks and waiters and ticket-takers, anonymous members of the serving cohort who expected nothing in return but prompt payment and the occasional tip. He listened to the radio obsessively and watched news on television and trolled on line, piecing together the miserable debacle of the religious conflagration that had featured 187 deaths, including the spectacular flame-out of two sacred leaders, and the ignominious collapse of an entire spiritual movement.

One hundred and eighty-five of the chosen had evaded the spectacular cancellation of the Rapture. They did not have access to the computer feed from Greenwich or they did not understand the message or they were depressives taking advantage of the Apocalypse and determined to die or because they were zealots so far beyond rational thinking that death seemed preferable to revisionist evasions.

Harry and Queequeg had travelled out to Heathrow together. They had decided they could contribute nothing to the chaotic investigation into religious suicides in countless jurisdictions and they chose not to become involved in the flamboyant demise of Severence and Tess in Greenwich. Harry walked Queequeg to the Air France line-up in Terminal 4 before proceeding to Terminal 3 for his Air Canada flight, which he took under the flimsiest of chauvinist obligations, despite their general discourtesy.

The two men had held each other at arms length, the burly man with the golden face etched in permanent and meaningful sorrow, and the other man leaning on his beechwood and buffalo-horn cane with its silver band, both looking for all the world that swirled around them like lovers on the verge of unbearable parting. And yet when they embraced, Queequeg crushing Harry against his massive chest, they would have struck the observer, if anyone among the cosmopolitan crowd had noticed, as brothers at arms, soldiers, fierce and passionate comrades.

"You take care Harry," said Queequeg, suddenly thrusting Harry to arms length again, then drawing him close and hugging him and kissing him vigorously on both cheeks, and standing back so the rare winter sunlight streaming in through massive windows illuminated his face like an exquisite oil painting.

Harry reached out and shook Queequeg's hand, it was his way, not kissing, and each man thrusted a hand over the knot of clasping fingers, squeezing and pumping so it hurt. Harry was miserable. Tess had died less than a full day before. He felt proud and disoriented and infinitely sad and his friend was leaving for the South Pacific, where fantasy was real.

He abruptly turned and walked away.

"*Au revoir, mon ami*," Quecqueg called after him.

Harry waved a hand over his shoulder but did not look back until he rounded a corner and entered the tunnel leading to Terminal 3. He paused, pivoted, and saw only crowds of anonymous people. He wondered if any of them were survivors. He supposed they were, of one sort or another, whether their lives had been touched by Tess or not, and he walked on.

Now, in his condo, as he moved back through his living room dressed for the midwinter cold in his extra long sheepskin coat, his light brown cashmere scarf that Karen had stitched into a möbius loop, and the black wool toque that had belonged to Miranda's dad, he paused and glanced down at the letter that had arrived two days previously from London. He had set it on the coffee table but it remained unopened. He knew who it was from.

When he returned from his walk, which took him up past the Saint Lawrence Market, north along Jarvis to the point where it veers off into Mount Pleasant Boulevard, then west along Bloor over to Avenue Road and down around Queen's Park onto University and eventually south, back to the waterfront, there were a series of phone messages waiting for him. He chose not to delete them, and to begin responding to his accumulated email.

For the next two and a half months, Harry signed over his authority to a phalanx of Public Trustees around the world for the return of whatever monies could be traced back to donors who had turned their wealth over to The Church Absolute. What could not be assigned was pooled as a charitable fund for victims of religious extremism.

The unopened letter from Tess lay all this time on the coffee table, haunting Harry and reassuring him. He did not want to hear her last words in his head. He needed to know she was there.

Sometimes at night he had vivid dreams and woke up emotionally depleted. He could always remember the strangling anxiety, the sorrow, the moments of peace, the exhilarating explosions of laughter, but he couldn't remember whether he had dreamed of Karen or whether it was Tess. The two had merged but they were separate, like the sides of his Marquesian friend's beautiful ornate face.

Miranda Quin and David Morgan insisted on taking him out to dinner several times.

"Why?" he had asked.

"You're depressed," said Morgan.

"How do you know?" he demanded.

"We're police," said Morgan. "We know things."

But they didn't know more about Tess and The Church than Harry had previously explained. They didn't question him. They assumed any pertinent details he would share without asking, and only three Canadians had died in the abortive Rapture, not enough to generate professional interest.

"There was nothing I could do," he explained.

"You did your best," said Miranda.

"She stopped it," he responded.

"She was a strange one, your Professor Izett," said Miranda.

"Tess."

"I'm sorry, Harry."

"Yeah," he said.

Their dinners were not successful and soon came to an end.

It was early May.

Harry picked up the envelope from Tess and stepped out on his balcony, breathed in the spring air, and contemplated tearing the letter into pieces and releasing them on the updraft to waft away over the harbour. The Presbyterian legacy of his beloved Aunt Beth was too strong; littering even from twenty-three stories was offensive and leaving a personal message unread was profligate. At the risk of breaking the bond between himself and Tess rather than strengthening it, he opened the envelope and read her final words.

Dear Harry,

Promise me you will return to the Anishnabi River. Bear witness to the lives of your family, to your own loss. Let them go, make your peace, set them free.

Martin Heidegger said that to live an authentic life we must accept it will end. Saint Paul, who was also a fascist, declared the last enemy to be destroyed shall be death. Mary of Galilee admonished in the apocrypha suppressed by the Paulenes, sing when darkness falls to bring back the sun.

Remember me sometimes, Harry. Step out from the shadow of death and into the light. Consider what Pooh might have said, and Wittgenstein more or less did, thinking can obscure the very best thoughts. Relax, be well, forgive the professorial rant.

Forgive yourself, dear Harry.

Forgive yourself.

Love,

Tess

Harry shredded the note into tiny bits and released them into the air where they fluttered and dispersed like crystals of snow in the spring sunshine.

Three days later, he rented a red canoe at the ESSO station on the edge of Algonquin Park, the place where he and Tess had finished their midwinter adventure and where he and his family had set out on their doomed canoe trip. The sign for 'Virgil's Outfitting Emporium' had been altered with pragmatic economy. The words 'Virgil' and 'Emporium' had been painted over so that it read quite simply: 'Outfitting.' Harry arranged to be dropped off at Lake Divide and for a pick-up on Long Pine. The first night on the river, he crawled deep into his sleeping bag to escape the persistent blackflies that had infiltrated his tent. The downy space was stifling but he picked up the scent of Tess as it wrapped around him. Karen; he consciously thought about Karen. He slept and dreamed but when he woke no lingering images swarmed through his mind.

Over the sharp rise at the beginning of the long portage, the forest opened like a majestic cathedral and he walked through towering red pines between moss-covered boulders and approached the Devil's Cauldron from the middle of the trail. He was filled with wonder not dread as he braced against a rocky altar and gazed over the swirling water, immersed in the thunder of its falling, and he felt Lucy and Matt deep inside and he smiled. Karen was close, he could imagine her snuggling into his shoulder. He stayed for a couple of hours, his mind empty of thoughts but teeming with feelings and images that made him content.

When he left to set up camp at the end of the portage where the Anishnabi opens out onto the sprawling silver reaches of Long Pine Lake, he was wistful rather than sad, and filled with the uncanny feeling of being somehow whole and complete.

He sat for a long time at the edge of the smoke from his cedar fire, trying to keep the blackflies at bay. They were unseasonably early this year. He stared into the orange-red flames, regretting Karen wasn't with him to share. It wasn't her voice he missed, not her ghost, but the person she had actually been. He cried a little and wiped smoke from his eyes, then he crawled into his tent, ignored the few blackflies that crept in with him, and listening to the falls in the distance he fell asleep and slept soundly through the night.

The next day on the long paddle to the take-out point where he and Tess had camped with hand-shovelled snow piled against the walls of their tent, he noticed an unnaturally rectilinear plane of grey cedar shingles far off to the north, visible among the pines and cedars and spruce before the hardwoods came into leaf. He paddled through rivulets in the floating swamp over to the cabin that stood in a clearing beside a small stream flowing out of the bush.

The cabin where Tess must have borrowed popcorn and tea and recovered the paisley shot-silk bandana was made of ancient cedar logs squared roughly with an axe or an adze and was well put together. The chinking had been repaired with oakum and hemp, with mud and clay and cement, by generations of occupants. The windows were boarded up and the place looked boldly forlorn. He called out but expected no answer.

Beaching his red canoe, he walked up to the cabin and tried the door. It was shut securely but as a courtesy to travellers was not locked. He stepped inside. It was impenetrably dark. He backed out and removed a shutter from one of the windows and returned inside where despite the gloom it seemed homey. Immediately, his eye went to an orange lifejacket hanging on a peg inside the door. It had a large jagged tear along the left side that no one had tried to repair. This didn't surprise him since few of the old woodsmen he knew from his camping days would have bothered with lifejackets at all. Most couldn't swim. If they dumped their canoes in the ice-cold water they mercifully drowned.

He touched the jacket but did not remove it from the peg.

There was a note beside the sink from Tess with a folded $20.00 for the popcorn and tea. Both had been pushed to the side and were flecked with water stains. Someone had been using the counter and had not bothered to collect or was just passing though.

Through the smeared glass of the shutterless window he could see a storm was blowing up over the lake. He went out and hauled his canoe into the trees, flipped it over, and carried his gear up to the cabin.

There was lots of split wood inside, including cedar kindling, and he started a fire in a cast iron stove that marked the boundary between the kitchen and living area and a larger fire in the stone fireplace against the north wall.

He settled in with a fresh brewed cup of camp coffee, grounds in a bag dipped in boiling water, and was about to relax when suddenly he decided he needed more light and went out to remove the board shutter from the other window, returning inside just as the rains came scooting across the marsh and began lashing the cabin door, which he pulled closed behind him. Finding a half-filled kerosene lamp, he lit the charred flat wick and replaced the glass mantle, which cast a warm glow against the rough polished log walls. He sat back in a huge leather armchair that must have been hauled over the ice and smelled vaguely musty from extended disuse but soon began to exude warm aromas. He surveyed the entire interior from where he sat with satisfaction. There was nothing to read.

By early evening Harry decided that he could easily slip into Old George's life and miss little of the outside world. There was a small bedroom behind a partition of vertical poles off to one side but he chose to sleep on the worn sofa within sight of the open fire. Despite the outlier lifestyle, he knew the owners would be accommodating if they showed up while he was here. He had seen enough of them at the trading post to recognize the natural grace they shared with indigenous people who had once lived on these lands now administered by the park authority, but natural modesty seemed to demand the courtesy of not sleeping in their bed.

Since he had given up trapping, Old George and the woman he called his 'missus' worked winters at the ESSO station, repairing canoes and tripping gear, making a grubstake to keep them going through a seven month 'summer' when they lived on the land. They kept a low profile because residence in parkland was restricted. The cabin while older than the park was inside its boundary. Harry envied their self-contained existence, but he suspected its appeal would diminish if there were no alternatives. Thoreau had travelled much in Concord, Blake had seen the world in a grain of sand. Harry Lindstrom decided he would rather, like the poet Marvell, throw open the iron gates of life and make the sunlight run.

Queequeg, his friend, was evoked by the flourish of literary allusions. He missed Queequeg. He looked around. The cabin was comfortable and familiar. Solitary sanctuary had its appeal. But Harry knew for himself he needed a world with room enough for the Queequegs and Miranda Quins, for the David Morgans, for Karen Malone and Madalena Strauss, Hannah Arnason and Tess Saintsbury, a world where Harry Lindstrom, skimming the surface of time, like Janus of old, could look both ways, and balance between.

The storm lasted into the third day, with high winds running the length of the lake, churning up whitecapped rollers that could swamp the most skillfully handled canoe. Harry was competent but no expert. He sat tight, enjoyed the fire, and during breaks in the rain chopped wood. He ate the last of his own food and cracked open a few large jars filled with whole wheat flour and smaller ones with powdered milk, powdered egg whites, and a single small jar of smashed prunes for infants, exactly the ingredients Karen used to use to make campfire flapjacks. There was a kerosene double-burner but he cooked on the woodstove. He found a jug of maple syrup and made up batches of flapjacks for successive breakfasts and dinners, skipping lunch altogether and feeling not the least deprived.

On the last morning, he cleaned up and paddled out, reaching the pickup point by early afternoon. A man from the outfitters was waiting for him. It turned out to be Old George who was about the same age as Harry but seemed ageless, both younger in his movement and older in his reticent demeanour, grizzled appearance, and economy with words.

"It's good to see you," said Harry, feeling exhilarated, exhausted, and a little shy, as if he had just completed a major expedition.

"Figured you'd hole up in the cabin," said George. "Didn't come yesterday or the day before."

"Thanks for being here now," said Harry. "I owe you."

"You pay the boss?"

"No, for the food and fuel."

"You chop any wood?"

"I did."

"You have a good time?"

"I did."

"Well you don't owe me nothing, then."

Old George smiled to himself. They drove in companionable silence to the ESSO station and Harry went into the trading post to pay his bill. He took out a couple of fifties from his wallet, folded them in an envelope and asked the outfitter to give it to George.

"You'll have to do it yourself," said the other man, amiably. "He won't take it from me. Says I pay him too much already."

"He's a bit strange isn't he?"

"Oh yeah."

"You known them long?"

"Old George's been around for years."

"Living out at the cabin?"

"Yeah. That's his home."

"When he's not living with you."

"He don't live here, he just stays when he's working, he and his missus."

"You bought this place three years ago."

"That's how long I've known him, three years and four months. He used to do some guiding, ran traplines in the winter, like outside the park boundary it's important to say, but pelts aren't worth crap no more. He started full time the winter I come, I think his missus wanted the critchure comforts, so when I took over he helped with the transitional, and they done over a homestead in the back of the shed. Come the breakup, I'd say that year it was April 15th, they packed up and left and we didn't see her again until the end of October. George come in from time to time for supplies, said he wouldn't do guiding no more, said he had to stay around home. I think his missus turned simple or something so he had to keep watch on her, but she's not retarded with the old timer's disease, she's too young, she don't say much, but she understands, you know, you can tell. She understands everything. They can use the money even if they don't say as much."

Harry walked out into the twilight and around to the long low wooden shed beside the rickety canoe rack and entered the darkened repair shop, walking through until he could see into the living quarters at the back.

As he approached the rectangle of light beaming like a theatre stage he slowed, then he abruptly stopped. The proscenium door was like a portal into another world. He knew instinctively he was violating a space that was private. This was not something he thought, it was something he felt, but he felt it with a sharp urgency that pushed at his chest like a heavy weight, pressing on his heart, constricting his breathing, threatening to knock him backwards off balance.

The woman, wearing jeans and a comfortably oversize sweater, walked past the interior door in the fully illuminated room with its sparse furnishings and gleaming rough-plank walls. Her left arm was drawn up against her body. She moved with a limp. She smiled at another person who was hidden from view. She turned and looked into the darkness, staring straight at Harry but not seeing him. She looked back at the concealed person, it had to be George. She smiled again, this time turning directly into the light source. Her face was deeply scarred on one side. Harry gasped, transfixed, filled with horror and joy. His throat burned dry, he tried to swallow, time stopped.

The fingers on her left hand were twisted, her arm had been crushed, the ring had torn free—the brown paisley bandana, the orange life jacket in a backwoods cabin, the absence of human remains. Tess must have known.

Harry watched. The man came into view. They moved together. There was low music from a radio, they moved in each others arms, they danced, their feet hardly moving. Harry wept. She was happy, she was happy beyond words.

Time slowly kicked in and he became aware of himself standing in the dark. He knocked on a workbench with his knuckles and stepped forward. George looked over as Harry moved into the light. The woman ignored him. Harry handed George the envelope. George took it reluctantly then shrugged and handed it to the woman.

"The missus is good with figures."

Karen looked up and Harry stared deep into her eyes. Green and brown and golden. A fracture in her skull showed beneath her left temple as an elliptical dent, the flesh on the left side of her face had been severely battered and crudely repaired without sutures, her eyelid drooped and the corner of her upper lip pulled away revealing two missing teeth, but as Harry looked at her she was still beautiful beyond imagining.

"Karen?" he said. She touched the back of her good hand to her injured cheek. She stared into his eyes. He knew she saw nothing.

Then she stepped away and started to peel potatoes at the sink.

George looked at her, then turned to Harry.

"Is there anything else?"

"No," said Harry and backed out into the darkness.

His rented car was out front. He drove straight through, breaking gently between tears and laughter. He was home before midnight. By daybreak he had booked a sequence of flights that would get him to French Polynesia late the next day. He left a message for Miranda, he didn't know when he'd return. He would miss the seasons, he'd eventually come back. He planned to call Queequeg from Papeete. Then he would begin searching the Islands. He had no idea what name she would use. He thought he would start on Huahine and look for a diver who called herself Tess.

CPSIA information can be obtained
at www.ICGtesting.com
Printed in the USA
LVHW040048070819
626741LV00001B/5